9/09

19.95

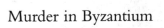

Murder in Byzantium

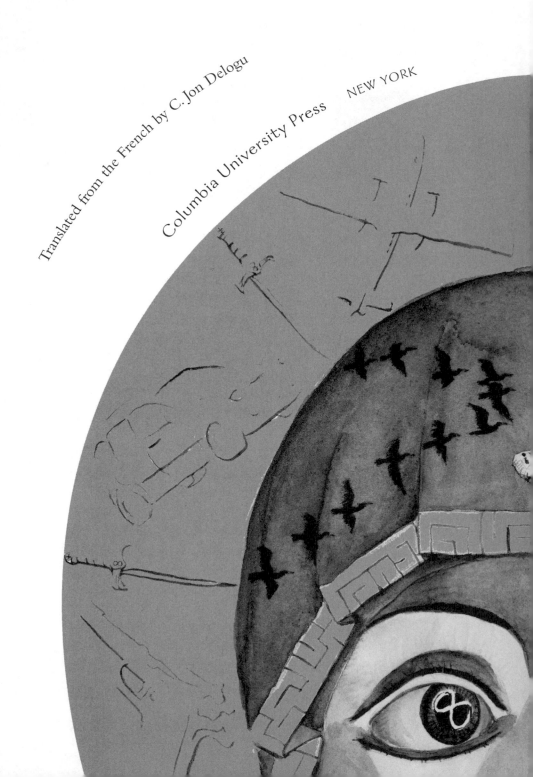

Translated from the French by C. Jon Delogu

Columbia University Press   NEW YORK

JULIA KRISTEVA MURDER in BYZANTIUM

COLUMBIA UNIVERSITY PRESS
Publishers Since 1893
New York, Chichester, West Sussex

Library of Congress Cataloging-in-Publication Data

Kristeva, Julia, 1941–
[Meurtre à Byzance. English]
Murder in Byzantium / Julia Kristeva ; translated from the
French by C. Jon Delogu.
p. cm.
ISBN 0–231–13636–6 (alk. paper)
I. Delogu, Christopher Jon. II. Title.
PQ2671.R547M4813   2005
843'.914—dc22   2005051851

Printed in the United States of America
c 10 9 8 7 6 5 4 3

CONTENTS ❧

If any man will come after me, let him deny himself, and take up his cross, and follow me.

St. Matthew 16:24 (King James Version)

Mystery at the Whale Lighthouse

The ocean slapped his face with a thick salty mist—gusting, breathless, dizzying. Piled up in curvy lines of gold and gray on the wet sand, this memory of the waves fading in the distance threatened to swallow his steps. Alone, hanging down from the sky, the green-black peaks of the cypress trees that the wind had spared held the attention of the runaway and helped steady his shaky balance.

After completing his work, the man liked to take off his knit mask in front of the victims and then leave with his face uncovered as though he were showing off his clear conscience. But this was pointless since there was no chance of meeting any living soul before the high tide at dawn near the Whale Lighthouse. The moist dunes bordered an empty expanse of salt marshes, sleeping under the frost and visited only by the occasional North-ern shoveler duck. Desperate or teasing cries of the birds known as laughing gulls filled the solitary scout with a rude joy. A few miles away, the body of Reverend Robertson, one of the leading worms of the New Pantheon, lay abandoned in the Seaside Temple, the group's winter residence. Number Eight had carried off only the blood-stained shirt knifed into ribbons. Hav-ing arrived at the lighthouse, the killer put on a second pair of latex gloves before taking the plastic bag that contained this vestment out of his army surplus rucksack. He placed this trophy at the foot of the old entryway that was now closed off and served only as a storage area for the garbage cans of the cafeteria that operated on the top floor during the summer season. A single thought was bothering him: were these two pairs enough to pro-tect him from AIDS, hepatitis, tuberculosis, and meningitis, which certainly were not rare—quite the opposite—among the members of this cursed sect? Next time shouldn't he use those wonderfully medieval-looking gloves knit with stainless steel fibers that autopsy specialists used? Gloves of steel, steel gloves, gloves of steel, steel gloves—the words filled his mind. No other thought had been able to etch itself on the cortex of Number Eight from the moment he had sunk his dagger into the throat of that bastard.

He tucked the shirt under two large stones so that the wind could not blow it away. Now his face lightened up: the *8* traced with the blood of the dead man covered the back of the shirt and he was as pleased as a little boy who had just taken revenge for some insult by means of a particularly gory prank. This *8* recalled the same shape that he had carved into the fatty flank of the depraved dead man. Infinite were the corruptions of this gangster, and infinite was the vengeance of the purifier! Number Eight put away his dirty gloves, put on his usual intense birdwatcher's face, and strode back across the marshes to his Range Rover imitating the song of the cormorants. He plopped down behind the steering wheel, drove like a zombie, and tucked his car neatly into a vacant space in the parking lot of the Tour Felicidad, a high-rise that overlooked an ordinary neighborhood of Santa Varvara. Back in his apartment on the thirty-ninth floor he turned on the television.

An anchorwoman with a platinum-blonde crew cut, the local version of Lara Croft or Ananova, was announcing, with an affected shudder in her voice, that the naked body of Father Robertson, one of the leaders of the famous New Pantheon sect, had just been discovered, thus bringing to seven the number of victims chosen from among the leadership of the group. "It seems that this seventh murder bears the signature of the same killer because the body, savagely stabbed but with no other marks or sexual violation, was undressed, and police are already convinced that somewhere in Santa Varvara they will soon find the customary shirt with the number eight painted with the blood of the stabbing victim, just as in the cases of the other assassinated leaders of the New Pantheon group . . . as our TV listeners are well aware," insisted the platinum-blonde anchorwoman. "Journalists have nicknamed this unusual serial killer 'Number Eight,'" mouthed the TV Barbie with her full red lips. When asked if he expected to find an eighth and hopefully final victim, Police Commissioner Rilsky, who has been directing the investigation, confessed that the police still had no leads as to the identity of the killer or killers, nor any information about possible motives, and that therefore he would not offer any theories about an eventual conclusion to this macabre series of events.

On that note Number Eight turned off the television and went to bed with a smile on his face that indeed suggested these events were far from over.

Murder in Byzantium

I approach the task with no intention of flaunting my skill as a writer; my concern is rather that a career so brilliant should not go unrecorded in the future.... Some Normans ... ravaged the outskirts of Nicaea, acting with horrible cruelty to the whole population; they cut in pieces some of the babies, impaled others on wooden spits and roasted them over a fire; old people were subjected to every kind of torture.... If I had not been made of steel, or fashioned from some other hard, tough substance ... a stranger to myself, I would have perished at once.

ANNA COMNENA, 1083–1148?, *The Alexiad*

CHAPTER ONE   The *Événement de Paris* Sends Stephanie Delacour to Santa Varvara

Once again my editor lays it on thick: the *Événement de Paris* needs Stephanie Delacour in Santa Varvara! Our very special foreign correspondent better hurry up! Here's your story, Stephanie: sects, do you follow me? That's all there is today, and frankly no one else could get to the bottom of this sordid affair, I mean no one else in Santa Varvara, you understand?

Whether I understood or not, I had no choice. As usual. Moreover, to put it bluntly, this case was definitely not going to be a vacation. Still trapped in a stage of economic and political transitions that was eating away at the rest of the planet, Santa Varvara had, on top of everything, become the paradise of various mafia groups and sects, with the latter continuously morphing into the former and vice versa without end. Of course you might reply that this strange paradise is not confined to Santa Varvara; it is everywhere. Exactly, and so good luck if you are able to identify the particular Santa Varvara that I am speaking about right now!

Thanks to my previous assignments, I knew this area by heart: sunny air saturated with hydrocarbons and jasmine, skeletons in the closets of political parties and petroleum companies, women decapitated, such as my dead friend Gloria Harrison, who devoted herself to translating literature in a country where no one reads any more because of television, her son Jerry, who finally became my son, a fragile flower who escaped, God knows how, out of this hellhole, the child I saved and who is saving me, but that's another story that I've not finished writing and that keeps me going. So, Santa Varvara, I know it well, I'm telling you!

Spiritual leaders with more or less imagination would troll the world's religions for any esoteric ingredients that could be mixed into the much needed elixir that would allow the clueless citizens of this fucked up country to forget the runaway inflation, the dizzying corruption, the chaotic administration, the absence of political direction, and therefore the absence of any future. Drug dealers would keep these amateurs of the Absolute high, and even with their sky-high prices they would come back for more, while arms dealers would manipulate clergymen of all sorts when they weren't dressing up and passing themselves off as men of God. These juicy schemes that profited everyone involved would not have been brought out into the open if the bitter rivalry between the mafia and the sects had not degenerated into murders and denunciations. But since the government needed the financial assistance of the international community to limp along from year to year, it found itself having to organize investigations, hold trials, and even appoint a Special Council of Sages—in a word, to crack down.

Everyone realized early on that this was not child's play. My friend Larry Smirnoff, the editor in chief of the local paper, the *Times,* lost one of his journalists, Gianchiotti, who had been covering the sects. He was found in his bathtub with two bullets in the head. "That's why he hadn't called in for three days. Dead as a doornail," snapped Larry over the phone to me with zero humor.

Things were so bad that, back in Paris, Audrey, the editor of the *Événement artistique,* who secretly loves me, I think, was trying to discourage me from going to that country on the other side of the world. "No one comes back from there unchanged, Stephanie. I am saying this because I care about you," she murmured while caressing my forearm.

Whether it was because of this last murder or simply an excessive show of courtesy that would take on unexpected proportions—but, after all, I was hard up and one only gets what one deserves—Chief Inspector Rilsky came out to the airport to welcome me. Rather gaunt, tan, surprisingly attractive—serious. The change in his appearance surprised me. He had traded in his double-breasted Cary Grant outfit for an oversized suit of untreated silk. I have never seen old Northrop nervous. He hates psychology and pretends not to have a soul. Under his cop's mask he is a model of discretion. Was it fear then that had made him appear so youthful and almost giddy today?

We had hardly set off in his black Mercedes before he started warning me how dangerous my assignment was. Damn Gianchiotti over at the *Times* got his brains blown out in his bathtub, and not once but twice. I made a small nod to let him know I knew. No way was I going to go back to Bob's loft in the loosely patrolled hippy neighborhood where I had stayed on my previous trips to Santa Varvara. I had my routines—I wasn't some tourist who was going to stay in hotels like some cub reporter fresh out of the mailroom! Northrop saw no other solution than to offer me his guest room. His apartment was no three-star hotel, of course, but he assured me that I would have peace and quiet and my own bathroom. Because I knew his habits, or so he thought, I should have expected that he had prepared for his guests a perfect bower of privacy. "Goes without saying," he said.

I became more flushed than I should have. The torrid heat and dusty air perfumed with jasmine made me dizzy each time I arrived in Santa Varvara. I struggled without conviction, asking myself if I were not yielding more to the unexpected charms of Northrop than to the arguments of the careful police officer. In fact, without giving it much thought, I noticed that he gave me admiring glances out of the corner of his eye while driving. I suppose I am in pretty good shape these days. The other day Audrey remarked that I didn't stop getting younger. "I think it's the writing," she said with a slight smile. That little Audrey.

The inspector led me as though for the first time into the vast penthouse apartment of his parents that he had moved into after their death a few years ago. He then took me down one wing that he had transformed into a private space for houseguests. It was rather chic, pleasant, and the domino design of the bathroom tiles didn't clash too much with the old-fashioned, exacting bachelor tastes that I always associated with Rilsky. Until now anyway. There was a distinctive touch. Perhaps. With the ceremony of a papal reception he introduced me to Minoushah, a rather wild-looking tiger cat that first rubbed his master's ankles and then bit them lightly to punish him for his absence. No sooner had I showered and dressed than Rilsky called me to come and choose a weapon. He served me a gin and tonic that I drank in one gulp and then he opened a safe that was hidden behind a fake fireplace.

"I understand that you were once handy with a gun, my dear Stephanie, but I would bet that you've never carried a gun around with your pens and pencils at work."

My talent at riflery, a sport I practiced as a teenager, had revealed itself at an amusement park arcade. According to my mother, I had received this gift from her father, who had inherited it from his ancestors, all distinguished hunters in the steppes of Russia. "It's genetic, my dear," cried my mother in almost teary admiration of her progeny. Since then I'd used a Browning that Rilsky's deputy inspector Popov had handed me while we were visiting the new firing range one day during my last trip to Santa Varvara. The poor guy wanted to impress me, but I was a better shot than he was, and the holes in the center of my target cards made Mister Golden Gun's jaw drop.

A nine-millimeter Smith & Wesson, a Colt, a nine-millimeter Glock, a Browning, and a nickel-plated Remington made up Rilsky's arsenal. After hearing his advice and Rilsky's nervousness, I chose the Colt with no comment. This passivity was not like me, but I didn't mind it for once, and I thought I sensed a certain tenderness when the inspector's hand brushed mine as he gave me the gun. But it was probably just nerves.

"You have a meeting tomorrow morning at ten at the central bureau of the New Pantheon. We think that this powerful sect is involved in the assassination of Gianchiotti. But this mafia-of-God looks like it's going to go after the serial killer too, and you can see why. He's knocking off the scum one by one! So put your gun in your bag, even though I don't think you're in any immediate danger. Not inside their own building at least. But keep your weapon with you wherever you go. I've put Popov in charge of your safety, and don't be surprised if he's a little unsubtle at times; you know how he can be!

Normally so much pushy kindness would have gotten on my nerves or bored me, but I decided to simply refuse the dinner invitation and give my host a big hug before going to bed. It seemed to me that he responded with uncustomary emotion, but I was dead tired and did not lose any sleep wondering about it.

The Robed Rogues of the New Pantheon ⨳

I was received by the New Pantheon PR director in their flashy, ultramodern downtown building. I had no hopes of getting anything out of this petty spin doctor charged with presenting a reassuring public image of the New Pantheon so as to hide the secret dealings of one of Santa Varvara's most scandalous sects. Except perhaps the chance to set up an interview with the head guru himself. The sect's leader reigned over his faithful flock from his stronghold in a wooded seaside area that was off-limits to non-members. Guessing how much these bandits were interested in spreading a positive image of themselves with the help of a Paris newspaper, I suggested that only a personal interview with Reverend Sun was likely to dissipate the persistent and worrisome rumors concerning the illicit activities of the leader who was hidden away in the sect's Seaside Temple.

"Illicit activities!?" The PR man put on an indignant look behind his professorial wireless spectacles.

"Business activities, including the sex business," I replied dryly. "We have video cassettes." He stared at my large bag.

"No, I don't have them with me. The *Événement de Paris* has the originals." I was lying, but the rumor had come from a reliable source, and I was there to detect confirming signs, of course.

"Impossible! It's all made up. You can do anything these days with digital images." The PR man was no longer quite so kind as he had appeared upon welcoming me.

"You realize how important my eyewitness account will be under these circumstances." I went on in this way for several more minutes while invisible cameras filmed my every word and gesture, and the glassy stare of the PR man was telling me that I would be very lucky to get out of the present situation unharmed.

"But of course. Reverend Sun is a pious man and you will be impressed by the fervor of his followers. The only fear I have is that you will not want to leave the temple once inside," he added with a half-smile.

"Me too," I replied with my most charming smile while thinking of moving toward the door.

"Allow me to see you out," he said with icy politeness. The staring looks of his henchmen, marked with hatred, fear, or fanaticism—I didn't know which—followed me down the hallways, to the elevator, and out to the parking lot.

"I will communicate your request to the reverend this evening," he said before kissing my hand and opening the door of the taxi.

I had just told the driver my destination and was beginning to lean back when a series of shots rang out from a semiautomatic weapon firing its full round from somewhere behind a row of parked cars. The PR man was lying on the ground, his glasses nearby. With my Colt in my hand, I crouched down to his level while aiming in the direction of the hiding sniper. The half-open eyes of the professorial man stared at the wavy hot air above the blacktop. There were holes in his white shirt and blood was pouring out of his right temple. A bullet had gone right through his skull.

"Get down, get down!" Popov slammed me to the ground between the taxi and the nearby Ford behind which Rilsky's able assistant had been hiding.

Just in time, too, because a new round of shots was fired, but from the other end of the parking lot, followed by the noise of two cars taking off fast.

"Let's let them settle their accounts and get the heck out of here," said Popov, seeming a bit more relaxed as he led me to an unmarked police car.

We were glad to leave the scene of the crime.

"Put her in a taxi and get back to the station immediately! Change of program! Step on it! Stephanie, wait for us in my office!" barked the voice of Rilsky out of Popov's cellphone some minutes later.

The assistant officer dropped me off at a taxi stand and drove off at full speed with his siren blaring.

Sebastian Chrest-Jones: A Migratory Bird, Lion, or Vulture?

The airplane took off in the direction of Stony Brook, where Sebastian Chrest-Jones was to receive an honorary degree in recognition of his studies of mixed populations over the past twenty years at the Institute of Migratory History. An honor that did not take into account the twenty years of carefully hidden—or so he thought—personal research on the First Crusade and Byzantium. This private passion had only a thin connection to his official duties and only his ambitious assistant knew of the secret hobby, the "little vice" of his professor. His obscure laboratory within the institute was operated under the authority of the University of Santa Varvara. It had been officially assigned the task of clarifying the history of the nation, especially as concerned the well-known but ill-understood logic of the "melting pot" that had lately been the subject of revisionist attacks. Under cover of this patriotic mission, no one suspected that Chrest-Jones had been able to pursue even more arcane investigations without any government support, investigations that somewhat relieved his congenital depression and satisfied an intellectual vanity that was second to none. Without knowing the real reason behind this doctorate *honoris causa* from Stony Brook University, Sebastian Chrest-Jones couldn't help feeling a mixture of sincere emotion and mocking derision.

The Fokker Friendship F-27, a little turboprop with World War I–era propellers that carried no more than twenty-five passengers, made those not used to flying nervous, even before 9/11. Nevertheless it managed to cover the three hundred miles that separated the two cities without a hitch. The award recipient had accepted the additional honor of being offered the airfare instead of going to the ceremony in his own car. After all, a ceremony of this kind required a certain solemnity even for destructive personalities such as his.

As he flew at low altitude over the flat expanse divided into fields and industrial parks, Sebastian Chrest-Jones, far from experiencing the incomparable detachment from all earthly things that one feels from inside a Boeing 747 or an Airbus A300, was seized by the feeling that moving along in midair like this was the only situation that suited him, the only time in his life where he could say he was in his element. Not because he was free in the sense of being untouchable, unreachable, and above the crowd—feelings that any celebrity passenger might feel. No, that wasn't it. The historian had a sort of midflight revelation up there, no doubt occasioned by the upcoming event that would glorify him in front of thousands of graduating students and their families, but it took him by surprise nonetheless.

In this Fokker plane, known for its military stability, and despite its age and small size, Sebastian Chrest-Jones realized that what he thought to be his attachment to sorrow, his "morbid inclination for nihilism," as his smart-talking wife Hermine—a jovial, seductive, and hopelessly superficial creature—always put it, was really nothing but an inseparable, insurmountable strangeness. Between earth and sky, within the loud hum of the propellers being turned by the axles and engines—the reliability of German engineering softened by the Dutch name *Fokker*—Sebastian Chrest-Jones sipped a Diet Coke served by a hurried and humorless flight attendant and thought to himself that he was nothing but a migrant. If he were to be reincarnated one day, as the Buddhists believed, he would be a bird. In the meantime he could immerse himself with a serene joy that was close to mystical ecstasy within the spirit and body of this intimate space, a space that was nothing more to him than a place of transit. He could abandon himself to this endless movement, a radical incapacity for the sedentary life or even for rest.

Many times the historian had felt this trouble that wasn't really troublesome, since his familiarity with feeling as though he belonged to another world took away the fear to the point of reducing it to something evident to him but unspeakable to anyone else. That was it: he was from another world. The night before, as he walked up the five flights of stairs to get a little exercise while Hermine, who had taken the elevator, was already fussing in the bathroom, he was suddenly hypnotized by his foot striking the red carpet with its blue designs. Whose carpet was this? Whose shoe? Who was taking this step? Where was he? Someone was walking up a stairwell in a life that was not here and not now, a Chrest-Jones who was not in that shoe there, on this carpet here, between these two steps. But who was it then? Where did he come from? Where was he going?

Sebastian was certain that this delightful and distressing dizziness that made him feel as though he were rising off the ground had nothing to do with the very moderate amounts of champagne and red wine that he had drunk at dinner, nor with the rather amusing irritation caused of late by the flamboyant habits of his wife at dinner parties with their friends. From the very beginning of their married life, Hermine had taken to complaining that Sebastian did not listen, speak, or communicate—the "lack of conversation" being the most sadistic blow for a woman to take, she insisted. This led her to take a lover—something she kept secret and was convinced, the silly woman, that he didn't know. That primate, Pino Minaldi, Sebastian's lab assistant, abused her physically and mentally, but Hermine confided to Estelle Pankow—and since everything that goes around comes around, Sebastian eventually found out too—that she'd rather be treated like a whore than be totally ignored. After all, disputes were a species of discussion, and discussions were part of that vast domain called conversation, which indeed was hardly Sebastian's strong suit. In the other extreme, the pleasure that Hermine received from a taut volley of words was comparable to the drug user's dose of cocaine or heroin and always culminated in light-headedness, jubilation, and uncontrollable laughter.

For her dinner parties with the Pankows or elsewhere and Pino Minaldi too were only pretexts for bursts of laughter, onanistic orality, and noisy epileptic fits offered to the world or rather the worldly with an inflated, exalted, unalterable word from her mouth—Hermine's true sexual organ. Sebastian knew this and would let the storm pass. How long ago had he stopped noticing this tall thin body barely clothed in her fine black silk dress with her angular, provocative gestures and her unruly blonde bangs? With his ears ringing from abuse, what else could he do up against this spastic hurricane of flesh and words except take his distance with a bored smile? So he opted for the role of silent sage, a role that men today have increasing difficulty holding on to, as everyone knows.

The night before Hermine had put on her fireworks, which for Sebastian meant rising into one of his customary zone-out cruises. Her opening move was to retell the latest holdup story from the nightly news. That story reminded her of another holdup that she had witnessed as a child: "Hooded men, machine guns, sacks of money, everyone on the ground, mother behind an armchair hiding me underneath her, can you imagine? I almost suffocated. And everything seemed to be frozen like in a still life, and the police, who arrived late, started interviewing the witnesses instead of going after the crooks, who had cleared out by that time, of course." Inhale. "À propos . . . " Of what? It only took Sebastian a second to link "à propos" with the expression "to clear out." " . . . I suppose you know this crazy story . . . No, well listen: this boy had run away and his mother, this typical Jewish mother, you know what I mean, calls the train station. 'Hello, train station? Has my son arrived?'" At this point Hermine's face was turning purple as she tried to keep from laughing. "Of course at the train station she expected everyone to know her dear little boy, where he was going, the time of his arrival, everything! But the son had run off, he'd cleared out! With this kind of mother, his home a kind of ghetto, you can understand why, don't you think? Ha ha ha!" The Pankows didn't really get the connection between the two stories, but so what? Estelle, a true Jewish mother, was not simply unruffled by Hermine's lack of manners—"as conscious as a canary," she thought to herself—but actually listened with a certain friendly attention. Or boredom. As a woman and a psychoanalyst, the hostess well knew that there is no stopping the verbal orgasm of a frigid hysteric and merely continued to observe her with a tenderly mocking eye.

Hermine made her glottis vibrate with such conviction that ripples of laughter soon overcame her whole audience. At the end of her run she insisted on weighing down her stories with didactic clarifications on the off chance that someone might not have kept up with the subtlety of her humor. Her conversation was one endless ribbon in which she was continually wrapping herself with nonstop excitement at the sound of her own voice. But Mrs. Chrest-Jones had already changed subjects. "Speaking of mothers, surely you've heard the news—in Santa Varvara no one's talking about anything else—it seems that homosexual couples are going to be allowed to adopt children." Well, Hermine didn't see what was so "shocking," as some shrinks had called it. "Can you imagine, even shrinks! Personally she was all in favor of this kind of adoption, believed that everyone around the table was aware of the solid legal and psychological grounds for such a thing, right, Estelle? After all, Freud and Lacan proved that we're all bisexual, mentally I mean; therefore, whether one is a man or a woman, there's always going to be a bit of the other sex in each one of the adoptive parents, even if they are homosexual. So the kid won't be missing out on anything, you understand? QED, right, dear?"

Hermine was convinced she was preaching to the converted. In fact, no! His colleague in the department of clinical human sciences had always struck Sebastian as a conciliatory, sensuously distant woman, such a rare commodity among the distinguished university faculty. But for once the politely ironic Estelle came unglued.

"That is laughable, my dear Hermine, really! Look, let me tell you, let's play a game, no, no, it's not complicated. Imagine I have you adopted, you, yes, you, by a homosexual couple, would you like that? Ask yourself and tell me. Me, I wouldn't. There, you see!" Estelle was not laughing. Her face was red with anger, definitely more a mad professor than a poised hostess face. Everyone else stared down at their cheese. "What's more, you'd do well to just leave Freud and Lacan out of your theories, which you have every right to defend, but really!" My, my. Estelle had no intention of backing off, and Pankow himself, her usually unflappable economist husband, looked up at her wide-eyed. "Bisexual, OK, but it comes from our bodies, don't you think?" The *body* was Estelle's specialty, Sebastian had almost forgotten, but of course didn't now given the circumstances. "Bodies of men and women, do you know about them?" Tanned and massaged, Estelle was radiant. No doubt just back from some water therapy vacation. Nothing like ocean water to firm up your bust and thighs, slim your waist, puff up your lips, and sculpt your whole body with vitality, even if you are a shrink, in fact, especially if you're a shrink. She had curly dark hair with a touch of gray and a fine sheen from some algae-based conditioner. She paused to savor her physical well-being, catch her breath, then resumed. "For me there's a difference between a woman's skin and a man's skin, a woman's voice and a man's voice, a woman's scent and a man's scent, and I can assure you it is not the same physical and verbal presence. You accept that the language of your parents—bisexual, certainly—is forged from their *entire* physical being, right? And then, bang, you get rid of the body with one swipe of the hand? But the child doesn't, believe me, and I know because I've got kids!" Estelle had gone from defense to offense with a direct hit below the belt of her dinner guest. "And I know that they grow up with all the perceptions that they receive from both sexes, father and mother, each of whom has, despite their bisexuality as you say, chosen a dominant way of being, male or female. OK, a woman can imitate a man, and vice versa, I know, and there's more and more of that going on—you don't need to tell me. Caricature, sure, why not? I am not homophobic, don't think that, but kids adopted by these sorts of caricatures will turn out to be caricatures themselves or another human species. Is that what you want?—excuse me, how did we get on to that?" Estelle was apparently at the end of her diatribe. The professor had spoken and the hostess could now get back to serving her guests. "I tend to get a little serious after midnight. It's time to cut this tarte Tatin. I can see that that cheese wasn't a big hit!"

"She made us her tarte Tatin! The cook's upside-down apple tart surprise! I've been waiting for it all evening! But really, we need to meet together—just the two of us, you know? Honestly, psychoanalysis has really fallen behind; you've all become so frumpy, my dear, if one compares you with the boldness of your sect in the early days. Excuse me for saying so, but are you the most backward of the fundamentalist religions in Santa Varvara, or what? Seriously, to think that certain rabbis and parish priests, yes, even priests, are changing their minds about homosexual couples . . . You'll see, my dear, adoption's not the end of the world, don't get upset, onward and upward."

Sebastian Chrest-Jones was used to it. He had not found his wife amusing for some time and Estelle's lessons bored him just about as much. He detested these end-of-dinner conversations for or against homosexual couples, for or against Jewish mothers, abortions, sexual liberation, pornography, public safety in low-income areas, government arrogance, grassroots opposition. Everything about Santa Varvara made him think about turning into a bird of prey or a wild beast and destroying it all. But only in secret, of course, because instead of committing a crime, the height of bad taste, our scholar had set himself a spiritual task, and one not that difficult in fact. He pasted a pleasant forced smile between his cheeks while before his mind's eye he secretly projected the screen of his laptop, and within that suspended state he even managed to resolve certain complicated problems that, despite his intense concentration, eluded him back at the lab or at home in front of his open window looking out on the bay.

His "transit zone," which more and more often would literally pluck him out of time—the night before between two steps and today aboard the Fokker—had nothing to do with the feverish cluckings of Hermine, his failed marriage, or the yapping at the Pankows' dinner parties. Sebastian was certain he held a truth, his personal truth, the truth that Hermine criticized him for being entirely without. His research on migrant populations, which, after all, had earned him the title of doctor *honoris causa* from Stony Brook, certainly had something to do with it, but for reasons very different from those that would be solemnly and objectively enumerated by the dean. The transit zone was his secret garden hideaway whose uncertainties he savored during his out-of-time hallucinations, which migrants frequently experience at irregular intervals. But today, at this high altitude above the irregularly cut squares that divided up the Santa Varvara plains, this state had already gone on for more than a quarter of an hour. The cool sun of autumn poured in through the plane's small window and began to heat up his Diet Coke. What time could it have been?

Finally the Fokker made a slightly bumpy landing at the airport in Stony Brook. The ceremony went exactly as planned, with the graduates kneeling and filled with emotion as they awaited their diplomas and scarves. Sebastian gave his speech and the dean placed around his neck the traditional hood, this one trimmed with white and cardinal red. These ornaments linked Sebastian's merits with those of imaginary monks from time immemorial, a link that every university in the United States, Canada, and elsewhere wanted to cultivate so as to extend the honor of its vocation. Then came the school anthem, followed by praise for the man and his works. While the historian was thinking of his father, a few tears came into his eyes. Then the newly honored doctor pulled himself together, and there were flowers offered, congratulations, hugs, a banquet, more speeches, smiles, promises, projects, everything, nothing.

At around two o'clock in the morning Sebastian left his deluxe VIP suite on campus and took a taxi to a suburban motel where Fa Chang was waiting. She had sent him an urgent e-mail. She absolutely had to see him. It could not wait, she insisted. That she had driven three hundred miles to speak to him piqued his curiosity. Chrest-Jones was not one to give in to the whims of a charming laboratory colleague, even one who had become in the past months a very pleasing mistress. Fa was not ignorant of his indifference and considered it his general attitude and by no means aimed at her alone. She did not let it upset her. "Of course," he smirked, "she's Asian." He set aside the insistent e-mail, wondering what this unaccustomed show of emotion was about, and was ready to let it be engulfed by the transit zone that he had earlier experienced on the plane. But the cumulative fatigue of the last forty-eight hours did not allow the very satisfied doctor *honoris causa* to sleep—so, Fa Chang, why not?

As soon as he entered the room, and without turning on the light, Fa kissed him softly in her childish whorish way—the ancient talent of the Chinese, he thought to himself, with a dry mock. He liked her androgynous body, dry and hard, with smallish breasts but wide, firm buttocks. It was a muscular little body like those of medal-winning Asian gymnasts. He was becoming more and more excited by Fa and this desire frightened him. Sebastian had the feeling that he would never be able to get rid of her, that she would never let go, never leave them alone, neither him nor his field of dreams, including his research, his precious investigations that led him to Byzantium and his novel: *The Story of Anna*, a Byzantine princess, the world's first female historian . . . psst! his obscure quest.

Had he read her last message? Of course, hadn't he entered this motel that wasn't all that discreet, though had Fa even noticed? There were fluorescent wall coverings, posters of loving kittens on the wall, fake flowers in fake gold-trimmed art nouveau vases, as well as subdued lighting just right for the sport-sex of salesmen far from home. Sebastian wondered about escaping all this, sliding into Fa, deeper in until he broke her open, opening her open, taking her to a zenith, exploding her, disappearing inside her, with her.

"No, not yesterday's, my dear, the one from this afternoon, after the ceremony." Knowing his emotional side, despite his usual oysterlike reserve,

Fa had organized a surprise for him. No, Sebastian had not looked at his e-mail since the morning.

"Well, dear, you'll hear it live then. It's the best thing that could have ever happened to me. Of course, you are under no obligation. I know how important your freedom is to you. But it's important that you know, and I prefer telling you on this very day, such an important day for you, for both of us, even though it concerns only me in a certain sense. So, guess what? I'm going to have a baby! Isn't that fabulous?"

She murmured it all in a breathless ripple. Women—Hermine, Estelle, Fa—they always have something to say, many things, rather urgent and generally painful, uninteresting, and nonsensical. She would not stop kissing him as he roamed over her medal-winning gymnast's tummy that performed so outstandingly on the balance beam, the uneven bars, and the pommel horse. And now she was the pommel horse and he went back and forth, but so far away, a migrant, a nowhere man, a man who takes his leave, goes, wanders off, a male of another world, abruptly inaccessible, an animal. A bird of prey, a wild beast, a brute. He stopped. Blood had invaded his mind. He no longer saw her, but her body continued to vibrate; it didn't know that Sebastian was no longer there, that Fa's lover no longer existed. The fear, anxiety, and anger of the emptied man changed suddenly into rage. A need to defend himself, to get free, to hit, to escape.

He squeezed Fa's throat and lost all sense of time.

When he realized that he had strangled her, he felt no particular emotion. Just indifference toward this crumpled little body lying on these wrinkled sheets, this pretentious motel for middle middle-class adultery, and this lawn sleeping its dewy sleep until morning. The mirror above the sink was empty—no image, nothing but the sound of running water, water splashing on hands, ordinary hands, the hands of no one. He was indifferent toward them too, like everything else. He went up to the dead body, delicately took the head in his hands, and thrust his thumbs into the eye sockets of the foreigner. See no evil.

A calm boundless force came over him and he lifted the body and wrapped it in Fa's coat, which she had used as a dressing gown. He then brought it outside standing, as though he were helping the young woman walk, and placed her in the car. No lights went on. Everyone was sleeping, even the motel's night watchman was slumped down in front of his television. Sebastian jumped in behind the wheel and drove quickly toward the lake that separated Santa Varvara and Santa Kruz. He then placed Fa in the driver's seat and pushed the Fiat Panda over the cliff. The car bobbed and spun over a few times before sinking into the deep water of Big Stony Brook Pond.

Still indifferent but possessed with a savage force, Sebastian Chrest-Jones calmly walked away and continued for several hours without knowing where he was going. Headlights flashed in his face; one car slowed down but he turned away. He stopped at a gas station and tossed back a double espresso. It was dawn. No project, no idea. The gas station was warm—that was enough.

"Professsor Chrest-Jones, what a surprise to find you here! Don't you recognize me?" Seeing the astonished look on Sebastian's face, he continued.

"I am one of the students who graduated yesterday along with you. There were a lot of us, it's true. Well, I know you—that is, I know your work, at least what I can understand of it at my modest level, I mean. Pardon me, but I truly admire you. I drove my parents back home. They live in the next village over and I'm going back to Stony Brook. Your car broke down, I suppose?"

The little redhead's obsequiousness was like candied fruit. Sebastian hated this sickly sweetness that the university secreted quite naturally, like the saliva of a famished person. Nevertheless, he decided to play along.

"Yes, bad luck, and it won't be ready before tomorrow. There's a shortage of spare parts in this outback, if you don't mind my saying so. What did you say your name was?"

"Tom, Tom Botev, sir."

"Yes, well, as you can see, Tom, I'm seriously stuck."

"It's your lucky day! I mean, no problem because I can take you back to campus, that's where I'm headed."

By noon Sebastian had reached his VIP campus suite. Tom would brag, no doubt, but about what? These young airheads don't know how to think. As for suspecting something, making some connection, or leading an inquiry—"Not a chance," thought Sebastian calmly as he packed his bags, said farewell to the dean, and flew back to Santa Varvara.

On the return flight the murderer napped. All scenes of the motel had vanished from his mind. There was only the agitation of surprising dreams to ruffle a powerful hypnotic tranquillity. The theory of inseparability, developed by a certain Jim Iks who worked at the university, impressed itself on his mind like a hallucination. He saw the lines of the article as clearly as if he were holding the review in his hands. Under certain circumstances, claimed this quantum physicist, if two objects came into contact just once, it sufficed for them to remain inseparable for all eternity. Forever, even if appearances showed them to be absolutely separate in time and space. Under what circumstances? Sebastian couldn't remember or didn't want to remember. Iks's article had irritated classical physicists, but the rudest primate in heat would have spontaneously agreed with this thesis back in the Stone Age! You can't imagine the hoopla that Iks's disciples orchestrated on the Santa Varvara campus and all over the planet. To hear them tell it, their genius leader had upended received ideas and raised troubling, very troubling questions for any rational ontology! Were they puffing things up so as to seem dramatically original in the eyes of the world? Perhaps campaigning for a Nobel Prize? With his novel on Byzantium Sebastian held the truth: Anna Comnena was inseparable from Sebastian Chrest-Jones, and vice versa, thanks to a family ancestor of his who had once crossed her path. The historian snuggled into his airplane seat feeling very pleased with himself. It was absurd to try and live anywhere but in the realm of inseparability. Iks and Chrest-Jones possessed the key to the only possible reality: the absolute time of the afterlife and therefore of life itself.

"Your Coke, sir," said a smiling, attractive attendant with a professional but unpleasant curtness. He watched the soda as it fell over the ice cubes making little bubbles that would burst and subside. A madness of lovers this inseparability? Maybe. "An intrauterine osmosis, an infantile collage inside the primitive mother that creates the madman, the passionate, the mystic, and the criminal," Estelle Pankow would no doubt have pontificated, had he shared his secret with her. Unless it were a dream that came secretly to haunt the sleep of every one of us? And at daybreak no sooner forgotten so that the person thus separated from his desire may confront objective reality with his indivisible compact self? Was it necessary for a second scientific folly such as that of Jim Iks to run against the grain of the lovers' madness and prove what the dreamers knew all along and what Sebastian was experiencing in writing his *Story of Anna*? There was something that Hermine would never understand and that little Fa Chang, with her recently impregnated tummy, would have endangered and surely altered, prevented, or destroyed. By getting rid of the androgynous gymnast Sebastian had become forever inseparable from Anna, from her ancestors, from her memory. He had returned to Byzantium.

Byzantium Is Where I Am; or, *The Story of Anna Comnena* ☙

Byzantium . . . As soon as he set to work, glued to his PC, Sebastian would reach that state of mental combustion, rare for a researcher, in which the life of the mind, or to put it more modestly the professional life, initially intended to flee anxieties, actually made them grow, would meld with them, aggravating and pacifying them at the same time. The result was not so much a thought process as a kind of flammable material that certain individuals would submit to like fate, others would seek to tame within the cage of their diaries, and that Sebastian Chrest-Jones simply pursued as his research. Granted, his job as a medievalist had always been the one and only passion in his life. Never before, however, had his investigations into the obscurities of Byzantium joined up in such absolute terms with the mysteries of his own existence. For several years now ancient history and contemporary life, documents and hypotheses mixed together and propelled him into a new reality whose place was neither Santa Varvara nor Byzantium, neither in the eleventh century nor in the twenty-first century. But where was it then?

Was it among the traces, so improbable but for him so necessary, of one of his ancestors from Thrace and probably from Provence, Boulogne, or Normandy originally? Or among the multicolored lines drawn by the software of his laptop computer, a virtual mapping of the First Crusade launched to liberate the Holy Sepulchre? From one hypothesis to another, from one chronicle to another, from one site to another within the vast web spun by many generations of scribes and now available on the World Wide Web, Sebastian fluttered. Of all the creatures in Santa Varvara and Byzantium, only the Lepidoptera seemed to him worthy of his esteem: innocent and gracious messengers with their multicolored wings, uncapturable and free of all bitterness, unlike birds who could be rather mean and overly noisy. Butterflies have neither body nor face, only a little hollow filament to which its membranous soul is attached, those wings of space, those sails of the countryside. One imagines no home for them, no nest, no house. Their only shelter consists in folding up their wings like praying hands and sleeping alone on some stamen, petal, or bud. These leaping Lepidoptera live in light and color, provisional fleeting crystals of the cosmic pulse. Man can only capture them by pursuing them with an aesthetic innocence whose cruelty is exacted against the migrant insect's unique human trait: its head and bulging eyes. He only needs to crush these vitreous globules between his fingers for the animal hidden inside its celestial jewel-like form to die. He can no longer enjoy the vibration that has been killed by his loving gesture, but instead the work of art itself in which lay condensed the mysteries of its journeys, the memory of its species, the quartering of the continents both icy and torrid, the magnificence of the flora and fauna, and finally the least upset series of diverse humanoids. Our historian is a butterfly chasing butterflies in search of new prey, multicolored spaces, dead eras, magnetic intervals, perfect errors, and obstinate wanderers—all that trembling Time shakes out.

Butterfly of butterflies, Persephone, with black spots of sadness . . . Vulcan, striped red and black . . . and Anna herself, this Stendhalian dreamer before Stendhal, in these warring times that don't let up . . . Sebastian clicked every day on his file "Anna Comnena Story":

"Me, I was overcome by many different feelings—to my friends still living and to men who in the future will read this history I swear by God who knows all things that I was no better than a madwoman, wholly wrapped up in my sorrow. . . . When I looked again to my father and recognized that all his strength was going and the circulation of blood in the arteries had finally stopped, then I turned away, exhausted and cold, my head bowed and both hands covering my eyes. Without a word I stepped back and began to weep."

Of all the chronicles of the First Crusade, only the *Alexiad* by the porphyrogene princess held Sebastian's attention. An accident? In love with her father, the emperor, or basileus, Alexius I Comnenus (1081–1118), Anna knew how to combine her melancholic admiration for the great man with a Byzantine taste for intrigue. Political power made her think; her attention to detail suggests a military mind, as does her gift for scrupulous geopolitical observation mixed with sarcasm that spares neither the sacred expedition nor the palace. And all of it, written in a style that is as erudite as it is contagious, made her, in Sebastian's opinion, the first female intellectual, perhaps even the first modern historian.

Of course some of his colleagues, the serious pedantic ones, preferred William of Tyre over her—William the eminent scholar who knew Syrian, Persian, Arabic, though the canon's primary interest was crusaders, Sebastian was entirely convinced of it. They also preferred Albert of Aix, the chronicler of the Lotharingians who furnishes modern scholiasts with many wonderful small details that they can use to retrace the itineraries of the first Crusades. Naturally there is also Raymond d'Aguilers, irreplaceable for understanding the Toulousians, no? And one must not forget the *Gesta Francorum*, that very lively chronicle of the Norman Crusade. Knowledge from the servants, all that—from archivists, herb and insect gatherers, gray men in the shadow of power, while Anna sat round about a throne—porphyrogene! Ah, the Porphyrogene! History passed through her very body—her tears, her moods, the intrigues of the palace, the battle with her brother John, the future basileus, who would snatch the throne from her even though she could have had it herself. However, in Byzantium, even in Byzantium, after so many empresses, a woman on the throne during these times of war was by no means automatic. To be a historian was mostly acceptable, but not entirely, although it was more discreet—go write in a convent if you want! And then there were the jealousies of her pathetic mother and the love rivalry of her grandmother, Anna Dalassena, Anna the Great, the perfidious politician. As for the male crusaders, no one else at the time describes them like Anna: too rustic, too wild, too handsome, too dangerous, awesome! This band of barbarians pushes her to write so as to conserve a record of the great Porphyry in those troubled, uncertain times. She would take refuge in a monastery to mourn the great basileus her father by writing the *Alexiad*, a work that would make historians jealous for centuries to come, and finally dies, no one knows where. In Sebastian's view Anna's history had the advantage of not being enclosed within the Latin perspective, a fact that led him to question its truth and to weigh on his own the views of opposing camps as good scientific method requires.

Flambé and *Apollo*, white butterflies, wings of time, microcosm and duration, species and history, hyperboles of my memory, Greek parchments, myths and science, combustion, magnets: Sebastian would not stop clicking on the pages that he loved and had read and reread from the fifteen books of the *Alexiad*. Raised on Homer, Plato, and Aristotle, Anna wrote in a language close to modern Greek. She had become a historian so that she could continue the work of her husband, the caesar Nicephorus Bryennius, who died young, but, more important, it was to be able to justify the reign of her father. Should her *Alexiad* be read as a "Chronicle of a Princess" or as a "Search for the Lost Father"? Sebastian did not need Doctor Freud to be told that his own secret motive that had attracted him for so long to Byzantium—despite the great astonishment of his university colleagues who considered it to be a dead, overworked field without the least relation to contemporary history—was essentially the same as that of Anna Comnena. No need to blush. Or perhaps more generally it was a common feature of eras in decline where the horizon appears wilted, such as in the eleventh and the twenty-first centuries, this hope to recharge oneself by investigating origins. In which case one goes back inevitably to an absent father, to the primordial enigma, which one must solve in order to retrieve him and, if possible, give him at best a certain shape and weight, to some dream of acquiring in this way an identity.

Tirelessly, Sebastian scrolled through the passages that he had recopied from the *Story of Anna* and paused to reread those where the princess cries for her father. The basileus Alexius dies in 1118 and his daughter is devastated. Our historian likes to find her mournful today, since, melancholic himself, he can be cheered by then following her to the earlier books of the *Alexiad*, considered more sober and useful for contemporary research. Anna does not spend all her time crying by any means. She needs to be taken seriously, presented in a "selected passages" section in school textbooks, and to become required reading, the subject of university courses, and respected by feminists who have also forgotten her. With great energy and talent this woman describes the defeats and conquests of her father, the basileus, pitted against the madmen of Porphyry, against would-be usurpers from across the seas, an awesome man! She adopted very often, alas, the father's point of view. Sebastian's approach is not very orthodox; it will irritate Byzantium scholars. Good.

He will have to verify and expand carefully, but it would seem that Anna is not fooled by the distress that overtakes Alexius I during this great swell of crusaders coming to Constantinople. Listen:

"He heard a rumor that countless Frankish armies were approaching. He dreaded their arrival, knowing as he did their uncontrollable passion, their erratic character and their irresolution, not to mention the other peculiar traits of the Celts, with their inevitable consequences: their greed for money, for example, which always led them, it seemed, to break their own agreements without scruple for any chance reason. . . . What actually happened was more far-reaching and terrible than rumor suggested, for the whole of the West and all the barbarians who lived between the Adriatic and the Strait of Gibraltar migrated in a body to Asia, marching across Europe country by country with all their households."

Seen from the sumptuous capital of the Orient at the end of the eleventh century, where have we gotten to in Santa Varvara, in New York, in Paris? All of these crusaders were for Anna nothing but a swarm of threatening insects, a sandstorm that unfurled itself for better or worse, only God could tell. A random assortment of Celts, Franks, Latins, and Barbarians mixed together and appearing all the same to Anna who, it seems, did not distinguish between the popular Crusade of Peter the Hermit and those of the noble barons and did not suspect the role played by Pope Urban II behind this massive wave of tribesmen. For Sebastian his female historian is a modern figure because she has her opinion, an opinion that comes through her storytelling. How many colloquia from San Francisco to Milan were necessary to decide whether history is subjective or objective, cold annales school or hot narration? Anna did not ask herself that question because she had already answered it—such is the undiscoverable way of truth. She feared and hated at once the cupidity and dexterity of the Latin chiefs who would not wash and could not write, but she did not underestimate their numbers or their courage.

"These men had such ardor and energy that all paths were laid open to them. The Celtic soldiers were accompanied by a multitude of unarmed people, more numerous than the sand in the sea or the stars in the sky, and each carrying a palm branch and a cross around their shoulders—all women and children who had left their homes. They looked like various streams flowing together into one river. . . . The arrival of all these people was preceded by a swarm of locusts that spared the grain harvest but destroyed and devoured the vineyards."

Sebastian in Search of the Lost Father ☙

The historian Sebastian Chrest-Jones would be perfectly capable of speaking before a scientific tribunal and explaining, for example, why his investigations were better furthered by the historical novel of Anna Comnena than, say, by the prose of William of Tyre or that of Foucher de Chartres. When he is at his PC, totally aborbed in this novel, he has no thoughts for those others. And too bad for Minaldi, his assistant! Ever since he became the lover of Hermine, Sebastian's wife, this fellow has seen fit to make wisecracks about the Porphyrogene! Sebastian ignores this drivel. He is reading his princess with a finely trained eye. He is enchanted by the locusts as well as by the swarms of people, the seeds and stars, and the confluence of these streams. It is there, surely, that the one he has always been looking for, his very own ancestor, is hiding. In search of this secret mirage—perhaps since he has no friends he had unwittingly leaked his quest to Hermine—the obscure historian of Santa Varvara had left for Philippopolis in Byzantium, present-day Plovdiv in Bulgaria, the birthplace of his father Sylvester, the patriarch of the Chrest family of immigrants who had traveled to the United States at the beginning of the twentieth century. From church records, rumors, folklore, and legends, Sebastian the son devoted himself to reconstructing the family saga.

Logically, he had first investigated the family name, Chrest, since a patronymic is a tomb, a papyrus, a live spring. The common noun *chrest* means "cross," which is hardly surprising and the name "commemorates the Crusades that had passed long ago somewhere in the area." Ah, these dictionary definitions! "Somewhere," "long ago"—but where and when? None of them gave specifics, and yet the songs and stories and proverbs all attested without the least doubt that a crusader had stopped at Philippopolis and had married the beautiful Militsa, his great-great-great- . . . how many "great" Bulgarian grandmothers would he have to go back through? This crusader, admired for his beauty and manly force, was no less hated for the same reasons, and because he was a barbarian invader. Anna Comnena said it better than anyone from the heights of her royal rank, but the villagers thought the same thing, and thus arose a plot to kill him sooner or later, because those who come from elsewhere, etc. . . . Hell is other people. Harvesting peasants found the intruding outsider stabbed in his field, even though the warrior had himself become a peasant. He had thought it best to stop crusading; he had not suspected that he was the only one to think so, or perhaps he had, but maybe he didn't mind either way. A strange character indeed, this first Chrest! Did he want to know what would happen if he settled down and stopped crusading, like a sort of experimenting alchemist? At the time, as everyone knows, alchemists were philosophers, revolutionaries, you know what I mean? His murderer was never discovered. It was in no one's interest to solve the mystery. Thus, since earliest times, a troubling legend surrounds the Chrest family and its descendants. A family of restless wanderers.

"You, Mr. Historian of Santa Varvara, you ought to know what your father was like, this father who left us behind, no? Still very young, we knew him then, I tell you, just as my grandfather told me: that man was an ambitious ball of energy. . . . " Sebastian did not know very much about his father Sylvester Chrest, and it was precisely to learn more about this person that he had undertaken his first expedition to Philippopolis (Plovdiv) back in his student days when he first felt inclined to travel further in time and space, today or tomorrow, if necessary. It was crazy to look for a shred of truth among these backward storytellers—all tall tales, myths, and mad distortions! A serious researcher must sift through rumors. He had found the tomb of the mother of Sylvester, one Mithra, and had taken a little of the earth from the cemetery back to Santa Varvara. "Your pilgrimage is grotesque," declared Hermine. Upset, he had stuffed the packet in a drawer but never forgot about it. Never.

But how long ago did this first crusader, the ancestor of the Chrests, this hypothetical forefather, live? Nine or ten centuries before the start of the third millennium! A long, long time ago! But Sebastian would not give up the search. He devoted himself to pouring over the documents that spoke about the passage of the Crusades through Philippopolis (Plovdiv). Back at Santa Varvara he spent years reconstructing the itineraries, examining the maps, and gradually letting go of the other Crusades to concentrate exclusively on the first. Thus came the fiery energy for his saga.

One click on the file "Routes of the First Crusade" and the screen filled with the lines traced across a map of medieval Europe. The Chrest ancestor surely arrived with the armies of Godfrey of Bouillon. They had gone via Hungary, crossed the Sava, and passed through Nish, Sofia, and Philippopolis. However, the loyal followers of Bouillon hardly scattered at all. His Lorraine and Norman barons and their followers would not have stayed in Thrace, where it was too hot and too bright. It was difficult to imagine Chrest stopping there all alone.

So had his ancestor come instead with the troops of Hugh of France? Perhaps. These insolent savages amused our dear Anna. After having planned a triumphant arrival, Hugh of Vermandois, the younger brother of the king of France, Philip I (himself excommunicated for having left his wife and

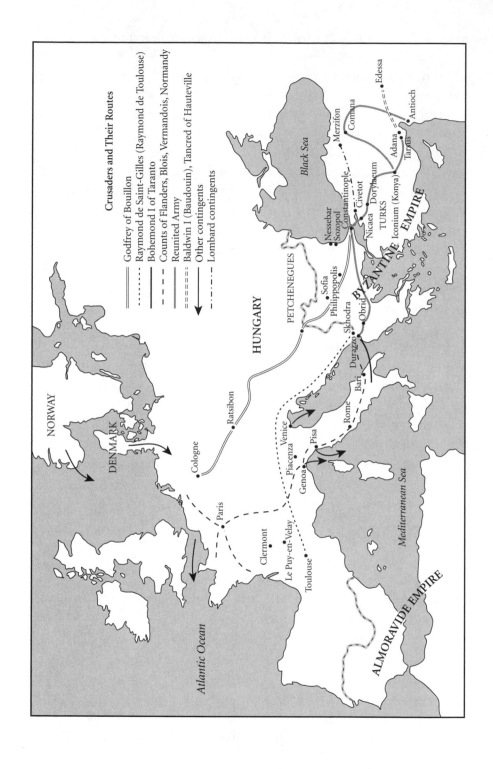

Crusaders and Their Routes

—————— Godfrey of Bouillon
············· Raymond de Saint-Gilles (Raymond de Toulouse)
– – – – – Bohemond I of Taranto
———— Counts of Flanders, Blois, Vermandois, Normandy
———— Reunited Army
= = = = = Baldwin I (Baudouin), Tancred of Hauteville
→ Other contingents
–·–·–·– Lombard contingents

NORWAY

DENMARK

Atlantic Ocean

Cologne

Ratsibon

HUNGARY

Paris

Clermont

Le Puy-en-Velay

Toulouse

Genoa

Piacenza

Venice

Pisa

Rome

Bari

Durazzo

Skhodra

Obrid

Sofia

Philippropolis

Nessebar

Sozopol

Constantinople

Civetot

Nicaea

Dorylaeum

Iconium (Konya)

Merzifon

Comana

Adana

Tarsus

Antioch

Edessa

Black Sea

PETCHENEGUES

BYZANTINE EMPIRE

TURKS

Mediterranean Sea

ALMORAVIDE EMPIRE

thus unable to lead the Crusade), landed as best he could after a terrible storm not far from Dyrrachium, also called Durazzo or Durrës. Alexius Comnenus fished out the Frenchman, or Frank, if you prefer, offered him a sumptuous table covered with gifts, and conducted him to the capital "not along the most direct route, but via a detour through Philippopolis," explains the storytelling princess. Chrest might have been a part of this band of adventurers. Unless, that is, he had come with the count of Toulouse, Raymond de Saint-Gilles, whom Alexius appreciated the most even though the count did not swear to be his vassal but only promised his loyalty.

Enigmas are not as impenetrable as science would have it, everything becomes rational for the mind of the historian brought to its kindling point. If he looked hard enough, Sebastian would find out where he came from. On the other hand, there was no need to set out on an investigation of the plot of Cain, the farmer, who killed his brother Abel, the nomadic shepherd and first ancestor of the Chrests. It was of no interest, a regular story, a plain, regular story. But, so, who was he, this pilgrim in search of the Holy Sepulchre who had the strange idea to become a Thracian peasant? Where did he come from? What migrant group did he belong to? Follow the path, trace the voyage, that is all we can do, we who are still here—for who knows how long?—slumped before our computers and already inscribed within the maps on our screens. We are on the little dotted lines, in the barely identifiable camps, we are the blinking shadows who believe we can go extravagantly, beyond memory, vagabonds within the routine human procession, crusaders of nothing.

When Sebastian was plunged into his saga, two paths interested him most: where had the troops of Hugh of Vermandois and those of Saint-Gilles originated? From what region, from what city did they come, these barbarians who were for Anna, all agree today, her real passion (just as they were for her father the basileus, as is well known, but perhaps in her case a somewhat different passion, more animal, dirty, and mean)? What famine, what distress, what madness, what faith drove these men and their troops?

The route of Saint-Gilles passes very close to Philippopolis. Having left behind Croatia, these Provençals crossed Durazzo, and then reached Vodena and Salonika before arriving at Christoupolis, present-day Kavalla. Many of them, discouraged or defeated by the Bulgarian and Petchenegue mercenaries of Alexius, scattered and did not pursue their quest to the very end:

the Holy Sepulchre. So did the first great-great-great . . . -great grandfather Chrest push on as far as Philippopolis?

History has preserved some of the illustrious names of this Provençal advance: Raymond de Saint-Gilles of the house of Valentinous and the bishop of Le Puy, Adhémar de Monteil, whom Pope Urban II had once considered putting in charge of the Crusade. In fact, Adhémar was the shadow director, the spiritual force behind the broadsword that he had left at home in Auvergne but that was carried here with pomp and prestige by the valorous Saint-Gilles.

"Adhémar and his band of clerics, a curious company, to be continued . . ." Sebastian had noted to himself as he clicked on the icon of Le Puy-en-Velay, at the left of the Crusades of Europe map that he worked tirelessly to complete, little by little each day, as he advanced in his readings.

He had not yet found the person he was looking for, but he already imagined the space of his quest, his saga: from Santa Varvara to Philippopolis the path would unquestionably pass through Constantinople with Anna Comnena and perhaps also through Le Puy-en-Velay . . . to be continued.

Feeling overcome with fatigue, Sebastian opens wide the window looking out on the bay and takes deep breaths of the gusting air. He cannot stand stale air, the fetid feeling of confined mammals overly warm, even if only his mind's impression—especially when it is his mind's impression. In the offices it always smells of confined bodies with sweaty and unclean orifices. Fresh air! A band of cormorants flies over the lagoon, and one hears the joyous cries of these unwelcome predators. Sebastian likes their laser-beam stares. How might a man obtain the same fine gaze over time and space, the piercing lucidity of dreams, of gliding in flight? They scrutinize the infinitely small. They see him here, at his window with his computer and simultaneously with no border between Santa Varvara and Byzantium. Besides butterflies, birds are the only creatures in the world that one can admire without making mistakes. There are no others, certainly not cats, dogs, and all those that allow themselves to be domesticated and form attachments. Sebastian could not understand those who did not trust birds with their armless, distant bodies. Herring gulls, Eurasian kestrels, western march harriers, and common terns—these immaculate killers would often swoop down and harpoon their prey, swallow bottom fish and eels on the rocks opposite before taking off again, innocent and elegant savages that they were, toward the shore of an other world. He observed them. Today they are a noisy band, as though sensing a coming storm, but no cloud was on the horizon, nothing but the red disk of a scarlet sun, and the cries of these drunken cormorants, agitated and off course, swirled already within the magnetic field of the storm.

Rilsky; or, How Not to Be a Purifier &

Rilsky and Popov did not show up at police headquarters for over an hour. I was trying to calm down, but the noise of the shootout would not stop ringing in my ears and I was freezing or boiling, I didn't know which. From the calls coming in over the police radio, I could tell there was trouble at the Seaside Temple site.

"You are courageous but careless! Jeez, there's no need to put your life in danger. We've got enough cadavers in Santa Varvara as it is." Rilsky took refuge in his spacious office, pale under his tan, almost handsome. He was trying to minimize the incident. "But rest assured, for the moment—and I insist, for the moment—you have nothing to worry about. The principal target is, or, I should say, *was* Reverend Sun. He has just taken leave of this world. More on that later."

Despite his presence and this good piece of news, the shootout from which I had just escaped, even if I was not the main target, was still making my heart beat and my palms sweaty. The death of Reverend Sun did not seem to please Northrop, however. In fact, it seriously bothered him.

"Found dead in his bedroom at the Seaside Temple site. We received the information just as the bullets started flying over at the parking lot. Same scenario: one bullet in his head and cut open as if he had done a hara-kiri, upper body exposed, and a signature written in blood on his back of a kind of number *8*—one of their sacred signs, I suppose. We'll find the shirt, like we did for the other victims, with the same figure and a name. Last week an arms dealer and high dignitary in the same sect was killed in the same way in his villa. We found his shirt miles from there with the figure and the name *Bell* on it. The pimp of ten days ago, also a New Pantheon member, was killed in the same way with the number *8* and the name *Rocky* on the shirt."

"Signatures *Joe, Bell*, and *Rocky* bring the total to eight now. It's the same psychopath, Boss, it's clear as. . . . " The boss clearly didn't see much that was clear about the situation.

"That's what they want us to believe, Popov. He or they. After all, perhaps there are several 'psychopaths,' as you say, maybe an entire rival sect trying to get even. And, you know, that *8* is maybe supposed to be read sideways as a ∞, the sign of infinity, do you follow me? In that case, your idea that our murderer might have set out to tally up eight victims is perhaps a bit optimistic."

I was trying without success to concentrate on what Northrop was saying, but it was all going by so fast and my hand was still nervously holding an imaginary Colt while the real unused weapon sat at the bottom of my handbag. Northrop noticed my condition and had someone bring me a glass of ice water, and he tapped my wrists with an awkward affection that bothered me all the more.

"The signature is a sign both to the police and the New Pantheon. This guy, if we suppose that he is acting alone, is at war against the mafia, the state, everybody!" said Rilsky in a voice that was both annoyed and overwhelmed.

"That's what I'm saying, Boss, because the day after each murder we receive a scrap of paper with the same black ink signatures that are on the shirts of these bastards . . . I mean victims. It's as though this message were for us too, except there's a difference between blood and ink, don't you think? For you, I mean for us, the message is less . . . bloody, get it?"

It goes without saying that Rilsky had picked up on this nuance. I understood the commissioner's predicament better now that I knew this detail. The enemy of these reverend bastards was no Good Samaritan. He was hostile toward everyone, starting with the police chief. He didn't respect anything and defied authority, it's true. It was a classic murder-the-father case in which the commissioner was the best approximate stand-in, let's say. But who was he, and what did he want to accomplish?

"These guys, or this guy, would seem to know the inside operations of the New Pantheon. I'm telling you, Boss, this can only be a guy on the inside. Look at this perfect setup today. He kills this asshole Sun while the PR director is receiving Mademoiselle Delacour freshly arrived from Paris. What great publicity! I don't believe in coincidences. This guy is on the inside."

"I think so too, Popov, though for now there is no proof. Today might have been a coincidence. Someone may have simply discovered that the PR director had some stain or other. Or else there is a group and they're acting together. On the other hand, murdering these hotshot dignitaries of the sect has all the signs of a solitary maniac or some tenacious avenger. Where is the report that I assigned you to do last week on the New Pantheon malcontents, dropouts, and turncoats? There must be some Judases and Iagos among the faithful who have gone into business for themselves, no? And the henchmen of this old Sun, have you followed up on them? Between sniffing coke and sticking homos the high road is sometimes narrow. The extinguished Sun proves it, you know what I mean?"

"I've got a list of them, Boss. There's nothing solid. They're a bunch of lost down-and-outers. None of them would be capable of carving up that rotten guy and adding calligraphy to boot."

"Well, keep at it, buddy boy. What are you still doing here? Get back to work!"

He'd gotten upset—I didn't know why. Did Popov have any idea? Maybe not. It was only much later that I was able to reconstruct the facts, if one can speak of "facts" to describe this dizziness that had seized Northrop and that he later explained to me.

SOMETIME AFTER HIS MEN, Rilsky himself entered the bedroom at the Seaside Temple compound and saw the body of the Reverend Sun, Number Eight's eighth victim. The odor of blood made him gag. He had never been able to stand the sickly sweet smell of decomposing human bodies. Northrop still had difficulty accepting that the fishy perfume of death was the ultimate secret of the living. With time the commissioner ought to have gotten used to the nature of things. But no. And yet, human flesh is never too solid, nor can it melt, thaw, or resolve itself into a dew—no matter what that poor idealist Hamlet may have wished! A fastidious fellow at heart, the Danish prince got it right when he observed how flat and unprofitable are the uses of this world. Flesh reveals in death its smelly truth that the living try to perfume away and cover up. Infected limbs and crawling worms disgusted the crime unit officer to the point of nausea. But, repulsed or not, Rilsky was committed to confronting this truth as often as possible, as if deep within his soul a naive vitalism stubbornly believed that death was not the inevitable fate of all sickening humanity.

However, since the scourge of Number Eight had begun, the closer encounters between the commissioner and rotting bodies plunged him into a troubling maelstrom that he could in no way master. Never one to be overwhelmed by compassion for the victims—far from it—Rilsky was usually able to block out his feelings so that he could search pitilessly for the criminal who had cut the throat or the balls of one of his fellow men. Today he was no longer able to. Somewhat shamefully, this officer of the law was surprised at his own joy upon seeing the fat and flabby bodies of these corrupt petty priests whose various crimes, misdemeanors, and other depravities he knew well but alas could not prosecute for lack of any solid evidence to submit to a justice system that couldn't give a damn anyway. The dead bodies mostly deserved the treatment they had received, if not worse. Rilsky could not help admiring the elegant bloody signature and the delicate carving of the figure 8, or ∞, into the skin of these miserable, lacerated men. The virtuosity of this purifier deserved at least a snickering nod, one that the commissioner was careful to hide from his men and the press, of course. But the shame disappeared rather quickly and the boss found it more and more pleasing to replay in his mind the sequence of the massacre, to threaten, and to stab the point of the dagger into the eyes, throat, navel, penis, and anus of these chiefs without feeling anything, or so he thought, besides the calm good conscience and glacial precision of a purifier beyond good and evil. Wasn't the iciness that he believed belonged to the serial killer, to the one nicknamed Number Eight, becoming more and more his own? Of course we are dealing with a psychopath; we must arrest him and we will arrest him. But how could one deny that the Exterminating Angel had come right on time, as though sent by providence itself, and that without him Santa Varvara would have no doubt continued with its lot of crimes? Therefore . . .

. . . The sharp blackness that overtook him, this hole in time, was it that of the serial killer? I would have done the same as he—and more. Who is the killer? Is each of us a potential killer? If not, how could one ever guess that an irreproachable police officer might hold within such murderous impulses? Am I a sadist in reverse who only wants to be revealed? Who knows? Or perhaps this potential has already expressed itself in some other life? I might have been in his place, perhaps I was: twin, double, brother. To mix, in this way, blood and ink, the murderer must be beside himself in an infinite black time. I was the one who busted your face, you rotten reverend. It was my not-me me, but go and try and prove that it was me. You will never be able to, nor will your comrades. But no one in the world will be able to guess the answer as intensely as you, while it may just be me who could state the contrary, but not even me. An endless rupture, a fat pleasure in the corner of the eyes, a smile on the lips, silence.

"Pardon me, Boss, but sometimes I wonder why you joined the police." Popov had witnessed how disturbed the chief of police was before the body of the dead Sun, and, asking, as usual, the wrong questions at the wrong time, he attributed it to the chief's exaggerated sensitivity and class-related refinement. "I mean, since you were born with a silver spoon in your mouth and all."

The incongruousness of this image did not bother Northrop. There were reasons for Popov not to feel privileged himself. The older sister of the assistant inspector had been sucked into the New Pantheon sect at fifteen, when he was only ten years old. Brainwashing, drugs, sexual abuse. Her body and her belongings disappeared without leaving a single trace of her life or her death. Ever since, their father, a mechanic, never stopped shaking his fists at the television and railing against the powerlessness of the government. Their mother, who worked herself to the bone as a cleaning lady in the immense IBM building, cried endlessly while waiting for her cirrhosis to carry her off too. For the young Popov, who wallowed in all this, the choice was clear between cop or thug. An average student and good son chooses cop. But how and why did Rilsky, with his orchestra conductor father and pianist mother, fall into the police? Where's your bruise that explains that, Boss! That's what we're wondering, damn it!

The chief obviously did not reply. With the look of those young grandfathers in American movies who delight women and children, the do-gooder who triumphs over the evildoer, my Cary Grant turned into Clint Eastwood. Over fifty, slightly heavyset, cultured, the perfect marriage of intelligence and pragmatism. Gifted with a refinement that suggested a musical sensibility or pathology, some would say, and the whole so patiently constructed over time. No, Popov could not understand, and Rilsky no doubt hardly understood himself.

At the highest extreme of beauty, it can happen that one suddenly hears a false note and that even all the notes begin to sound false to your ear. Is then this *luxe, calme et volupté* enjoyed by the innocent audience of the peaceful concert that would be your family life, or entire social life, no more than a plaster cast over a wooden leg, a bandage over a gaping wound, a beautiful mask over a monstrous face? I know well that the plaster cast, the bandage, and the mask are called civilization. There are families that, like the Rilskys, often want to know nothing of evil. No traumatic events, nothing, ever happened at the Rilskys, nothing happens now, a nothing that is not everything, one that whispers the unsaid that will never be spoken, but only communicated through headaches, fevers more or less acute, and ulcers. His conductor father died of it, of nothing. Northrop had begun to listen to this opera of false notes, a music inaudible to the hypocrite ears of the well-mannered, the music of the flood, of *Apocalypse Now.*

As for the purifier, you know, not only does he measure the horror, but this figure confronts it with a certain jubilation, one must admit—a jubilation unknown to his parents and beyond his own superego, which lives on all the same: his DNA heritage, an indelible fate. He is the purifier of abjection, and if he were not, who would eliminate it, remove it in broad daylight? The world would be divided plainly into assholes and ninnies. The law itself would not exist with these two sides, the pure and the impure, because the law is necessarily schizo, it was Northrop's job to know this. But it was no use to say this to Popov, who was still too young and simple-minded for the moment.

"Did you read today's *Times,* Boss?" Popov was trying to fill the silence. Rilsky finally managed to clear away the macabre thoughts of Reverend Sun's chopped up body that obsessed his mind. "The media hounds are on our tail for sure. They say that our investigation has become 'suspiciously slow,' you know what I mean? They are even insinuating that if the killer is a purifier, as all are prepared to say, then he might well belong to the police! They are so predictable, these guys—their way of turning attention from the petty corruption among us, if there is any, I mean, well, I don't know . . . suppose. . . . Only in Santa Varvara could you read something like that, don't you think, Boss?"

"The local rags aren't saying, by any chance, that Number Eight is me?" asked the commissioner with oracular calm.

"Christ, that's you all over, Boss! Only you could joke about stuff like this, pardon me," said Popov, stifling a burst of laughter and controlling his smile.

Rilsky was not sure he was joking. He was no longer sure of anything. If the press itself was having doubts. . . . Something led him to believe that he could very well be the purifier, that he could have been, or may have been, because he sensed this serial killer in his skin, his muscles, his head.

In a novel one might have said that Number Eight was his alter ego. Surely Rilsky was sliding downward toward a certain proximity. Whence did this arise, how did they know each other? Was Number Eight a delinquent that the commissioner had nabbed in another affair, whom he'd sent to court, or had convicted for life? Or even sent to the electric chair? Was it guilt that was pushing him to identify with this unstoppable aggressor, a crafty rogue like him? Or was he his unconscious twin, the dark double of Northrop who killed after midnight without remembering a thing, nothing but the baggy eyes and red lids of habitual insomniacs?

"You look tired to me, Boss. You should take a break," said Popov in a tone that suggested he sought some vague pardon.

"Don't give it another thought, my friend. The *Times* must have its reasons for writing that I am the accomplice of Number Eight. If my investigation is slow, it must be because I am he. Go on now! I want you to gather me more fingerprints, interview all the witnesses again, and fast, do you hear?"

Me, the Commissioner, and Scott Ross &

I decided to wait a few days before contacting the New Pantheon again. The police had cordoned off the Seaside Temple compound, and I had no chance of gaining access even if I might be able to wring some sympathy points from the new PR director. The person who had been quickly chosen to replace the cold cadaver lying in the parking lot proved to be a talkative chap in an early press conference and particularly attentive to foreign journalists.

Apartment, nap, sofa. I needed some down time to try and understand things. Northrop was not in a hurry either. His habitual casualness was compounded by a lazy fatigue that was not his custom. His deputies returned to the scene of the crime, but he was content to receive their reports via fax or e-mail. He let Popov filter the incoming calls. The commissioner seemed out of it, as though the crime unit he was in charge of were definitively overwhelmed, perhaps even impotent in the face of this disaster, and maybe for a long time. A war among the sects worked to the advantage of the government—an unexpected abscess to hold everyone's attention! It was a Christmas present in the summer that allowed the apparent powers to drift peacefully along. What did it matter to them if this somber Sun had been snuffed out by enemies within the New Pantheon itself or by the Universal Church, the Jade Paradise sect, or the Spiritual Science group? The cocaine and Kalishnikovs would still pass through Santa Varvara, and Rilsky had not ruled out that members of the government profited directly from the generosity of this rainbow of reverends. The police themselves were not above suspicion, he well knew, all the while defending the integrity of his unit, for the most part, that is. But everything was getting muddled. It was already the second summer the serial killer had eluded him, and still no hot leads. For the first time since I'd met him, Northrop appeared more concerned with my comfort than with the pursuit of the indecipherable "Joe-Bill-Rocky" that signed the seppuku robes of these guru dealers. To get him out of his daze, he spun out the idea of an artistic psychopath, a unique kind of drug user who was into doing macabre "installations" in public while secretly rejoicing at being the one and only actor-spectator of this vengeful series of happenings.

Should we eat out? Where? He prefers to eat at home. What if we order in Chinese? Of course that suits me fine!

We were both in shock, and thus together, but differently, "at home."

Ginger shrimp, sweet and sour pork, Cantonese rice—nothing out of the ordinary. This student meal allowed me to avoid calf's head, the preferred dish of my host, who had too often taken me to order it at the only French restaurant in the area. It was their specialty—mine also, it turns out—anyway, that's enough foodie talk!

"This man is a purifier, my dear Stephanie. He's doing the cleaning up that we've been unable to do with our beautiful legal procedures, and it doesn't make me feel good to say so. What's more, it's obvious that he thinks the same way as his victims. He's God-crazy too, an absolutist, but one who's gone off the deep end. Why? Too much crack, no doubt. You've got to be on some high, or coming down from one, to carry out such exercises so coldly. He's clearly getting a glacial pleasure out of it. But why has he turned his anger against his own tribe? He's got to be one of their own, otherwise how could he get into the Seaside Temple compound? Or else he was one of them at some time, since he knows how to maneuver without getting caught."

The boss was trying to convince himself. He seemed distant. Either he was really spinning his wheels or he was hiding something from me. Once again. But of course it was my job as an investigative reporter to find out what. I had to lead my own inquiry. I looked at him with tenderness: a man perhaps more mysterious than the role he gave himself.

We were late going back to our rooms that evening. He casually touched my forearm with his hand that played along to the harpsichord music of Scott Ross. The telephone rang—not the professional line, but the old Rilsky family number Northrop kept for the guest studio. He pinched his brows, somewhat surprised since he had not given out this number to anyone. My bureau chief in Paris only called me on my cellphone or else used e-mail. The ringer was insistent and my host decided to respond. He came back looking perplexed, as though he were burning to tell me a secret and fighting against the imprudence of spewing it all out. I acted as though I weren't paying attention by keeping my eyelids closed and pretending to concentrate on the music of Scott Ross.

"That was Hermine," he said, sitting back down opposite me, "Hermine Chrest-Jones, Sebastian's wife. He has been missing for a week, and she thinks he's really disappeared or dead." The commissioner was even more pale than he was yesterday, after the shootout that I had narrowly escaped.

I didn't know this Hermine, and the name Chrest-Jones rang only a vague bell: was it some distant relative of the commissioner? I was also suddenly feeling troubled by another thought: had I drunk my gin and tonic too fast or did I simply want to kiss him? I was thinking it was the latter when he put his arm around my shoulders, tuned out the harpsichord, and there in semidarkness I was made privy to the shaggy dog saga of Northrop's family. I was well aware that among sensitive souls these kinds of confidences were a prelude to erotic effusions. I was no dummy: ever since I'd arrived he was expecting nothing else. With his still young face framed by tufts of gray hair, his pragmatism, and the new spontaneity that went along with the intelligence that I had always admired, Northrop now pleased me. Stranger still, the ridiculous image I had created of a humanist holed up in a police department—something I now considered a cheap trick to shield myself from his paternalist charms—melted away as quickly as the ice cube in my drink that I held between my tongue and palate. I no longer resisted, kissed him everywhere, and finished by pulling him to the large bed in the guest room, shameful and eager as I imagine one feels during incestuous relations.

I did, however, half listen, barely, to a vague story about an unfound father: everything began with a legendary ancestor named Sylvester Chrest whom Northrop resembled to a very great degree, physically anyway. An orphan, the commissioner's grandfather fled the Balkans and the misery of that region to reunite with distant relations who had recently moved to Santa Varvara. He was from the start a devilishly hard worker. Waiter, logger, errand boy, and general handyman, Sylvester Chrest miraculously found time to complete his medical studies and, what's more, Doctor Chrest set up his practice in the center of Santa Varvara. Handsome and well liked, he had the idea of marrying the daughter of Henry Spencer, the hospital director, and thus moved up the social ladder. Suzanne and Sylvester had a daughter, Griselda, Northrop's mother. My friend, host, and now lover was thus the grandson of Suzanne Chrest-Spencer and Sylvester Chrest, a Balkan immigrant. Griselda, Northrop's mother, became a piano teacher and married the talented conductor of the Bourgas orchestra, Boris Rilsky, Northrop's father—that much I knew already. Sylvester married Suzanne when he was about thirty and had his only daughter, Griselda, but Northrop's grandfather no longer seemed content with his social ascent and his family life. Northrop had his own vivid memories of a majestic and enigmatic patriarch.

"So what was your grandfather like?" I asked, more interested in Nordi's voice than in his obscure Balkan saga. He murmured something close to my ear. Some men take up their childhood voice again when they are in love. He was no longer looking at me, his eyes were turned inward, and it was his voice that was kissing me.

"Sylvester? He was a tall, hard man with fair skin and blue eyes. He wore a beard, rode horses, and took care of his patients, but, you know, he also used to disappear without leaving any forwarding address. And yet he adored his wife Suzanne, their daughter Griselda, and of course Northrop himself, his only grandson, who was born when he was approaching sixty. Ten years later, a short time before his death, this respected and revered grandfather told his family some news that they had been suspecting a little already—namely, that he had just legally recognized a little five-year-old boy, the result of a love affair with a twenty-five-year-old waitress named Tracy Jones. This forbidden fruit then went by the name Sebastian Chrest-Jones."

"Hermine's husband?" I asked. I was listening while kissing him at the same time, so I'm summarizing here a bit. Neither his wife Suzanne nor his daughter were scandalized by the announcement of this bastard's existence, but all of Santa Varvara was gossiping wildly about it; and Northrop, who had just turned ten, thus found himself with an uncle half his age, little Sebastian who was made the legal half-brother of Griselda, Nordi's mother. This was a little complex for the time, which was not yet used to such reconstructed or, I should say, deconstructed families. Old Sylvester died shortly thereafter, and naturally the legitimate family was not pressed to develop further ties with the supernumerary child whom the family patriarch had seen fit to saddle them with like a kind of joke present before leaving them all. For their part, Tracy Jones and Sebastian were content to benefit from the comfortable inheritance that the patriarch had generously left for them, but they did not seek out ties with Sebastian's "true family" either. This was naturally the case with Suzanne, who lived to be ninety, but even more so with the Rilsky family. This made some sense, since the latter was branching off from the family line and neither carried the family name, Chrest, nor were they concerned with their memories, preferring instead the universal memory of music. Mrs. Rilsky, my commissioner's mother, neglected this half-brother whom she had hardly known, and after her marriage to the conductor she saw nothing, absolutely nothing, in common between herself and this little person.

Nevertheless, the disturbance of it all stayed alive, like a scar that remains irritating despite the cooling effect of time and manners. The uncle (Sebastian) and the nephew (Northrop) would greet each other politely when they met—the former being five years younger than the latter, let's remember—since they both belonged to the tight-knit circle of Santa Varvara's upper class whose members were always running into each other. Otherwise, however, they avoided each other deliberately, and each did his best to know as little about the other as possible. When they became adults this little game continued, but for Sebastian (the uncle) it was no doubt difficult since his nephew the head police inspector Northrop Rilsky often made the front pages in relation to the criminal cases he had helped solve. On the other hand, Northrop the nephew had no trouble completely forgetting the existence of his bastard half-uncle Sebastian, who, as any psychiatrist will tell you, had gotten the most out of his bastard status by becoming a historian, a profession he had exercised up until then without any particular distinction.

"You've never met up again?" I asked absently, still lost between his voice and his lips.

"Yes we did, once, at a cocktail party celebrating the fiftieth anniversary of the criminology department. He introduced me to Hermine, a talkative and not unattractive blonde. But that was twenty years ago." He then added with an air of perplexity, "A guy like Chrest-Jones must have already been a little nuts for him to crack up totally. But there's a difference between cracking up and cracking heads and carving people up. But, who knows, maybe for a long time he's been plotting to take his revenge on the human race disguised under the calm demeanor of the little professor. Why not? Don't run away, get even!"

But really the commissioner was not paid to be astonished, and any scenario was possible, even from the closest and most familiar sources, including himself. The disturbing familiarity with the killer had overtaken Rilsky like a fatal destiny hinting at an implacable program or genetic fraternity. Was he a sort of Sebastian, this Number who-knows-how-many? Rilsky was grasping at straws. Anything was possible.

Thus the telephone call from Hermine was neither a whim nor an accident, but part of a deliberate strategy. Maybe. I tried to gauge the different feelings that this call may have provoked in my friend, besides jarring his apparent serenity. Did this intrusion, interrupting as it did their tacit agreement, arouse in him some slight remorse? An anxiety about origins? A social disturbance? But, concretely, what was at stake? Was he wondering about their star-crossed paths as only children? Or, more painfully, was Sebastian's disappearance reviving the pain he felt over the loss of Martha, the only woman in his life? Years ago, portraits of her were everywhere in the police commissioner's office. I seem to remember it was Popov who told me how Martha had died of leukemia shortly after their marriage and left Northrop a bachelor for life.

I thought I knew him. "One knows more about people and oneself in the heat of crime than in the heat of love," joked Rilsky, back when we were looking for the missing head of Gloria, which was also being sought by drug dealers disguised as art dealers, and when networks of pimps who were killing prostitutes in Paris led us to the doors of certain embassies. "Our special embedded reporter knows everything," read the headline in the *Événement de Paris*, but I have to say that, although it bothered my bureau chief, this compliment was as much the result of my stubborn logic as of the twisted genius of the commissioner.

But on this night I discovered another man. The commissioner may have grumbled and complained about this nutty Hermine bothering him when she ought to have gone and made a report at the nearest police station like anyone else—since everyone in this fucked up city knew that Police Commissioner Rilsky didn't get involved in every missing person case in Santa Varvara, especially the cases of missing husbands—but he was unquestionably and deeply affected by the news. His upset feelings had nothing to do with the regular moral anxieties of his job. I was divided between the desire to love him and the shame of entering into an obscure and perhaps forbidden terrain. I sensed, however, that his story of a lost uncle came just at the right time: our paths had now crossed again at one of those confusing moments in life when, because we don't know where we are, the past falls down on us—our past, that of our extended family, of preceding generations. Despite what the majority of lost souls imagine, this resurgence of past times is hardly surprising since it has always already been there. And the secret of origins asks only to be a part of our investigation, to make sense out of the insipid present that, without them, would only be treatable through suicide.

Nordi was getting me wrapped up in his family saga; that was all I needed! But I preferred to fall asleep to the music of Scott Ross, Scarlatti, ah!

CHAPTER TWO   ❧ A University Crusader

The laboratory of migration history occupied one whole floor of the asbestos-filled towers that stood with no grace whatsoever on the University of Santa Varvara campus and offered the press its latest made-to-order story of ecological scandal. "Danger on Campus," "How Many Students with Cancer?" and "Many Already Contaminated, Three Asbestos Deaths Suspected" were some of the newspaper headlines that also called for trials and public demonstrations. Why was this happening now when the danger of asbestos has been known for seventy years and the campus ecologists have been fighting against it in vain for more than a decade? Nervous souls were asking, Why now? And eyes turned to the presidential palace because all suspected as usual that the evil and manipulation were coming down from the top. Rilsky knew this type of "humanitarian protest" wouldn't last more than a month, that the fever would subside and be forgotten, as in all such episodes. One couldn't level a campus that had cost millions to build just to please the Green Party! After having got lost once or twice in the labyrinth of badly marked hallways, he eventually found his way to the door of the asbestos-plagued lab of Sebastian Chrest-Jones, who, like everyone else on campus, must have marveled at being transformed into a media star thanks to this killer dust.

Since a scientist is, for all intents and purposes, his work, Rilsky thought it reasonable to begin by investigating his computer files and disks in hopes that they would perhaps reveal insights into the personality of Sebastian Chrest-Jones, his now absent uncle.

As the members of the lab pretended to read the newspaper while impatiently waiting in the tea room, Rilsky locked himself in Sebastian's office to conduct interviews, the first being with Hermine, who, as he expected, said nothing of any interest. Sebastian's wife was one of those women called "still attractive" and "independent." She was a thin, flat-chested, fake blonde whose distress did not prevent her from drawing attention to her long straight legs that were unaccustomed to anything but pants. The commissioner had no trouble identifying her type: the well-preserved former feminist always intent on putting herself forward on her own. Her manner clearly reminded one how much "her" generation had paid in blood, sweat, and tears for a liberation that most people didn't give a damn about today, wrongly, as they would soon find out! Hermine made her speeches with an amused air punctuated by cascades of laughter, persuaded as she was that laughter was the sole index of the good health and common sense of people who took the trouble to express themselves. Even if it were in the mode of mourning as it was here where the worst had indeed happened.

"It's unexplainable, Commissioner. An intuition, a certainty, you'll see." Rilsky, however, noticed without marked surprise that the voluntary widow expressed her intuitions through bursts of laughter. He didn't yet know that this jocose delivery was her normal speech pattern—practically genetic.

"Here's a piece of news"—or a letter or person—"that will make you laugh," she would say to all those present before serving up the most ordinary of stories that she invariably considered most extraordinary. Hermine had had many lovers and several abortions. She would recount the details to anyone who would listen with the conspicuous good humor she deemed always necessary. Of course one is scarred by it all, such as the inability to have a child, and one accumulates a host of minor sentimental wounds, but, she chuckled, this was no reason to play the victim. Besides, Sebastian didn't like children. What luck! What's more, he seemed pleased to rely day-to-day on a woman who had some experience. It had not taken her long to realize that in truth he took no notice of her at all.

"You can't imagine, Northrop . . . You don't mind if I call you Northrop, do you? After all, we're family since you are, or were, his nephew; and if I choose to speak in the past tense, it's because I am certain the irremediable deed has been done. You see, Northrop dear, over our thirty years of married life Sebastian has called me at least twice a day—proof that even though there was no communication between us, ha ha, hee hee, I mean no human communication, only codes, technical signals, and rituals, proof that I was nevertheless his safety belt! I know you'll find it hard to believe, but he could spend hours with you without listening or answering. When I say "you" I mean "me," of course. So I preferred to argue with Pino, Pino Minaldi, my friend, his assistant, ha ha, hee hee, rather than live cooped up with my curfew-and convent-loving husband. Pino is a brute, it's true, but at least he reacts, you know what I mean? People will try to tell you those two hated each other; some might even insinuate that Pino, ha ha, hee hee, rubbed him out. But I tell you it's impossible, and you should believe me. Why? Because Sebastian suspected nothing, I mean nothing. He was oblivious. Their fights? Nothing but professional debates—funny, don't you think? Yes, Pino was his assistant, but he no longer followed the master, that's for sure! In the sciences, you know, it's routine stuff. They call it research but in fact there's nothing more ordinary, ha ha, hee hee. I'm speaking in the past tense again—that surprises you, but my hunches are never wrong, I have strong instincts; women often operate instinctually, you know? This disappearance is no game, ha ha, hee hee."

Hermine was intent on placing Pino outside any blame in case the police chief should hear about the frequent quarrels between her lover and her husband—disputes that no longer interested anyone in the lab. They had become so routine that the team of researchers, when asked, barely seemed even to believe they existed. OK, Popov could explore that angle later, as usual, one never knows, but the wife's fears seemed to be more about the possibility of being considered unfaithful than grounded in any real threat to her husband that might come from his young and jealous collaborator. He had a big mouth this Minaldi, the kind of person who would make fists and hiss insults through his teeth such as, "I will kill that idiot crusader. This loony Pierrot is unbelievable. I will break his face one of these days!" But to go from insults to actions was unlikely, no?

In the adjoining library next to Sebastian's office, the lab assistant seemed totally at ease. He was certain that he had taken possession of the premises since the disappearance of the professor, perhaps even before.

"I won't deny that there were conflicts between the professor and myself," said Minaldi to Rilsky in an obsequious and evasive tone. "But they were only professional disagreements, I would even say ideological. Professor Chrest-Jones had altered his philosophy of immigration in recent years, and I must say that this had shocked me since we saw things the same way at the time he hired me to work in the lab . . . how many years ago now? Hermine must know—I mean Mrs. Chrest-Jones. At the time the professor was a firm believer in *métissage,* like myself or like you, I suppose. But he changed positions radically and now believes that it is necessary to halt population movements, develop local economies so as to eliminate one of the main causes of immigration, and therefore nip the exile in the bud, so to speak, as though this were possible! It was his way of saying that for him emigration had become a danger, *the* danger, you see? A conservative, right-wing position, and of course antirealist. People want to move, and not just for money, I'm telling you, and no one will stop them, not even Professor Chrest-Jones. Nomadic hordes will march over his research and his new title of doctor *honoris causa*, because that is where History is headed. We should face up to the reality of illegal aliens with as much humanity as possible instead of trying—in vain—to induce them to go home with miserable little stipends. But what do you expect? As one gets older, one no longer dares to think. One begins by speaking a lot of rubbish, and a little while later one has gone completely bonkers."

Pino Minaldi realized that his remarks had gone beyond the restrained attitude that he had hoped to maintain with Rilsky. He stopped brusquely and fixed his black eyes on the face of the commissioner like a child surprised at having broken something.

"Uhhh, Commissioner . . . " He hesitated, as though he had forgotten his name. "You are Police Commissioner Rilsky, right?" Then he started mumbling while backing up slightly. "I've never had a chance to meet you before today; hence my surprise. How shall I say it: there's a family resemblance between Professor Chrest-Jones and yourself. I suppose people must have already said that to you? The same facial features, the same expressions, even the same eyes, except the color."

Of course people had said that to him. On the memorable day when the young Sebastian was presented to the Chrest family, his blond nephew Northrop found himself standing before a little five-year-old with black hair, but with the same eyebrows and smile as his. The resemblance and the source of unease was especially in the almond-shaped eyes that had the same morning mixture of malice and timidity. Only the color differed—light blue for Northrop while Sebastian's were dark brown. Their mouths were fine and mocking, always balanced between a frank pout and an unreadable smile. The similarities were obvious, but none of the Chrests spoke of it. Had it been from the first meeting or gradually over the many Sundays that Sebastian would spend as a guest in the home of the patriarch that Northrop studied the differences between himself and the intruder? Thus it was, for example, that one day, while the young boy was painting with watercolors on sheets of paper set on a table by his half-sister Griselda, Northrop leaned over the back of his neck to see if his uncle had the same red birthmark behind his left ear that he himself had since birth. Phew, what a relief! The seal of the patriarch Sylvester Chrest did not show up in an identical way on the bodies of the two male descendants of the tribe. Northrop was also proud of his height, and was much more lanky than the more burly dark-haired boy. On the other hand, the coal-colored hair and dark brown eyes of Sebastian gave him a serious and manly appearance. "He looks much older than his age" and "perhaps a little wild," people would say. "He's quite the little man," Griselda would say, with some ambivalence, since Northrop's mother had a hard time getting used to the idea that her half-brother was younger than her son.

Fortunately for him, Northrop's perplexity did not go on for more than a year because the dark-haired femme fatale Tracy Jones, who was rumored to be a drug addict and, in any case, always thoroughly detested by the Chrest family ("poor Sebastian!"), died in a car accident that was "rather dubious" according to Griselda. Sebastian was then sent to a boarding school where he remained through adolescence. Over the years Northrop heard less and less about his uncle, the dark clone of the blond patriarch Sylvester Chrest, who made an elegant departure from this world at the age of seventy-five.

"We are distantly related. His father was my grandfather," said Rilsky who was upset at the idea of saying too much about this distant relation that was not so distant, but not unhappy to have unsettled Minaldi, who was noticeably at a loss to understand the genealogical twists of this family that continually baffled him. "Let's see, Mr., er, what's your name?"

"Minaldi, Pino Minaldi," he replied in an eager-to-please voice.

"Mr. Minaldi, Inspector Popov, whom you've met already, will continue the necessary questioning with you. I expect you to cooperate with him fully, of course. We need to know the professor's agenda, recent contacts, and any other details that are relevant to his disappearance. As for me, I would like to be shown his files, his archives, his disks, and his personal computer and access codes, in other words, everything!"

What exactly had he been doing, this double who had been so troubling in the past and so quickly erased now? Rilsky knew absolutely nothing. A specialist of the history of migrations, OK, but migrations of who, from where to where, when, and how? Today everyone is more or less divided between two countries, two women, two men, two languages, two chairs, two waters—Northrop too, especially Northrop, who went from one crime to another, one law to another, but it wasn't something to write a history about.

"He must have taken his laptop with him because it's not at home, according to Hermine, nor at the lab. This is not surprising since Professor Chrest-Jones went everywhere with it. But his documents are available to you, of course. I have all his disks going back four years, ever since he started us working on his obsession. You can look at them all you want. Documentation is my specialty in fact. I helped him in this area, so much so that you might say I compiled it myself. You will learn all about the Crusades, Commissioner, if you're interested in delving into this treasure trove."

In the stream of Hermine-speak Northrop heard some snatches mentioning the hobby of the professor that the commissioner must surely know of. Hermine was certain that Rilsky had heard about Sebastian's passion for the Crusades—everyone knew about it, how could he not? He was not going to confess to her that he had no idea, no idea whatsoever! After all, they had barely known each other as children, and what they did know was vague and distant. Well, to make a long story short, Sebastian's bent for history turned in the direction of exploring his father's origins, Hermine insisted on reminding him, and he even visited the region of Plovdiv in Bulgaria, formerly Philippopolis, where the Chrest family originated. No one knew exactly what he discovered there, but, according to Hermine, he supposedly kept a detailed travel diary with interviews, testimonials, and notes. The whole thing was rather a hodgepodge of this and that and naturally top secret. The only significant piece of information shared by Sebastian about it all—even though Hermine found it rather far-fetched, "fantastic, I would say, ha ha, hee hee!"—was his discovery of the exact hidden meaning of the patronymic Chrest.

"The Crusaders were *crucesignati*, 'marked with a cross' or *milites Christi*, 'soldiers of God.' You know, among all these German and French barons who mingled with the poor in elaborating their project to reconquer Jerusalem and liberate the tomb of Christ, some left traces of their passage from West to East, notably at Philippopolis. He liked this whole idea, you see, Northrop, and he even discovered a document, no doubt rare for the time, that attests to a great-great-great-grandmother—we're talking fourteenth century here, the time of the Turkish Occupation. You'll notice that the history reconstructed by Sebastian takes place long after these mythical Crusades—so it was a woman, a certain Militsa Christi or Militsa Chrest, it doesn't matter, the pronunciation gets altered, you understand, from Latin to this magma of Slavic languages and then finally to Santa Varvarois. Well, Sebastian, he was a dreamer, a romantic. This discovery was enough for him to change directions and become a specialist of the Crusades." Hermine concluded her summary with rather more aggression than compassion in her voice. Minaldi then gave the commissioner a sweet-toned and fuller account.

"Of course you know that Plovdiv is in Bulgaria, Commissioner." Minaldi continued to play the obedient servant. No, yes, well, the commissioner knew something about it, perhaps. "Well, those guys are experts when it comes to computer viruses. They can hack your security system like nobody else in the world. I tell you, they are such skillful troublemakers, they can go in and steal the most protected databases. That's why Sebastian, I mean Professor Chrest-Jones, hired me in the first place, because I know about computers, viruses, antiviruses, and so forth. It's my specialty, after history, that is. I was asked to make his screen and computer security system foolproof so that no one else could use it, and my system is impenetrable, I'm telling you, Commissioner. Of course for you, given the circumstances, I can get you around the system—that is what you're asking, isn't it? As soon as you need access, everything will be available to you. You can count on me." Minaldi rounded out his speech in an excited gallop.

"Are you telling me, Minaldi, that Sebastian Chrest-Jones conducted a secret research project?" asked Rilsky, wide-eyed.

"You could put it that way if you like, but if you want my opinion, Commissioner, it wasn't really research, but more a dream, his personal faith as a man who was rather . . . lost, I mean fragile, always upset, never at ease, and difficult to understand." Minaldi paused to let his melodramatic presentation sink in.

"I see. Well, Popov, let's get all this stuff under police surveillance: files, computers, disks. Let's get the experts going on this. We want it analyzed piece by piece and up and down, and fast! I will be overseeing this personally, here and wherever it leads. As for you, Mr. Minaldi, I don't want you leaving the country without informing me. We'll meet tomorrow at nine o'clock. Be on time. I may need to make use of your talents," said Rilsky with self-importance and some condescension.

The Missing Person's Journal &

Where is one when one is nowhere? Northrop had experienced this odd lightness, and the thought that Sebastian had experienced his own version of it, even odder than his own, made him feel more neutral than truly happy. It was the serenity of indifference. The commissioner was convinced that all relations are indirect and none are necessary. There was no familiarity, only an uncanny strangeness. An unhealthy suspicion? Paranoia? Perhaps. Self-exile is not enough to experience this feeling of continual uprooting. So many foreigners leave their native lands and crowd together among themselves, in their "communities," as they say, really clannish family enclaves, over which their host countries keep a close watch. For their part, they prefer to ignore their host countries because their presence as refugees is humiliating, even if they are nourished better there than these poor nomads ever were at home. This is by no means Northrop's situation. He was born in Santa Varvara and all his roots were Santa Varvarois, with the exception of Sylvester Chrest, of course. But there has always been a foreign import or two in every family, if one looks closely, especially in Santa Varvara where everyone is an immigrant of either one or two generations back. However, there are immigrants and then there are immigrants. The Rilsky clan, for example, on his father's side, that is, was of immigrant stock just like their neighbors; but the Rilskys are distinguished people, musicians from father to son, for whom music is the elite language. They don't waste their time dwelling over genealogies day and night; they simply live their lives as Santa Varvarois, period. It is true that the patriarch Sylvester was a bit of an odd duck in these waters; but why not let him alone finally? Since one can see that his path has nothing in common with Commissioner Rilsky's, if one takes an honest look instead of splitting hairs about this or that. That was it: Sylvester Chrest was completely different from Northrop Rilsky, and the latter had been convinced of this for a long time.

What about this migrant's anxiety, however, this restlessness of body and soul? Too bad, there was nothing to be done about it. Was he then like Sebastian? Poor Sebastian—looking for the genetic origins of his fate as a supernumerary child in the chronicles of the Crusades! Looking for them, moreover, in the middle of Santa Varvara, where no one had ever heard of Godfrey of Bouillon, Peter the Hermit, or Anna Comnena! Byzantine it certainly was! What's more, the police commissioner, this rational man whose good judgment was supposed to protect the country from all possible and imaginable wackos, was being sucked into the favorite game of his strange double, the scavenger hunt of the obscure Professor Chrest-Jones, a man who would never have come out of the shadows, had he not hit on the strange idea of disappearing.

The next day, this time without losing his way in the corridors, Rilsky went to the university lab. He was very pleased to see that Minaldi was there waiting for him already. The commissioner hated to waste time as much as he hated when others wasted his time.

The missing person's journal was at the bottom of three stacks of documents that the experts from Rilsky's crime unit had assembled on the white formica counter in the corner of Sebastian's office. Rilsky thumbed through it quickly before packing it up for a closer and calmer inspection at his home. There were two notebooks, of one hundred pages each, filled with a large romantic cursive script that one only finds nowadays in the love letters of elderly women, letters decorated with dried flowers pressed between yellowing pages that have not been reopened since the death of their grandfathers. In other words, a handwriting totally unlike Northrop's small, compact handwriting, which can only be read with a magnifying glass. There was no point in reading it all immediately, neither closely nor chronologically. He only wanted to take a general sounding of it all, just like any cop who leafs through the depositions of witnesses and defendants or like an experienced wild animal that knows how to size up its prey right away: a bizarre contradiction here, a suspect piece of information there, etc. Above and to the side of the journal were various labeled folders: *Amiens-Pierre l'Ermite Coucoupêtre, Gautier Sans Avoir, Godefroi de Bouillon, Bohème de Tarente and Tancrède, Puy-en-Velay, Anna Comnena* (again), *Vézelay, Urban II, Innocent III, Kaloyan, Enricho de Leiningen and the Jews, Nish-Philippopolis, Fréderic Barberousse, The Crusade of Children.* Byzantine indeed, this mix of exotic medieval names and eccentric scholarship. Northrop was dumbfounded—only God could make heads or tails of it all.

"To make things easier for you, Commissioner, you have the possibility of consulting all these materials via the files on the hard drive or on these disks that I have specially prepared for you." Minaldi had a tendency to repeat himself. "The same goes for the pictures that I have classified. You will see photocopies of original documents, slides of tapestries, frescoes, sculptures, and even some computer-generated images representing important events of the First Crusade. There are also some materials devoted to the three following ones that especially concern Philippopolis. But the professor was mostly interested in the First Crusade—that was his obsession!

Was it really necessary to view this mess in order to pick out a few clues that might illuminate the foggy bottom of Sebastian's brain and thereby provide a coherent plan of investigation for the rational mind of the commissioner? It was very easy to get lost in Byzantium, especially since the vulgarization provided by this computer geek who claimed to be Hermine's lover was of no use at all. He had absolutely no confidence in Minaldi, though he would have to test this impression all the same. If he proceeded by intuition, should he begin with the journal or let it drop? Rilsky hesitated. Was Chrest-Jones's escapade of sufficient interest to merit a personal investigation by the chief of the department's crime unit while other, more urgent and mysterious cases, especially that of the serial killer, remained unsolved? The mafialike behavior of local sects had led to the much publicized dispatching of the special reporter from the *Événement de Paris*, OK; but wasn't the disappearance of Sebastian just a stunt, the melancholic whim of a cheated husband who simulates leaving home to rekindle the waning desire of his wife? And what better way than to make use of the media's constant need for "news"? It was a perfect fit! Then there was the chance that Sebastian was mixed up with the serial killer, was perhaps the killer himself. Why not? What better cover for a killer than to be disguised as an innocent medievalist? The idea was a little strange, but Northrop could not rule it out entirely.

Sebastian had written notes in Greek, Latin, French, and German. He had also used the Cyrillic alphabet, but for what language? Bulgarian? Serbo-Croatian? Macedonian? Perhaps a mixture of all three? At the middle school where Sylvester the Patriarch had enrolled his supernumerary son, of whom he was very proud, the lad won all the foreign language prizes. This happened, not surprisingly, after the death of his mother, Tracy Jones.

During a family dinner Griselda once mentioned Sebastian's gift for languages, which had been pointed out to her by a friend. No one around the table seemed to see anything exceptional in it—in Santa Varvara and elsewhere these days everyone speaks several languages. Being an ace at foreign languages would do nothing to lift him out of the obscurity he'd been consigned to. The same friend later told another story—and Griselda took a secret pleasure in relating it to all the interested parties—of how the young prodigy was not affected by the death of his mother, but had instead become attached to his paternal grandmother, whom he had never known, to the point of going to seek out the grave of this ancestor in Bulgaria.

He even brought back a handful of soil in a tea tin and showed it to his college roommate, who happened to be the son of this well-informed gossip. Having listened to the account of this odd show of fidelity, the Rilsky family stared wide-eyed and in the next instant lowered their gazes toward the contents of their plates, and the information was thus eliminated by the good manners that smooth over everything in such circumstances.

Rilsky leaned over the pages, which had taken on a bluish tint from the outdated inky lace, an exaggerated cursive script that clearly communicated the almost nauseating womanish sincerity of his missing uncle. "*To speak all languages and yet to speak none is to speak a language of silence. I am not one of them; I speak the way I imagine they want me to speak. This is not necessarily a false language, but it is already a role. From one role to another, I'm surprised at my talkativeness. The sensitive child who remained quiet has become a chatterbox who speaks a language of silence.*" When could he have written these sentences? After some romantic failure, a dispute with Hermine, or perhaps an encounter with Rilsky himself, who would not have even recognized him? Without any temporal reference points, the notes did not fade away but remained frozen in a kind of vertical presence. The tête-à-tête with his journal allowed Sebastian to launch into lyrical effusions. These more or less inspired reveries were interspersed with factual accounts of peasants whom he met around Plovdiv having to do with geographic descriptions and poetic references and concluded with page after page of quotations in various local idioms. And yet, even though the manuscript achieves a minute reconstitution of a very old history, that of the Chrest family, it would seem, and makes use of various precise documents relating to the Crusades, none of the journal's pages is dated. Its time lacks all tenses.

Northrop thought of the silence that was overtaking his deepest self, or what he, like anyone else, thought was his deepest self, and that he brushed against at the end of a day of interviewing hardened criminals and victims still stunned at having survived events of savage aggression. Or a day spent meeting with bored and overworked judges and cynical legal counselors. Bodies filled with holes and those freezing in their steel filing cabinets at the morgue had more to say, surprisingly, than all the people he had to deal with day after day. It was more accurate to say he had to "speak with" this world of crime than to "speak about it." As a policeman he was content to decipher the dialects and pursue the essential, which, more often than not, was only silence. It had nothing to do with what is popularly called "monstrosity," "animality," or "human nature." Those who have not crossed into the circle of crime like theater and noise—their disgust is itself spectacular and chatty. At the heart of human beings where horror resides, Rilsky had only bumped up against an opaque silence, an incommensurable strangeness that is more nerve-wracking than madness itself; the latter being, after all, satisfied with those pathetic but innocent disturbances at the surface that so intrigue the psychiatric community.

"I am a disenfranchised citizen of nowhere," wrote Sebastian. *"All exiles come from someplace that they prefer over their adopted countries or that they hate so that they can more easily fuse with their second home. I know some who have become amateur poets and speak of 'frail birches stooped with snow' or 'warm scents of spicy dishes that rock the blue of the eternal sea' whenever they think of their native lands. Others burn with indifference. Still others, who come to be stamped as victims in their land of exile, lament their state as though complaining were the ultimate price to pay for a degree of freedom one thousand times preferable to the slavery they had fled. I neither fled nor chose. And yet in my home I am not at home. And when I travel abroad I recognize on the faces of strangers the familiar look of being from nowhere. Is it really how they are or only my momentary impression as an uprooted passerby? I am of no place, and, as for time, perhaps I am of a time that shrinks into something outside time."*

He could sure pour on the lyricism, my brainy little uncle, when really he was just carrying around the weight of his bastard status, certainly not enviable, but at least he was a recognized bastard, spoiled even, I witnessed that myself! OK, everyone's not stuck being a bastard, but so what? Did he perhaps read too much Sartre while pretending to be the engaged public intellectual in his asbestos-filled towers? Whatever, but I won't be crying over him, that's for sure! As for foreigners, they are everywhere in the world; even in Santa Varvara one sees all kinds and colors, and they're not all illegitimate children as far as I know! The professor tended to think of himself as a prophet of the human condition. Perhaps even its redeemer. Interesting, no? But, what does that have to do with his disappearance? After all, "citizen of nowhere" could apply to a lot of people. For his part the commissioner had no nostalgic feelings and truly had no wish to live anywhere abroad. Leaving one place and settling someplace else would never solve anything. Sebastian had his arguments. He, Northrop, belonged to nothing, except perhaps Stephanie, but their relations were so recent, and then, too, love is more a kind of music than a bond, the symmetrical opposite of crime's silence.

"Professor Chrest-Jones had a lot of imagination, don't you think, Commissioner?" *He* had a lot of gall, this Minaldi, leaning over my shoulder and making remarks like this! With a crewman like that, it's no surprise that Sebastian wanted to jump ship.

"You think that he's not dead, that he's run away to the country of his research obsessions?" Rilsky, fighting against his revulsion, played the expert adolescent psychologist, the popular prophet of truth today.

"I have no idea, but what I do know is that Hermine, I mean Mrs. Chrest-Jones, is overworried. Lots of people disappear without leaving any address, and no one sends the police after them just because their own families don't care or don't exist. Take, for example, our young Chinese colleague from Hong Kong, Fa Chang, who's been in our lab for two years. I've not seen her for a week. She must have told the professor that she was going somewhere, perhaps to see her grandmother in Taiwan or her boyfriend in San Francisco. But since her family doesn't live here and her friends don't know any higher-ups in the police department, no one has sounded any alarms." Minaldi's airs of superiority were becoming more and more obscene.

This Fa Chang was just what this dull puzzle needed! Were there only foreigners in Santa Varvara now, or "citizens of nowhere," as Sebastian put it? Rilsky would have to test him, but Minaldi, whose arrogance freed him from all self-doubt, seemed the perfect vainglorious Santa Varvara native. But, in fact, he too was the son of foreigners, though no doubt the only one not to dwell on the matter. The worst of it was that there would always be Minaldis—monarchists, nationalists, populists, and more or less convincing academics who never openly oppose today's métissage fashion—oh, not that!—for fear of looking like backward extremists but who never miss an opportunity to defend the purity of the republic or the declining monarchies. These thoughts passed through Rilsky's mind as he opened and then quickly closed again the folder labeled *Pierre l'Ermite*. He'll have to wait, that hermit! The experts were continuing their work silently: sealing, stacking, and boxing folders without paying the least attention to Minaldi.

Rilsky was beginning to get seriously annoyed. OK, that will do for today. Luckily there was Stephanie, his airmail surprise, and their unexpected agreement, and the pleasure of seeing her again later.

It was odd, but he had been immediately certain about this passion that had been always locked inside his dreams—only waiting to blossom, wrong but essential. It was as extraordinary and familiar as the sensation of being the serial purifier that had come over him the day he saw the body of Reverend Sun. Stephanie and Number Eight: the light and dark faces of the same abyss possessed this civil servant, this guardian of law and order, this notorious bachelor and melancholy dandy, this brainy cop and doggerel poet. Taken too seriously by some and not enough by others, Rilsky was well over fifty before his controlled facade began to crumble. Was it worth getting worked up over? Should he see a police psychologist or think about undergoing analysis? That wasn't his style. Despite his taste for introspection the commissioner preferred action. He was going to live; that is, do what is called life, not necessarily his duty, even though the one did not exclude the other. He would see.

All the same, Stephanie's confidence did not put an end to the maelstrom that carried him off now and then with a passionate jubilation. There had never been any Number Eight—the serial killer was really him! For how long had he been Commissioner Rilsky and Mr. Hyde? Was it in another life? Or now, last night again, midnight on Saturday, or possibly Sunday at dawn? He made an *8* with his finger. What a joke, the dead don't have eyes, every avenger is an innocent, without regrets but instead a big blade to saw bones, veins, and livers such as those of Reverend Sun or Nordi—a black hole. He escaped from this dizziness of feeling cramped, surrounded, and sick. Only the young woman's presence brought him back to reality. Finally another Rilsky was beginning to exist, maybe—or so, at least, he wished to believe. Good-bye Dr. Jekyll, no more crazy hypotheses: out with the logical constructions and the family tradition of playing at the astute negotiator. Perhaps that was love, after all—the simple certainty of its *being* communicated to you by the body, gaze, and voice of the woman whose pleasure you possess and who possesses yours. And this without grand words, even if in the spasm of excess the two lovers might babble to each other things that would then be immediately reabsorbed by a slight, shame-filled discretion during a moment of silent smoking, gin drinking, and listening to Scott Ross.

Is Communism a Descendant of Byzantium? ᛭

"The professor must have gone there in the seventies sometime, perhaps as early as 1970. After May 1968, no one believed in communism anymore. It wasn't yet like the Berlin Wall coming down, rather just the start of revisionism, as they called it, such as the exposure of the gulags, you remember?" Minaldi was explaining Sebastian Chrest-Jones's journey to his father's native land while Rilsky studied a computer model of the itinerary of the First Crusade that traced the path of the troops of Adhémar de Monteil, the bishop of Le Puy-en-Velay, through Philippopolis in 1096–1097 and on toward the tomb of Christ. "Believe it or not, Sebastian Chrest never saw the modern country; he simply didn't care about it, according to his wife, who of course knows him well. In my opinion he was indifferent to politics and still is. Yes, that exists, Commissioner, even among historians, perhaps I should say especially among historians. Was he cynical? No, but depoliticized, you might say. Everything in the here and now bores him; he lives beyond it or before it all—we realists might say nowhere." Minaldi's pronouncements were half Hermine and half the mimicking of his former thesis director's journal. Rilsky was quick at detecting the parrot mode among witnesses. People who thought and spoke for themselves were so rare one could wonder if any existed at all.

"The Bulgarian communists obviously thought Chrest-Jones was a spy. Here's this person who buries himself in the archives of Plovdiv doing research on crusaders—you can imagine their reaction: he's either nuts or a spy, who naively thinks that he'll divert attention from himself in the archives, but who, of course, only attracts more attention. The local police concluded that the nuclear power plant must be the real interest of Professor Chrest-Jones. But how did he manage to camouflage so completely his interest for the plant? They assigned a seductive young communist party member, bilingual of course, to help him with his work, improve his Bulgarian, and spy on the spy. Nothing came of it. Total indifference." Minaldi's juicy storytelling was fueled by the intimacy he shared with the professor's wife. The commissioner let him rattle on, waiting for the tip-off that would lead him to the serial killer. Nothing had come of it so far, just a waste of time.

"Even toward death, Commissioner. Not that long ago, Sebastian told us, er . . . told Hermine, I mean Mrs. Chrest-Jones and myself, that as a teenager he knew he would never be able to believe in God because he had no fear of death. Absurd, don't you think? Everyone is afraid of death, right? Much later, just before disappearing from his marriage bower, he'd discovered that if he had no fear of death, it was because he lived constantly by its side."

"'Here, you see: my wrinkled hands with their varicose veins. I am watching them die now, but I know that I've been sensing their coming death forever. The journey has been going on forever. One cannot be afraid of the journey, it's inevitable—it's all there is.' 'You're tired,' was Hermine's diagnosis; she also suspected cancer. Someone had told her that a victim of major illness has a premonition of the end that causes melancholy long before the first physical symptoms of the illness appear. 'I am not tired and I do not have cancer. This is not a decline; I am simply on my way,' replied the professor to the utter stupefaction of his wife and her lover.

"You see how, with ideas like these, he was afraid of nothing, not even communism; he barely knew such a thing existed," said Minaldi almost sympathetically.

"Excuse me, do you mind, Pino? Indifferent is false. And cynical, certainly not. Actually, after the first trip to the tomb of his grandmother, he returned one or two times, it seems to me. I don't keep a close count of his professional travels, but I know that it was Byzantium that interested him—its Orthodox faith, though not for the sake of glorifying it, that I know!" Hermine was already casting herself as the widow of the runaway. It might be necessary to rehabilitate the image of her husband and not leave everything to Minaldi. "Do you mind?" And what if poor Sebastian were worth more than this Pino who is pushing himself forward to grab everything? OK, it's human, but really! "He thought them excellent mystics, but so dependent, so unfree, you understand. They were sort of half slaves and half rebels, the pope and Stalin: the submissive son and the tyrannical father—no way out! Dostoyevsky said it all: 'The Orthodox Church fosters the nihilism that prefigures communism,' he used to repeat. Original, don't you think? It all made me sick, and with good reason. Can you make anything of it, Northrop? He wanted me to read *The Possessed*—what an idea! It's so badly written, don't you think? It's as clear as mud, of course I mean for a thinking person such as myself. I wasn't the audience they—Dostoyevsky and Sebastian—needed. But he had ideas, my husband, I can assure you of that—religious and political ideas in a certain way. You go too fast Pino, I'm afraid, you see. . . . ."

She had sat down on a corner of the desk and was swinging one leg back and forth as she spoke. Pino gave her a cold stare, the prelude to other future exchanges, but she returned his evil eye with her own and continued on, her swinging leg keeping time with her mouth.

Sebastian would only have shared two or three memories of this Bulgarian trip with Hermine, who wondered if they were indeed the traces of strongly felt experiences or simply the clichés of any tourist. First the opulent greenish copper copulas of the Saint Sveta Nedelia Church in Sofia and the deep sound of the bells that one could hear from the apartment in the narrow Saint Sofia Street where the last members of the Chrest family—distant cousins of the patriarch Sylvester—still lived. Who knows why this memory brought tears to Sebastian's scared little squirrel eyes? Then there was the portrait of the svelte noblewoman Dessislava painted in the twelfth century and now hanging in a church in Boyana, if Hermine remembered correctly, a small town outside the capital. Sebastian believed that this work already broke with the style of the Byzantine icons, though it did not yet display the suppleness of the Giotto frescoes—no, not quite, but it came very close, I think. And finally the Baudouin tower in Turnovo—the former capital—that held captive certain crusaders from among the troops of Baudouin of Flanders, among them the very first member of the Chrest family according to one of Sebastian's early theories, though he abandoned it eventually; Hermine didn't know why. The ruins of this well-known tower pleased him enormously, he was always pointing it out in postcards—it was pathetically boring, really. But luckily that obsession didn't last for long and he was soon on to something else.

"For once he was speaking, Commissioner; he wasn't speaking to me, as I've already said, and really you'd wonder if he even saw me there next to him like I am next to you here, but he was speaking at least, in his bubble." Hermine was intent on adding her psychological testimony about the missing person to the investigation. "He spoke with that kind of lover's voice that seems to be sharing secrets with you while at the same time listening to his own words. It was a way of speaking passionately to oneself. OK, why not, but it did nothing for me except make me yawn! However, you can see that, having been subjected to this over and over, I have retained a few things. In the end he realized that I could care less about his family pilgrimage, his efforts to redeem his bastard status, or whatever else was motivating him; and he laughed a good long time—I can still hear that crazy laugh he let out—ha ha, hee hee. And then he never spoke about his trips again. A shadowy man, that's what he was. A man who chased after long shadows in every direction until they belonged only to him. Sebastian was certainly alone, but he was a mole, not the migrating bird he thought himself to be." Hermine's voice struck an almost tragic note before punctuating her remarks with another "ha ha, hee hee."

Rilsky listened to her closely while going through the files on the disk entitled *From "Le Puy-en-Velay to Philippopolis,"* one of which showed a map of Europe bisected with a dotted red line tracing the itinerary of Raymond de Saint-Gilles. He left off following the path of Adhémar. Was it possible that this woman, who definitely was not his type, nevertheless knew Sebastian better than anyone? The commissioner only believed in the absurd, especially the absurdity of married life; and therefore was quite pleased to follow the meandering digressions of this widow. They partially confirmed him in his thinking as a new hypothesis formed itself out of the darkness.

For Rilsky went much further than the chattering spouse. He recalled that as a child Sebastian never stopped running, falling, and hurting himself—always without crying. Already living in the shadows, alone and unhappy. That was something his grandmother Suzanne or his mother Griselda had found striking, if the nephew remembered correctly, and given his own shaky hold on his remembrance of past time, he really was not sure it was Griselda or Suzanne who had passed along this detail. Perhaps it did not even have to do with Sebastian, but rather another boy they knew, or perhaps he had made up this miserable story about his poor little uncle for consistency's sake—to make him more interesting for the investigating commissioner that he was, as well as nephew of the victim, but, first of all, police commissioner, let's not forget! The role of child-king the family had bestowed on Nordi allowed him to absorb without risk the traumas of criminals as well as those of victims. Moreover, after years of collaborating on arrests, trials, and the testimony of experts, Rilsky's career had taught him that unlucky babies—as many criminals happened to have been—are bruised long before birth. Fate beats up on them early: the mother's anxieties bombard it already in the uterus and it suffers the shocks caused by all of these hormones gone haywire. It's a miracle that such creatures manage to be born more or less normal seeming. But the warring does not let up. Hence the awkwardness and the additional bumps and bruises. In any case, one thing was certain in his memory now: the stories about Sebastian falling down all the time could not have come from his grandmother Suzanne, because she was so embarrassed by the illegitimate child of her husband that she could not pronounce the little boy's name, although on rare occasions she did put up with his presence in her house.

The sun had begun to shine through the historian's office window. The team of experts sent out for coffee. Rilsky returned to his mostly random examination of the routes of the First Crusade. He thought about the missing person and, hoping to see more clearly, tried to recall, as best he could, the few memories he still had from their childhood.

One could imagine—Northrop certainly could—that someone who so mistreats his body is even more punishing on his mind. As he relived them in his own mind, Rilsky greatly exaggerated Sebastian's now distant trials and tribulations. It would not have taken much for him to imagine poor Sebastian as a little not-quite-normal handicapped kid with a funny gait and a habit of bumping into every table corner and door—a boy with swollen knees, a fat lip, and covered with bruises that never went away and thus permanently hinted at the invisible psychic bruises of his soul. The most painful of all being the inability to express himself—of feeling misunderstood and unloved. Northrop suddenly began to grow fond of this imaginary Sebastian, while still remaining mildly revolted by his sufferings. He slid willingly into the kind of tender yet hopeless relationship that may form, who knows why, with invalids whom one finds charming.

Sebastian the unloved. Bringing kids into this crazy world was already incomprehensible, and Rilsky would never have taken such a risk, not even with Martha and God knows if. . . . But illegitimate children to boot! They're running on one leg from the start! It was hardly surprising if Sebastian had become a solitary wanderer, an egotistical adventurer, or, as it looked now, one of the police's "cases."

Minaldi had left the lab and taken Hermine to lunch. Rilsky went out to buy himself a sandwich, which he ate outside; he then decided to walk back to the police station. When he had the time, walking helped him organize his thoughts.

"Our incorrigible nomad," sighed the grandmother, Suzanne, in admiration of her husband, the patriarch. She was forever charmed by this blond Balkan man. Her romantic soul did not want to acknowledge that the nomad lives a feverish and unceasing struggle beyond any moral boundaries to outdo himself. It is no accident that the overwhelming majority of delinquents happen to be recent immigrants and their children. This was generally the case, and the commissioner had the statistics to prove it. But then there was the particular case, and Northrop Rilsky never overlooked the particular case. The suffering individual who comes out of this adventure, the unclassifiable Sebastian Chrest-Jones, for example, takes his blows, falls silent, and then ends up projecting himself into the role of a crusader, a purifier—now fusing with the expeditions of earlier examples, now peeling off from them and living his own calamity.

He descended the large shady avenue that buzzed with noise, then another, crossed the park, and walked up the street opposite the police station, thinking to himself all the while. Did Sebastian consider himself a social reject, a throwaway, or did he take a more resigned or even mildly heroic view of his life thanks to his research on migrations and then on the Crusades? Had his work provided him with a comfortable equilibrium that put an end to the drift of the ill-conceived child? Had this come through the annulment of sainthood itself and the erasure of his own exceptional status—as though he were an unconscious Christ who evolves out of the banality of the poor child, then the modest historian, to become and remain the end of a particular line? Had Sebastian finally recovered from this mute pain that he articulated in various ways with the half-silly crowning of himself as doctor *honoris causa*? But where was he living this recovery? In flight, suicide, or in crime?

Rilsky entered the police station. Despite all his work and the many calls, the rest of the day seemed to go by slowly. Neither Minaldi, Hermine, nor anybody else could understand this omega point that the commissioner had come to through his identification with his missing uncle. It was his own very personal way of conducting this investigation, and for once he was throwing himself into it totally. Well, perhaps not exactly totally, like Stephanie did; but then, well, to each his own. No, no one else could understand, except perhaps Stephanie Delacour, the woman whom the commissioner hurried to rejoin in the evening in the guest studio of his apartment, where she would be listening to Scott Ross and sipping her gin and tonic—eager to see her unexpected lover again.

> Ever he would wander, selfcompelled, to the extreme
> limit of his cometary orbit, beyond the fixed stars and
> variable suns and telescopic planets . . . he would some-
> how reappear reborn above delta in the constellation of
> Cassiopeia and after incalculable eons of peregrination
> return an estranged avenger, a wreaker of justice on
> malefactors, a dark crusader, a sleeper awakened.
>
> JAMES JOYCE, *Ulysses*

CHAPTER THREE ❧ Stephanie in Love

I have the ultimate and irrefutable proof of the savageness of Santa Varvara. This place even makes me forget Jerry, the delicate child of Gloria, my decapitated friend. I adopted this child and set him up in Paris with Pauline. Nevertheless, the fragile existence of this adolescent computer nerd and his whole world that I consider to be very real shrink and almost disappear as soon as I arrive here. That world is incompatible with Santa Varvara; I know nothing from it translates here. Perhaps that is one of the unspeakable forces that suck me against my will further into this muddle? Perhaps I am being protected by the kind of grace that one comes across at certain turning points in life when it risks turning into who knows what. Is this grace making me softer and more maternal, someone hardly recognizable as the same person who signs those columns for the *Événement de Paris*?

"You can play with your video games as much as you want on my computer!" I said this many times to Jerry, since he preferred staying home with his games to spending Sunday afternoons in the rue d'Assas. "You are so out of it, Steph," he would reply to put an end to my endless telephone calls and avoid pacing up and down. These quips were haikus, witty digs, voluntary or not, within the terse language of this bright, private person. "My fruitcake," he used to say after kissing me as a way of saying that I spoiled him and that he loved being spoiled. Am I to believe that his tenderness is an unbearable challenge to me? At least I can take a break from him here, in the arms of the police commissioner, for instance, and, besides, the feeling doesn't last long. Jerry is regularly popping up on my computer, not pleadingly but in a way that recalls to me less his problems than me, myself, I: Stephanie from nowhere. Whether through his inward turn or his outward embrace of me, we meet our needs.

"March 22. Lux's bees have replaced the pigeons under your windows." He knows that I observe these kinds of changes.

"May 24. Pauline complains that you don't publish very much in the *Événement de Paris*. Love, Jerry." What a declaration. Suddenly I miss him.

"June 3. Macha doesn't call anymore." The spurned lover doesn't sign his name. His girlfriend makes him suffer too much.

E-mails from Jerry are like coded messages from the days of the Resistance: "The castaways speak to the castaways." Only my son belongs to another world and tries to belong to ours—the reverse is not true. I try, and sometimes I succeed, when things are going well in my life: to be a mom. Today is different. His e-mails are like contagious eclipses; they block out the obvious realities of Santa Varvara, including those of my new lover, and I forget about the "special reporter." No more role-playing. I trip over the wounded voice of Jerry, I go deeper and write.

Me Stephanie Delacour, I am writing this metaphysical—or is it psychological?—crime novel with my dubious sense of humor, I'm sure you'll agree, and here I pause. Am I going to pursue a traditional-style investigation into the sects or follow my natural preference and immerse myself in the human condition of wounded souls? Perhaps I've become overly influenced by melodramatic reality shows. Who would have believed it?

How did I fall in love, to use the standard expression, with this geezer Rilsky, who's almost old enough to be my father, and whom I've known and never cared about at all ever since I started coming to Santa Varvara, which is to say forever? Talk about a love story! I guess you could say a love with no story, one of the unexpected pleasures that take place out of time. I am curling into some inward space and let the serial killer and the New Pantheon drop. My boss in Paris can call my cellphone all he wants. It's switched off and so am I: out of order. For once Stephanie Delacour has gone into her secret hideaway here in Santa Varvara—incredible, no?

Do you want my address? I'm living among the geraniums and their soil, which was wet yesterday and dry today. I pour myself into the fresh water with which I moisten their feet; I drink alongside the full-leafed branches above the rocky beds; I knead them into timid little purple flowers in the heat of the sun. I seep into this lively amber scent that overpowers the heavy fragrance of the neighboring rosebushes and chases away the mosquitoes sickened by the taste of seaweed that increases with the coming storm behind the low wall of stones; and I fill my mouth with the most delicious plum jam that my grandmother flavored with these full-shaped citronella-scented leaves. But the taste is only a memory and I am no more than an earthling at the edge of the ocean.

The tenacious flowers that grip the crust of the earth's volcano are only a temporary refuge for me, a momentary borderland. I hold onto them like an energetic or drunken bee or fly, the ephemeral lover of perfumed pollens of innumerable colors. The geraniums will not let me go; I know well their rooted stubbornness—and yet I'm forgetting them today because I'm overcome with the conviction of belonging to a long line of travelers. I only feel really at home on airplanes—far from roots and surrounded by strangers, not borders. At those high altitudes space belongs to no one.

I am of the rootless race of the knights of the steppes, the knights of the desert, the migrants of airports. As soon as I land, as soon as my foot hits the ground, as soon as my ears detect what seems like a comprehensible language, and my eyes cross the looks of others who seem to know me, I absent myself.

I don't hunker down inside myself because that deep center gets found out. I pass instead into the in-between, neither depth nor surface, and take up residence in that emptiness that I call strangeness. I've been loaned many languages but I own none. I do not express myself in either words or sentences, as others do in their mother tongues, even though I like to trace rhythms and visions more easily in French because it is the language of my son, a language of childhood, for him and for me, and nevertheless meditated upon cautiously, like the language of children who were for a long time mute—oysters who were mistaken for stones.

More and less than words and sentences, it's the underside of the language that I sense flowing in my mouth and running out of my fingers as I write my pieces from Santa Varvara or elsewhere. Some of our readers, being native speakers, sense that my language is borrowed, cold, and distant. "You go too far, my dear Stephanie," complains my boss. How happy are the limited! Me, I don't really forget the juicy inside of this shell of words as other native speakers forget their maternal babblings. But, always held back by the vowels, consonants, and syllables, I go to meet the ungraspable little flame underneath the outer covering of signs: humor and meaning, mean and naive goodness, fluid fleeting river forever changing, where the famous old sage would never bathe twice. In my wildest and most triumphant dreams I do not take myself for one of the pre-Socratics. I am, if it's possible for me to speak of such things in the present tense, just a Byzantine. What is that?

A foreigner and a woman, I know that I come from Byzantium, a place that has never existed with any credible reality except in my soul. After Greece—which, for the first time in world history and better than anyone else, celebrated the Good and the Beautiful in the name of the gods and God inside splendid temples and before the arrival of the barbarians that they continually fended off, spawned, and absorbed—my own Byzantium must no doubt be the most crucified country, I believe, because it lavished on itself a level of sophistication never before attained. That's it, you're there! The never ending incongruous debates about the sex of angels, that's Byzantine. The damage wrought by iconoclasts and the sanctification of images carried out by icon lovers, without which the world would never have hit on television or known the likes of Guy Debord, *Survivor,* and all the Bin Ladens on Al Jazeera . . . that's Byzantine. The first religious war in the Old World, those legendary Crusades that later inspired President Bush with a duplicate set of pogroms, looting of local treasures, failed (already) attempts at European unification and globalization beyond Europe—yes, "globalization" since the Crusaders went beyond Europe to the tomb of Christ invaded by the miscreants, remember?—all that still always happens via Byzantium. From this point of view, I believe, Byzantium is what remains most precious, refined, and painful about Europe, that which others envy about it and which she has difficulty realizing herself and extending—unless that is . . . who knows? In the meantime, Santa Varvara expands in all directions.

Everywhere? But where exactly? You want to locate Santa Varvara on a map? But it's impossible, you know. How can one locate the global village? Santa Varvara is in Paris, New York, Moscow, Sofia, London, Plovdiv, and in Santa Varvara too, of course—it's everywhere, I tell you, everywhere where foreigners like you and I try to survive, we the inauthentic wanderers searching for who knows what truth, against all the money-soaked mafias peddling the easy life in this crime novel run wild, this *spectacle* still called for now—but who knows for how much longer—a "society." The nonstop exhibition of intimacy, televising of values, and execution of our passions. The criminal investigation bureaus that, when they're not rotten like the rest, try to determine "where the desire comes from"—a desire that all children who've been raised on video games since birth know full well is a desire for death. Just as journalists sometimes—after all, the spectacle can boast that it is made of scenes, screens, and behind-the-scenes surprises, very rare, it's true, but who does it better?—journalists, as I was saying, if they can render their work academic, try to unravel what's going on, how the world works, and what it all means. The flutterings of the heart have been taken over by the flutterings of spectacle, and we spend our time distinguishing gradations of lesser and greater evil. What I'm saying is that the best Byzantines, like the best citizens of Santa Varvara, can be found among detectives, children, and journalists. Among certain detectives, children, and journalists.

Look around you: cannibals clone themselves, kamikazes set nurses on fire with candles and eat dead children off roasting sticks—it's a disoriented human race that has lost all sense of what crime is. "All is permitted," my dear Fyodor Mikhaylovich, but "nothing is interdicted," said the delicious Lacan, and you heard it here from your special embedded foreign correspondent! If I don't do it, or someone like me, who can get the job done such that there will be no indulgences made to either the "difficult" neighborhoods or the skinheads? I am even inclined to think that it is precisely from among the transitory beings that we are—we vulnerable Byzantines and recorders of the modern Crusades—that the question of the future, if not the future, will come. Articulating the problems, asking Byzantine questions—is there anything else to do while the natives are hunkering down underneath the footer of their corporate bottom lines, selfish and macho, French, Russian, American, gypsy, Palestinian, feminist, Catholic, Muslim, Jewish, Korean. . . . Go on, complete the list for yourself. Is there anything else, I'm asking, when angry immigrants and random fanatic shahids boil with humiliation while waiting to blow up your buildings, ransack your banks, disfigure your people, and torch your houses and vacation homes? Until the G8 countries succeed in creating prosperity within all the new emerging countries, this goes without saying.

Let's speak about them, the foreigners, whom you fear or glorify in this "multicultural age"—don't pass up this fashionable pleasure! I know what I'm talking about, and you do too. All of you who listen, as I do, as everyone does, to Jean-Marie Le Pen, don't tell me that Speedy Sarko has passed him, swallowed him, or modernized him—No![1] The seductiveness of tradition, of roots, of the purely native will return because it's always been there, in the fear factor gene. That seductiveness turns into a talent for predicting, governing, and telling us, long before anyone else, about all the present security dangers and the severe retaliation that will come. But you hesitate about letting it run its course out of fear—yes, fear!—that these tough remedies will be used against you. When it comes down to it, you're not as naive as you look. You prefer letting someone else do the dirty work, a foreigner if possible—clever, no?

We understand each other, you and me. I listen to Le Pen and Sarko too. And I've heard the same from Kristeva speaking at the Arab World Institute—a foreigner diagnosing the new maladies of the soul, as she calls them, maladies that afflict immigrants more than others, according to her. For once, this crowd of multicultural enthusiasts was not comforted by what they heard, but actually came unglued and left feeling hung over and guilty. She told them that the world's migrants and homeless who have fled their mother languages and are excluded from those of their adopted countries spontaneously become addicts, false nonbeings, and prey to psychosomatic illnesses and delinquency. Is it possible? Is it possible? More than the rest of us? Does this mean there are no saviors left to look up to within the International?

And why is that? One wonders. Because these guardians, these watchmen of the night, these insomniacs who are not tricked by any borders or comforting shelters, these new earthling nomads cash in on the advantages of eternal discontent and permanent revolt and thus do away with all pro-

---

1. Translator's note: When this book was first published in France in early 2004, Jean-Marie Le Pen was the leader of the country's infamous extreme right party, the National Front. Nicolas Sarkozy was French minister of the interior—a position comparable to that of then U.S. attorney general John Ashcroft. Mr. Sarkozy became minister of finance later that year and was replaced by Dominique de Villepin, who had been the foreign affairs minister during the run-up to the Iraq war. In June 2005, after the French rejection of the European Constitution, Sarkozy was reappointed minister of the interior and Villepin was named prime minister. The text is mocking the then popular perception that "Speedy Sarko"—a derisive nickname that winks in the direction of cinematic toughness à la Shaft or Scarface, while also linking the immigrant Sarkozy to the famous "ethnic" cartoon superhero Speedy Gonzales—offered a pragmatic and less repulsive version of the over-the-top brutality commonly associated with the racist and xenophobic positions of Jean-Marie Le Pen and his party.

tection. You want security, and you're right. Did you know that it begins with the mother language, man's first seat belt that protects him against all attacks from the inside as well as from the outside world, and that it extends to those famous values—monetary and aesthetic—that have acted like a guardrail for us but now are crumbling like the churches in Italy destroyed by earthquakes. (Everyone saw that on television. Everyone has his or her Agadir.) With no seat belts or guardrails, all foreigners, myself included, are subject to all excesses, explained the psychiatrist at the Arab World Institute. Unless they make up some false forms of protection: Homesickness (with a capital *H*), a newfound and more fervent religious devotion, fundamentalism, etc. Thus newly constituted, the foreigner's only remaining task is to sabotage the false personality that accidentally existed before—through suicide, for example, preferably in view of the television cameras of the hostile world to which he will never really belong. Too easy! Do you see another solution? And all in the illusory hope of returning to the authentic origin where the mother is awaiting him, that unknown mother squashed by the Powers-That-Be, all the powers, starting with that exercised by the martyr himself over his own people. All that to attain, beyond the umbilical mother and the dreams of happiness, the paradise and supreme joy that the compromises of this world disallow but that will be wildly available in the afterlife—thus the traveler, like the believer, is always hoping for another world. The psychiatrist had truly shaken up her audience that day.

Afterward it's easy to claim that foreigners are not my religion, that I have none, or, if I do, that it's only about keeping myself in motion—a passerby. One who doesn't hope to ground oneself via stories, articles, and inquiries but rests content instead with simply rephrasing the question: if the desire is a desire for death, how shall it be written? It's a question with no answer, a question to be asked up until the thousandth-and-first night that has not yet come; it's a question of the last reading of the last writing—let's go, I'm going, everybody gets a turn, his right, his loss!

Thus it happens that while I am investigating a series of crimes in Santa Varvara, the opposite of Byzantium and a place where I recently arrived and fell in love with Commissioner Rilsky—that's all I needed, as I think you understand—I, Stephanie Delacour, am addressing you, with all due respect, if you'll allow me that expression. Newspaper lingo, memories, pamphlet prose, stories, essays, free association, dream, study—who cares? No genre, only a diagonal passing through. My words are only circumstantial companions to me—a transparent film, a momentary obligation, an absolute necessity and yet somehow disloyal—my means by which I am determined to make public that which is hardly said at all, or, if it exists, then only with the help of figures, allusions, nonsense, and stories. Before or beyond language, my wanderings among perceptions and ideas are confined to no specific habitat such as the one that still shelters certain of my contemporaries: the habitat of their native idiom.

I knew a writer who only felt secure when speaking, reading, and writing his national language. All other situations, encounters, or possibilities made him feel in danger, angry, and bellicose. I knew a philosopher who thought that language, especially his own, could not become mad even though the world around it was sinking into the maddest of nightmares and a Führer was using it to galvanize crowds and incite crimes. Along the same lines, I have known women who clung to their local heritage and would only eat and prepare meals that they had tasted in the kitchen of their mothers, rejecting everything else and incapable of creating a recipe that was not already in the family repertoire.

I freely concede that I am a bit of a paradox, though a very explicable one.

But I won't tell you everything today. I know perfectly well that there are only mother tongues and national texts. That there *are* or that there *were*? Recently a humanity in transit has sought to express itself—burdened by its "no man's language" and feeling more at ease with video clips and music samples than with the pleasing oral rhetoric that dignified the ideas of our ancestors. Am I exaggerating? Of course! Nabokov was fully capable of leaving Russian, passing now and then through French, and taking up permanent residence in a comfortable English that was saturated with Slavic vibrations.

Did Beckett not achieve his matricide by parachuting into the language of Voltaire—a language that he never ceased emptying of its substance as a way of taking revenge on the effusions of Joyce and waiting for Godot within the narrow confines of—take your pick—Protestant or Catholic doubt? Finally Naipaul, who translates the Indian continent into an English that resonates like a cosmopolitan code quite beyond any Shakespearean pathos or music. Listen to the rapping of globalization's lost rap artists: this one, that one, this one, that one.... For my part, I inhabit the French language, but it closes me more than it discloses me and, through its knightly armor, I am only trying to get across these secrets of Byzantium.

If I tend to believe that the truth is couched in an invisible sublanguage, would this be Byzantine resurgence, a latter-day biblical graft on the body of the miraculous Greek achievement that preferred circumventing Homeric clarity at the risk of creating chasms of necessary and tragically useless complications? My Byzantium, you will have understood by now, is not the land of plenty that is popularly associated with this somewhat jarring name. My Byzantium resolutely names the unnameable or whatever it is that you wish not to reveal.

I knew a colleague who enjoyed writing erotic fiction, with heavy doses of petting and pawing, to attract today's essentially female reading public. What's more, he invented lovers for himself, magnified his amorous exploits, and bragged about having made *mille e tre* conquests—a portrait that was exactly the reverse of his romantic reality, something I well knew from first-hand observations was genuinely mediocre. Me, Stephanie Delacour, I'm just the opposite. Like "our" Colette, I indulge the unintense but honorable pleasure of not speaking of love. Along with my Byzantine atavism, however imaginary, I have a culpable preference for not revealing my burns, my men. Whether out of faith or perversity, I hold on to my prudery, for I am convinced that intimacy blossoms in the unsaid. Intimacy speaks indirectly, transmuted into figures and parables, numbers, symbols, and allusions, and all that is Byzantine.

There Are No Happy Foreigners ❧

Next to me, my new lover, this old friend, is still deep within his postcoital sleep. I'm just the opposite: erotic acts first calm me down but then keep me wide awake. Lost and found, things and words, neither arid nor ardent: always between the two, the tearing away. Because it's in the mounting pleasure that I discovered this coming out that ends up annihilating me, muscles and blood, before and after the consciousness of language and that I call my strangeness. The joy of coming is the intimate strangeness that we seek amid the ordinary order of our lives—a strangeness that constitutes us and that can rigidify into a painful fate or, with a bit of luck, transform into a marvelous openness. This is what I try to be and do in my own way:

a journalist, a world traveler, an investigator. I am trying to mix in with the sects of Santa Varvara, for example; this is openness itself, though not "marvelous," it's true, even though Commissioner Rilsky would not discount this adjective, and he knows about sex, believe me.

I am no longer taking Donormyl since we've been together, and yet a dream has awakened me and I have been restless ever since. I dive into my notebooks. NR (or Nordi as his friends call him) put a copy of Sebastian's journal on the nightstand. I don't think he's going to read it; he says he's had enough. Is he leaving it for me to look at? For now I have other things to do. Me first. There is not much left of this happy and rather absurd dream. I moonlight as a surrealist. The snouts of rather ferocious dogs have graceful rosebuds at their tips. Wow, some would wake up at less than that! Something to do with my childhood, but what?

It's true that, long before I discovered a talent for supposedly dangerous liaisons, two moments of my so-called childhood that occur to me now had drawn me toward these foreign zones, which I ended up adopting as my secret home. They have taken on all their resonance with the weight of time that has telescoped them and charged them with meaning for me in a contagious loop between then and now. One is a family photo shoot, the other a bombardment. In both scenes I am immersed in politics, as one says now, which is where I want to take you, of course!

I don't recall the exact circumstances of these earliest pictures of me that are lovingly preserved by my parents among their albums. However, I do remember something about the group photo that came before. I am sitting on a table with my parents standing behind me; my cousin is in the same pose, with her parents behind her as well. There is nothing remarkable about this game of matching families except for my wide-eyed expression and my o-shaped mouth out of which no cry of horror, the horror that's making my eyes pop out, will come. I can still hear the melodious voice my father would use in order to avoid getting angry: "Will you allow me to capture this moment?" he sang as he set the camera's timer and positioned the tripod before running behind me.

Capture the moment? It was inconceivable to me, and I must have looked rather stupid because my mother quickly offered her two cents: "Look at the little bird coming out of the lens!" That a little bird could come out of a hole in the black box that was in front of us was even more inconceivable. I remained petrified between the fidgeting of the adults and this gaping dead eye that we were expecting to capture us, or was it the other way around? The instant went on interminably, the hole was swallowing me up, I almost fell off the table, my father caught me, and the flash blinded me in the same instant, capturing my dizziness forever. I didn't belong to the bodies that were around me, and the little threatening bird inside the blind lens was nothing but a mechanical thief or sorcerer who would catch me and eat me just like the big bad wolf who ate little Red Riding Hood. I wasn't on the family table, nor was I in the little hole. I was nowhere and my situation seemed unbearable, but I held up as best I could. It even pleased me a little, thanks to my father who had kept me from falling into the void and the ridiculous. But there is the ridiculous expression on my face that my cousin has never failed to point out over the years, and still does every time these old photos are brought out at the laughable and mournful family reunions that bring us together.

Next, the bombardment, a rather grave incident. The capital is bombarded and we flee to the shelters. I am three years old, perhaps. My father is carrying my little baby sister in his arms while I walk valiantly next to him holding my mother's hand. The sky is lit up with rockets as on Bastille Day, though these fireworks don't make big pink circles. They tear through the sky like brightly colored gladiolas. I stare at one of these fire flowers and I don't want to continue toward the shelter. When one of the big gladiolas abruptly lands on the ground, I let go of my mother's hand and run irresistibly toward it as my mother screams after me. I saw a burning tongue, an electric scar, cut its way through the middle of the square and illuminate a round object, a sort of puffy brioche with ridges, like those of a scallop shell, that I can still recall. I run toward this madeleine cake, I want to eat it, when someone—it was my mother, she told me much later, as no one in my family wanted to remember this crazy moment—stopped my progress and knocked me to the ground. The thing explodes. The madeleine was really a bomb, and I was no longer there, but where was I? Miraculously, no one in my family was hurt. I heard sirens, the smell of blood made me nauseous, but I was not present. In my dreams I always go back to the fiery gladiola and the sweet bread that attracts me—and then nothing, the night. Sexual symbolism? Of course. And warlike on top of it all or underneath. I am a child of war.

This same absence could at times take on rough edges, let's say. Avoiding all mysticism, I prefer to go right away to my disconnections and strangeness. Often on Sunday afternoons I would accompany my father to soccer matches. We would cheer on "our team," the valiant "Blue Lions," against the "Reds," the formidable players of the army team; and we liked thinking that we were defending Civilization against the Barbarism that surrounded us. It was an act of both political and cultural courage according to the murmurings of the gentlemen in the stands around my father and me. And I was very proud of their confidence in me. I didn't understand the rules of the game, which went too fast; and the occasional unclear explanations of my father, who was not much of a teacher, were more confusing than enlightening. Transported by the rhythmic movement of bodies and the quickness of the kicks, I cried my lungs out shouting "Goal!" along with all the fans of "our team" whenever the ball went into the net of the Reds. However, this state of sweaty hands and beating heart did not reach its zenith with those cries so much as in the mute, overwhelming condition where I, with no voice, lost my sense of self as I became literally transfused by the magnetized crowd within the stadium.

"Losing one's I"—there's a pretentious expression that I usually abhor, but at that moment there was really a transfusion going on; I was without personal borders, a mere vibration that faded out as the sensation of calm took over. That's what happened; it was confirmed for me the next day when I studied the photo of the winning goal in the newspaper. It wasn't at all the star player, though he was idolized and I still remember his name, who impressed me. From the stands where I was watching, all that the photographer captured of this exploit of "ours" was a moving mass, a gray blur, forever frozen by the grainy snapshot. The minuscule little point there, right there, was me—my head like a little pinprick, a micron-sized iron filing held by the magnet of the stadium and the indifferent newsprint. I have never enjoyed any photograph of myself taken by lovers, friends, or professional photographers—though some have been very talented—as much as this one, nor have I ever felt so certain about the absolutely faithful representation of who I really am as I did when I saw that grainy gray photo. Beyond or short of the real me, across family conflicts, political crises, erotic exchanges, virile enthusiasms, and the drunken triumph that my father had wanted me to join while still keeping me in my place as a simple witness, it's the annulment of myself that I celebrated in exquisite peace looking at this speck that finally revealed me to myself.

If later the endless traveling—up to my complete absorption within the errors of the virtual and complete unreality—was never cause for depression, it's because I never doubted my status as one of the chosen. Certain as I was, thanks to my father, of always having my place in the stands at game time—next to him, with him—I could take pleasure with no risk to myself of being exiled within the invisible of the image, something that these days is worse than a tomb. There was, however, no altruism in this effacement. It was more a detachment, though might detachment be precisely the underside of altruism?

Other women exhaust themselves trying to equal the power of fathers or the performance of males. I gave up such pursuits from the beginning because my father convinced me, even before I realized it for myself, that I was capable of being one of them, of fusing with his enthusiasm, all the while remaining definitely someone else and somewhere else. Shored up in this way, the pleasure of my strangeness knows no limits; I can melt with no fear whatsoever into the anonymity of the masses. Are you afraid of being a banal "one"? If so, it's because you have not enjoyed the rush that comes from being alone, next to and separate from your father, different from the men and all the others, no matter who they are, lost and with them.

There's a packet of cigarettes on Nordi's bedside table. He doesn't smoke anymore, but I do, exceptionally, on this night. It's the trip, the stadium, this old diary that smells like the Camels of my father.

I knock myself out trying to be the best instructor at a summer camp. I want "my kids" to eat better, sleep more, wash the fastest, and be the cleanest. I want their rooms to be tidy and spotless, their skits to fascinate, their singing to enchant, their medals at swimming and archery to be numerous. In short, I want them to be the best at everything, God knows why, but it's absolutely essential to me. And I manage it, to the consternation of my colleagues who are green with envy. My kids are as exhausted and happy as I am—my drive to be first having kept me from getting any sleep. One afternoon during a heat wave I tried to recuperate with a little nap. As though sensing that the tyrant was weakening, my kids went nuts, shouting and indulging in the most ridiculous pranks and battles against each other. Between my anger and my impotence, which was going to win out? Abruptly, this tension gave way. A central pillar crumbled and absolute indifference made me feel lighter. It was neither a renunciation, because I still felt guilty, nor a defeat, because I was still filled with bitterness and dreaming of a storming revenge. I had simply cut loose all lines—nothing held me to anything; suddenly there were no desirable or detestable objects,

therefore nothing to perfect, no subject either, nothing but an infinite floating that modified my perceptions of space and time. I couldn't even hear
their yelling anymore. My ears gradually became attuned to the laughter
of swallows and my nose to the salty scent of seaweed. I was elsewhere,
detached from everything and more present than ever.

How long did this last? Perhaps hours. The others thought I was sleeping when really I had only drifted off a bit. The distant cries of the children
eventually reached me. Amusing but of no interest. Some white butterflies
entered and exited out the open window, as real and unreal as a film. The
inside and the outside, the wind, the sea, the sky, the herons, the butterflies,
the room, me, and the children rolled into continuous twisted coils without
edges, borders, or fixed points, only a rustling of sounds, scents, tastes, and
touchings that overwhelmed what "I" was—formerly so vigilant and now
finally pacified. No excitement, the relaxation after pleasure, the sense of
nonsense that fills a surface with shimmering sensations. A sea of possibilities,
but reserved, waiting, no blossoming this time, only an infinite germination,
no acceleration, an unseen multitude, ticklish, enveloping. There is no fatigue
such as one experiences with drugs or alcohol after this sort of disconnec-
tion. My cutting out costs nothing; it is priceless. There is though the cost
of being overwhelmed at any moment and of allowing oneself to be just as
easily taken over by whatever comes next. And it's not without scars. No
other word comes to me, to name the outer lining of my ardent tenacity, but
"dispassionate." Dispassionate, I find words heavy and people irremediably
phony. My self survives this annulment, but in a grotesque state. I lighten up,
thanks to those indifferent butterflies who carry off what remains of me.

Period.

I kiss Nordi's forehead and lie down on my side turned away from him.

"Rebounds": An Unpublishable Opinion &

Is it these states of vibration, these optical dramas, these moves inside, outside, and beyond the box that I seek when I wander to the ends of the
earth? And not just recollections of those conditions but the conditions
themselves that accompany me as I travel and work now. In the end it
seems to me that they confer, if not exactly a coherence, at least a logic of
their own to my rather chaotic existence.

No one has understood how I, the brilliant student of philosophy turned sinologist, then extreme structuralist (a role that interested me for a short time) could have morphed into a globetrotting investigative reporter-detective that the *Événement de Paris* sends off in a flash here or there, whenever a new crime—preferably one against human rights—hits the pages. Since any crime is by definition a crime against human rights, you can guess that I'm sent out all the time; my boss doesn't hesitate an instant and I'm off again with no time to catch my breath.

Not satisfied with overseeing the police's crime unit throughout this universal Santa Varvara, Northrop Rilsky can now flatter himself that he is my lover. I admit that I find the whole thing rather titillating; I smile just imagining the expression on my boss's face back in Paris were he to know about it. On his side Northrop Rilsky puts forward a narrowly political and ultrarational explanation that I try out on my mother in order to justify my "wasted life," as she calls it, which of course worries her.

So Rilsky's theory is that it's only France's decline, especially the withdrawal from its universalist ambitions, sold paradoxically, it's true, under the label "cultural exception," that could explain why a woman like me could flee Paris to roll around in the mud of Santa Varvara, New York, Toronto, Tokyo, Melbourne, Moscow, and other places. In a certain way I agree with the dear man. Once upon a time I used to string together my erotic highs as an intensely intelligent young woman, intense and intelligent, with a variety of intellectual performances. In the Latin Quarter you believed in theory, the avant-garde, and then in the extravagant tastes and sexual temerity of Mr. X, Ms. Y, or Mrs. Z—so long as it had style. It was very French, this game of style, practically nonsensical, but it even became an export commodity, though sales are less strong today outside France, especially when compared to perfume and champagne, two musts that have always done well, with or without style. Don't remind me again that today they are pouring these national treasures into the gutters of Santa Varvara. That vengeful mood will pass, but not style, they'll never touch it, not there or in Paris. All that's "Old Europe," finished, curtains!

With the expansion of the media and of democracy, traditional-style bourgeois families abandoned the habit of reading as did of course families in working-class areas, though at one time it had a strong following, at least within the red circle of the capital. The children of the overclass nowadays only dream of becoming the CEO of Microsoft or Vivendi Universal, golden boys or television producers, and the rest become delinquents or rap stars, but as for reading—a big fat zero. The rush toward science departments is over, and literature departments and the other so-called humanities absorb those who scraped by on the high school exit exam, people who can barely spell their names, and ragtag bunches of third-world refugees with garbled French seeking cover while they wait for their resident visas to come through. Editors only publish hard, get-even confessions or else soft get-yours romances designed to hook the fifty-year-old housewife, that eternal Madame Bovary, the only one left who still thinks it her duty to open books in this speeded-up world of images.

This wave had been coming on for the last fifteen years—"since Mitterrand," Rilsky would spit out bitterly—without my being able to tell if he thought it was more the Right or the Left that was to blame. I've felt I'm living in an occupied country for about the last two years. There is no film, television show, newspaper, or magazine that doesn't try to pitch me a lifestyle of lowest common denominators; none that doesn't call some paranoid creep a writer when all he or she does is mimic the rhetoric (or absence of rhetoric) of last year's Blahtity-Blah Book Prize winner that everyone has already forgotten twelve months later; none that doesn't serve up the cold, prefab edginess of some "emergency," "frontline," or "firing line" claiming its orgies of this and that to be the latest victory for women's liberation. And everything always 100 percent thought free! The smooth, frictionless "platform" of any group is a must, I tell you; and it even gets marketed to you as "minimal art" these days, or even, by the most ballsy, as "spiritual"! You don't like France anymore, my mother sighs as she sees me packing my bags for the umpteenth time. "Who's talking to you about France? And what France? You mean those arrogant little bourgeois pricks who are dying to stir the pot?" I try to please her by using some of her own vocabulary. But that's what I think.

A sharper image? Yeah, baby! They label me an archaic puritan—that kills me!—but I'm going to pick you some pixels, my friend, buckets full, including the negatives. I will go to the heart of the darkroom and we shall see what we see! I'm diving into the media business too, so look out! I'm not going to tell you that the image is the devil and that it must be forbidden or encrypted—no, not that, that's not me. The devil is dead. There's only opium and cocaine now. The media generation is full of druggies, and I'm not thinking of the star anchor who snorts, the writer who shoots up, or DJ junkies and druggy technicians. It's more than that. The whole society wants to ignore everything; it drowns its anxieties and its conflicts in a worldwide seductive stupor that the miserable scandals and loudmouths calling for Crusades feed into without causing the least bump or bruise—far from it.

"There is no way out of the spectacle, Stephanie; no exit is provided for in the program, so stop dreaming, my dear." My boss at the *Événement de Paris* lectures me—patronizing from head to toe. It was precisely because I knew there was no way out that I joined the team of this little cynic. Or rather because I believed there was in fact a way out, one that passed through the interior, through the underside of all the cards, and through the cards themselves—in other words, through playing the game.

You think I'm on the side of the house, that I'm a cheater, too, and want to sell easy, false vulgarity, no? Well, I'm not! I'm off to beat you at your own game with my little investigations. We're going to dismantle the secret networks of the bourgeoise that sparkle with grotesque lies and pretend to make love a full-time job; we're going to expose the rosy dance of the austere deputy who decries the breakdown of the family; we will present the circuitous paths of money laundering that have enriched the prostitutes of the Republic. None of that will bother anyone, you'll make a new movie about it, a new television show . . . I know, I know. The embezzler of taxpayers' money and the convicted former CEO billionaire will turn their "affairs" into novels and made-for-TV screenplays. Of course. I know the business better than you now. Philosophy, linguistics, semiology—they do count for something you know. And now, to top things off, journalism! It was to be expected. But my investigation does not stop here. Let's continue.

Is there something underneath the image? It's the drive, my friends, that the image strives to put to sleep, and since there is really only the death drive, go calm down between the covers of some collected Freud. "Stop, drives are no longer in!" one of my lovers used to snort, exasperated by my swagger, before popping another ecstasy tablet that turned him off of sex entirely. Should I have gone on Lexomil? Certainly not! I changed lovers. "Watch what you're going to say, your drive to think is making me ill!" complained another who had a very low resistance to castration anxiety. But he's not the only one, the whole spectacle society has a very low resistance in this area: one is advised not to think, it curbs the appetite of every consumer, and it hurts. Let's play *Who Wants to Be a Millionaire?* instead. Let's win at *Jeopardy,* on *The Antiques Road Show,* or the stock market. Let's win our insatiable demand for narcissistic gratification that humans no longer address to the Father—where is the Father?—but to the imaginary Mother of the Spectacle Society and the big silicon-enhanced tit of speculation. Why pout? Try to play. Yeah, baby! Bravo, that's the way, you're bound to win one of these days, better luck next time, bye-bye Céline, I've got ten, who says twenty? OK, hands off my hobbyhorse. I investigate, therefore I am—that's my motto as a complicit player. I'm just trying to give this screwball game one more turn, if I can. My little own surplus enjoyment—nothing more, child's play, the thinking person's Halloween.

Under the screens, the crime. Morbid Stephanie rejoicing in the hell that she's made all by herself, *povera disgraziata,* no paradise, just this detective novel obsession. And not even matronly enough to make one of those big tomes that Anglo-Saxon women put out with all the bile and bitter vaginal juices coming in razor cuts and gunfire, the erections of psychopaths and bad boy policemen. Nope, not capable of that, not TiVo friendly enough, not enough necrophilia and alcohol, not lewd, psychotic, or scopic enough. A little too ironic, skeptical, and laconic. But yes, yes, you will see. Only the voyage is worth the detour, the movement. It's in writing the crime that one avoids it, not before, never without that, only in uprooting, in transcending appearances, undoing the ties, the suspense.

Nordi is still sleeping, not me. I have all the time in the world at night, especially at night.

My Encounter with Anna Comnena ❧

So let's place the images vertically now. But not exclusively, because my investigations take me toward every horizon: Paris, Santa Varvara, Moscow, Istanbul, Beijing . . . and even to Le Puy-en-Velay, Vézelay, and Philippopolis. My map of the world has been shaped by my trips, meetings, and the new networks that weave an open community around me and that has nothing crazy about it. It goes well beyond e-mails and the Internet, across the cliques of journalists and the other professional clans that I have dealt with, further than the disciplines that I have had occasion to work within. More than the beliefs of some and the States of others, it's really just a little International of Byzantines like me, Stephanie Delacour, trying to understand and sometimes coming up with some answers. How could I, without their help, have found the head of Gloria Harrison, uncovered the nuclear proliferation mafia and its links to the Medellín Cartel, and managed to protect Jerry as well? Nordi being his usual phlegmatic self, at least outwardly—nothing like the real man that I know now—I had no choice but to strike out on my own and invent an alternate reality, one much more real than that of the alterglobalist thinkers, by spreading myself out in all directions. This exercise offered definite advantages, the first being the gradual sloughing off of all clannishness, which in Paris and everywhere else imposes a vigorously repressive logic of exclusion when faced with anyone who hasn't got the message.

Read *Le Figaro* to dispel the false impression that you live in the same world as *Le Monde* readers and then come and read my *Événement de Paris* to discover yet another world. That's normal, you will say. It's normal that each editorial team, clan, family, or sect has a right to its own vision of things and tries to impose it. How lucky we are that "competition" saves us all from the threat of Jacobin centralism, not to say totalitarianism! What else can one do but encourage this free play of democracy via pluralism? There is no better alternative as any Sciences-Po student will tell you without batting an eye. Of course! Naturally! Yes, except that within one country and the confines of its media, within the limited time of one term of office and one generation, robust pluralism is reduced to a ferocious battle of clans and Big Brotherish brainwashing. An example? Look at the *Événement artistique*. In less than two years Audrey, my colleague and dear friend, has fallen under the influence of a guru, a seer; not one from among the New Pantheon crowd, thank goodness, but a nonaligned, independent person, she says. But let's face it, it's so obvious, she secretly loves him to the point where she has begun to speak, write, and think with his mannerisms! And since her guru loves Wagner, Herr Wagner, *Parsifal*, and the news from Bayreuth have taken over her *Événement artistique*—"nazism with a human face," whisper the envious. Without going as far as that, let's just say that Audrey's paper has become a broken record that repeats the loaded messages of the guru, who now, thanks to the efforts and fawning of the editor, controls most of what passes for the last word in music criticism and on the arts in general! Don't tell me I'm just jealous! I don't have a jealous bone in my body. "You are incapable of hate, my girl, and lacking that you will not go far." My mother has said this over and over since I was a little girl, but it's done no good. Between us, none of this is all that serious, since the media-manufactured culture is only a gigantic outpatient clinic to treat the narcissistic pains of the middle classes—OK, but it still irks me to see how easy it is to pull the strings and how many twisted people profit from it all! Audrey's clan has discreetly amassed a lot of power and her griot is rejoicing on the top of her pyramid! Of course "the competition" denounces her and her team for sucking up to this guy so shamelessly while at the same time they carry on with their own tactics of favoritism that haven't paid off as well so far despite being equally underhanded, rabid, or both. And so it goes within the little world of music lovers, art lovers, and avid readers who know without knowing that they are being manipulated and love it anyway!

Air! Inhale! Exhale! Keep moving! Trips and provisional networks happen and dissolve in the time it takes to untie the knots of passions that are generally solved by murder or murders. Have you noticed it? Today, more than ever before, the event of the day is death.

And because in tracking the secrets behind appearances I take soundings of memories, my networks that piece together again the map of the world become layered with labyrinths that lead back to History. Against a past rediscovered, the present recomposes itself differently, forgotten little islands return and run into the stream of current events, the time of individuals is borne away on the floes of collective destiny, and, while believing that I am crisscrossing the globe, I am actually losing myself in Time as I go back in Time. It is a time that is reconstructed, like families that are pieced together again after multiple divorces and remarriages. So I'm next to this lunatic Rilsky who definitely needs my pragmatism to put an end to his intimate speculations and solve this serial killer mystery, just as I need, without knowing quite why, his erotic hunger as a mature and underemployed older man. This is the difference between the "foreign correspondent" and the "supercop": my wanderings have taken me today to another European era, nine centuries before the problematic "Union" of the present day that still hesitates to extend its reach from the Atlantic to the Black Sea, with or without Turkey—perhaps without, in my view as a woman with no Islamic headscarf.

While waiting for news about my serial killer, I am reading the notes of the missing uncle that dear Northrop has taken to studying with a mute passion and a distracted air that is most disturbing. Every evening he brings back photocopies of the notebooks and looks at them casually or closely, I'm not sure, with no comment. They are piling up on the nightstand, and all I have to do is help myself.

According to our obscure historian, it was the troubling times of the Crusades that inaugurated this Euro-Mediterranean project that we're lectured about now, not without good reasons but with a lot of backfiring and blockages too, although they didn't exactly conceive of it in the same way at the time and simply covered the whole thing with the unique symbol of the cross. For better and worse, one could say, the Crusades attempted to unify our angry, irreconcilable differences by declaring war against them, humiliating them, crushing them, and ferociously killing them, not in the name of Democracy, as we do today, but in the name of the Resuscitated, the risen Christ; that is, before the project collapsed on its own, the dead bodies of the crusaders piling up on European roads and around the Holy Sepulchre exposing the failure of this will to power.

Since his laborious thesis appears not to have sufficed, the mind of our scholar, who for now is still missing, took a passionate turn, and that is where the manuscript begins to interest me.

Chrest-Jones glorified a Byzantine princess as the premier historian of the Crusades. Born in 1083, there is no trace of her after 1148. Anna Comnena, the esteemed daughter of emperor Alexius I Comnenus and the tearful wife of Nicephorus Bryennius, had read Plato and Aristotle as a young girl and eventually became the leading intellectual of her day, chronicling what was told to her as well as what she saw and heard. More than eight centuries after her death, Ms. Comnena becomes the leading lady of our missing professor. He starts to admire her because to him, despite the family bias, this woman was able to describe events from the perspective of both a military strategist and a depressed psychologist. She told of the harsh battles, the twists of fate, the stakes for this and that group, the confrontation of different habits and ways of thinking. She examined every thread and knot of this ongoing set of conflicts that were endlessly breaking down and reconstructing themselves; but she did it in a way that also revealed things about her own Byzantine soul. Any historian would admire her; Sebastian was fascinated by her. His descriptions of her take on the lyrical expansiveness of a true hymn because the scholar, quite simply, had fallen in love. Is he dead now, as his jittery wife believes? Maybe knocked off by the serial killer. There's a wild idea! It came to me while I was reading his notebooks and would not go away. Did Chrest-Jones have any contact with the New Pantheon sect? Not that I know of, but who knows? Rilsky, maybe.

I reread the passages from Anna Comnena that Chrest-Jones had chosen to copy out. Not bad, the uncle was on to something. Questions: could one repeat what Anna did, write as she did, here and now, one millennium later? Would it be possible for our brains and bodies that we think of as so new? Would we be capable of following the Brownian motions of men and women to the point where they would stabilize—roughly speaking, but you get my point—and define themselves as peoples of nation-states with stable borders yet still at war despite their treaties and their laws? If Princess Anna Comnena were to wake up in our world, would she be all that surprised? She would learn how religions, ideologies, and technological advances have put a lock on migrants: the Renaissance, the Enlightenment, capitalism, communism, the new world order. Would she also understand that, as our beliefs dissolve on the stock market, it is not the brutality of the Crusades that is coming from the depths but the worries of a nomadic humanity not searching for the tomb of the Savior but for any community possible? "But are the two so different?" the learned Porphyrogene might have wondered on her own, even before I could ask the question myself.

I am intrigued by the lamentation of this complex and precocious Comnena.

Beyond his uncle's fanatic quest, my affair with the commissioner has got me dragged deeper into the passions and imaginary mistresses of the runaway historian who has made his wife Hermine jealous and made me, Stephanie Delacour, dream about a Byzantine princess. That's quite an accomplishment! I am coming to accept that my mother was not far off the mark when she said to me the other day as I got ready to fly off: "You're in the wrong line of work again, my girl. I wonder if you're ever going to get a job that suits you." Who knows? Perhaps I'll be a detective in Byzantium if I can't reincarnate myself as Anna Comnena.

"To each his own Byzantium. There are only imaginary Byzantiums." Back at our place, NR, Nordi, puts on his oracular tone after a day of looking for the missing person, the serial killer, or who knows who else?

I serve myself more gin. I like the word *gin,* and the rest—violet and quinine, the light, round bitterness.

"Are you sticking with J&B?"

"Always."

I serve him his drink. No remarks. I'm floating off.

My own Byzantium is the color of time; don't look for it on a map. Modern misanthropes who nurse their depressed feelings with tourism believe they meet up with it in Greece or Turkey—some go as far as the Balkans, but they don't love, they flee, they run away. "Away from Byzantium!" my friend Joseph Brodsky shouted again yesterday. A mistake! Can one get away from the passage of time? Today Byzantium is nowhere; it is noplace, except perhaps on the tingling skin of the Bosporus, like a brownish-green grape that hints of both seaweed and wine, or perhaps the sulfur exhaled by the Black Sea around Nessebar when the sun goes down and the women depart—women with bitter smiles and jet-black eyes fixed on their children who babble happily in English—what else?—with surprised tourists. Only passing epiphanies such as these I have described give an idea of what this odd future anterior of Byzantium was, is, and will always be. A wine of intrigue and tenderness, savors and pains, an intuition of mixtures and meetings. But not a place, no, not any place—"our special reporter" has been around the world, but not there, believe me.

I met a Russian poet who believed he was in Byzantium when someone shined his shoes in Constantinople. It's a cliché—Constantinople is overflowing with shoeshiners of all types, each armed with brushes and brilliantly shiny tins of shoe polish. An emblem for the world's misery could be the shoeshine boy in Istanbul. This poet liked to do his shopping in the grand bazaar with its famous catacombs filled with bronzes, bracelets, crucifixes, yatagans, samovars, icons, and rugs. NB: to the eyes of the tourist, the rug is the very symbol of Byzantium—and a bargain! What blindness, what myopia, what a lack of metaphysical discernment and sense of history to have mistaken this vaulted labyrinth for an Orthodox church and to have rolled it and ramified it as though it were a citation of the Prophet! It's normal though—Russians are always looking for evil outside themselves—in Chechnya, for example. And what could be more outside for these snowy melancholics than the passing wisp of my Byzantium that they take to be some fatal Arabia?

"It seems that Sebastian cites a German philosopher who's an expert on Greek miracles. This thinker claims to have discovered these beliefs intact today among the peasants of Kaisariani in a little Orthodox church whose low ceilings, he rejoiced, were hardly bent by the juridical spirit that dominates the Roman Church and its theology."

Nordi is leafing through the notebooks of Sebastian that I'm forcing myself to read too. He's teaching me. We're rather far away from our serial killer, and we like it like that.

For sure, philosophers and Germans in general have little regard for the spirit of laws and dream of romantic peoples so as to rehash their jealousy of the Greeks—under the shadow of Roman theology, of course. That's what I think to myself anyway.

This has no bearing on my own Byzantium, which is neither Roman- nor Koran-based, has no rugs or opera, no samovars, and no orgy of frescoes. By transposing Greek serenity into the crossroads of the crucified, my Byzantium would offer human passions their political incarnation as the permanent crisis of power. But it would also invest it with unbearable flashes of conscience, a lacerating rethinking through endlessly recommencing heresies.

Nordi continues to absorb the prose of his uncle or pretends to. Now and then he raises his eyes and smiles at me. I know he's off somewhere else; I am too. Shah Minoushah, the third member of our new family, seizes this moment of the day to meow comfortably against Nordi's thigh. I'm dreaming and reembroidering Sebastian's lace—my own investigative quest.

History books will tell you that from its founding by Constantine the Great as "New Rome" in 330, Byzantium was more Asian than Latin and that it already cultivated the cruelty of the Oriental satraps while ignoring Roman law. This vice turned the court into a band of killers, stranglers, and even castrators—all institutionalized criminals drunk on power, so much so that they would found a Third Rome in Moscow and transmit its faith through Stalin himself. You will also hear that this Oriental Christianity does not recognize the human person. Ah, the person! You know that the human person is only Occidental and universal thanks to manifest reason and the rights of man; while Byzantium can only know elegies of pleasure, ecstasies of death, the erudition of the senses, heretical hagiographies, and political subterfuge. It's a detective story written long before Agatha Christie, Patricia Cornwell, and other Mary Higgins Clarks came on the scene! Byzantium is a maze of legends and half-knowledge, a dead end with no way out, the definitive softening of the Christian soul, all kneaded and ready to stretch out on the Arab rug, a fake Occident hung out to dry, delivered up body and soul to the Muslim hordes. You will also hear that the sinister cavalry of the Prophet could have held off massacring the heretical Byzantines, blinded under the mosaic-filled cupolas of Saint Sophie, because the intricacies of the Byzantine soul had already flowed into the arabesques of the same Oriental spirit, at once decorative and flat. You only need to look at their endless and cunning plots—no elevation toward Truth among these fast-talking dealers of easily exchanged chirpings and trippings, no more than in these incredible councils and other theological mumbo jumbo!

You don't care about the speculations of poets and philosophers? You only want to peruse the historical literature? OK, let's go and try to reconstruct the twisted and often broken genealogical trees of the emperors: the Theodorus-Arcadius-Martial-Pulcherie-Theodosius, Leo I or II, all the Justins and Justinians, Tiberiuses, and Constantines, up to the usurper Phocas—indeed, there's no shortage of usurpers here!—Heraclius I, and the Constantines III and IV. Then come the Isaurians with Leo III and the others, and I must not forget Nicephorus I the General Logothete, Michael II the Amorian, Theophilus and Theodora, Michael III the Drunkard, and of course the series of Basils, beginning with Basil I, the Macedonian, and then Basil II, the Bulgaroktonus (we'll come back to him!). And that's not all. Who could ignore the empresses? Especially the Theodoras, of which there are quite a few, my favorites, before arriving at the Ducaian-Comnenan dynasty and the Angelans.

You know, Byzantine history is rather similar to Chinese catalogs. I'm not kidding, because since one can't see the necessary reasonable progression, some believe that they're already dealing with the Orient. If we're stopping here, it's because of Anna and Sebastian; and we're not going to whine about not knowing whether the brothers John and Andronicus, or Theodora, Irene, and the other sisters of our intellectual princess, were more or less dignified than she was. Just because they're hardly mentioned, or not at all, doesn't mean there wouldn't be some research to conduct on those points—perhaps a round-table discussion—our missing Sebastian was big on round tables. Because this John II Comnenus, the one who sent his plotting sister to a convent where she became the illustrious writer whom we know thanks to Sebastian Chrest-Jones, this John, despite what Anna says, was, according to some historians, one of the greatest figures of Byzantium, a man distinguished both as a statesman and as a moralist, a rather rare combination among Byzantine emperors, one has to admit. The proof is that he crushed the Petchenegues—you don't hear any more about the

Petchenegues today, I'm sure—pacified the Balkans, tamed the Seljuq states on the north coast of Asia Minor, and even won the respect of the Norman principality of Antioch!

You see, they want you to believe that Byzantium is a chain of wars, one bungling basileus after another where instability becomes a way of life. Don't listen to these carping pragmatists and middle managers working for Cogito Limited. I've told you, my own Byzantium is only a way of being styled after the colors of the time. Past, present, and future fused in the written form of the Attic language that was then breaking down, already damaged by Latin derivatives and other popular idioms that would keep it from ever being a true modern Greek language. Not being able to become the sovereign herself, this true daughter of her father used her proximity to the sovereign to memorialize his as well as her own projections: Anna the transition, the prescient, the precursor. A one-woman show—rather surprising, don't you think, at the beginning of the twelfth century. One person who was already, despite what the critics of Orthodox faith say, a crossroads, a shock of civilizations, a clash of cultures, woman and man, weeper and warlord, singular and universal, unconsoled and proud, incommensurable. Anna, my Byzantium.

Hers was the Occident turned Oriental, the most advanced of the eastern countries, the most sophisticated of the western ones—like France today. We, the French, we still think of ourselves as a great power when really we're nothing more than a causeway to the third world and, ironically, hold in contempt the migrant pariahs who only want to fleece us. We're no less suspicious of the fourth Rome inhabited by the noveaux riches across the Atlantic who, at least in Washington, believe they can do without our senile and sneaky arrogance! Too Froggy, these Byzantines? Very Byzantine, these Frogs? Byzantium did not last, and France itself is fading. That's the way it goes; all we can do is leave traces like the princess with her chronicle the color of time. Is it the end of a cycle? Or is it instead the eternal return of a perpetual recommencement? The Kafka-like art of taking one step to the side, of not quite adhering, of beating one's head, of questioning the questions, of not forgetting one's own crimes, of obsessively hairsplitting, of wondering about the sex of angels, of being a Monophysite, and, let's see, an icon lover, icon hater, unreconstructed intellectual, Byzantinist, feminist . . . we understand each other, proud historian!

No one knows the date of her death. The princess finished writing in

1148, so she is dead, period. It would take a Byzantine to believe that the body of a woman concludes like a text, like a scholarly exchange, a heresy, a historical chronicle. Dust of dusts, all is dust. They were rather biblical, these Byzantines, but not Jewish enough. Not persevering enough, not straight enough—no, they didn't have a nose for the goal. Too doubting, these people vaporized into a mist of questions, a cloud of problems, an odd perfume that makes one wonder how they could ever have put pen to paper.

Today the region from which Anna's chronicle emerged is falling to pieces. I've been there; I've felt its wind spreading a sticky powder over the porphyrian city. It's as though the earth were separating from itself so as to caress its surface, migrate as far as the Bosporus, diffuse into the Marble Sea, and dissolve finally into mud with the first rain—the Russian poet and I spoke about this. I choose to believe that it is indeed this dust that is definitively overwhelming the actual inhabitants, Greeks, Turks, or Slavs—no relation to Anna these people, these usurpers, these impostors, these numskulls. But is one ever sure? Even sleepers wake up one day or another. All of them are paralyzed, however, by a congenital slowdown that explodes into deadly fighting—until the NATO airstrikes calm them down for good—because their torpor leads to melancholy, to bitterness, to an unshakable pouting against the whole world, a world that could care less and goes about its business with an eye on the black gold.

The same rusty cloud is in the chai and the mouths of the Americans who yawn into the sun, while at the same time the star is falling into the Golden Horn irremediably. It envelopes everything in a brown film, including the pages of my *Alexiad*, the only known tome of Anna, her paperback cadaver, her perpetual life, a contagious existence, one must say, since it has already become Sebastian's and mine too a little. My Byzantium is in her fifteen books, an imaginary chronicle; has it ever existed any other way?

"Like France!" Nordi chuckles; he thinks he's pleasing me. "An imaginary construct. The exact opposite of Santa Varvara, no? You don't just think that we here are only real and virtual, and what's the difference really? but that we totally lack imagination—we zap and click from video games to bombing Baghdad. You believe that it's this inaptitude for problematizing the questions and questioning the answers that leads us to crime? To total, indiscernable, perfect crime?" I don't say anything, I'm dreaming, this gin. . . . "Maybe. But my dear, since there is crime, and because people talk about it, in fact they talk about nothing else, well, Santa Varvara will still need me and you. You see, Santa Varvara is good for us. So you stay with me, promise?"

Dear Nordi might be in love, but he shall always be on the side of the world's masters—a police commissioner, a cop. And me, the Byzantine, I'm going along with him, I'm following. I lift off from myself—like that dust that leaves the ground and is carried by the wind around the Golden Horn, like a spirit separating from its body, like a body that spreads out its odor in the heat—while I pretend to read the *Alexiad* as though I were on the shores of the Bosporus or Lake Ohrid or the Aegean Sea or the Black Sea. No, don't look for me on the map, my Byzantium is a matter of time, the very question that time asks itself when it doesn't want to choose between two places, two dogmas, two crises, two identities, two continents, two religions, two sexes, two plots. Byzantium leaves the question open and time as well. Neither hesitation nor uncertainty, nothing but the wisdom of what happens, of time passing and knowing it's passing, a passing passenger, future anterior.

Perhaps I have a strong criminal tendency buried deep within me, otherwise I wouldn't be so interested in criminals and
I wouldn't write so often about them. . . . A suspense novel is
quite different from a detective novel. . . . Its author will take
a much greater interest in the criminal mind, because the
criminal often takes up the whole thing from start to finish
and the writer has to get down what happens in his head.
Unless one is attracted to him, one does not succeed.
PATRICIA HIGHSMITH, *Plotting and Writing Suspense Fiction*

CHAPTER FOUR ☙ Sebastian the Crusader in the
Footsteps of NATO

Sebastian's Fokker finally touched down at the airport in Santa Varvara.
The other passengers were mostly people on Easter vacation who, as usual,
would rush to the seaside or to the mountains or to some other locale they
hoped was still exotic. No more than they, the doctor *honoris causa* had no
idea how to continue the story. No thoughts, no weight. All that remained
of Sebastian was the interval between one man observing another ordering
two Bloody Marys at the bar. No self.

He pulled his little rolly-wheels bag and walked by the windows of
the various shops of duty-free luxury items, hardly distinguishing one
from another. Ordinarily the professor did not hold back and behaved
like all the other anxious travelers who tried to calm themselves by
emptying their coin purses and exceeding the limit on their credit cards
in order to purchase some useless gadget as a pleasing gift for whomever
it was who was waiting for them somewhere on the planet. Nothing of
the kind now crossed his mind, which had been taken over by a perfect
neutrality.

He walked mechanically toward the international counter and asked for
a one-way ticket to Milan on Alitalia. Time seemed contracted—Sebastian
had no idea how long a flight it was. A second, an hour, eight hours—what

did it matter; he held himself erect, perpendicular, for an instant. Then standing in a white lucidity without self or sleep—how long had he not slept?

He left the intercontinental airport of Milan Malpensa in Varese to rent a four-wheel drive Fiat Panda from the local dealer. "The perfect car for youth" chimed the salesman repeating the slogan of the advertising campaign. "Not expensive, *signore*, this jewel costs the same as the Suzuki Samurai, you know—but what great handling; it's absolutely the car for you! I knew the moment I saw you, it can practically climb up trees, it's the mountaineer's friend; I'm telling you it's the car for you, and you can thank the Virgin Mary and my dealership!" Sold! Sebastian was no longer listening to the man's chatter, he simply needed a four-wheel-drive vehicle.

He stopped in the city center near the Duomo to buy a suitcase and some necessary items: a change of clothes, socks, a pair of hiking shoes, two pairs of sweatpants and two sweatshirts, a suit, three dress shirts, and some toiletries. His toothbrush, pajamas, laptop computer, and box of floppy disks had been in his rolly-wheels bag since his departure for Stony Brook. Now he had only to go down the Dalmatian coast as far as Durazzo and then take the Via Egnatia. No one would think of him following this itinerary, if by chance anyone were still thinking of him or searching for him. Hermine? He doubted it; after all, she could console herself easily enough with Minaldi. Sebastian felt that he had plunged totally into a clandestine existence. Sebastian? Sub-self? *C/J?* He was not following a paper road map but instead the wrinkle of another time, the time of Adhémar.

ON AUGUST 15, 1095, Pope Urban II made a stop at Le Puy-en-Velay to converse at length with the bishop there, Adhémar de Monteil, a spiritual leader who carried a big sword. The pope called the bishops together for a council at Clermont before haranguing the crowd, the nobility of the region among them. Shock and Awe! No baron of any significance was present, but Raymond de Saint-Gilles, count of Toulouse, had sent his messengers to deliver word of his allegiance to the papal sovereign. The pope vigorously condemned the habitual violence and injustices of the knights. Then he invited them to defend their brothers, all of their brothers near and far, those who had been looted in the region and especially those who had fallen victim to the infidels in the East. Did they understand, the barons in search of adventure and the younger siblings in search of an inheritance, that the rewards they hoped for would prove illusory? To be absolved of their sins was the only thing guaranteed by the expedition, but this was not unimportant.

C/J did not imagine that the crusaders were drawn solely by the incalculable riches of the Orient. Formerly, famous preachers such as Peter the Hermit and noblemen such as Walter the Penniless, a great and powerful lord despite his name, already knew how to incite the fervor of highly diverse masses of men. A new impulse was beginning now. Wasn't the pope sending his troops to reestablish Christian unity barely forty years after the schism of 1054 that divided Rome and Constantinople, the Occidental and Oriental Churches, over the question of the status, divine or human, of the Son? *Filioque* or *per Filium*? Does the Holy Spirit proceed from the Father and the Son or from the Father by way of the Son? This was the question, a crucial one in the history of the world, that now stymied a contemporary citizen of Santa Varvara but led inevitably to divorce. So was it now a matter of making peace? Urban could be called an early advocate of the first European Union—know what I mean? Delusional and tragic, certainly, but prophetic and so timely. Unlike obtuse chiefs of state who propose naive crusades of Good against Evil to television audiences used to grazing on idiotic programming, wasn't Urban launching a sublime, transcendent dream of multicultural unity?

C/J did not leave out of account the staging of it all. He imagined himself in the mass of Urban II's followers, who demonstrated their immediate enthusiasm for the plan by shouting "It is the will of God!" and by adopting the placement on their garments of the cloth cross that had up until then been worn by pilgrims to Jerusalem—a practice that led the crusaders to be called the *crucesignati*. The indulgences promised exerted an enormous influence as did the charters and other documents that Sebastian had acquired; they indicated a society that had been sucked up en masse into an attitude of conversion so as to escape the Last Judgment and the end of the world. Both had been announced by certain preachers and widely feared at the start of this new millennium, even though, according to the recently honored doctor *honoris causa*, fears of the Apocalypse did not seem to preoccupy the people as much as some lightweight and peremptory medievalists tended to suggest. Nor did the good doctor share the thesis that said the Crusades were at war against Islam. Whether Occidental thinking had any notion at the time of a politically and religiously unified

Islamic entity seemed doubtful to him. He had found no explicit proof of a unification agreement between Rome and Byzantium, Urban II and Alexius I Comnenus. Certainly negotiations never stopped, even after the excommunication of Alexius Comnenus by Gregory VII. The Byzantine basileus was waiting for aid from Rome, aid he had requested to help fight the Saracen invasion. Did the pope envision using the military force he had rallied together in Clermont in 1095 as a way to restore Rome's authority over all eastern Christians? Or was his goal only the reunification of the Greek and Latin Churches so to speak? There was no proof either way, but C/J believed the former. It was the most noble, in the eyes of this modern observer, and the only project capable of attracting someone of the caliber of the bishop of Le Puy, Aymar Adhémar de Monteil . . . the first to swear his allegiance and receive from the hands of the pope the red on white silk cross that would become the emblem of the crusaders.

After his pledge of allegiance, Adhémar, who had become the spiritual leader of this first Crusade, set off with Raymond de Saint-Gilles and the French of Languedoc. They chose a route through the Alps, crossed Lombardy, cut to the south toward Brindisi and the Dalmatian coast and present-day Serbia, which was then Bulgaria. Eighteen months later, on April 26, 1097, he entered Constantinople after Raymond de Saint-Gilles solemnly agreed, after tough negotiations, to respect the life and honor of the emperor. Another route through Bari was chosen by Hugh of Vermandois. He had departed before Adhémar, however several misadventures caused him to arrive later on May 14, 1097. Already present were Godfrey of Bouillon, the duke of Lower-Lotharingia or Lower Lorraine, a tall, imposing blond-haired and bearded Nordic, and his brother Baudouin, a dark-haired giant and legendary ladies man. They had traveled via Austria, Hungary, and Bulgaria and arrived in the Oriental capital six months earlier during Christmas in 1096. However, Anna Comnena directed her real thunder at Bohemond I of Otranto, the leader of the Italian Normans, who arrived on April 9, 1096, and C/J could not help laughing whenever he recalled the venomous sarcasms of the princess: "Because by nature this man was a fox, flexible in the face of events, superior in calculation and cunning to all the Latins who were then crossing the empire, though he had the fewest troops and the least money; but he surpassed everyone else in perversity. Inconstancy, the natural characteristic of all Latins, was his trademark." Alas, who is reading her now in the lands of the former Yugoslavia of Tito, in Santa Varvara, or in Paris?

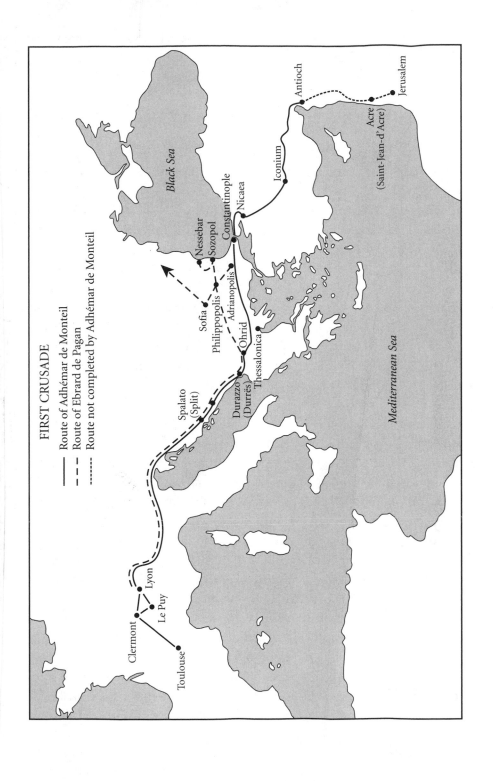

FIRST CRUSADE

—— Route of Adhémar de Monteil
– – – Route of Ebrard de Pagan
· · · · · · Route not completed by Adhémar de Monteil

Black Sea

Mediterranean Sea

Antioch

Jerusalem

Acre
(Saint-Jean-d'Acre)

Iconium

Nicaea

Constantinople

Nessebar
Sozopol

Adrianopolis

Sofia

Philippopolis

Ohrid

Thessalonica

Durazzo
(Durrës)

Spalato
(Split)

Lyon

Le Puy

Clermont

Toulouse

Indeed, the bitter Kosovars who followed his Panda with unpleasant stares might have taken some comfort from her words, know what I mean? In fact, Anna and her contemporaries were in a panic over these waves of arriving Latins: "One might compare them to the stars in the sky or grains of sand spread over the shore." But her contempt was such that she refused to name them: "Despite my goodwill, I prefer not to give the names of their chiefs. The names do not come to me, partly because I am incapable of speaking these unpronounceable barbaric sounds and partly because I am put off by their great number. What point is there in pronouncing the names of all these men whose very existence severely bothered all contemporaries?" Bothered? Or terrified? Or fascinated? In his heart of hearts that was now the sub-self of the traveler, C/J had made up his mind: he was certain that Anna said neither all she knew nor all the unspeakable things she had felt. To shed light on these mysteries was precisely the explorer's goal and the reason he was driving his Fiat Panda across the Dalmatian coast, Serbia, Kosovo, and through the Macedonian region devastated by the allied bombardments in 2000 to Philippopolis. For example, why is Adhémar not mentioned in the *Alexiad*? How should one understand this particular silence by a historian who elsewhere is so precise?

He drove like a zombie without stopping. Once in a while a sip of San Pellegrino, a nap on the backseat, or a night's sleep in a room at a rural boarding house. The kilometers went by but he saw nothing and no one; he was caught in his dream, crushed by the ineradicable fatigue of crime, held in the vise of a hallucinating memory. Little by little, however, the war-ravaged countryside pressed itself onto the attention of Sub-self.

Tons of depleted uranium had been spread over the land and its inhabitants. Graphite explosives detonated near the ground caused millions of microscopic carbon fibers to disturb electrical plants, transformer stations, and high-tension lines as well as communication systems. The result was a gigantic short circuit that left all of Belgrade and 70 percent of the rest of Serbian territory without electricity. Bridges over the Danube were out and all of the region's traffic was disorganized. C/J was obliged to take alternate routes that he had not been on before. Kosovo seemed to have been spared, but all along the way, as far as Macedonia, peasants complained of ill effects—true or false?—the respiratory trouble caused by these carbon and graphite fibers was similar to asbestos-related ailments.

Children and elderly men and women held up heads of lettuce and tomatoes to the windows of his red Panda that could hardly pass unnoticed—vegetables poisoned by the Americans, they said. The road was nothing but a string of burnt houses, abandoned fields, and scorched forests and pastures. "NATO estimated the cost of Yugoslavian reconstruction at 35 billion dollars." These figures, useless and opaque, occurred to him along with a vague memory of a certain Professor Chrest-Jones who had supported, along with his colleagues at the University of Santa Varvara, the Western crusade against the sinister Milosevic. He remembers savoring an ironic remark by Warren Christopher: "When Milosevic puts on his charm, one can easily see how if he had been born somewhere else he would have become a successful politician within a democratic system." Thank the stars in the sky for protecting Santa Varvara from Milosevic! But the border between here and there was not as clear as they say—history doesn't advance without some breakage after all. Well, of course, seeing the damage firsthand is not the same as reading about it on the Internet. So it's true, melancholy, the famous melancholy of the Slavic soul, is flourishing in the area. After the fall of the Wall, the Balkan peasants wanted everything right away; hence their increased bitterness, now and forever. These people hate us, it's only logical, and fortunately for us they hate the Muslims even more because they are truly afraid of them just as they were nine centuries ago, and even longer ago if it's possible, and they must know why. Human lives turn round and round like the ice cubes in my glass of slivovitz; each one does its ring around the rosie and all fall down.

C/J drove on without noticing, the foot of Sub-self held the accelerator pedal down to the floor; the Panda bumped and jumped over the potholed roads, the countryside flew by; he barely felt tired, though his shoulders were in knots. Who was he, this Adhémar? A mystic? No doubt, like all the crusaders. Only the Holy Land, the birthplace of Christianity, and the Holy Sepulchre, that object of intense veneration, could have made this aristocrat who was devoted to holy shrines and figures, especially the Virgin of Le Puy, join the expedition.

And the damage done, you ask? Let's reformulate the question: Were the Crusades as devastating as they say? Arab chronicles of the eleventh century took pleasure in exaggerating the devastation and even claim that the invaders were cannibals—you see the heady potion! But when free nations want to rally around shared values today, a sort of collective pledge of allegiance, aren't they absolutely right to launch their crusade with drones, MOAB, and antinuclear armor? And prepared to drop planeloads of bombs, destroy bridges and electrical plants, and contaminate the fields and air of "Old Europe" and elsewhere?

The Jews, a prime example of nomadism, showed the world the productivity of a wandering culture. C/J sincerely praised them for that, no problem, and Hermine could vouch for it. And yet in their search for origins, these decidedly intransigent people who imagine themselves to be the absolute originals, and why not—"to be" or "not to be," the verdict is still out, let's calmly remember, but even so—are the Jews not eternal crusaders fighting tooth and nail now more than ever to remain the one and only group of settlers in the Holy Land, their land, which nevertheless also belongs to Muslims and Christians? It's not the same thing at all, you snap back: they're just getting back the land that was taken from them and building a secure place for themselves after the horrors of the Shoah. OK, but the Palestinian kamikazes make exactly the same claim about exactly the same land and base it on their own origin story, know what I mean?

C/J saw hatred everywhere set one tribe against another. Have we really done anything besides repeat the massacres inaugurated at the time of the Crusades, if not earlier? That said, the gusto of Adhémar seemed to him the most just and pure as well as the most enigmatic. A crusader, certainly, and one of the very first, but transported or rather made tranquil by a different sort of enthusiasm. A special something before the spirit of the Crusade imposed its ways, which have been handed down to us and reveal something essential about human nature. Before the stains made by the brutal killing machines, always more sophisticated, always more efficient, that destroy men and land. C/J was unsure what it was; perhaps this journey would teach him.

Had he lived in the eighteenth century, C/J did not rule out the possibility of joining in the general laughter of Voltaire, who dismissed the Crusades as "a new kind of vanity," "an epidemic fever," "the madness of Coucoupêtre," the philosopher's amusing nickname for Peter the Hermit—touché! "They cry in Italy and we take arms in France," "We love our crosses," the mocking philosopher added. There's nothing more to say. But the question remains—why? Is it because this land was full of new lords who loved dissipation and war and thought nothing (according to this Enlightenment thinker) of diving into the crimes that debauchery leads to and losing themselves in a state of ignorance as shameful as their appetite for luxury? OK, but Adhémar was not like that, and *C/J* would turn to Foucher de Chartres, Anna Comnena, and other Ibn al-Athir types in support of his theories and dreams.

Adhémar sincerely believed it was his duty to safeguard the purity of the unified Christian faith, which is to say the European faith, according to *C/J*'s thinking; but this would be accomplished not by exterminating the Islamists but simply by exposing them to Christ's true message, which was, Adhémar had never doubted for an instant, more complex and more human than that of the followers of Allah. The bishop of Le Puy was even prepared to debate the matter with Alexius and—why not?—with his young daughter Anna who was reputed to be very learned, and even with the Saracen religious leaders. The rumor of this certainly did not make him a heretic but, more likely, a singular, unique figure who stood out from the rest—it was not impossible that this legend was true. It is generally admitted today that a specifically medieval man does not exist, though we do know that in those times the people feared animals and storms, ascribed the powers of both to God, and had an intensely strict sense of honor—OK, but what of it? Given his pure, pious, and independent spirit, this innovator, this earliest of reformers was probably reluctant to question certain dogmas, why wouldn't he be? *C/J* was inclined to think so, since it would explain certain silences in the biography of Adhémar. Did he want to combat fanaticism, as one says today; did he think that truth was essentially mysterious? Since Christ's message calls for peace, was it not necessary as true Christians to incarnate that peace through respect for each and every creature?

This papal legate, the first crusader, was perhaps an untypical crusader, and *C/J*, who subscribed to this theory, concluded that this was why the bishop of Le Puy did not survive the brutalities of the adventure. He died of the plague, or perhaps some psychosomatic malady, on August 1, 1098, at the gates of Antioch after having discovered the Holy Lance . . . jeez! His entire army mourned him. Even so, he did not lack for enemies, notably, among the most heated, one named Bartholomé, a jealous rival who claimed to have had a vision of Saint André wherein he was told the location of the same Holy Lance! But what to make of this saint who also, according to him, asked troops to fast for five days—though there was nothing to eat—or pillage enemy camps despite the strong disapproval of Adhémar who, unusually, was more tolerant and reasonable behind his outward exterior as a soldier of God.

C/J detested Bartholomé and all the other seen-the-light fundamentalists who pressed around the bishop of Le Puy. As the pacifier and unifier he seems to have been, Adhémar was clearly unlike the rest, and *C/J* became more and more convinced as he traveled across Kosovo. During his eighteen-year reign in Velay, had he not succeeded in taming the turbulent barons and persuading them to return valuable objects that had been violently seized from churches and abbeys without the need for any trials or other leverage? And did he not compose the *Salve Regina* hymn of the crusaders, Hail Holy Queen, in honor of the Virgin Mary?

Ad te clamamus exsules filii Hevae. . . . Et Jesum, benedictum fructum ventris tui, nobis post hoc exsilium ostende. O clemens, O pia, O dulcis Virgo Maria.

To thee do we cry, poor banished children of Eve. . . . And after this our exile show unto us the blessed fruit of thy womb, Jesus. O clement, O loving, O sweet Virgin Mary.

Did he live as though in exile, an exiled person among his own people, this Adhémar who wanted to conserve his passion as an exile and share it with other exiles, but who at the same time found himself on the road toward a general reconciliation of all in the One? A fascinating challenge, one had to admit, and *C/J* could not disapprove. Adhémar was certainly a precursor, a very distant precursor—alas! And dead for over nine centuries . . . jeez!

The road goes on and on—meager fields of wheat, abandoned pastures, dust and dirt. The gypsies had taken down the road signs; it seems they use them as fuel to cook their peppers and eggplants. All is poverty, penury, and scarcity at the beginning of this third millennium, the people complain; Balkan peoples no longer hope for anything from Europe, though perhaps still something from NATO, which is saying something. *C/J* stops, takes out his road map. No landmarks, tough! He'll forge ahead toward the south, then he'll need to branch off one of these days to the left and try to regain the road to Philippopolis farther to the east.

The bishop significantly left his nephew Ebrard Pagan (or de Payns, according to some sources) in Philippopolis. This was Sebastian's own discovery, though still a hypothesis for the moment, one that he had presented and defended at a numismatic conference in Budapest in 1988 and at the Palestinian university at Bir Zeit in 1993. His thesis struck like a bomb, and there was "heated debate," as they say. Some colleagues expressed favorable interest, others suspected it all to be pure speculation, the typical sort of attention-grabbing scheme designed to propel somebody to star status at these sorts of gatherings. Now he was going to offer them the ultimate proof; after all, science demands that one get personally involved, at least the human sciences do.

Sebastian believed that Ebrard Pagan was the son of a sister of Adhémar, Leuze, and the leading nobleman in Velay, Hilduin Pagan (or de Payns). What's more, he would be the nephew (or uncle, this needed to be confirmed) of the founder of the Order of Templars created in 1118 by Hughes de Payens.

Like the barons Heracle and Ponce de Polignac, and all the others in Le Puy, the father of the young man, Hilduin Pagan, was persuaded by Adhémar to return stolen articles to the local churches in Rozières, Sainte-Marie and Saint-Jean, and to the Abbey of Chamalières. And in order to make his new Christian faith even more official, as well as his loyalty to the bishop of Le Puy, he sent forth his son Ebrard to join in the march toward the Holy Land.

Ebrard (or Everard) adapted so well the uncle-bishop's attitude of free-thinking that he quickly abandoned both the uncle and the Crusade, fleeing toward Thrace. In Philippopolis this Renaissance precursor had a family, cultivated land, immersed himself in the study of Slavic languages, perfected his Greek, and debated the heresies that circulated at the time even more densely than they do today among the Byzantine philosophers who were as learned as they were numerous in that large city.

Immersed in his reveries and punchy from fatigue, C/J started singing the *Salve Regina*, "the anthem of Le Puy," as Saint Bernard would call it: "Ad te clamamus . . . O clemens, O pia. . . . " Was it indeed Sebastian, or his shadow from another time, that had merged with shades of Adhémar de

Monteil or Ebrard Pagan? He saw the hideous architecture of Serbia and Macedonia go by; soon he would cross the Bulgarian border. After all, what proof did he have, the insomniac of Stony Brook, that the papal legate of the first Crusade, this Adhémar de Monteil, was a sage who respected the singular man, the *ecce homo?* Or that this warrior, this intransigent administrator of the ecclesiastical wealth of Le Puy, was an early Renaissance man? Frankly none—he had nothing but his own dream of the *Salve Regina*—an artful interpretation by a bastard exile questing for Origins, with a big O, that were as necessary seeming as they were quickly repudiated, an interpretation that had led him to burrow into the parish archives of the diocese of Le Puy.

Yes, what proof did he have that the nephew Ebrard Pagan, who had loyally served Adhémar before devoting himself to his love for Militsa the Bulgarian, but also to reading Byzantine books, what proof did he have that he was really and truly the distant point of origin of the Chrest family, one of the genuine *crucesignati* named in documents he had consulted at the libarary in Plovdiv-Philippopolis, and thus the ancestor of Sylvester Chrest, the father of *C/J*, that is, of Sebastian himself? None except the fact that local chronicles discovered by Professor Chrest-Jones state that Ebrard Pagan was really and truly there in the eleventh century with the crusaders from the Languedoc areas led by Raymond de Saint-Gilles and the bishop of Le Puy. But what importance is there to knowing who descends from whom, me from you, you from Christ or Adam, from Mary or Eve? From Krishna, Shiva, or the Yellow Emperor?

The man at the wheel of his Fiat Panda knew that this quest was crazy, and yet it was the quest that firmly determined his route and made him advance. Without it he would have shot himself in the head after strangling Fa Chang who believed, the imbecile, herself to be at the beginning of a new chapter in her life! To become an origin without him, beyond him, despite him, Sebastian! To give life and what all else without first asking what it could possibly mean in this world today, this world of depleted uranium and women wearing veils!

Plovdiv. Finally a hotel. Suddenly he felt very tired. He was now allowed to feel tired, allowed to sleep. Our observer left the gap between the one who does and the one who watches others do, without place or time, a polytrope carried off in a flux of thoughts and uncontrollable words. And then he lay down, happy. Well, almost.

The Historian Is Dead, France Changes Direction, Maybe ℥

"I'm telling you, Commissioner, he's dead! Proof? Since he disappeared, he has not used his computer. It's been a month, doesn't that mean anything to you?" Minaldi had succeeded in getting one leg over the wall of disgust that Rilsky had erected to seal him out, and now after a dozen unanswered calls—the commissioner-will-get-back-to-you-as-soon-as-possible-please-be-patient-and-understand-that-he-is-very-busy-but-has-not-forgotten-about-you—the obsequious assistant of Sebastian Chrest-Jones had come down to the police station.

Rilsky couldn't let him wait in the hallway forever and Popov told the visiting lab assistant that his interview would have to be brief. Not being himself all that up on "information technology," Rilsky didn't find the argument based on the absence of computer use all that convincing, especially since from their very first interview immediately after the disappearance of Sebastian Minaldi's reasoning appeared to be aimed at little more than improving his position within the local clan of timid, small-minded academics rotting inside the conformist circles of their discipline.

However, since he had no new information about the disappearance or death of his mysteriously missing uncle, a disappearance that Stephanie had taken pains to link to his Byzantine love story and that he himself, because of bothersome memories, admitted was getting in the way of his ability to make progress with other investigations, Northrop decided to grant the intruder a few minutes of his time.

"I am very familiar with the habits of Professor Chrest-Jones, as you know, Commissioner, and I'm telling you that he never went anywhere without his laptop, a real gem of a machine, I might add! I'm sure you know what I'm talking about when I say that he was a true modern researcher who wrote everything directly on the computer, stored his data, did his e-mail, surfed the Internet, and even kept the accounts of the lab." The commissioner threw him a skeptical look that elicited no reaction from the talkative assistant.

"You are no doubt wondering how I know that he's no longer using his computer. It's easy, not that legit perhaps, but what is these days? Anyway, I think you'll pardon my indiscretion and perhaps even congratulate me since my little faux pas is going to further your investigation, do you follow me?" asked Minaldi with sly false modesty.

"Let me explain what I mean. Some time ago I set up a rather ingenious system—it's rather complicated and I know it's not your field, but it is mine and I'm pretty good at it—so anyway, with this system I can decode the professor's log-on information and have remote access to the professor's laptop. Chrest-Jones was a suspicious character, we could even say secretive, and he frequently changed his access codes in ways that he considered unhackable. But since I was the one who sort of taught him how to use his computer, it wasn't all that difficult for me to crack his codes and gain access. If I allowed myself this indiscretion, since I'm sure that's what you see it as, it was in order to know more about the minute workings of the mind of my master so that I, his disciple, could better serve him in his research—surely you can believe me since, after all, serving him is, or was, my job. He was a man of few words, Chrest-Jones, and one had to guess what he wanted since he often did not like to explain things, if you see what I mean. So, in my view, since he's not working any longer on his computer, he is certainly dead!" Here his Cheshire cat smile drifted toward a look of idiotic sadism.

"I think I understand you, sir," replied Rilsky while coldly restraining himself from throwing the man out of his office. The "sir," spoken without the least affect, hit even the tone-deaf ears of Popov as the most biting of insults, but Minaldi was totally deaf and utterly unable to decode any such subtleties. "Your argument is not without a certain logic. I will not comment for now on the ethical aspects of what you claim to know and how you came to know it, but naturally the possibility of the subject's death is one of the hypotheses under consideration."

"I considered this a hypothesis from the beginning, Commissioner; but I've come to you today because I am now certain it's true!" Minaldi triumphant. "If you're still investigating" (Rilsky, teeth clenched, murmurs to himself: "This jackass thinks he can insult my department!"), you should be looking for a dead body, not a missing person."

"Don't you worry, sir." He delivered as icy a "sir" as he could. "What is your . . . oh, yes, Minaldi. Have confidence in our men, Mr. Minaldi, they are more competent than they may seem or than the academic circles in Santa Varvara may think." Rilsky rose to lead out this opportunist who blushed slightly with a mix of pleasure and confusion. "Pardon me if I have to get back to my work; our department has no shortage of cases to attend to." He wasn't going to let this little prick think that the commissioner was stuck on a family matter that only interested Hermine and the microcosm of the academy that was always ready to consider itself the center of the universe anyway.

Northrop was fed up with the case of the runaway Sebastian, a case that merely confirmed him as one more middle-aged adolescent and pushed his wife's hysteria over the top. Granted, he might have done the very same thing in the professor's situation, but this was too much now. These university good-for-nothings wanted to make a big deal of it, an "affair" that you'd think they believed was more important than the serial killer or the New Pantheon leaders out at their Seaside Temple headquarters. The case of Number Eight was the only real problem at the moment, and, one had to say, a terrible failure for the usually brilliant Rilsky. Sebastian's was a banal case, a scandal more fit for psychologists and marriage counselors than the police. God knows how much Rilsky hated that snooty psychologist Dr. What's-His-Name who dogged him ever since the Chrest family's past had been resurrected instead of being left alone where it was. This family mix-up came at a bad moment and was now getting in the way of the investigation into the New Pantheon and its mafia-related tentacles—*there* was a scandal that promised to become a global story, but one that, alas, was hardly moving forward. Unless the mysterious Sebastian was somehow linked to the serial killer? Rilsky had not ruled out this possibility; after all, nothing was known about Number Eight, and judging from his notebooks Sebastian was perhaps enough of a lunatic to get involved in something this crazy. Who or what could stop a daydreaming tenured professor from thinking of himself as a purifier, or from disappearing, or from passing himself off as dead? No one and nothing. He could throw everyone off his trail and continue his invisible vengeance against the bad apples of this rotten world. So was it necessary to learn more about him, wade through more of his prose, and what more? OK OK, they would get around to it. Northrop forced himself to decipher more documents within his uncle's archives. It was a mammoth task, and Rilsky was worried blind from the first page: here again was the family and here again this black stain. Stephanie would no doubt see things more clearly. That was one more reason Northrop did not share with her his suspicions, but perhaps she had some too? Bizarre, this sudden passion for Byzantium. . . .

But there was the one bright side of this depressing labyrinth: Stephanie. Northrop was the first to be surprised by the new body that was waking up inside him and the commissioner let it happen, happy but also amused and wary. In fact, he avoided thinking about it because all thoughts on the matter—the idea of Northrop in love—were perfectly ridiculous. It was better not to dwell on it. He saw no other way to avoid the specter of ridicule than by letting his mind go blank. Or else by letting it fill up entirely with other matters such as events in foreign politics.

The night before Stephanie had made him dine with the French ambassador, who, like everyone else in the country, wanted to put in his two cents about the serial killer. Foulques Weil gaily offered his explanation, one that was about as useless as those of the local police, but that he humorously did not cling to and in fact altered several times over the course of the dinner, as though he were imagining various possible plot lines for a TV detective show. His excellency the French ambassador was a fine, spirited gentleman at least two cuts above the usual civil servants of the diplomatic corps who nevertheless had all been carefully chosen for the sensitive assignment in Santa Varvara. He knew how to suavely ingratiate himself among those gathered at the customary parties and receptions that served the customary champagne, crustless caviar sandwich squares, and other deluxe finger food. The reader must now be informed that for the first time in years—thanks to the pitiful snail's pace of this affair and the reinvigorated existence given to the usually placid, not to say flaccid, commissioner by the mouth, skin, and sexual organs of Stephanie—Northrop, yes Northrop, to his own great surprise, was taking an interest in politics. This went against an axiom that Rilsky knew well and expressed in the following way: "Politics is a promise that is only binding for believers, whereas love is a promise unto death between the lovers, and therefore politics and love are incompatible." In fact, the more his personal passion blossomed, the more he became passionate about events that he had formerly treated with indifference, though they were the standard nourishment of most other human beings. If he preferred to pay attention to foreign affairs, it was because as commissioner of Santa Varvara he was too familiar with the backstage workings of all domestic affairs to be surprised by anything. He therefore found it more and more necessary to add the following corollary to what he liked to call his "Rilsky axiom": "Since the one who loves lives excitedly outside of time, he takes his rest by laughing at the farces of history." As a man of reason Rilsky relied on such axioms to avoid the risk of his behavior appearing loose, lazy, or just plain wrong, as it would in the case of someone who lived day to day without such rules of conduct. Armed in this way, he could devote himself to other police work and professional matters that he was normally supposed to be in charge of (every system of logic being valid so long as one respects its coherence) but had lately pushed aside. Pushed aside and also allowed to be overtaken, as we have seen, by disturbing mental black holes and a dangerous doubling of the personality of the Dr. Jekyll and Mr. Hyde type that Stevenson made famous.

This was the state of mind that led the commissioner, one of the leading figures working in Santa Varvara, to discuss without any hesitation the recent ups and downs of the electoral process in France with His Excellency Foulques Weil. Anything to get away from that Minaldi! Between crime and love one had need of the legal perverse space known as politics. Having arrived at this sage attitude of general pardon, the commissioner took a keen pleasure in witnessing the motions of male and female politicians—the latter having become more and more numerous, though not enough for Stephanie's taste, in this margin of the human comedy that most people think of as decisive, a conviction that was not the least humorous thing about the whole subject. No one suspected it was a kind of joke therapy for the commissioner that resulted in his diving into the debates that regularly stirred up his fellow citizens and led him to lose his customary sense of distance and actually believe he had opinions on this or that.

Did he believe in them? Hardly, except when Stephanie spoke and he admired, charmed as he was, the beauty of her convictions. Even after a couple of whiskies he was still able to laugh a black laugh at his transitory lover's persona, smitten by the arguments of his politically involved journalist friend. Her habit of declaring her views and stubbornly defending them was nothing if not charming. Under the disguise of the disillusioned nomadic contrarian, there was a moral-breathing creature who would not give in to disappointments. Her spirit had something admirable about it, let's say unique and not speak about the rest, thought Northrop, smiling out of the corner of his eyes behind the tinted lenses of his glasses.

"Lionel's idea of politics was disconnected from what the French expect and probably from what any group of citizens hopes for." Was it timidity or fear of men, beginning with her boss? Stephanie talked politics as though she were writing a piece for her *Événement de Paris*: pompous, serious, zero humor. "The proof? Well, his politics didn't succeed." She called the prime minister by his first name, not so much because of a certain familiarity as covacationers on the Atlantic but because of her affinity for the rigor of this secretive man, often termed "psycho-rigid," a French code word for Huguenot. "He thought he was talking to a citizenry of adults intolerant of demagogy who preferred hard truths over traps and illusions. It was a noble thought! As though there existed, somewhere in the world, popular masses, excuse me, 'grassroots organizations,' that are not leaning toward know-nothing populism or even fascism. Or let me give you the soft version: who doesn't prefer the commonsense security talk of a father figure whom we like hospitality-minded and fun loving, if possible, though we'll accept the down-and-dirty lawyer in preacher's robes, if it comes to that?"

"You are so serious, my dear Stephanie!" In the downpour of words that showed no signs of letting up, Northrop had jumped on a momentary pause of breath to tease his friend. He wished only to egg her on and be drenched further by her driving verbiage, which he found bracing and absurd.

"Not at all! What disgusts me is not so much the media-driven spinning and churning imposed by so-called friends of the candidate that ended up pushing out any real political debate and that he was too weak to resist. What gets me is how any talk of the 'collective' has become a no-fly zone, do you understand? Instead, there's a permanent buzz, a gag on the individual, an egalitarian hive where the bees are on such a first-name basis that the fake bumblebee himself is surprised about having to move in every direction without head or wings." Boy, she sure could be tough on her friends, the sweet little Stephanie! "In a last courageous gasp he ended up even saying so in front of the cameras, can you believe the daring of this comrade? Too late though! The hive can't believe it! What's more, it can't even hear it! The champ no longer knows who he is; he is so dizzy he apologizes for having attacked his opponent, the old challenger whom no one thought could get it up anymore! The most timid beginning boxer would not have made such a foolish mistake. He left the door wide open, first to his fratricide-thinking brothers and then of course to all the retirees who miss their strong leader." Stephanie, feeling the anger of the just, turned bright purple, which was not justified but ravishing nonetheless.

None of this was found dull by His Excellency Foulques Weil, for whom Rilsky had had great esteem ever since the recently arrived fifty-something diplomat managed in just a few months to clean up the French consulate in Santa Varvara, which before his appointment had been rife with corruption and visa trafficking aimed at young women who dreamed of joining the Paris prostitution market. Discreet and well-educated, this aristocrat with his Jewish name and, through his mother, a permanent address in Bois de Lamothe, claimed to belong to no political party and to be as humbly ensconced as the furniture of the Republic by which he meant to insinuate his irreplaceability. It was striking how cares about the furniture and other belongings of the nation seemed to haunt the French mind. If he was furniture, he was certainly a luxury item and no doubt a high-ranking figure within the secret service as well. Foulques Weil was a man of the world who was attractive to women but had remained unattached and thus was able to devote himself to his job with the ardor of a missionary. He liked to compare himself to Proust's Swann, who, instead of failing to make a name for himself in art history as he had failed in his amorous affairs with Odette, had succeeded in his Career. In the company of Rilsky, who was charmed by this Parisian outsider, the ambassador liked to add color to his commentaries on the current politico-criminal investigations with allusions to James Joyce, the Irishman who ironized about the "sumptuous and stagnant exaggeration of murder" in human affairs, including and especially the affairs of modern man. This literary refinement, which generally went unnoticed by all except Rilsky, did not prevent his excellency the ambassador from acquiring a sophisticated knowledge of the history of Santa Varvara that included its mafia. In addition, Foulques Weil was able to express himself in Santa Varvarois just as well as the pope had done on his recent visit. Stephanie's harangue needed more nuance and refinement and his excellency was going to provide both with the utmost elegance:

"Madame, I am prepared to agree with you; however, permit me to remind you of the relevant international context. What do you consider to be the degree of freedom of action open to national governments, France's or others, in the wake of September 11? That is the question and one would have to be very clever indeed to try and answer it. What the press calls politics, all the agitation that the commissioner looks on with suspicion—is that not right, my friend?—and that is carried out by minions of the state such as myself, where does it really take place? Paris? Washington? Jerusalem? Riyadh? Choose between the Jews and the Arabs? Or neither one, but instead Oil with a capital *O*? Or let's try and make ourselves heard—'spoilers' that we are, no?—in the Security Council, for example, or on the streets of emerging nations or others. Whatever one might try, the margin for maneuvering is narrow indeed. This doesn't entirely discourage us, however. . . . "

Foulques Weil sipped his champagne and, before a Stephanie-momentarily-out-of-service and a Rilsky-who-was-increasingly-amused, passed without the least hesitation to the other side of the red line the commissioner considered to be diplomacy's exclusive privilege. Weil was not going to repeat the tricks of Paul Morand, who, long before the Gulf War and the campaign in Iraq, had predicted the battle for black gold above and beyond any pro- or anti-Semitism. His excellency took up where he left off and was intent on explaining to his hosts that political was overwhelmed by cases and affairs to a greater degree than ever before. He affirmed that the people were governed by the most demagogic political leaders who succeeded in seducing their constituents, all the while obeying certain mafialike cartels, which in the present globalized economy had amassed and divided up among themselves considerable financial and religious interests. And that civil servants like himself, disillusioned but still loyal to their role within public service, had seen their latitude for action drastically reduced. This he took as one more reason to do one's job well and whatever would be would be! "Good night noises everywhere!" was basically the ambassador's conclusion, in full agreement with the philosophy of Rilsky, who, since Stephanie's arrival, had been trying to shelter his private life from everyone else. Amusing enough, politics, up to a point.

"Besides that, you have no doubt observed the delectable and implacable pair of vise grips into which the French people have locked themselves or, if you prefer, French ideology." The ambassador did not want to let them think that geopolitics cut him off from the alleged cultural core of his native country. "We rock ourselves to sleep with enchanted castles and militant worker groups, ancestral gargoyles and Thai bordellos; by day we love the tranquil governance of a self-professed provincial, but by night we dream along with those who worship big dicks that never tire of multiplying themselves and filling all orifices according to the latest beaux arts fashions of Paris. Don't worry, I will say no more. For a longtime grunge delighted in provoking norms and laws to the point where the police were right about going after trash and backrooms. Well, the party's over now, ladies and gentlemen! No, it's not the end of history, there will always be histories, always more or less criminal, won't there, Commissioner? Everyone is or will be his own Hamlet, who walks 'reading the book of himself,' as the poet said. No, it's the nontime that is beginning; I mean the time of analysis." Foulques Weil was becoming threatening in a half-Freudian half-biblical way. His hosts stared back at him with questioning circumspection. "You thought of me as more modernist, some have even called me avant-garde? Reassure yourselves, at heart we are in agreement. French ideology is fond of extremes, this leads us to excel at the coup d'état, on the barricades, and in modern art; but it's also why we are less adept at the rational management of daily affairs. For lack of becoming Protestant or going global, our old Catholic country has perhaps finally decided to walk off to bed in its hand-knit slippers. After all, the air is a bit chilly when you open the windows, don't you think? And now we are pacifists, pacifist Atlantists, a variant on the third worlders, do you follow me? Complication will always be a French specialty. Isn't France the most advanced of Muslim countries?"

"You would be a troublemaker, Mr. Ambassador, if you were not a poet." Rilsky could think of no better compliment to express his feeling of complicity with this perhaps timeless and certainly matchless civil servant. However, he would not commit the low faux pas of leading his excellency into a debate over France's position in the Iraqi crisis. Francophobia flowed like French wine in the gutters of Santa Varvara; it was best to stay on the level of men of taste and understand each other by allusions. "Yes, yes, you have understood me, a poet such as the author of the *Flowers of Evil*. He understood that glory is showered on riffraff. Did he not write long ago—with apologies to Miss Delacour, who is a fan of democracy—'They are imbeciles who believe that glory can only be founded on virtue'? Because—and it's proven by the events that we've been discussing this evening, no?—even those in your homeland of France, which shows, admit it, that you French are not as exceptional as you would have us believe—'Glory is the result of the mind's adapting itself to the idiocy of the nation' and 'Dicatators are the janitors of the people—nothing more.'"

Foulques Weil would certainly not follow the commissioner into what seemed to be, behind the Baudelairean smokescreen, the beginnings of an attack against the current French government, perhaps even against the president himself. Ironist though he may have been, his role as an ambassador required that he acquiesce to the reason of the state, and he would take no other tack. He knew from experience that one had to be a bit of an assassin and a thief to survive in politics and that one doesn't become president without a large dose of passionate humanism that electors can smell a mile away—who knows how—and that takes up residence in one's guts so as to become, if not the bed of fascism, at least the deathbed of democracy. One had to realize it and put guardrails around it, that was all. But why get into politics when one is not the type for playing Beauty and the Beast? By sticking to diplomacy, with a little wit and, if possible, a little culture, one could get by—that at least was Foulques's recipe.

The ambassador managed to recover his diplomatic reserve and was not sure he wanted to share in this latest lyrical display of his host, the kind of poetic wizardry whose secret was known only to the commissioner and that he reserved for after dinner and only for selected guests. All the more so since these flowers of evil had a whiff of something elitist about them, perhaps even an antidemocratic or antirepublican slant, but were in any case something an ambassador needed to be wary of in public no matter what his intimate convictions might be, even if the latter were rather evident in the relaxed atmosphere at the end of a reception. But Stephanie Delacour seemed so impressed, though in total disagreement with his remarks, that the ambassador, as a true gentleman, could only agree tacitly with his host. It seemed that politics did indeed turn into a sideshow, Rilsky was yet again shown proof of that, when, that is, it didn't result in surgical strikes—but it hadn't come to that in the present case. Afghanistan was far away and it was better not to bring up Iraq.

So it was that, having rid himself of Minaldi, the commissioner, on his way to his apartment, where Stephanie was waiting for him, turned over in his head the repartee of the previous night's dinner—far more amusing than the university man's repetitious babblings. Like a detective novel, life itself needs detours and subplots to be readable, livable. Not to follow the same leads, the same ideas: a good investigation does not follow the laws of parthenogenesis but instead requires a second angle if it is going to develop. Patricia Highsmith even made this into a rule of thumb in the art of suspense. Rilsky applied it to existence itself, whenever possible: Weil, therefore, and the byplay of a political society dinner were the complement to dealing with Minaldi, Popov, Sebastian, and even Stephanie, whom he was delighted to see again upon his arrival.

"What's new?"

"The car of Fa Chang, Sebastian's assistant, has been found. Remember, she disappeared at about the same time he did. They found the car in a lake near Stony Brook. There's no sign of the body for the moment, they're going to dredge the lake. And something else. Minaldi thinks that Sebastian is really dead because, get this, my dear, this gigolo assistant thought nothing of hacking into Chrest's computer, and because he says that the professor has not logged on since he disappeared, he concludes he's dead because a professor who doesn't use his computer is a dead professor, thus Sebastian Chrest-Jones is dead: QED. That's the logic of this Minaldi!"

Stephanie looked at her lover with a hagard, incredulous air, forced to descend from the heights of the previous night's conversation at the ambassador's residence to the cogitations of this university midget.

"This little apprentice detective is as abject morally as he is physically ugly, don't you think? Leave him to his envious undertaker impulses, I have another idea, do you want to hear it? I've consulted all the notes and video documents of your historian uncle, you see, including the disks and files he made before his disappearance, which your department printed and you're supposed to be studying."

"Mmm." Out of fear or hope, Rilsky felt his throat tighten. Had Stephanie discovered a clue? The trail of the purifier? A connection to Number Eight? The commissioner looked at the journalist, pale and silent.

"I know. I know you've glanced at them, but I'm telling you they're worth taking a closer look at. I can tell you one thing for sure, my dear commissioner: Sebastian Chrest-Jones was in love with Anna Comnena!" Stephanie spoke without the least smile of doubt or derision and had totally forgotten about Number Eight.

Having up until now considered Mademoiselle Delacour to be generally reasonable, although—to her credit—somewhat passionate, Rilsky now suddenly observed her with a decided tenderness, which, coming from him, was the equivalent of the greatest caution. It would seem one couldn't count on anyone in this damn investigation!

The Story of Anna Comnena, as Told by Stephanie Delacour ❧

In Santa Varvara the humid summer heat spares neither geraniums, cats, or women. No one is free from it. In August the wind halts, bodies melt into puddles of sweat; no jasmine-scented breeze can displace the acrid smell of petrol that hangs in the air, and the foul emissions from the nearby refineries fall on all that is living, or barely living. The only solution: air-conditioning, if you're lucky enough to have it at home. Wearing only a T-shirt and underwear, Stephanie is immersed in Sebastian's archives. She rises from her dreamy torpor. Hotter than ever, the tiger cat walks silently, breaks a vase, disappears like a woman, no, like a man, the same nervous shivers go down her back, the same perplexed stare as Nordi's, poor cat, oh, what heat! Leave me alone Shah, there, you'll stay locked in the kitchen now. Stephanie is following Sebastian, she tracks him through his papers, she reinvents the runaway and his phantoms—after all, it's her work as an embedded journalist while waiting for new news of Number Eight.

Nordi leaves the apartment early. He gets back late. Stephanie is working for him still, it's important to support him psychologically, no? He looks a bit undone, in his shoes anyone would be; and the journalist, it goes without saying, does not underestimate the shock that she herself has occasioned in the life of this hardened bachelor. With her dry cheeks, wide temples, and triangular chin, she takes possession of Sebastian's prose with an appetite the Parisian had never before experienced, something between lassitude and aggressive gaiety, the soft ardor of a woman in love, but with whom? The Shah cat is she, Stephanie: the iced tea descends in her glass, she goes over immense scenes and strips of time, she unravels Sebastian's yarn and makes of it a beautiful history in the shape of a heart, dedicated to Nordi, who suspects nothing.

"You ask me what Sebastian saw in Anna Comnena? Well, everything, don't you see? If not, why would he go and bury himself here at the dawn of the third millennium in the books of a Byzantine princess who lived at the beginning of the second? There's an elegant symmetry, don't you think? What could he have possibly seen in her? You don't see it? Something of no value to the modern-day women of Santa Varvara but for which Chrest has the highest esteem: an austere black-haired beauty, the spitting image of her father the basileus, with the pride of a sovereign and the mind of an intellectual! First raised on the teachings of ancient cultures, she further enriched her mind with studies of the quadrivium of the sciences: astrology, geometry, arithmetic, and music plus the trivium—grammar, rhetoric, and dialectics—that is the foundation of all cultures, as I'm sure you know. Who could ask for more? In addition, instead of withdrawing into a monastic order as her Western equivalents would have done—if, that is, other learned women existed elsewhere at the time—she gets involved in politics, plots and counterplots, in order to save the family's honor. Beginning with her father, Alexius I, whose character and reign she magnifies in a style that recalls Homer or Plato, but softened by her Porphyrian manners. Because the princess is nevertheless a woman, a detail that one ought not forget, Nordi, and even though Byzantium had known formidable empresses long before her, Anna did not begin to write until she was fifty-five, following the death of her husband, the caesar Nicephorus Bryennius, in 1138. Bryennius had already begun a chronicle of the reign of Alexius I, but it is Anna who will continue and complete it. She was more inspired than her husband, more gifted in relating court intrigues, more precise about the armed confrontations, more in wonder at the Byzantine accomplishments, and more romantic, her pen thoroughly soaked in an inexhaustible nostalgia.

"I'm exaggerating? Do you know how big the *Alexiad* is? Fifteen books. They are tomes that only diehard bookworms read today to form an idea about those times. You think, with an anticipated readership of such modest proportions, Anna would not go far? Ask yourself instead who still reads, say, *The Three Musketeers*? The most curious have seen the film and take Depardieu for Alexandre Dumas, who, by the way, can thank the movie business for opening the doors of the Pantheon to him! Anna, who falls into disgrace in 1118 after failing to depose her brother John in favor of her husband, fixes on the idea of her oeuvre after the husband's death in 1138. She writes for ten years and, just after completing her work, she dies, alone and disgusted with the turn history was taking. Sebastian has doubts that 1148 is the true date of her death. Of course, ever since encountering her, our Santa Varvara historian lives with his wise colleague there, in her pages, in her skin, in her time. . . .

"Can you see? Can you imagine it? He has got inside the little tan body of the princess, his mind took up residence behind her big black eyes, which he took pleasure in embellishing with highly lyrical phrases composed on the liquid screen of his laptop—phrases that would sound ridiculous if the story were less tragic. Just listen a bit to how he describes Anna's eyes from the moment of her birth in the Purple Room of the royal palace in Constantinople—a room decorated in red and gold, the place where the future sovereigns of the empire came into the world. He says they are eyes that would have "entranced one like a bolt of lightning, like a gift of Athena, or a charm of Eros!" In fact, he's mimicking Anna, he speaks like his idol. Close to the newborn child, our man sees the two matrons, the empress Irene Dukas who has given birth and the paternal grandmother Anna Dalassena, stomping about with feverish impatience as much as he, Sebastian, does nine centuries later! He describes the female historian as having been crowned since her birth with an extravagant affection, with a love that he, Sebastian, had not received. And so it happens that under the golden cupolas of the Queen of Cities the mother and grandmother, who are rivals in their affection for the infant, are joined by a third noble woman, the famous Marie of Alania. The name means nothing to you? Marie was the wife of the former emperor, Michael VII, removed from power by Alexius I. Get this: Marie of Alania had hired this very man, Alexius I, to protect her only son, Constantine, and later takes Alexius as her lover! Alexius took advantage of the situation to neutralize the opposing camp, a typical Byzantine intrigue! The affair was an open secret at the Byzantine court.

"I suppose you can guess that this charming stratagem, convenient for all parties, was to culminate with the marriage of Constantine, Marie's son, with Anna, the daughter of the adopted son who was also Marie of Alania's lover. Anna was engaged to Constantine at birth and shortly thereafter, at the age of eight, the gifted child was handed over to her future mother-in-law. The latter saw to it that the child acquired all that was necessary for a woman one day destined to become an empress. Having been nourished in this way on the affections and jealousies of her three female teachers (are you following?—her mother, her grandmother, and the lover of her father), Anna flourished and went further than any of them in wisdom. The quality of her mind stupefied the entire court.

"Her wet-nurse Zoe informs her that the myrrh that flows from the tomb of Saint Demetrios has the most wonderful curative properties: 'provided one approaches the tomb with the proper faith, with the help of God, and without provoking the displeasure of Athena of the sea-green eyes,' answers the princess in the presense of courtiers, who are amazed by this wisdom that comes so close to pagan heresy—certainly nothing that one should repeat to the Orthodox patriarch who rules over the souls of Constantinople! And when the young scholar asks her teachers to teach her the art of astrology, she says, 'It is not to practice it, God forbid, but to better understand its futility and better judge those who do practice it.' Is the little princess sly or already extremely rational? Sebastian thinks of her as an early Madame de Staël, can you believe it? What's more, until the end of her life Anna refuses to believe that events are determined by the stars and mocks those who allow their actions to be guided by their dreams. Nonetheless, she persists in her admiration for her father, who claimed Saint Demetrios appeared to him in a dream to say, "Do not worry. Do not waver. Tomorrow you will be the winner." The very next day the basileus wins the battle at Thessalonika. Bingo. However, if one believes Sebastian, only the mother of the Word could inspire in princess Anna a true Christian devotion, and he exclaims over the passages in the *Alexiad* where one sees the father of the narrator waiting four days for a miracle of the Virgin that doesn't happen and then returning to the sacred temple of Blachernes to offer the customary hymnody and the most fervent supplications in order that the usual great event finally take place, so that the basileus can embark with the highest of hopes.

"Anna was a woman of her times, if you like, Nordi, but already an intellectual according to your nephew. The word shocks you, I suppose, because you cannot imagine a female intellectual before Simone de Beauvoir, ignorant as you are! Am I wrong? Oh, you go back as far as Germaine de Staël too? Bravo. This is just what I mean: you cannot admit that this freak of nature, this miracle of the human species—a female intellectual—defying the laws of the uterus to participate in those of the mind, begins with Anna Comnena? Well, your uncle Sebastian is persuaded that it is true! And so, like a painter remaking his model, he remakes her history at the same time that he remakes the body of the princess as well as her entire destiny—in short, everything that touches on her thought. Think of Renoir, who transforms meaty maids into Venuses on the half-shell. Or think of Cezanne's bathers, whom he depicts as androgynes, some say as transvestites. And I am not forgetting Picasso or De Kooning who seem really to like these cruel and crushed female faces that of course only come from their paintbrushes, except, when let out obscenely, that they're "from their bushy tails"—the pigs! Yes, Sebastian has transfused into Anna, he loves her for the memory she wills to him of the Crusades, especially her description of the First Crusade from 1095 to 1115, though she was only twelve at the time it started. She relies for her narrative of this adventure on third-person accounts and the testimonies of chroniclers and courtiers, and she especially follows her project of unfailing paternal glorification, but so what!"

"All that's well and good, my dear Stephanie, but what do you expect me to do with it for my investigation?"

The night had lowered the temperature, as Stephanie tried to share with Nordi small doses of what she, like a greedy cat, had been consuming on her walks through the brain of the missing person. Neither his glass of J&B on the rocks nor the intimations of future intimacy that he read in Stephanie's eyes could persuade the commissioner of the relevance of Sebastian's love story. Except perhaps, if Stephanie was right and this guy's head was totally immersed in Byzantium, he hardly fit the profile of Number Eight! They didn't match up, so it was one scenario that could be abandoned. Rilsky didn't know whether to be happy or alarmed at the thought . . . but what thought? Are you sleeping, Minoushah?

"O ye of little faith! Come on, Nordi, his delirium—his passion, let's say—that may be what made Sebastian disappear, do you understand? It's obvious if he got so interested in the First Crusade it's because he wanted to know how reasonable Christians, as he puts it, could get involved in a holy war, a sort of counterjihad, if you like. He likes the vision offered by Anna's pen writing from the other side of Europe, from that vestigal Greece of the orthodox and sovereign empire that pursued the impious worshippers of the Crescent, with the help of confident and conquering Latins like us, but not without also mocking our barbarous pretensions while already sensing their own imminent demise. No, to be sure, Anna does not predict the defeat of Byzantium, but her final tears allow one to read in them something much graver than the mere distress of the daughter orphaned from the father she loves. And Sebastian projects himself into this black sun—ah, the sweetness of Byzantine sorrow: it's music to his ears. Stretching from the twenty-first century back to the end of the eleventh and the beginning of the twelfth centuries, an entire historical cycle has been completed; that is his prophecy. Is he wrong? Is he right? Here is what he says, 'All of Europe today is one heady Byzantium, too proud of itself and already in peril, too poor to play alone the role of global policeman; ready to make subtle compromises and fatal procrastinations, she is condemned. Today only Santa

Varvara appears able to combat Evil, but who can in all reasonableness seek salvation in Santa Varvara?' That's what he thinks, your missing uncle, thanks to his pilgrimage along the forking paths of Anna's garden. You should read him—I know it's asking too much of you, you don't have time, you've already read a little, you've got the point, that's what you're thinking. . . ."

"No it's not." Northrop sighs. He's never going to get a word in. His Stephanie lights up while speaking, her eyes brilliant, her cheeks a peachy pink. She's traded in her T-shirt for a slinky purple silk dress, and one strap has fallen off her shoulder.

"It's not? Well, listen up to what I'm saying. His love for her blended with his reason as a historian and opened up his eyes to a new perspective—he now sees our world through Anna's eyes. His love, blind and no doubt distorting, perceives truths that science doesn't see, do you follow? For example? While waiting for you to arrest the serial killer of the New Pantheon—no, I'm not teasing, I know it's not easy—I read the *Alexiad*, that's right, the whole thing, what else am I supposed to do cooped up in this heat with only Shah kitty for company? And I can tell you this: Sebastian is cooking his data, he fabulates dreamily over this word, embroiders on this sentence, that allusion, and remakes Anna's history as he pleases to fit his own story. If that is not a fool for love, I don't know what is. And of course he erases everything that would cast the least shadow over his beautiful princess.

"Thus, he says, the incomparable intellectual, who supposedly only lived for the pleasures of the mind, was contemplating suicide and, says Sebastian, even wanted to retire to a convent out of disgust with politics; in fact, as I've told you, she really did try to get rid of her own brother, John, who was barring her from the throne. From the moment he was born there was no way for her to become sovereign, so it was useless to marry Constantine, you remember, the son of the mistress of her father, Marie of Alania. So, of course, the engagement between the two was broken, and the strong-headed young lady sent back to her mother and her precious studies. That's how being a woman sets you on a path to becoming a writer and a writer of history! Having John on the throne, a male heir and of Comnenan blood (unlike Constantine) was better than the alternate scenario imagined before his birth, even if he lacked his sister's mind and was, according to sources, somewhat agitated, incapable of controlling himself, and a shameful embarrassment to his family! It should be noted that in the *Alexiad* of his sister the future basileus only receives a few choice lines, believe me. Anna's ongoing plotting does not escape the attention of rival factions, but she herself does not back down from her project of assassinating her brother as soon as he took power, with the death of Alexius, in 1118 so as to place her husband Bryennius on the throne without the least effort on his part. Our female historian doesn't mention any of these elegant schemes in her book—you can easily guess that she would not be going to brag about them—and they don't at all get in Sebastian's way. That's how politics works, period, he thinks, and Anna's a politician. Besides, she makes up for it by writing her fifteen volumes that her brother, not really the vindictive type, lets her scribble away in her convent—books that would earn her a type of royalty far superior to the perishable political power that patriarchal customs had stolen from her."

Nordi was listening to her with one half of one ear while he caressed his cat Shah-Minoushah, who regularly snuggled on the commissioner's lap when his master "got back from his crimes," as he would say. The cat was of the other wordless world, an obscure animal, and the man loved to pass his hand like a hard comb over its three-color coat: white, chicory, and a reddish-orange stripe over the forehead. The teats on its white stomach no longer bore milk. Despite its advanced age, it was still active and jumpy, and its little strawberry-colored tongue lapped up whatever milk or meat was proposed like a gluttonous kitten.

The insistence with which women could talk on and on always struck the commissioner as something inexorably cruel, even in Stephanie's case. She was in the process of pulling apart Sebastian or Anna Comnena, or both, like an autopsy specialist who pokes his scalpel into the spleen, liver, duodenum, and prostate of his "clients" that have become immovable slabs of muscle, fat, and bone. This exercise was accomplished with the minute application of a lacemaker and not without a certain heated passion Rilsky had noticed whenever he overcame his natural revulsion and forced himself to contemplate these sorts of gruesome investigations. Stephanie seemed to behave in the same animated careful way, and the commissioner was suddenly afraid, as it seemed clear that his female friend could probe with the same smiling attention into the head of Shah-Minoushah; she could dissect its emerald eyes, white teats, cherry-velvet paws, and even take out one by one the little claws with which Minoushah was at that very moment poking and pricking the commissioner's knees.

Bizarrely, this absurd idea had the effect of rendering the tidal wave of words that Stephanie poured over him suddenly more interesting. It now made perfect sense that Sebastian had gone in search of this Byzantine princess among their ancestors. It didn't seem at all impossible this dream, this intense sensation of proximity, this osmosis between two bodies, two times, two destinies. It was the starting point of madness and crimes, as Rilsky well knew. He felt almost relieved. One of a kind, OK, but could he really be a serial killer, this bothersome uncle? Maybe. Speculations. But the proof—where is the proof, my dear harlequin romancer?

As Nordi looked suddenly rather more awake, Stephanie hit the pause button for only a second and then went back into play mode.

"You want more proof of Sebastian's passion? He changes things at will, and often to his own advantage, including on the subject of the princess's affections. Our scholar does not utter a word about the extraordinary and precocious attachment of Anna to Constantine, her little fiancé, whom she describes with the consummate elegance of a Greek lover. Listen to this, Nordi: 'He was charming, not only in his words but in his movements, and incomparably dextrous at games, as others who knew him then would also later say. He was blond and had skin as fair as milk, with a lively color in all the right places like a rose that was just beginning to open. His eyes were not light, but like those of a falcon, shining under eyebrows like a golden kitten's. His numerous charms were so fascinating to those who saw him that he seemed to be a beauty of heaven and not of earth. In short, to see him was to see a painting of Love.'

"You see, Nordi, how after a poem like this by the world's first female troubadour our little repudiated fiancée-for-a-day would write nothing on the death of her beloved Constantine. I don't think she ever got over this first love, what do you think? Sebastian will have nothing to do with him, and for good reason—he's the lover! And his hallucination tells him that Anna loves him as though *he* were Constantine the irreplaceable! What's more, he completely inverts the sense of Anna's words of praise for Nicephorus Bryennius, whom she marries in 1097 at age fourteen and glorifies in her chronicle much more than Constantine—as is only normal: she's a woman who has entered into the marriage contract and become the good noble wife. Her Nicephorus is therefore a marvel, even though the terms of praise are less Homeric and more responsible than the lyrical strains reserved for her 'golden kitten' Constantine.

"I grant you the marriage with the caesar Nicephorus may appear very strange. Why? Well, because this Nicephorus was the son of another Nicephorus Bryennius, an illustrious general defeated by Papa Alexius when he was still just a novice emperor. You see what I mean? The daughter of the conqueror married the son of the conquered in order to make peace between powerful families, yet again, and assure the succession of the Byzantine throne, in this case the throne of Anna's father, who will hold on to his daughter no matter what happens or what she does as his leading and most necessary servant, you see? How does the girl serve her father from birth? By submitting, like all women of her time and since, to the constraints of marriage, or, as I think, through her pen, which goes well beyond the reality of things and even of words? That is the question. Anna exploits these two possibilities, neither of which seems to bother her, because all signs seem to indicate that she too loved plotting. Yes, like Sebastian, I think that she enjoyed playing since she exhibits such enthusiasm for rhetoric, as one can see. Love of words was for her the one true passion that counted above all others and maybe even took their place. Listen to this: 'I was united by a legitimate marriage to Caesar Nicephorus, a man who, by the spark of his beauty, the superiority of his mind, and the perfection of his eloquence, far outdistanced his contemporaries. He was truly marvelous both to see and to hear. What harmony, what exquisite grace came through in every sentence of this caesar!'

"There's no need to smile. Those people knew what a couple was, unlike the liberated fellow you think you are, though as I get to know you . . . but we can talk about that later. Anyway, nothing prevents one from supposing that Anna was locked onto both Constantine and her husband, since in both cases she had the blessing of her father, don't you think? Bad luck though, sickness carries off the adored husband, a sickness 'caused by excessive fatigue due either to very frequent military operations or to his inexpressible sollicitude to *ourselves*.' So, 'overwhelming tears flood *our* eyes,' 'compassion' for this lost caesar is 'an infinite pain' that overtakes her like 'the smoke of furnace fire, a daily flame whose heat burns words . . . '

"Just a little purple prose, this royal compassion? What do you think, Nordi? Or a brainy memory of Euripides? Or a nice application of her trivium lessons, which our studious princess had learned to exercise since childhood? Probably, but so what? Words were things for Anna; she had taken over and completed the chronicles of her caesar husband, which most agree she outdid hands down. But here your uncle goes off the rails a little, I think. What a modern, decadent idea, what stupid resentment, when he attributes to our Byzantine princess the bitterness of modern feminism! According to his commentaries, Anna would have revolted against her husband and had contempt for his obvious mediocrity. He writes that she would have kept silent about this, out of respect for conventions, all the while taking her revenge on a less than satisfying companion (in all senses) by writing her own text! This reminds me of the supposed 'martyrdom' of Charlotte Brontë, a sacrificial victim of the Victorian egoism of her father Patrick, the misanthropic pastor, and—why not?—the incestuous alcoholism of her brother Branwell—Charlotte, who dies during her pregnancy, the poor female genius turned flag of melodramatic feminists through the writing of her own texts! Or Madame de Sévigné, imagined by the same partisans to have taken up her pen in protest against her pale husband, if not against the so desirable and so elusive libertine general, her cousin Bussy-Rabutin? Or Beauvoir writing against her macho, pissy, ugly anti-Semite Sartre (sure, not possible?—everything's possible that crosses your mind!), and who was it then who wrote *Being and Nothingness* or *Nausea*? Come on, come on, this vision of history is not so out of line with ideas professed at the University of Santa Varvara and elsewhere, and I can understand how Sebastian was not able to pass them up. But the pages that he wrote afterward suggest a revery that is much more personal than this politically correct echo of feminist-oriented courses taught by other departments down the hall from his lab. His passion, his fantasy leads him, get this, to alter Anna's genealogy!"

"Interesting," Nordi mumbles. "Continue. The unloved bastard, the extra son of papa Chrest would then have never gotten over his own past? Listen, Minoushah, listen please, this story won't harm us, neither you or me. On the contrary, don't you think? To me it's evocative, it gives me ideas. So, you were saying, Stephanie?"

"Wow, Nor, I forgot how much you like Shah-Minoushah! No, it's not an insult, I adore her too, except I bug her, with me she breaks vases, now where was I? You've not forgotten, dear, that we now have two cases to solve: Number Eight and Sebastian, and so, at the risk of boring you . . . OK, here goes. Anna Comnena was, by her mother Irene, a Ducas; that is, of the illustrious family identified with a certain Michael Ducas, duke of Dyrrachium, then duke of the navy, and our historian does not hesitate to sing the praises of "my maternal uncle" in book 5. But he's not the one who interests us here. The richest of them all was John Ducas, Irene's grandfather, brother of the emperor Constantine X Ducas. The Ducas family plotted first against the Comnenus family before joining forces with them, a typical Byzantine story that doesn't concern us except that Sebastian invents something here. It is one of his inventions I'm sure, I was able to confirm this with the meager knowledge I've picked up from cross-checking in Anna's own book—you know, when I get into it, none of this Byzantine stuff can hold me back! So he pretends, get this, that the son of this filthy rich John Ducas, one Andronicus Ducas—in other words, Anna's grandfather—married a noble Bulgarian, Maria of Bulgaria, who would therefore be Irene's mother and Anna's grandmother. Got that? Let me remind you that at the time, we're talking 1096–1097, after complicated wars between the two countries that don't need to concern us either, the Bulgarian kingdom is nothing more than a Byzantine province. Maria of Bulgaria is a rich landowner, a voluptuous and simple beauty, more peasant than aristocrat. She puts up with the escapades of her husband Andronicus who plays Don Juan around Lake Ohrid where she resides in an old manor house left to her by her Bulgarian family and is interested mostly in money and a pagan cult of nature far removed from Hellenic refinement. Given all that, you can understand that no one is rushing to welcome Maria to Constantinople, in fact she's never invited to imperial receptions, her wheat-scented perfume and heavy laugh are thought ridiculous. Her type just would not fit in! The mother of the empress Irene was supposed to just stay on her estate and hand over her daughter's dowry, said to have been considerable, at the time of the marriage between Irene and Alexius. It was of course necessary that this significant stream of money continue to arrive with little or no show of thanks or courtesy.

"But now here is Princess Anna, the superb adolescent whose whims include running around the capital with poets and other writers of questionable morals. Anna begins to fall apart, according to Sebastian. Since the death of her golden kitten Constantine, the dark gaze of the princess is covered with tears, and her face becomes more sallow every day. 'It's her age,' says Italos, the palace doctor, but Irene doesn't believe it. The pious mother comes to meals every day with the works of Maximus the Confessor under her arm, but that no longer interests Anna, who at one time used to adore theological discussions. The adolescent girl has given up all her outside interests and is now turning her mind inward. Irene thinks that her little one is contemplating her blood, her stomach, and the nothingness that is deepening within her. Anna is said to have admitted to Zoe in strictest confidence that she was ready to enter orders, and the nurse apparently repeated this to the girl's mother. So, as a last resort before consigning this body over to God, they would send Anna to vist her grandmother, Maria of Bulgaria—there she could get some fresh air and discover nature. After all, there is more to life than the world of parchments within the patriarchal library where the princess had been agreeably going moldy from the age of thirteen. A compromise for sure, perhaps even a strategic error, this idea of allowing Anna to go over the river and through the woods to the peasant grandmother's house as a nice distraction before imposing on her a daughterly destiny in conformity with furthering the affairs of her father.

"So what? you ask. Well, there's no trace of this trip to Ohrid in the *Alexiad*! I don't think so; anyway, I've not read every word of it, but, if I remember correctly, Sebastian cites a Bulgarian historian, a certain Vera M., who recently proved that this trip of Anna's to see her grandmother did really happen—at least your nephew has convinced me to go along with his idea, and things are far from simple when it comes to these details, as you shall see. Our runaway scholar claims that at Ohrid Anna Comnena met, get this, his own ancestor! That's right, his and your great-great-great . . . grandfather, can you believe it? Forget Constantine! Round file Nicephorus! Long live the noble knights!—or at least one of them, a crusader unlike all the rest, the one whom Sebastian is pleased to claim as his ancestor. Hold on a second and you'll understand.

"Do you remember Hugues de France? The count of Vermandois and the younger brother of King Philip I of France, who was denounced by the pope for abandoning his wife and carrying off another man's, is blocked from joining the Crusade. Therefore, Hugh of France becomes the leader of a group of barons who set out on the route leading to the Byzantine capital at the very moment when Peter the Hermit's men have camped outside the walls of Constantinople. Hugh goes through Italy, traverses Rome where he receives the banner of Saint Peter, then reorganizes in Bari, for his crossing of the Adriatic, but gets caught in a terrible storm and only after great difficulty does he arrive on the Byzantine coast in the area of Dyrrachium or Durazzo (present-day Durrës in Albania) sometime in October 1096. The Byzantine governor of the city, John Comnenus, nephew of the basileus and Anna's cousin, welcomes him with a semblance of the honor to be shown an ally against the Seljuk Turks. Curiously, however, these Byzantines, like Ulysses, seem always to have an extra card up their sleeves to outdo these upstart Latins! John Comnenus sends Hugh to Constantinople, but via an oddly circuitous path and under the close supervision of a Byzantine escort that has him pass through Ohrid and even further north through Philippopolis! As one might expect, Anna's *Alexiad* does not fail to mention the clownish arrival of these Frankish knights, more bragging barbarians than distinguished and courageous noblemen. Indeed, her account is so condescending toward the poor Hugh, whom she calls Ubos, that Sebastian thinks it can only be a smokescreen that hides—guess what? I'll tell you what, a love story!

"Yes, so it seems Maria of Bulgaria, in charge of entertaining her granddaughter, takes advantage of all opportunities, of which there are many in this heavily traveled area, to have the girl presented to any noble knights passing through. The region was in total confusion because of the diverse contingents of the First Crusade who were more or less following their intended routes with detours here and there to acquire food and supplies. Imagine the situation: before these mighty barons there had been Walter the Penniless, who descended from the north and passed through Hungary, crossed the Danube, then the Sava, marched on Belgrade and Nish, then toward Philippopolis. Peter the Hermit had joined him after having burned the mills around Sofia, on July 12, 1096—Sebastian discovered the exact date. Soon after the barons of France led by Hugh, Godfrey of Bouillon also arrives from the north, crossing Hungary, then Nish, Sofia, Philippopolis, Adrianople, always in the direction of Constantinople. Bohemond of Otranto arrives a little later via Italy, traverses Rome, also organizes ships and supplies at Bari and eventually arrives somewhere between Avlona and Dyrrachium with the two Roberts—Robert of Normandy and Robert of Flanders. Some go through Brindisi and head toward Vodena and Thessalonika.

"Look, I've traced the routes, are you following, Nordi?" She is leaning over them, serious, didactic, passionate. "Can you imagine this massive debarkation and wave of overland movement? Anna speaks of ten thousand knights and sixty thousand infantrymen, and even if these numbers are ex-

The double line indicates the route of Godfrey of Bouillon.
The dotted line indicates the route of Raymond de Toulouse.
The line of dashes represents the route of the two Roberts (of Flanders and Normandy).
The solid line is the route of Bohemond I of Taranto.
The bold line shows the altered route of Hugues de France.

aggerated one can easily imagine the Byzantine functionaries overwhelmed and unable to feed and care for so many troops.

"What's more, remember that a large number of the pilgrims are far from kind toward heretics such as the Paulicians, for example, and they think nothing of burning their city on the banks of the Vardar River. Remember also that on their side the local population typically refused to sell food or furnish guides to the outsiders. Even though the majority continue to make progress to Constantinople with the hope of eventually reaching the Holy Sepulchre in Jerusalem, some knights and their attendants begin to get discouraged, hesitate about pushing on, or turn into outlaws. Some, disillusioned by the difficulty of the expedition, as well as by the skepticism and sometimes outright resistance of the eastern Christians, finally come to the realization that these Byzantines are quite different from people in western Christendom. Not only are they richer than had been imagined, but they aren't easily pushed around. They're suspicious, proud, and often hostile toward these conceited Latin barons who don't even know how to read. Other crusaders allow themselves to be seduced by a way of life that is more refined than their own, one that mixes peasant simplicity and theological disputes within a complex hierarchy whose opulence and intrigues are to their liking and one that is ready to convert barbarians who've come from faraway into salaried vassals of the autocrator. Alexius had only asked Urban II for competent and obedient mercenaries, not these pretentious hotheads who had set out on a holy war toward Jerusalem with the secret intention of taking over Byzantium!

"Are you all right, you two? Yes . . . you and Shah-Minoushah are kindly invited to tune back in to the tale of our sad little princess and Maria of Bulgaria. One more word about the history of Maria. Anna's grandmother remembered that Byzantium had assassinated her ancestors barely a century before, not to mention the gruesome murders the Byzantine noblemen carried out among each other as though for sport, all the while organizing marriages between enemies all across Porphyria. Go figure! Byzantium, the region's leading producer of perfidy! Maria's family line went back to Aron, the brother of the great czar Samuil, a Bulgarian whose eldest daughter eventually married a Comnenus, a paternal uncle of Alexius I, a certain Isaac Comnenus, the brother of Alexius's father John. There is no doubt about any of that. Am I confusing you? I'm just trying to point out how the Porphyrian genealogy was also a skillful mosaic of wars and weddings between nobles and invaders, Greeks and Slavs, proud lines and insolent neighbors. It had to be that way. The dynasty of Samuil extended from the Danube to Thessaly and the Adriatic, and therefore, as this vast outback of its great Byzantine neighbor, it threatened the reign of Basil II himself, the greatest sovereign of the Macedonian dynasty. Was Samuil so powerful and so dangerous that Basil had to deploy the barbaric cruelty all of the peasants around Maria still feared? After many battles the Byzantine leader won a decisive victory at the pass of Kleidion (Belasitsa) on the Strymon River in July 1014, taking over fifteen thousand of Maria's compatriots as prisoners. Fine, but why have all their eyes been gouged out with the exception of a hundred and fifty who will be spared one eye each and ordered to lead the rest of their comrades back to Samuil? The latter dies of sorrow and shame at the sight of the Byzantine spectacle of these blinded troops, and ever since that day these sinister events have been retold to generation after generation of Bulgarian children.

"At the very name Bulgaroktonus (the Bulgar slayer) Maria herself can only cry; her heart turns to ice; her eyes empty—it's the blindness inflicted by the pitiless Basil: the humiliated cannot see. But the eyes, oh, the eyes, this is the key to Byzantium! So many debates about the visible and the invisible, about making images or not making images, you know. Maria is too much of a peasant to follow any of that, but she knows that in Constantinople the people are crazy about seeing and being seen, while others claim that the invisible can only be felt, that one must only inhale it, taste it with the heart by immersing first one's face and eventually one's whole body, just as one embraces an icon, for example. You are devoured by eyes in Byzantium. Look, my granddaughter Anna, at the piercing eyes of the scholarly books that devour you! Do they go as far as the invisible? Perhaps not. She knows all, this child, except about inhaling, eating, sensing. Not really, not yet; we shall see one day. Byzantium may have blinded Samuil's soldiers, but the eyes remain, eyes that live in the look of Anna, the unlikely witness Anna, above all others. The eyes of a Byzantine, you will tell me, but what do we know . . . about eyes?

ANNA COMNENA, A BRIEF TIME LINE

December 1, 1083:	Born in the "Purple Room" in Constantinople. Engagement to Constantine Ducas a few days later.
1088:	Birth of younger brother John II Comnenus to whom the rights of succession are transferred. The birth of this male heir causes Anna's engagement to Constantine Ducas to be dissolved.
1097:	After the death of Constantine, marriage to Nicephorus Bryennius.
1118:	Death of her father, Alexius I Comnenus. Anna falls into disgrace after a failed attempt to dethrone her brother John.
1138:	Death of Nicephorus Bryennius. Anna begins the *Alexiad*.
1148:	Living in modest retirement, Anna completes the *Alexiad*, a bittersweet conclusion of a life that had shown much promise.

"Are you listening to me, Nordi, or are you contemplating Minoushah's eyes? I am speaking, but I can still see you, so watch out! Shall I continue? So, as I was saying, the loyal but nonetheless bitter mother-in-law of Alexius, Maria of Bulgaria, surrounded herself with scholars and extravagant priests who flirted with the Bogomil heresy, if they didn't outright support it, and their curiosity led them to welcome the most commendable of the knights errant within their territory. Some of these foreign barons were accorded some provisions, and the cleanest among them and those with some semblance of manners were even welcomed at table, with interpreters providing a running translation since very few of the foreign guests could speak Greek. Now and then a cleric passed by, it's the spring of 1097, when there suddenly emerges this young Ebrard de Pagan, an early scout within the ranks of the Count of Toulouse.

"Ebrard de Pagan, also known as Ebrard de Payns, preceded the armies of Saint-Gilles. Or more precisely of his uncle, Adhémar de Monteil, the papal legate who was supposed to accompany the French of Languedoc. You remember, don't you? OK, let me remind you then. Raymond IV de Saint-Gilles claimed the cross at the Council of Clermont in November 1095. After lengthy preparations he departs only in October 1096 with his wife Elvire d'Aragon, who had participated in the holy wars against Muslims in Spain, and his youngest son Alphonse; the eldest, Bertrand, being charged with tending the home fires back in Toulouse. They cross the Alps at the Montgenèvre col and traverse northern Italy until they reach the Gulf of Trieste. They then follow the coast east via Istrie and Dalmatia. The Dalmatian road is poor, the population is hostile and rough, the Languedoc troops prove to be highly undisciplined and as a result it takes them forty days during which they must endure famine, the Petchenegue escort, as well as the antagonisms of John Comnenus, their hypocritical host, before they finally arrive, severely worn out, in 1097.

"Our scout was a timid young man. Ebrard could speak Latin as well as his native tongue and Anna's language. That at least is what Sebastian believes. A blond beauty with an athletic build and a fluid tongue—like honey, says Maria. The traveler seems not to have been indifferent to the somber adolescent Anna, who, for her part, seems finally to have been interested in one of the many distinguished visitors whom her grandmother would introduce, up until then without success. It did not escape Maria's notice that her young relation remained in the company of this young cleric instead of running off to contemplate in solitude the shores of Lake Ohrid or to reread her favorite passages of Homer in the privacy of her own room.

"It's as though the scene took place yesterday on the country estate of Maria of Bulgaria; Sebastian reshoots the whole scene. Are you with me, Nordi?"

Priests and bishops do not carry sabers in our land; they are men of faith. I do not shock you in saying this, I hope? The ebony eyes of the Byzantine princess intend to be fiery toward these Latins, but Ebrard sees in them a provocative softness or at least an invitation to further conversation.

In our land, in Auvergne, this began with the peace of God. A curious peace, I grant you, because the councils, such as that of Le Puy in the last century, permitted the bishops to arm themselves to protect the treasures of the church that had been ransacked by warlords, but also obliged them to defend the people without arms, the *inermes*, against the violence of knights, the *milites*. When you say that the bishops attempt to replace the weakened royal power, do you think they are wrong? Grant me on your side that one may view these things differently. The right to make war was requested by peace assemblies composed of both lords and the people. From that point the war was sanctified, but only to the extent that it protected the church and the poor from pirating knights such as those who had carried out the earlier pillaging. Without this peace of God accorded in this way, we Occidentals never would have crusaded to help you combat the impious, do you understand? (Did Ebrard's long lesson risk boring Anna? She allowed herself to be seduced by the foreigner's words that spoke of other customs. And by that hungry mouth, a rosebud surrounded by the blond beard of the traveler.)

That is what I meant, knight. War has become sacred for you, just as the jihad is for the Muslims. But then, what difference is there between your barons who invade our lands, threatening our capital while claiming that they are here to deliver Jerusalem—an outcome we hope for, believe me—and these anti-Christs, descendants of Abraham and Agar, the Islamists, the product of the bile of Sodom and the bitterness of Gomorrah? (Anna was getting worked up. Although young, she was not ignorant of the large numbers of Allah's followers who threatened her father's borders. She had read John of Damascus, who condemned the Muslims as pagans and false prophets, and John Kameniates, who had witnessed massacres and Islamic-sponsored pillaging of neighboring Byzantine cities such as Thessalonika, and *The Life of Saint Andrew the Fool*, which classified as Evil the perverse religion of the sons of Ishmael. Sebastian had no doubt that Anna had read all of these texts, and it was precisely because she read too much that her mother had sent her to Ohrid in the first place and also why her poor grandmother couldn't make heads or tails of the girl.)

"Under the stone arches of this comfortable and reassuring rustic citadel, the glimmering light from torches and candles gave a golden orange color to the cheeks of the daughter of Alexius, and Ebrard wondered how he could agree with her without shutting down their exchange. The Saracens were pagans, heretics, and impious, there was no doubt about it. However, the French peace of God was not only about the right to kill, whether as priest or bishop, with the aim of reversing the fateful course of history by which God punished Christendom by sending forth the Muslim apocalypse. On the contrary, and Adhémar had transmitted to his nephew Ebrard the eschatological meaning of this peace of God: it was God's cease-fire that was to suspend vengeance whenever necessary. Was not the original doctrine of Christ's teaching and of the early church the affirmation that in the beginning was love? In Christianity, said the bishop, holy war is not fundamental . . . as is the jihad for the Muslims, added Ebrard. We must go back to the wars of the eternal one spoken of in the Old Testament, but to use these arguments to construct a new attitude. Is the Crusade to reconquer a holy war, as our Pope Urban II affirms; an extension of the peace of God that we introduced in France? Or must it be taken as an act of love, and if so, how? That is the problem. A real torment for men such as Adhémar and Ebrard, the princess was sure. However, if Ebrard had given in to this doubt, would he have committed himself to the Crusade? But if he had not, he would not have had the chance to meet her, Anna Comnena, that evening, in the home of her grandmother, God bless her house!

"This Latin lacked the elegance of Bosporus courtiers, Anna remarked, but his words seemed so sincere, so honest, that an unknown trouble slid into the mind of the Byzantine girl, made her blush, and she interrupted their conversation.

"Safe journey to you, knight! Think about this though: true servants of Yahweh are not warriors; reread your Bible more closely. Leave fighting to the military and to politicians; they like to live in the impure and nourish themselves on it with gusto, I can assure you. Goodnight!" She stood and adjusted the diadem on her forehead, not to make up for her small height but to mark the superiority of her Orthodox faith.

"Until we meet again, princess." Ebrard was only able to murmer these hopeful words long after Anna followed her grandmother out of the room.

"Now listen closely to this, Nordi. It also sounds like it happened yesterday on the shores of the lake:

"Early March 1097, here the sun is as warm as in May, just enough to smooth the water into a mirror and invite the swallows to skim its surface with their wings and so quench their thirst after their winter migration. Anna has exchanged the Indian silk tunics of red, mauve, and gold typical of the Comnenan palace for a white peasant shirt of simple embroidered cloth. Who will criticize her for this? Not her faithful Zoe who tirelessly chaperones her, nor the very physical Maria, and certainly not the aged Radomir, the fisherman who serves the grandmother and views the world exclusively through the eyes of his lady.

"No one in Constantinople would believe Anna if she told her noble entourage that she had spent time on board Radomir's fishing boat, had listened to his heresies, which were rather amusing actually because he claimed he was a Bogomil, "loved by God" in his Slavic language. This peasant also claimed that Good and Evil had an equal share in the Creation, that women were creatures equal to men in certain circumstances (a logical consequence of the preceding principle), without specifying which ones, something that first made her chuckle and then saddened her. Or that she had breathed the salty odor of carp and trout—called here korans!—wriggling still in Radomir's nets, and tasted their tender flesh, a taste unknown on the banks of the Bosporus. Or that she had even touched them, sliding mercury, the visible entrails of the sea, flexible and fleeting between her fingers, in time to her laughter. That Anna had wanted to do as the korans do, and that she had laid on the water in her white embroidered shirt as Radomir's boat approached the shore, the new cotton sticking to her skin tight around her breasts and buttocks, a heat never before experienced streaming between her legs.

"With the water, only Helios, the son of Hyperion, was witness to her, and he closed the eyes of other humans, curved them inward, invisible pleasure, 'Two eagles sent by large-voiced Zeus arrived, diving down from the top of the mountain. First, riding the wind, they flew forwards, side by side, flapping their large wings. Soon, however, above the cries that pierced the blue sky from who knows where, they banked suddenly in a few hurried flaps and their gaze downward at the heads of all seemed to be sending death. Then, skimming the mountain face and the col with their claws, they flew off to the right, above the houses of the upper village. Everyone's eyes followed this terrible omen. All wondered in chorus what would follow.' The verses of the old blind man filled Anna's spirit while Athena, the goddess with sea-green eyes like an ocean fish, caressed her breasts, stomach, and pubic area.

"Zoe, Radomir, and other servants, who were waiting behind pine-covered rocks, were right to cry out with abandon. Anna righted herself in the water and saw, not far from the shore, a small group of foreign soldiers, Frankish crusaders certainly. Some of their rather courteous leaders had been welcomed just the night before. But no, these disheveled men were only thieves, dirty and evidently famished, who wanted the food and gold coins of the careless picnickers. Once again Anna regretted not being a man, even if it was always repeated that she resembled her father. No one had ever taught her how to fight—why was that, holy Virgin mother of the Word, why not draw one's saber and stab the enemy, face death like her father did, and as poor John was being taught to do? No, Anna feared neither barbarians nor suicide. Since breaking off her engagement with Constantine, was her young life not already a sort of death, a life beyond life? But for the first time since her body had discovered the water, the earth, the swallows, and the korans, Anna was ashamed of her breasts and her hardened nipples outlined under the wet cotton, as foreboding as the eagles of Homer, and of her long loose hair, and of her naked arms and feet. The Latin barbarians advanced. Anna did not retreat. Zoe gave out one more strident, witchlike cry to invoke who knows what magic power of Zeus or the Savior, perhaps of both. Anna implored both, too, when she was very afraid. The bandits hesitated but still advanced, slowly, black with rage. Anna saw no more, she slid and collapsed in the warm, shallow water—no, it wasn't her marble bathtub in the palace—she fell into another world, the end of the world. Evil is as powerful as Good, what good is it to be a woman, just as well to finish in this way as another, what did it matter!

"When she opened her eyes she found herself in the arms of Ebrard. The young knight in the army of the Count of Toulouse, this cleric in the service of his uncle, the prelate Adhémar, whom he had preceded in his perilous traverse of the Balkans, had not slept at all the night before. After having left the country house of Maria of Bulgaria, he waited until dawn with his horse. He knew that pillagers crept out of his camp in the early hours to attack the local population. Ebrard was determined to pursue them. Unless it was that he had already noticed the bather, offered like Aphrodite to his timid curiosity these past seven days, and wanted to see again her body after having heard her sweet words? Sebastian hesitated about which script to follow.

"They could not have had a worse meeting. A modest nobleman from Auvergne would never have dared to come so close to the daughter of the basileus. To have his wet arms around her neck, her mouth next to his male skin murmuring 'papa,' her fishlike body coming out of its torpor and curling against his body with all its force. This accidental rescue eliminated the possibility of seeing her again on simple terms as he had done the night before when he looked into her eyes and spoke with her at her grandmother's home. Anna looks at him. The young man sees in her eyes the reflection of his own gaze of pleasure and fright. How long does it last: two seconds, two hours? It does not cease from that moment on. He sets her down softly on the ground, and Anna does not turn away her bright eyes, admired by the whole court, from the tanned foreign face under its mop of straw hair, from the broad shoulders unadorned with armor and dripping with water that carried her out of the blue lake and through the blue air. Then she does turn away and feels the tears pouring over her cheeks and onto the hands of Zoe, who hurries to dress her in a long dry gown.

"Ebrard waves from a distance. He is already departing on his horse. He was never seen again. Some believe that he rejoined Radomir, that he wandered for some weeks with him and the Bogomils around Lake Ohrid, and that he later reunited with his uncle in Thessalonika. The prelate was convalescing there from a wound sustained in fighting against the Petchenegues, Byzantine mercenaries whom he had encountered when he left his route in hopes of understanding and establishing peace with these foreign communities. Ebrard Pagan asked to be freed from his responsabilities with the uncle's pardon and blessing. Ebrard felt he no longer had the heart of a crusader, he did not have the drive to continue on to Constantinople, Antioch, and Jerusalem. All the more since, without the moderating influence of the wounded bishop, the Toulouse army was already rampaging through the towns and villages of Thrace crying, "Toulouse, Toulouse!" with the intention of arriving at Constantinople for the start of holy week on April 21, 1097. Ebrard did not see himself continuing in that direction. He could no longer see himself in that role at all.

"Rumors of massacres committed by the crusaders all along their route were already circulating. No, Radomir knew no more about the brutality of the Saint-Gilles soldiers than what Ebrard had been able to see with his own eyes. But Radomir had heard it said that some trembled with horror at the sound of the name of Count Emich of Leisingen, who boasted of having a cross miraculously impressed on his skin and had attacked Jews far away in Spire, Worms, Prague, and Volkmar. A thousand Jews massacred at Mayence, the synagogue at Cologne torched. All this happened in the spring and early summer of 1096, as I've told you. The unhappy victims in Cologne took refuge in the cathedral, and the archbishop seized the opportunity to convert them, but the leading rabbi grabbed a knife and threw himself on his host. Radomir took a sinister pleasure in repeating these atrocities. 'I'm mispronouncing the names of your cities, you will excuse me, but, you see, you crusaders ... ' No, Ebrard was unable to follow his uncle's men to Jerusalem. He had been misunderstood. He had not understood. The handsome cleric broke ranks with his own men and was never heard from again.

"The defection of his nephew weakened Adhémar. Thus deprived of a loyal family member and a rare confidant among this crowd of superstitious knights who could speak of nothing but holy war, the bishop of Le Puy died prematurely, very shortly after having recovered the Holy Lance at Antioch, either of the plague or of a dagger wound inflicted by a hotheaded crusader, no one is sure which.

"The impression of Anna's body rested forever on Ebrard's chest, like an invisible, intimate covering over the cross sewn onto his clothes, which, despite everything, he never stopped wearing. But he had retreated far inside this cross, within the hug of the fainted princess. Cold caress, burning fish ιχθυς, an anagram of Christos, the mystical emblem of the Savior. Ebrard became a missing person among his troops. No one ever saw him again. Since that time, since the scene that took place only yesterday from Sebastian's perspective . . ."

Basil the Bogomil: The Continuation and Conclusion of Anna's Story ☙

"And Anna? Nothing. She doesn't say a word to anybody, ever. Only Zoe and Radomir knew, but they also keep the secret. You could say it stayed an absolute secret. Her body, which was suddenly opened to Ebrard in the waters of Lake Ohrid, closes again forever. Her eight children, of which only four survived, merely passed through her dried-up body. She no longer dressed in white cotton or linen, nor ever went bathing in open waters. She put her blood-colored brocades back on and responded without delay to the messenger sent by her parents who urgently requested her return to the capital. To marry her off, of course! And right away, by her birthday, December 1. At fourteen a young woman of her rank can wait no longer, especially when the Comnenus family is in need of trustworthy allies such as the Bryennius family. We the winners will make peace with the family of the losers. In short, you are destined to become the wife of Nicephorus, the Bryennius son, a military man, of course, and exactly what your father needs. Anna put up no opposition, it was unthinkable that she do so, the Holy Virgin keep us! Anna did not even consider it. She was thinking of smooth-skinned korans and of Ebrard de Pagan, but no one knew it, including her. She did her duty by marrying, then by writing for all eternity. The rest is her own affair, deep in her own guts, in the moisture between her legs, in the hardness at the tips of her breasts, in the rose of roses. Who was he, this Ebrard de Pagan? A man, a crusader, a messenger of Christ or of Apollo? She, Anna, is a great intellectual, and only that, a sealed woman that future generations will never know how to break open.

"As you can guess, Nordi, Anna's story is nothing but Sebastian's story. Do you believe me now when I tell you that he is in love with Anna Comnena? He's a dangerous man, you must understand. He's pursuing a dream, he's in love with love, and everything else, and I mean EVERYTHING, can only disappoint him. What can this exalted figure that no reality could satisfy possibly do? He runs away, he commits suicide, he 'crosses' himself and embarks on a holy war, becomes a terrorist, a fundamentalist, a kamikaze? You can see I don't have the answer, but a murderous path is open before him, for him, and we have only to follow him in order to come upon it. Love turns to crime. Don't object, you will see—I can sense it—call it intuition. 'Stephanie our leading detective,' isn't that what you've said yourself?"

"Hmmm. Hmmm."

Nordi falls silent, but his thoughts are still following the Anna-Stephanie-Sebastian stream of consciousness, the princess got him hooked on her story even if the commissioner still has no idea how any of it could be put to use. Get Popov and the whole department working on this lead? But what *is* the lead, for crying out loud? What's the outcome of this Crusade or of this professor's disappearance? Shah-Minoushah has been asleep for some time; she has nothing better to do. But not Rilsky, who needs to decide what case he is going to make to Interpol and why. What is he going to say to Foulques Weil, who recently asked again for news of the serial killer? In Paris they're asking questions; they're always asking questions in Paris about stuff that is none of their business.

These are matters that Stephanie doesn't have to think about, obviously. She's content to build her card castle chronicle of Anna out loud; this young person always needs to be telling a story, even during a heat wave; it's rather charming, isn't it Minoushah?

The cat purrs, rolling its r's. Minoushah has a Slavic accent when she is sleeping soundly.

"Of course, Anna does not say a word about this meeting with your supposed ancestor in her *Alexiad*. This does not prove the meeting did not take place. Sebastian is right about that. Anna does not relate everything, and her silence is not simply ignorance. Vicious, politically savvy, and engaged, the *Alexiad* is clearly her propaganda outlet. Do you want examples? Here is one of the worst. She seems not to take into account Pope Urban II's role in the Crusade. Doesn't she write that these Latins, who for a long time have been eager to take control of the Roman Empire, and then the Byzantine Empire, wanted to seize it 'thanks to the pretext offered by the sermon of Peter the Hermit'? *Exit* the pope, Porphyrian orthodoxy requires it! She also says that the Latins, who are under the pressure of famine and a continuous blockade 'came to consider Peter their bishop.' She stubbornly refuses to mention Adhémar and always ascribes the spiritual authority of these greedy and brusquely violent crusaders possessed by a 'folly worse than Herod's' to Peter—who is perhaps the 'Coucoupêtre' that made Voltaire laugh. Then there's the Provençal cleric Pierre Barthélemy who intervenes in the matter of the Holy Lance. He'd be called a loony today and was already in his own day, quite the opposite of the clear-sighted Adhémar, and quite incapable of speaking to the pillagers as Anna claims he did: 'You promised to remain pure until your arrival in Jerusalem, and you have, I believe, gone against your word. You ought then to turn to the Lord and cry out your mistakes day and night, and demonstrate your repentance with hot tears and vigils devoted to regaining God's favor.' Only Adhémar de Monteil could have lectured his soldiers in that way, but he is never mentioned by the Byzantine historian. Does she intentionally forget him because of Ebrard, his nephew, his messenger to the waters of Lake Ohrid?"

Here the novel must be interrupted by clear-eyed reason, and, why not, by the eye of the police commissioner of Santa Varvara.

"Hold on there one second, Stephanie. You, or you and Sebastian, want to make me believe that at the time there was a church opposed to the holy war of the Church?" In truth, Rilsky could care less about the theological debates of the Crusade-era Church or any other. His only concern was this double-sided portrait of Sebastian put forward by Stephanie: on one side a hopeless romantic whose love translates as a "crusade" on behalf of a nine-hundred-year-old woman writer and on the other a dark runaway murderer, why not the serial killer himself? The commissioner will say nothing for the moment, he will simply file this possible lead within his revery with Shah who has always led him in all essential matters. He will allow other superficial possibilities to circulate. For instance, he will let Stephanie believe that Anna's story and Sebastian's story and Stephanie's story interest him, Police Commissioner Rilsky, passionately, and leave no doubt about that. He's already thought up one of his comeback lines: that Stephanie underestimates his erudite side as an intellectual cop. He'll then play the professor himself a bit, then he'll. . . . "It seems that specialists have established that there are more and more massacres of Jews starting with the First Crusade, you yourself alluded to them. It's not my field, but this seems like the mother of all holy wars! Isn't our dear departed professor trying all available means to get away with something, and why not by making up a love story?"

"Don't believe it. Sebastian is also conducting a real research project. An honest one, I mean. He also uncovered the Jew hunts starting with the First Crusade, and do you know how? It's all recorded in his computer files. *Primo:* Yahweh's faithful in Orléans, pushed by the devil, supposedly bribed with money a fugitive serf of some convent or other and sent him to the Fatimid sultan in Cairo carrying a letter written in Hebrew! This letter warns the powerful Al-Hakim of the imminent threat of invasion of his country by Christians and counsels him to demolish their "venerable house," the Holy Sepulchre itself! Al-Hakim does it without having to be asked twice. In other words, it's the Jews who manipulated the Muslims who destroyed Christ's tomb and thus provoked the Crusade! This rumor supposedly circulated from the very beginning, Sebastian has proof. *Secundo*: at the time of the presumed encounter between Anna and Ebrard, in 1096 or thereabouts, Pope Urban II—assuming it was he, there is still some doubt, according to Sebastian—but anyway, this pope calls on God's aid in attacking and killing the Agarians: 'We will be victorious as in the days of Titus and Vespasian who avenged the death of the Son of God. After their victory, they received the honor of the Roman Empire and received pardon (*indulgentiam*) for their sins. And we, if we act in the same way, will without a doubt receive eternal Life.' Translation: these pagan Roman emperors were, if not exactly baptized into the Christian faith, at least pardoned in its eyes because they massacred Jews, which for the Christians of the day was a good way to avenge Christ. Conclusion: we, crusaders, must do the same! Jeez, don't look at me like that, you think that Sebastian is out of his mind, OK. But before becoming infatuated with the princess, your uncle does try to see things from all sides, you understand? He even recopies the chronicles of Shlomo bar Simeon and Eliezer bar Nathan . . . wait a second while I find the pages, here, I've got it . . . these guys didn't mince their words back in the twelfth century: 'The pope of infamous Rome, having launched a call to march on Jerusalem, raised a spontaneous and formidable horde of French and German volunteers to set off for Jerusalem to the tomb of the hung bastard (here: *sic!*—it's Sebastian's underlining). The following call is put out: He who kills a Jew will have all his sins forgiven.' You see! Let me continue: 'They affixed on their garments a most visible sign, a cross. Satan came and mingled among them all, they who were more numerous than the grains of sand on the shore or the number of locusts covering the surface of the planet.' In the margin Sebastian writes, 'Same remark in Anna's text!' Do I need to spell it out to you? He's a nervous one, this Chrest-Jones; he's a researcher. And just because he bugs you is no reason to underestimate him, believe me.

"That seems twisted to you? But you can clearly see that our Sebastian is far from pardoning the medieval Church for an anti-Semitism that did not exactly go by that name at the time. But if the name wasn't there, the deeds certainly were. I've already told you that according to Sebastian Ebrard himself supposedly knew of this behavior. Did Adhémar and Ebrard share these obsessions and conspiracy theories? There is nothing to prove they did not oppose them, nor that they did. What we do know, though, is that the prelate from Le Puy-en-Velay, a moderate on other points, does not follow the fashionable belief in miracles and other apparitions that push the crusaders to exterminate the miscreants; and he even dares to question the revelation made by Pierre Barthélemy on the subject of the Holy Lance. The chronicles of the time say that for his doubt he will be passing some days in hell after his death!

"There is no mention of Adhémar in Anna's text, as I've already said, and I share the surprise of Sebastian on this. This huge omission does not fit the overall picture of the extremely well-informed scholar that she was. Even if there's an Orthodox caution when it comes to the subject of the Vatican, why remain silent on the subject of this papal messenger? Because of Ebrard who must be discreetly erased, effaced from the glorious world in which the princess is establishing the personal glory of her father and of course her own, no? She can, however, not keep out of her *Alexiad* a portrait of Raymond de Saint-Gilles, the count of Toulouse, who accompanied Adhémar and Ebrard. According to Sebastian, Anna would have crossed them all and their troops forty years earlier at the home of her grandmother, Maria, the same troops who then swarmed toward Philippopolis—don't forget that name, I'll come back to it, you'll see. All this took place before Raymond de Saint-Gilles returns to Constantinople, participates in the siege at Nicaea, receives the Holy Lance, assaults Damascus and Tripoli, is asked to be King of Jerusalem, etc.

"Anna calls Saint-Gilles 'Isangeles,' and while saying nothing about Adhémar, you'll see that our author embroiders elaborate praise for this distinguished Toulousian whom Ebrard served: 'The Autocrator favored Isangeles because of the superiority of his mind, the uprightness of his heart, and the purity of his life. Also because he saw how much this man cared about truth above all else on every occasion, and how on every occasion he went forth with a truth that was greater than that of the other Latins just as the sun's light is greater than that of the other stars.' Well put and well placed, no? So Saint-Gilles is made to play the sun who will block out the hidden shadows of Adhémar and Ebrard. The record shows, and Sebastian touches on this, that Alexius I often received Saint-Gilles. The count of Toulouse was a friend of the basileus, the only one from this band of barons who will remain forever suspect in the eyes of the Byzantines prior to their eventually becoming outright hostile to all the crusaders, as their arrival in wave after wave came only to mean wave after wave of horrors and pillaging. A treaty will even be signed between the emperor and Isangeles's crusaders, which goes to show how much he had the inside track. Anna interrupts her account to give full expression to her joy at this event. Is it the politician in her speaking or her secret that can only speak indirectly? Was she burying the trouble at Ohrid under silence on intimate matters and under the hyperbole that she used to overlay official state business?

"This enthusiasm for the Languedoc people of southwestern France is quite symptomatic, as is the brusque hospitality she shows toward them and how much it contrasts with the Byzantine sarcasm she deploys to make fun of the notorious Ubos. Sebastian knows that this is the name she uses for Hugh of France, the brother of Philip I, king of France, as proud as Novatian for his nobility, his fortune, and his power. At the moment he left his country to travel to the Holy Sepulchre, he addresses the autocrator, telling him in advance of his plans in a ridiculous message designed to guarantee his own brilliant welcome. He wrote, 'Know, basileus, that I am the basileus of all basilei, the greatest of all who live under the sky. Know also that when I arrive it would be best that I am met and welcomed with the honors that correspond to my high birth.' You see, Nordi, long before Napoleon and de Gaulle, Hugh, this little brother of Philip I, thought he was at Versailles already, a sun king awaiting his dawn! No wonder that pretentions of grandeur is the preferred mark of distinction among the rest of us French. In any case, Anna makes note of it. Providence will not permit such arrogance, as you can imagine. God or Athena with her sea-green eyes, who knows, sends a violent storm that destroys most of the ships of this insolent man along with most of his crew and passengers. Only one boat in which, by chance, Hugh happened to be managed to be spared and finally arrived half broken on the eastern shore of the Adriatic somewhere between Dyrrachium and a place called Palli not far from the domain of Maria of Bulgaria, says Sebastian. So the shipwrecked Frenchman is rescued in a rather pitiful state. The local duke consoles him with reassuring promises and treats him to some fine meals. After these gifts the proud man is left in peace but not exactly set free because the Byzantine escort forces him to make a long detour, as I've said, one that also leads him to traverse the estate of Maria of Bulgaria where Anna must still have been living. Eventually Ubos is joined by some of the remnants of the band of pillagers led by Emich of Leisingen, according to Sebastian, and later meets the basileus in person.

"'Alexius I received the Frenchman with all appropriate honors,' says Anna, 'and he showered him with delicate attentions.' But here is the dirty little detail: 'After giving him many gifts, including large sums of money, Alexius persuades him to immediately become his lieutenant by making the usual pledge of allegiance demanded of Latins.' You can see the perfidy of the princess. This Hugh of France is ridiculous. Ridiculous, there is no other word. Anna is unable to suppress her contempt for my ancestors!

"As if this Ubos caricature were not enough, the historian attacks the Latin religious figures, who, unlike their Byzantine counterparts, she says, do not respect the canons, laws, and precepts of the gospels. 'Do not touch, do not shout, do not attack, because you are consecrated!' And there is this reminder in the *Alexiad* that sounds like an echo of her discussion with Ebrard, if one goes along with Sebastian's story: 'The Latin barbarian transfers his shield to his left arm and holds his sword in his right, while at the same time he communes with the divine body and blood. He witnesses carnage and becomes a man of blood, as it is said in the psalm of David.' This 'witness of carnage' and 'man of blood' who claims to 'commune with the divine body and blood,' doesn't all that make you think of Adhémar and more specifically of the young cleric Ebrard? It would seem that Anna is avenging a personal pain by going after these pretentious invaders who supposedly lack the spiritual tradition that comes from the Bible and that according to her only the Byzantines know how to cherish. I agree with Sebastian on this one, you see. I think that the official line required for her chronicle allows Anna to cover up the wound of a compromising situation, those beautiful evenings when she could talk religion in the home of her grandmother Maria before encountering the swords of brigands, then the arms of Ebrard. What are they called again, this knight and his men, scary or fascinating foreigners, all similar, all Franks, perpetrators of the same sacrilegious acts . . .

"Do you want me to prove to you again that her *Alexiad* is a savvy camouflage of an ancient love affair? There's another symptom that subtly points to the Ebrard affair and the absence of Adhémar in the *Alexiad*. The heresies, the heresies that shook the Empire and that were spoken of at Maria's estate. Anna discusses them at length, and their troubling nature seems to have bothered her Orthodox purity as she traces the word *bogomil*. There are pages and pages devoted to this subject in her book. Evidently, 'we,' as reported by Anna Comnena, were against the Bogomils! Listen to this.

"A monk named Basil who deftly spread the impiety of the Bogomils and who was condemned to burn at the stake by the princess's father is roundly criticized by the history: 'With twelve disciples whom he called apostles, he later also inducted female disciples, lost and depraved creatures, and thus spread perversity everywhere.' Is Basil the diabolical double of the old brave korans fisherman Radomir? 'He constructed an exterior appearance, he adopted from all sides the skin of a lion, he who was nothing but a donkey, and remained recalcitrant before the advances of the autocrator (who pretended to accept his impious arguments), except he was swollen with pride from the flattery he received. The autocrator even welcomed him at his table.' So, to counteract this blasphemer, the clever basileus lights two fires: the first, over which a cross is placed, is intended for those who want to die for the Christian faith by rejecting heresy; the second is especially conceived for those who remain attached to the Bogomil beliefs. Was this really a choice? Since they were going to die, all the Bogomils threw themselves on the fire underneath the cross. The heresy was thus disavowed by its own defenders, what better proof could there be of its inanity? And Alexius is able to judge himself the winner.

"But here his daughter seems for the first and only time to disapprove of the autocrator. How could her papa believe it possible to sidestep the irrational? How could he block that which defies the *logos*, that which of course Anna herself abhors? It is nonetheless true that the demons of Satanael persist and fascinate, they make surprise attacks on one's heart and guts and take possession, like on that day fifty years before in the water of Athena or Aphrodite (or both, as usual), without leaving a memory trace, nothing but dizziness. These are things that defy understanding; they nevertheless really exist—better not to think of them, not to write of them, and it's certainly possible, especially when it's a matter of life or death.

"The monk Basil is a different case, he can be spoken of, poor heterodox that he was! It was evening when, after the judgment of the synod, he was locked away in his cell before his execution. The air was pure, the stars bright, the moon full. Have you noticed, Nordi, that the stars, sky, and moon that precede a miracle or tragedy are always remembered? Then, around midnight, 'spontaneously rocks began to fall like hail on the cell, but no hand was throwing these stones and no man was stoning this diabolical abbot. It was probably the vengeance of the demons of Satanael, furious and alarmed that this heretical monk had revealed their mysteries to the basileus.' The less she understands, the more Anna indulges in a description of this possession that rises up from nature itself, simulating the madness of man: 'They are just rocks thrown on the ground and the roof tiles . . . these rocks fell continuously one after another,' and 'after this rain of stones there suddenly came an earthquake that shook the ground, and the entire roof trembled.'

"But this is not all. More extraordinary than the earthquake is Basil himself, once he has thown himself into the flames. He begins by mocking the fire, citing a verse of David, 'You will not be touched and you will only look with your eyes.' As though she were accompanying the heretic in his loss of ordinary reason, Anna looks for another reason, that which drives him to defy the historian's father and God himself to become a Bogomil. Because 'to look at him was to see a man of steel,' 'the fire could not soften his iron heart.' Is Basil 'struck with madness' or is he 'sunk into the deepest darkness,' following the example of Christ's Passion, from which he emerged purified? The flame itself 'devoured the impious man so completely that there was neither odor of burnt flesh nor the least alteration in the fire's smoke except for a thin smoky line that appeared in the middle of the flame.' Was it a miracle then? Was he an impious man or . . .

"Were they heretics, these Bogomils, or even atheists? Anna reflects, she hesitates. We're in the eleventh century, you haven't forgotten, have you,

Nordi? How can you not fall in love with this woman like Sebastian, like me—yes, you can laugh all you want! She is not far from thinking that these Bogomils represent an as yet unrecognized saintliness, 'as earlier in Babylon, the fire receded before those people who were dear to God and encased them as though in a room of gold.' The prophet Daniel himself was supposedly a witness.

"Anna is almost at the end of her book. All that remains is to recount the death of her father. The writer is almost sixty-five years old and so why not let herself go and indulge her weakness for those who fascinated her back when she was thirteen resting at her grandmother's house, there with Maria of Bulgaria when she met Ebrard de Pagan? No, don't count on it. No further news, no last-minute declarations. The princess reasserts her formal side: 'That is enough on this prodigious figure. I would have liked to make a complete presentation of the Bogomil heresies, but modesty prevents me, as the beautiful Sappho says somewhere, because, although I am a historian, I'm also a woman born in Porphyria, the first-born and most honored child of Alexius, and it is best to remain silent about that which crossed many minds.' A sense of private modesty held her back, she says.

"Did you hear, Nordi? There's a whole program there! Anna tells us her code. Pass over the modesty of Sappho, there has been a better example since, and nothing in Anna allows one to suspect the saphist in her, and will we ever know? The essential point is in the 'it is best to remain silent' 'because although I am a historian, I'm also a woman.' Sappho herself never went that far!

"You think I'm too interested in Anna? That I'm seduced, bewitched, and trapped just like Sebastian and others before him? A little, not totally. I'm keeping a cool head and it's Sebastian that interests me. I have not forgotten that I'm in Santa Varvara and that we're faced with a situation that is 'largely criminal,' to quote my colleagues back at the *Événement de Paris*. Anna excises everything that does not belong to a daughter of Alexius Comnenus and only says that which would do honor to Porphyria for all eternity. Sebastian concludes that she dissimulates private political and theological 'affairs' behind public ones. Hence the misery of Byzantium, her empty coffers, her internal wars that have weakened the crown, and her obligation from the very beginning of Alexius's reign to seek the aid of the crusaders? Anna does not ignore these things, nor, however, does she really take them into account. Modesty prevents her, of course.

"And yet it's important to note that it is her own troubles that this first female intellectual walls into her secret crypt. There may have been a mystery to Anna, a passion, perhaps even a madness, as in the case of Basil the Bogomil who was encased in a flaming golden chamber, one similar to that in which the historian sealed a part of herself, sealed it almost out of her mind, keeping as the only trace an immense sadness, an incomprehensible distress in the daughter of a basileus as glorious as Alexius I for whom she likes to braid crowns to further highlight her own beauty. Without this secret crypt how can one explain Anna's tendency to lament as though she were not the last of the stoical elegists but the first of romantics there back at the turn of the twelfth century? This is the argument of our Sebastian. Listen: 'I dove into many other misfortunes'—she writes this at the death of her husband, the caesar Nicephorus—'from my first day in swaddling clothes in the Porphyria, so to speak, and I have been the prey of sad destinies . . . Alas, what sadness, what reversals! Orpheus, he with his songs, made rocks, forests, and even dead creatures move; the flutist Timothy, having played once before Alexander the Orthion, moved the Macedonian to run suddenly after his arms and sword; the story of my misfortunes will not incite any material movement or any running toward arms or combat, but may it nonetheless succeed in moving to tears its hearers and elicit the compassion not only of those with feelings but also of inanimate nature!' Do you hear that? A pure melancholy spirit calling out, across nine centuries, for the compassion of readers like us! And calling out to the mineral astral universe as well! 'A pure spirit grows under the surface of stones. . . .'

"But the essential point for me—for us, dear Commissioner—is not this. If Sebastian is smitten by Anna, as I think I've proved to you, it's because he is projecting himself onto her. He too is building a reasonable intellectual surface over an abyss of passions, perhaps even of mad delusions. Anyway, it can't be ruled out, but then again, what do I know? In any case, to run away like that—here one day, gone the next—and considering your family of homeless drifters—excuse me, migrants—it would not surprise me if our distinguished doctor was a disguise covering a superanxious schizophrenic! Someone trying to save himself by idealizing a thousand-year-old colleague, a certain Anna Comnena, with her broken heart (or body, take your pick), a wound that resembles Sebastian's, stitched together with more noble scar tissue, a starlike jewel and therefore pardonable and yet so close to his.

"So what are the consequences for our investigation? Unlike your pitiful little Minaldi, I don't think Sebastian is dead. That's what I wanted to get to. And if he's not using his laptop, it's because he doesn't yet have anything to add to his story. Do you follow me? He absolutely has to rediscover his beauty and her sighing fugitive or at least follow up every trace of them, especially, of course, on their territory, on the shores of Lake Ohrid, in Philippopolis, and on and on.

"So. Give me a few more days, I still haven't gone through all the paperwork and the video materials that Sebastian gathered together, films and photos. Let me go through it, I'm telling you, there's no hurry, is there? Still no word on the serial killer?"

Men flow into life, and ebb into death.

Some are filled with life;
Some are empty with death;
Some hold fast to life, and thereby perish,
For life is an abstraction.

Those who are filled with life
Need not fear tigers and rhinos in the wilds,
Nor wear armor and shields in battle;
The rhinoceros finds no place in them for its horn,
The tiger no place for its claw,
The soldier no place for a weapon,
For death finds no place in them

LAO-TZE, *Tao de Ching*

CHAPTER FIVE ❧ How to Set the House on Fire . . .

Today Number Eight decided to kill because he was feeling an irresistible urge to vomit. This relation of sordid cause to sordid effect, well-known to readers of detective fiction, will surprise no one. His liver was rotten, his throat was decomposing, even his brain hurt from liquifying into pus. Nothing in his body was intact. The mafia types who were still conducting their Crusade of Evil had succeeded in taking him over and attacking him from inside. The invasion of these new terrorists had begun as usual by word of mouth and ear: strident cries, saws cutting his eardrum, visceral buzzing, and an unstoppable implosion of the voice that turned his stomach. The complete opposite of the sweet peepings of birds that Number Eight enjoyed above everything else in the world because their songs were in harmony with their feathers and the wind and because man knew how to tame them such that he could practically fly himself and escape from other men. Human voices only barked threats now, slogans of war in American English and Arabic, the explosion of planes and the Twin Towers, a continuous sonic bombardment that shattered the cell walls, fragmented chromosomes, and tried to destroy the very root of his life; and because Number Eight was yet still alive, this sonic violence could only twist itself into a repulsive discomfort, the most disgusting of all—vomit.

For some time Number Eight had been convinced that the New Pantheon was the right arm of the world terrorism that now was punishing practically the entire planet and had succeeded in dominating Santa Varvara. His psychiatrist had done all he could prescribing him the latest neuroleptics: Lemental, Lozapine, Roleptan, Ponex, Spedral, Yprexa. Medical science had done everything in its power, but Number Eight remained untreatable and his conviction steadfast. Not only was he persuaded that his conviction had nothing to do with his sickness—even though his doctor tried to convince him that his sickness was precisely due to his belief that it had nothing to do with his symptoms—but the facts continued to stack up in favor of his conviction.

The latest revelations permitted one to extend the already large circle of the New Pantheon. Number Eight had new proof about the crazed leaders of the Axis of Evil that reached out to apparently rival groups. To begin with there were the fundamentalists of Al Qaeda who sought to one-size Islamize the entire free world but profited along the way from mafia money, which for the health of its own circulatory system needed all the dizzying connections to high finance and families as well as to clans, esoteric and spiritual groups, sex, prostitution, secret police, pedophilia, and drugs. This whole complex knot of associations had been around in the Middle East for thousands of years. Look at the Bible. You can't rewrite history, and history only evolves by means of the minutest of variations. The Muslim suicide bombers blew themselves up in the center of Jerusalem? But wasn't the laundromat for "dirty money" being allowed to function right there in the holy city, a service for both victims and executioners? Everyone got their piece of the action, the Islamic fundamentalists no less than the conservative Zionists as well as the extreme Orthodox who pretended to combat them, or was it the other way around? Number Eight had studied the "in" courses in political science at the University of Santa Varvara— naturally, everything comes back to the University of Santa Varvara—and he knew full well that globalization would lead to the end of the globe if steps were not taken to protect the disadvantaged. Clinton himself had said so at Davos, and the leaders of the G8 repeated the message here and there around the world. And one mustn't forget the left wing and their adversaries the nazi right and the druggies, the crazies, the poets, the intellectuals, and all the rest who rightly suspected the Establishment and who were all in agreement on this point. But Number Eight quickly realized that the "in" crowd had only one idea: force him to submit to their own mental program, without the least thought that from birth he had rebelled against all species of mental influence. Therefore he sheltered himself from their wavelength, disconnected his receiver from their propaganda antennae, and founded his own governing system. It made his liver hurt so bad he wanted to vomit, but so be it, nausea was behind an entire philosophical tradition in these modern times.

No one dared say the world needed a purifier, someone who couldn't stop vomiting. Of course, everyone in Santa Varvara was a foreigner, if not personally then at least one or two generations back. Number Eight was too, and a rather better one than others. This didn't keep him from seeing clearly that it was immigration, controlled or not, that constituted the originary heart of Evil. The New Pantheon was not just a crumby bunch of profiteers, on the contrary, these guys were responsible for amplifying and exploiting the irrepressible wave of immigration—Number Eight was in a position to know!—a wave that objectively speaking was much bigger than they were. You had to go back to the ideologues of rapid growth and souped-up migratory movements, to the apostles of that suicidal religion of humanity known as Exile that went back a long way but stretched on today without a blush.

Moreover, of all the crimes that Sebastian Chrest-Jones had committed on this earth—and Number Eight knew of a few of them—his academic cult around migration and multiculturalism was not the least pernicious and hypocritical, an untreatable poison that was hitting the species right down to its embryos. Justice should have dictated that the ornithologist take care of this nut long before attacking those so-called reverends. However, even Number Eight could not know everything, nor be everywhere. Better late than never, despite his head, which was throbbing with pain and ruining his health.

On Saturday morning the university was almost empty, and he was obviously not going to cover his head with his usual mask to cross the campus. With the casual gait of a doctoral student determined to obtain the latest document about which he had dreamed the night before and without which he would be unable to keep up the appearance of yet another studious weekend, Number Eight entered the history building and found his way to the laboratory of Sebastian Chrest-Jones. In his backpack was everything necessary to pick one of those simple combination locks that are supposed to protect university property and faculty. It wasn't necessary. The door opened easily when he turned the knob. The professor was working at his computer with his back to the door. He too seemed eager to dive into the latest document he had been dreaming of the night before. He didn't hear the visitor, who approached as quietly as a big cat. One karate chop on the back of the neck, one stab into the throat, and Number Eight removed his shirt, carved up the man's stomach, signed on his back, stuffed the shirt trophy into a plastic bag, put the bag into his backpack, took off his latex gloves, and left the lab as calmly as he had entered.

Minaldi lay in a puddle of hemoglobin. That Saturday morning he had let himself into the professor's office, which was graced with a beautiful plaque with the latter's name. He was still trying to send a "Trojan horse" into Chrest's laptop computer from the laboratory's main machine. There were not many zealous researchers on the weekends, even among the historians, and the body was not discovered until Monday.

Popov didn't know what to think anymore, and Rilsky had become more jubilant than ever, genuinely overwhelmed by the odd habit of twinning with the serial killer. It was clear: if he, Rilsky, had been able to knock off a human being, this piece of vomit Minaldi would have been the first on his list, without a doubt. Only a thin transparent film separated the consciousness of the commissioner from the certainty that not only could he have killed Minaldi, but that he had in fact committed this crime, a purifier justified by the simple ignominy of his victim and proud to rid mankind of such a creature.

Since the night before, the long history of Anna Comnena as told by Stephanie, with the revisions and corrections of Sebastian worked in, had strangely relaxed the boss, who, as a result, but without really knowing why, felt less alone with his anxiety about being someone else. Perhaps not a murderer exactly but a sort of psychopath like those that his job as a commissioner forced him to lock up. And so what? Rilsky certainly was not the first or the last complicated individual on this planet, one that already included a historian in love with a thousand-year-old princess, a historian of the Crusades who, Byzantine though she may have been, really had been in love with a Latin crusader . . . well, at least according to the reconstituted version told by Stephanie Delacour, who embraced the version of Sebastian Chrest, and it's well known that the journalist of the *Événement de Paris* is rarely mistaken. Ergo, let's take it easy!

However, standing before Minaldi's body the trouble resurfaced. The commissioner practically kicked himself for not having the balls of this damned Number Eight, who, while playing Mr. Justice again, also proved himself to be a man of discriminating taste. Ridding the earth of Minaldi was obviously an aesthetic act of the first order, not easy to outdo, one might add.

Given the manner in which he'd sent the victim into the afterworld, the commissioner had not the least doubt that the author was the same serial killer who had assigned himself the task of liquidating the New Pantheon. But the questions that followed like a stack of dominoes from that fact did nothing to simplify the investigation; on the contrary, they only served to complicate matters further.

Primo: why Minaldi? Because he was a secret member of the New Pantheon, as corrupt, if not more so, as the reverends who had been the earlier victims of the killer's moral mop-up? Or was it a deliberate red herring, an effort to confound the police and thumb his nose at everyone who stood for law and order in Santa Varvara, including the university community? Not very likely, but not impossible, because this anonymous killer was also an anarchist and a joker. This had not escaped Rilsky, but since the rule of irony is to feint with one's meaning and target, the good ironist must be highly discreet when it comes to revealing his intention. Unfortunately, this logic gives a certain depth (either overgenerous or thorough) to every banality and platitude since any one may contain hidden meanings, and a good ironist always works best with an intelligent public, often lacking, it's true, alas, alas!

Secundo: was Number Eight an ironist or a madman? Was he an escapee from one of those psychiatric hospitals that brag between themselves about their open-door outpatient services and thus make the police departments fill up with their overflow population of crazies? Rilsky hated himself for asking this kind of question since if it was true that the actions of this man were intimately near to him to the point where he was asking if he had not himself committed these murders in a state of improbable but not impossible impersonation, it was also true or at least logically coherent that no one besides this same Rilsky could know if Number Eight was a joker or a madman.

Last but not least, the hypothesis of Sebastian as the serial killer, something he was ready to abandon since listening to the story of Anna according to Sebastian, as edited by Stephanie, was now resurfacing. Who could and should have something against Minaldi if not Sebastian, the cuckold-professor delighted to add one more touch to his portrait as purifier by knocking off this university bum after having already taken care of the New Pantheon? That made sense.

To summarize: a junkie, a globalist, or Sebastian himself?

What's the difference? You don't see the difference?

Rilsky himself was losing his grip on the whole thing, such was the toll exacted by the infinite black whirlpool that was sucking him in again. At bottom, the boss was scared. He needed to get back to R-E-A-L-I-T-Y: verifications, interrogations, fingerprints.

He could begin by greeting the tearful Hermine, who was waiting in the next room, much more torn apart by the death of her lover than by the alleged disappearance—let's grant for the moment its high probability—of her husband.

"It's incomprehensible, it's too much, to lose both of them one after another. How do you explain that, Northrop?" She called him by his first name in the hope of gaining access to professional secrets.

Hermine was certainly not wrong. But Minaldi or Sebastian, where's the problem? Sooner or later, we all have to go sometime. Rilsky thought this, hesitated about saying it to her, then did.

She suddenly squelched her sighs and pulled herself back together, as though for once she were being herself.

"Now there's no need to stay any longer in this less than inspiring funereal atmosphere—I'm talking about the architecture." He pretended to embrace her in his arms as a way of showing that they were after all family—and so as not to forget R-E-A-L-I-T-Y. "You will feel better at home, don't you agree? Now, where's Popov?"

... Or the Infinite Is Written in Chinese &

"So, where do things stand, old boy?" Circumstances were worsening and Nordi absolutely had to keep a hold on his role as boss. "Still nothing. Things are going too slow, don't you think? Nine homicides on our desk and still no clue about who the nutcase is that started this all! Someone who is perhaps further honing his religious convictions even now, because this guy is obviously a fanatic and capable of sacrificing to his God of the Infinite! We were mistaken to read his signature as the number eight, it's ∞, the infinite, that he's playing at today with Minaldi—nothing more, nothing less, I tell you! And the bosses behind it all? Someone has got to be pulling the strings behind our artistic executioner, haven't you thought of that? Of course I told you, from the start, I've always said there are bosses commandeering stuff everywhere . . . don't play dumb . . . of course . . . rather . . . à propos, hasn't it come yet, the usual letter in which he tells us of his exploits?"

"Yes, it has, Boss. His letter, if it's really his, is there in the stack of this morning's mail. But it's Chinese," said Popov without laughing.

"What do you mean?"

"Just what I said. It's in Chinese."

Rilsky was ready for anything, but not for language games. Apparently with globalization anything was possible.

"Characters, let me see . . . ideograms to be exact. Translate them, and have everything analyzed for me, saliva, blood, hair, anything you want and anything you can—on the letter and in Minaldi's desk, I mean the desk of Professor Chrest-Jones. I know, I know we've had no clue up till now; the Infinite has been working with gloves on. But things change, Popov, and psychopaths too can sometimes change . . . at least some of them. So start everything over again and carry out each step as meticulously as I told you to do back when we started. Don't forget to report to me about the victim's daily schedule, and remember to interview all his friends and acquaintances, the known and the obscure. Don't waste your time on that windbag Hermine. Go over this lab with a fine-tooth comb and put out a call for witnesses to come forward. Naturally, you'll also want to go through the psychiatric hospitals and continue to keep tabs on all the known and probable members of the New Pantheon. The usual suspects, in other words. DNA analysis with electrophoresis if you come up with the least bit of analyzable material. I've gotten the go-ahead, of course; this case is serious, I hope you've realized that!" Bad sign: Popov was staring at the floor. The commissioner only got upset when he didn't understand a thing about a case.

"An intellectual on drugs angry at the whole world, starting with his own father, and including the professor who gave him an F on some exam . . ." Popov was making an effort to think.

"Listen, the trail is getting colder every day, and you can only tell me cock-and-bull stories. Here's a piece of advice: keep that crap for the journalists and don't bring me anything but hard facts. Go on, get out of here!" This was not the usual Rilsky, but Popov knew him well nonetheless.

The boss was never more himself than when he was beside himself. This man belonged to no known social category. It pleased him to fool everybody. This was the one true reason that Popov admired him unconditionally.

As it turned out, things advanced rather suddenly without anyone knowing why. When it rains it pours, they say, and so it was that on the very day that Minaldi was found assassinated, the body of Fa Chang was fished out of the lake near Stony Brook.

The lab assistant of Professor Chrest-Jones had been marinating a long time, no one knew exactly how long, lodged among the dense vegetation near the western shore of the lake, giving that side a rather marshy appearance. It was an unrecognizable swollen mass of water, gases, and decomposing solids.

"Drowning victims are never pretty to look at, but this one was nothing but a soupy mess." Popov was disgusted by the fragility of female flesh.

"You've had too much water already, dear Ophelia, so I won't add any more by crying." Rilsky doing his Shakespeare riff.

"How's that, Boss?"

"Lay her in the earth and from her fair and chaste flesh violets will grow." Rilsky still in his dream. "No regrets, Popov. Mess or no, you get me an autopsy. And DNA is everywhere. Do what's necessary and fast. Get me Ron Steiner, the chief of forensics, quick, and tell him from me to order up a PCR right away. No questions asked, and no administrative rigmarole, all right? We're talking extraordinary powers, you got me? Nothing to do with the New Pantheon? What do you know? When will you understand that at this time in this country everything is related to everything else, and that includes the New Pantheon and Number Eight, I mean the Infinite? Not so hot your report on the drowning victim—given how long we've been looking for this woman, all you can do is call her an 'insignificant person of no interest,' which is actually a little redundant, am I wrong? Are you pulling my leg and everybody else's? Chinese, thank you. With a name like that, what else would she be? Parents emigrated from Hong Kong in sixty-five, but why in sixty-five? You call that an investigation. Deceased in eighty and eighty-four respectively, no other details? The rest is equally bland! You've not taken this case seriously, it's obvious, when actually everything is serious in this stinking country—everything, got that? This is better: 'Twin brother, Xiao Chang. Studied math with distinction, then became a marginal character, reported to have frequented ecological and antiglobalization circles, perhaps a junkie.' What's that mean, 'perhaps'? 'Works part-time as an assistant for the Aviary Defense League in the wildlife refuge of Santa Varvara.' Now, that's amusing, no? A math geek who becomes a bird lover and antiglobalization activist? 'On vacation.' In other words, you've not interviewed him, have you? Understand that this is an urgent matter now and has always been an urgent matter, as with any big case. You haven't understood that yet! Now hurry up, damn it, and get this through your head: nothing is 'minor,' everything hangs together in Santa Varvara—everything is major!" Rilsky was finally breathing again, having momentarily shaken the annoying conviction of being the purifier's double. This drowning victim came just at the right time. No, the commissioner had nothing to do with this fetid Chinese Ophelia, therefore nothing to do with her assassin either, that at least was certain. He was reestablishing control over his beliefs and his reason for being, no small feat in Santa Varvara where everyone ends up doubting themselves now and then.

IT WAS CLEAR. The investigation was accelerating. The letter from the serial killer that was received after the death of Minaldi was indeed composed of Chinese characters. Was it pure chance? The letter was not long, only a few ideograms, "written in the hand of an experienced calligrapher," said the senior member of the university's Chinese department who occasionally did consulting work for the police, thus confirming the commissioner's intuition. Popov was shocked to learn that the Infinite considered himself a purifier.

"This Chinese specialist is giving me a headache, Boss. He makes a whole speech over every character. Try and make something of it yourself; this Chinese is Greek to me." Popov playing the whining schoolboy.

"Show him in." Rilsky was irritated but still curious to hear old Professor Lee, who had a reputation as a sage in Santa Varvara.

"Here, Commissioner, is the first character you have given me the honor of analyzing, thanks to this photocopy. He pointed to a mysterious piece of calligraphy with his bamboo baton: 淨化者 is to be read *jing-hua-zhe*, literally, 'pure-becoming-that which gives,' or, put more clearly, 'that which makes pure,' 'that which makes to become pure,' 'he who makes purity come.' We have the radical 'old' in the last character, because this arrival of purity certainly requires a long apprenticeship of authentic wisdom, don't you agree?" Rilsky was tempted to reply that authentic wisdom did not automatically inspire an impulse toward purification and that perhaps part of wisdom was a recognition of the necessity of mixing with the impure, but this was, he sensed, hardly the moment for metaphysical arguments. "We Chinese, we are philosophers, but not like you." Mr. Lee now made a face that was either a courteous smile or a complex pout of hilarity and disgust. "Confucians uphold purity, while for Taoists the question can hardly come up, right? The Tao, pronounced DOW, never presents itself as any one simple thing, if you see what I mean."

Fascinating. In other circumstances, Rilsky would have let the good professor talk on and on, but this was not a moment for scholarly discussions. Today he needed to get to the point.

"We'll say a 'purifier,'" the commissioner concluded in a hurry.

"If you like."

"What do you mean, 'If I like'? And you? What would you like?" Rilsky was afraid of getting angry again.

"If a translation were necessary, I would agree with you and say 'purifier,'" replied the professor in a tone of resignation.

"Of course it's necessary, my good man, We have to translate, what else can we do?" Don't anyone tell me that the clash of civilizations doesn't exist! "Could we please move on now? What does specimen number two tell us?"

"報仇, bao-chou, literally it means 'respond with hatred,' and you have in 'respond' or 'bring' the radical for 'earth,' while in 'hatred' or 'enemy' you have the radical for 'man.' To say that 'the earth responds' but that 'man is an enemy' would be a kind of poetry that we Chinese are fond of." This was the same soup as last time, perhaps a little more sugary.

"So here we have another riddle that is very exciting to the mind, right, Professor Lee? Now the translation?"

"You would say 'vengeance' in Santa Varvarois. I can think of no other term."

"That will do. You can't imagine how much your enemy of the earth suits me. And the last one?"

"The third ensemble, 無限, *wu-xian,* which is a variant of 無窮, *wu-qiong,* means 'not to have any limits' or 'never to be exhausted.' The first sign includes the radical for 'fire,' the second that of 'territory' in the sense of 'bounded area,' while the variant that I mentioned, which your correspondent does not happen to use but is used in the same way, contains the radical for 'cave' or 'habitation.' Someone has set the house on fire! There is a poem behind this composed word. But perhaps poetry doesn't interest you at the present time. Don't worry, I won't go on any further." Lee was having fun making the suspense last longer, but Rilsky was not going to get angry and thereby satisfy the feeling of radical superiority that lay underneath the professor's modest appearance.

"The translation? In a modern language such as yours, one would say 'without limit,' or, if you prefer, 'the infinite.'"

"So, if I get what you're saying, the infinite would be a pyromaniac? You have my sincerest congratulations and thanks, Master Lee! Your poems have revealed depths that a police commissioner such as myself could not imagine, as you may have guessed, and yet you have taken me exactly where I wanted to go. Now don't be modest. Thank you very much indeed; we shall probably be seeing each other soon. I would be delighted to speak with you again about your fascinating reading of the characters and of Chinese thought, even if it mostly goes over the heads of regular Santa Varvara citizens like me. May I call on you, on a day that's convenient, of course?" Rilsky was impatient. His dislike for Chinese poetry caused him to be almost arrogant.

He got rid of the old wise man in a flurry of excitement that only increased when he read a note Popov handed him. The crime lab just confirmed that the Chinese letter contained traces of sweat and saliva and they were going to see if these traces were sufficient to conduct the famous DNA electrophoresis. Had the purifier forgotten to use gloves this time? With a little luck, Rilsky might now have a real hold on his terrifying alter ego, the criminal who was making all of Santa Varvara and the *Événement de Paris* tremble.

Sebastian's Way: In Search of a Woman of His Type ☙

Stephanie was right, Sebastian was in love with Anna Comnena; but he loved her as though he were Ebrard Pagan. The historian of migrations had set out on the trail of the *crucesignati*, searching for this knight, this shadowy forefather and not for the Byzantine princess, not for Anna herself. The transfusion into his presumed ancestor had become such a strong hallucination and so intoxicating that he hardly took notice of real living people, seeing as he did the space around him exclusively through the eyes of Ebrard.

When one is strongly excited, in mourning, or under the influence of certain drugs, the world appears as nothing more than a cosmic landscape without any inhabitants. Too loved or too wounded, humans shrink or melt; they end up absorbed in the wave of color and form, smell and sound that composes a mountain, a forest, a body of water, a rosebush, a chickadee, a fox, or a cat. On the walls of the Chauvet Cave the prehistoric painter depicted the magical movements of bison and the serious looks of horses with flexed muscles. In the brushstrokes and the color that becomes each animal he projected his interior life and made it outwardly visible for the first time. Less archaic and less dynamic than the artists of Chauvet, Sebastian's intimate cave offers neither tension nor flow, nothing but the indifference of a landscape and the memory of an inhabitant who transformed dramatic blows of the past into a fairy tale. The seriously wounded man, the killer Sebastian, conserved no trace of the evil he had suffered or inflicted. He was now one of those strangely calm and disquieting individuals whose capacity to be beyond Evil and beyond time seemed like a peaceful existence.

To find refuge in this precise point of existence, one needs to have been annihilated. Certain people destroy themselves by destroying others, after which time stops or rather opens up into a space of ecstatic contemplation. Pain then irrupts, but without the reply of an act of vengeance or execution, with the attendant blood and tears. No, never again. Suffering is definitively transformed into an implacable accuracy of perceptions and unshareable beauty. One needs to have been as dead as a stone and then to have been remade as a self outside oneself to reconnect with the splendor of the outside world.

Orpheus, Eurydice, and the Bacchantes had earlier lived in the Rhodope long before Ebrard arrived with a handful of crusaders who had abandoned the Crusade and erected a large stone cross. Like everyone else, these dissident deserters feared the wave of Muslim invasion, the invincible Saracen warriors, cruel and clever heretics. Ebrard certainly had no wish to be wounded and die from the blade of their yatagans. All the more so since he had met others in the area of Lake Ohrid whose sole ambition was to cultivate the land and who seemed rather less ferocious than some of his own companions, the pilgrims from Languedoc. And then there were the Bogomils who integrated into their unusual customs all those who would listen to them and did not reject the Lord but also asked about the demonic such that they integrated both of them as well. Another man had taken over from the first Ebrard after he renounced both the Crusade and Anna. Not a survivor but a man on the other side of death, open, empty and therefore receptive. Like Sebastian.

Anna said that some of the ancients used to claim that pleasure is only the absence of pain. The *beate vivere* fell apart for Ebrard exactly at the moment when he realized that Anna would not be for him, that he would have to separate himself from her wet fire, her perfumed linen tunic, and her skin. So long as the body and mind of the Byzantine were alive, Ebrard would continue living, but a life now set apart from life, another life. He would continue it, he did not know how, but he would continue it. Would he know that the daughter of Alexius became a writer in her old age, that she was the world's first female historian, that she had constructed her body of work over the crypt of their love, a love that never took place and that she tried with all her might to forget with her pen? Ebrard would never know, but so what? He had chosen to belong to a history that is not written down, to a nothingness, one could say. "No one is a saint who leaves traces." Lao-Tze had been teaching that lesson for a long time. He was the opposite of Anna, leaving no trace, not a sacrifice but a survivor, a living being in the anonymous flow of living beings. Only his vitality, his passage through life will testify that their meeting did in fact take place. Anna lived it too, even if she wants to ignore it. Ebrard lived it but will not say so. He will let this swerve live on, he will transmit it simply by being, by enduring the voyage. His path will be the visible face of the chapel where Ebrard is entombed unknown. He will not continue toward the Holy Sepulchre, he will content himself with walking on the land of men and women. Living so as to testify that life existed and will exist, at other times and places, and that Ebrard had met it. A fairy tale of another time. Past and future. Now? Now it was necessary to be able to exist the way others steal from stores. It is not even a life, just as it is not stealing, for these homeless people. *C/J* had it on authority from Estelle Pankow, who read detective fiction and treated these folks: it was beyond everything.

At an altitude of over forty-five hundred feet there is an immense prairie fifteen hundred feet long, seven hundred fifty feet wide and surrounded by a wall of pine, beech, and oak. This sacred place carries a predestined name: Chrest Wood or The Wood of Crosses. Sebastian Chrest-Jones had to go there. Was it a sancturary of Dionysos, which, according to the ancients, rivaled the temple of Apollo at Delphi? Or, a more convincing legend, was it a Bogomil sanctuary? In this version the heretics would have chosen Chrest Wood to celebrate their infamous rites far from authorities and nearer to the gods, and there were at least two for the Manichaeans, a god of Good and one of Evil. The monastery of the Holy Trinity, now gone, used to house an icon of the Virgin framed with fragments of wood that came directly from Christ's cross. So it was said, and Sebastian was hopeful of learning more about it. Was this the booty of the crusaders returning from the Holy Sepulchre? Brought back by pilgrims? Or by tricksters? Time only teases myths out further. And rumor made Chrest Wood holy, his own wood, the wood of Sebastian Chrest-Jones; it made ferns tremble as well as strawberry plants, blackberries, blueberries, and currants. Healers had moved there, Chrest Wood became magic—miraculous even—for centuries it had made the blind see and the paralyzed walk. Princess Eudoxie herself, the sister of King Boris III, came one fine day for care not that long ago, and a one-hundred-foot-high iron cross was erected on the same site as the old stone cross of the crusaders that had disappeared. The people say what they like; *C/J* is not really interested in people. Time has shaped its economy in the grass and the rock, it has been bent into this open clearing, unusual and naked, a supreme communion with all and with nothing.

Did you know that the uranium contained in the rock under the ferns has been shown scientifically to radiate and thereby provoke the states of exhaltation and investigations into the sacred that today's media defend or decry according to their taste? Maybe. Memory is a very powerful uranium, it displaces the Savior's cross, broken into little pieces, and sets these scraps within the frame of a female peasant icon situated in a clearing in the Rhodope. Was it to pacify man with the sun, when his hungry teeth bite into the mauve skin of a huckleberry—teeth of man or teeth of the sun?

Time expanded in the clearing; it matured with the pinkish juice of blueberries, but only Sebastian could live in this suspension, this jewel. Santa Varvara now extends its reach everywhere. In fact, Sebastian Chrest had continuously crossed its path ever since Stony Brook, in Milan-

Malpensa, Belgrade, Kosovo, Durrës, Ohrid, right up to this sanctuary of Dionysos and the Bogomils, and Ebrard, the aptly named Chrest Wood. Suddenly the continuity of the trip was broken there and revealed a secret world. The World? Cataclysms had happened here and elsewhere, storms, wars, earthquakes, and the quaking of religious and political systems. They swept away inhabitants and their habitats, peoples and roads, children and cottages, without damaging the greenery or the light. The rain that falls suddenly is still there, as are the scared butterflies that flee. The earth is threatened, there is global warming and the hole in the ozone—OK, we know that. Worse, the war in Iraq divides former allies, and other wars will follow. The Chrest clearing is still immaculate despite its survivor's appearance, shaped by hatreds and nourished by deaths. *C/J* tells himself that it is being reserved, like a mature woman who seduces by her reserve. It is the World. Who sees it? Tourists? The faithful? Memory's wounded?

Ebrard Pagan came here scarred. Cut across the forehead by a Byzantine sword, he could no longer stand the Languedoc pillagers who claimed to be Christians but who very obviously were salivating over the land here as well as Oriental fortunes. His shoulder was pierced by an arrow shot by his own side, such was their hatred of his opposition to their pillaging! Radomir cared for him and then taught him how to walk on embers without burning his feet and to make love to both men and women without restraint. In leaving his Uncle Adhémar and fleeing Anna, Ebrard was free of God. What else could he do besides yield to the demons of his flesh? A banal fire for anyone who does not know Good and Evil because he believes them the same thing. Bogomil perhaps. The drunkenness of innocence certainly. He left these black masses convinced as a child, speechless, but seized again with the impossible desire to hold Anna in his arms and flee from her as well. Just as this white butterfly flees from Ebrard who prepares to capture it again as he runs through the ferns softly like a cat—bare-handed, of course. He holds his breath, extends his thumb and index finger. The butterfly is falling asleep, but not Ebrard, who with extreme vigilance holds Anna—breasts velvety, sex lively—let go, not let go?

In the past as a boy scout Sebastian enjoyed chasing butterflies without a net, simply with his bare hands—a strangler already. His goal, pursued with the pride of a killer, was to pin them on a corkboard that served as a multicolor collection of trophies. They say that marjoram, hebe, and honeysuckle love the butterflies that pollinate them. *C/J* adores them too.

Not caterpillars or cocoons. No, they were rather disgusting, those incomplete larvae. He only felt passionate about the adult butterfly aptly named *Imago*. First came the smallest, the Meadow Brown, for example, the color of the wood, Chrest Wood, the color of the oak, with two chocolate-colored eyes with dark pupils on the upper part of its wings. Also the Large Checkered Skipper, brown and white, the speckled rear part of its wings resembling the bark of trees, the earth around heather and leafless stems. But it was the airy Apollo that fascinated him most, with its white membranes that could bend the sun's rays, its red-orange spots on the rear part of its wings and gray hairs at the end of its abdomen that attracted the eyes of the avid hunter who hoped to trap the animal turned image. There was the light yellow Scarce Swallowtail with horizontal stripes, its wings covered with blue moons and its long black tail. The Spanish Festoon that looks as though it had escaped from a volcano with its red and yellow stains with black marks. The Purple-Edged Copper whose scarlet shaded into purple in the case of the male of the species and brown among the females. The Brown Hairstreak had a yellowish orange spot on a chocolate background, and the Silver-Bordered Fritillary had orange crescent edges around its brown wings. On hot days colonies of Large Blues with their pear-shaped sapphire spots blend in with the blue of the sky. There is also the Damon Blue, with its underside fuzzy opal tending toward silver in the male, and the velvety Chalk Hill Blue, the males bright violet and the females a pleasant light brown. Only those with the most powerful wings—the Red Admiral, with its black and red stripes, white spots, and marble patterns on the underside, and the Monarch, awesome with its energetic yellow and black movements—still fascinate the killer now: the ultimate image of the incommensurable superiority that lifts into the sky on its scaly wings, with nose and beard the two-footed pale faces that we are.

As a child, Sebastian pinched their little heads, first crushing their eyes, and then placed a sharp needle through their hearts before mounting them in rows in his box. In a similar way with the little Fa Chang, he first lovingly squeezed her neck before crushing her bulging eyes, once she had stopped breathing, and then stuffed her into her minuscule Fiat and pushed the car into the lake.

This was quite different from Ebrard, who lived a second life besides his real life, sealed off within the unsaid of the *Alexiad*. One could say there were two Ebrards, as there were two Sebastians, and it was not simple to make day mix with night. All the more since Ebrard and Anna believed they loved life, their mother and father, and above all God the father, or so they thought in those days. But Sebastian? He absolutely could not understand those who played at being progenitors. Hermine claimed he detested them. "A misanthrope, that's what you are." Fine, she got over it, emancipated feminist that she was. Sebastian's obsessions made her laugh, and Sebastian felt all the more justified in his convictions. To have a kid when you are Tracy Jones, waitress, with this transitory figure Sylvester Chrest, and to do it just for one's own pleasure without asking the child himself whom she would name Sebastian if it would be pleasing to him to come into the world! No one asks the butterfly its opinion when it comes time to leave its silky cocoon. Butterflies fly out as butterflies, and for as long as he can remember sunlight, Sebastian has adored strangling butterflies, Tracy Joneses, and Fa Changs. You call that murder? No, it's not murder, it's beyond everything.

The only human creation of any value is not children, nor is it the body—not even an aerobically trained body as that airhead Hermine, his legitimate wife, would have it, she who obsesses over her jogging, squash, and other exercise programs when she's not obsessing over the nutty diets proposed by her nutritionist. No, what's valuable are works, monuments, gardens, books, paintings, music, and archives. Such as, for example, the incommensurable stone cross, later of iron, that dominates and will always dominate Chrest Wood. Sebastian believed, moreover, that one needed only to look around, to travel and migrate in order to become tired of beauty and ruins. Today beauty is nothing but butterflies and ruins. He will stop over in Philippopolis, there where Ebrard settled, there where he met Militsa and founded a line. The line of Chrests, of which nothing remained. There was no trace except the speculations of *C/J*, doctor *honoris causa* of migration, in his story of Anna, which was linked to her own writings.

Anna certainly never came here, because when Alexius came to Philippopolis to combat heretics in 1113 or 1114 the princess had already been married for six years to Caesar Nicephorus, had already given birth to three of her eight children, of whom only four survived. Anna would have perfectly understood Sebastian the butterfly hunter, because the female author took very little interest in her offspring and signed over breast-feeding, baby food, daily baths, and the rest to Zoe—know what I mean? From then on it's politics that holds her attention as much as or more than books. The first female intellectual spent all her time in the senate building. Her expertise on the subject of state intrigues already surpassed that of her paternal grandmother, Anna Dalassena. Why then, if Anna never came around here, does her *Alexiad* speak of Philippopolis as though she knew it?

Superb Philippopolis, "once grand and beautiful," she writes, but somewhat ravaged by the Scythians and especially a favorite haven of the impious. "Because the Armenians possessed it, as well as the people called the Bogomils, and the Paulicians, a branch of the sect of Manichaeans, disciples of Paul and John, who were taken with the heresies of Manes." Alexius I set up shop here for a time because, proud as he was to combat the invading Muslims and outfox his opponents with the help the crusaders pretended to offer him in this perilous epic confrontation, the emperor also took pleasure in personally purifying his own religion, the true one, not to be confused with that of the arrogant Latins who moved dangerously away from the canon and who no longer celebrated the same Trinity: we'll see that later. He took pleasure in hunting down any and all profane types who would corrupt his religion. "On the margins of his official expedition, he undertook a more important task: he turned the Manichaeans away from the bitter principles of their religion and instilled in them sweet-tasting dogma. From morning till afternoon and sometimes until evening, and sometimes late into the night, he would summon them in order to teach them the Orthodox faith and refute the errors of their heresies. . . . Thanks to the continuous interviews and exhortations of the autocrator, the majority of Manichaeans were won over and received the divine blessing. The interviews typically lasted from dawn until well after dusk, and, far from ducking these conversations, the basileus most often remained, forgoing meals and enduring all, even in the middle of summer, from within his open tent." This is Anna's testimony.

Radomir, of course, accepts the exhortations of the basileus. The imperial tent, set up in the center of Philippopolis, is right next to the ruins of the former synagogue that was built here in the third century. It is one of the most imposing examples of the entire diaspora, and the basileus can still see the mosaics on the floors that include Hebrew letters and the seven-branched candelabra or menorah. The Jewish, Georgian, and Armenian merchants as well as other probable groups don't seem to bother Alexius. He makes use of them and they of him. On the other hand, heretics who pledge allegiance to Our Lord while committing blasphemy are much more harmful, and it is their troops concentrated in Philippopolis that Alexius addresses.

Radomir listens and pretends to be persuaded by the imperial condemnation. Inside the tent, hidden in the shadow of a pillar, Ebrard does not address the sovereign. Already for six years the Languedoc cleric has chosen the peace of God in a direction that his Uncle Adhémar would not have denounced. Ebrard of course believes that the Church must be armed against pillagers and infidels and that for the love of God holy war is necessary, but in his eyes this is not the only possible path. Speaking with Anna and Radomir, having one's body experience a renewing bath and the fire of a woman, searching for the peace of God in one's private interior Jerusalem all seemed to him sweet tasting, as the Hellenic Anna would say, a test far more difficult and no less dignified than bringing down the walls of Antioch.

In his tent at Philippopolis Ebrard can still hear Anna's arguments, which were more subtle than the exhortations of her father the basileus, arguments that went back to those evenings at the home of Maria of Bulgaria when the Byzantine princess first presented her thoughts to the knight by candlelight. No, Anna did not accept the doctrine of two principles put forward by the Manichaeans that had swept over the court because it was professed by Porphyry himself, the great adversary of orthodoxy in Constantinople. "For our part, we revere the divine unity, but not that which admits only one person," affirmed the learned princess, who was never more seductive than when she was philosophizing. "Nor do we accept the 'One' of Plato that is the 'ineffable' of the Greeks and the 'Mystery' of the Chaldeans, because they append many other principles from it, both cosmic and supracosmic." The historian of Santa Varvara is not a mad fan of the divine unity as expressed by Anna, although he is irremediably seduced by her reasoning faculty, her erudition, the clarity of her mind, and especially the determination with which she stood up to the Latin Ebrard so many years after their ephemeral encounter, without speaking of it overtly of course, but in writing, in the secret of a muffled love and in her exclusive loyalty to her papa and Byzantium.

"Both cosmic and supracosmic." The mouth that formulated these words had come so close to the face of Ebrard under the sun of Ohrid, and the Auvergnat cleric was persuaded, like Anna, that the divine unity did not admit only one person . . . but then how many? The Father, the Son, the

Holy Ghost, OK. Woman, added Radomir. Ebrard was not sure. And yet the body of Anna made it necessary to ask the question, know what I mean? The Father *and* the Son or the Father *by* the Son? Let's talk about it, but a cleric cannot speak to a basileus. Ebrard did not have the rank, and moreover he is for all intents and purposes dead within a certain world from the moment he leaves Adhémar and renounces Anna. Nor could he take on the role of peasant like that *nemes* Radomir, since in Auvergne Ebrard de Pagan was already both a *milites* and a cleric. From now on he had chosen to lead a new holy war that took place inside himself; he chose a sword that went through his heart, blood of ink, an invisible hemorrhage.

Did the basileus notice him? A knight from Languedoc, even one dressed according to local fashions, would not exactly have blended in. Alexius had not eaten in three days and was extra tired from the sun whose rays felt even hotter inside the heavy tent. Did his look register fatigue or surprise when he saw the green eyes of Ebrard? The peace of God is obtained only with the consciousness of orginal sin firmly lodged in one's mind, something that doesn't prevent one from combating the sins of others in armed attack. Does Alexius know of the burning sense of guilt that aggravated the embrace with Anna? Insolent and sure of himself, the Byzantine emperor wanted to eradicate all heresies. From listening to him, Ebrard would seem to be admitting that he is a heretic. How could one not be if one is made of flesh and blood, if Jesus was born to Mary who is not Eve, true, but not far from her all the same? (Ebrard has no notion of the Immaculate Conception. It would take seven more centuries for that dogma to be promulgated, as theologians know.) It seems clear to him, as clear as the waters of Ohrid, that the incarnation is a heresy. There is, therefore, peace only in the recognition of heresy—or heresies. Alexius could have sent Ebrard to burn at the stake for less than that and Sebastian along with him.

Today Philippopolis is a city like any city in Santa Varvara. No difference, the same Pizza Huts, the same Nike outlets. Sebastian has known this ever since his first trip here. Since the fall of the Berlin wall Santa Varvara has expanded continuously. A few old-fashioned houses still exist though. They are in the historic neighborhood that Sebastian walks through on every visit, feeling himself closer to the traces of his ancestors who burrowed themselves into the sides of three hills.

They are sumptuous homes, not necessarily a part of the ancient Chrest saga, but so what, they nevertheless belong to the same world, the same

habitat and atmosphere, the same oxygen, the same spirit that survives beyond the bodies of the ancestors and sometimes transforms them—in other
words, the same culture. No one speaks of Philippopolis in Santa Varvara,
New York, London, or Paris. This part of Europe has passed into the blind
spot of history. Why? Is it because of Orthodox Byzantium, which tied
itself in knots, like Anna, against the crusaders while still letting them pass
through, even asking for their help, yet tricking them, these Latins who
were not exactly heretics but already too worldly, too violent, and too
imperial with their pope who considered himself the center of the world
and who succeeded in surpassing the Orthodox Empire by imposing the
Catholic version of true faith and holding us in contempt? Or is it because
of the Turks, who cut us off from the rest of the world for five centuries?
Or is it because of the communist system that always thrived in Orthodox
territories from Russia to Romania and from Bulgaria to Serbia? And then
there are the Greeks who pass for marxist-nationalists today, if they aren't
fascists. What is the true reason? Is it due to the *per Filium* that subordinates
the Son to the Father, since the Orthodox believe that the Holy Ghost
comes from the Father by means of the Son who is under his authority and
not, as Catholics believe, that it descends equally from the Father and the
Son, *Filioque*? The Orthodox view makes the Son into a sentimental servant, potentially masochist and homosexual, and necessarily a worshipper
of the (little) Fathers of the people. This belief leaves you, the son, with only
a single way out: violence, anarchy, terrorism, revolution, murder, mafia,
Stalin to Putin—what a romp! These are the theorizings of a few Parisian
psychiatrists along with Julia Kristeva, but it's far from the dominant view,
faith is a lot more twisted than the successors of Dr. Freud imagine and can
tie you into Borromean knots for sure!

Whatever the explanation, it is true that today no one knows about the
splendors that Sebastian never tired of witnessing: the house of the Armenian Hindilian, since Philippopolis was a crossroads for Georgians, Jews, and
Armenians, traveling salesmen, cosmopolitan scholars who settled over the
three hills of the Thracian city among wine makers and tobacco growers.
This mixture has carried on through the centuries. Some, like the Chrests,
established definitive roots and stayed for at least several generations before
leaving one fine day, like Sylvester, for Santa Varvara. These Hindilians, for
example, were spread all over Europe; they traded with Vienna, Venice, and
London and then moved to Damascus, Baghdad, and on to the East Indies.

They were pacific crusaders who came a few centuries after the first round of belligerent barons. Trade was in the process of unifying Europe. Florentine furniture, Venetian mirrors, Oriental rugs, Victorian libraries—was it mere booty to be stockpiled or were these collections the noble sign of a Europe united for the first time? They pretended to forget the sword and the cross; they gathered the gold coins of as many kingdoms as possible while waiting for the birth of nations and the burst of technology—and perhaps underestimating both entirely. Under the protective canopy of their cool courtyards, in the shadow of smokers' dens, sheltered by large wall hangings of painted silk, they smoked water pipes and basked in the peace that money can buy, money that is not always easy to earn but that is the fortune of those who have taken up traveling as others take up residence in their good conscience. Except one is never at peace when one pulls at one's roots, and only a satisfied curiosity can occasionally calm the rushing waters of anxiety.

C/J's Fiat Panda could not get up the bare hills of the historic quarter where one found the accumulated opulence of these old nomads who had carried on, through the time of the rebirth of the capital and down to the wars of the last century, the same rich lifestyle that had caused his ancestor Ebrard to stop here so long ago. And the site attracted Sebastian now, a butterfly on the amber pollen of Byzantium. He would lose his way walking around, stop at antique shops of all kinds to exchange words with the unassuming guardians of traces of this or that custom, habit, or piece of lore that set travelers dreaming. He would rest under fig trees freighted with their honeylike cargo and next to rosebushes that no one seemed to notice.

Here the rose is a national flag and is no longer noticed. Blown by the dusty winds of Rhodope, red petals pile up on old stones, mix with the blue strips of some ancient species and tea-colored flakes that are more discreet and far more odorous before gusts disperse them over the heads and on the breasts of dark-haired women with fiery laughter. Sebastian paid no real attention to the rose petals or the butterflies of Philippopolis. He only had eyes for the municipal records. He would go and interview the Assomptionist brothers who were martyrs of the communist era; they would facilitate his access to parish records in France where they had originated, or so Sebastian hoped. Wasn't their founder, Father d'Alzon, from the Cévennes? To trace back as far as Hugh and Adhémar, to Vézelay and Le Puy-en-Velay, and farther still, C/J will make memory a fine art.

In the meantime the Panda had no trouble crossing the deserted countryside that was still being ravaged by the most terrible of economic crises, one that severely affected the land, eradicating grains, corn, and other crops including the cherries, the "juicy crowns of my country" as Sylvester used to say, salivating at the very thought of them. Today *C/J* saw there were none as he drove on to Mount Vitocha. No, Ebrard didn't come this way. There is no document that suggests he could have. However, two waves of the popular Crusade, separate from the path of the barons, did pass through Sredets, the present-day capital, Sofia, and they claimed to have been invincible torrents of God. Awesome! They were the troops of Walter the Penniless at the end of summer in 1096 and those of Peter the Hermit at the beginning of November of the same year. "The entire plain of Belgrade was covered with blood and bodies," writes the chronicler Ekkehard of Aura. Belgrade was at the time Bulgarian, but politically it was Byzantine. Naturally the Byzantines recoiled at opening their markets to pilgrims—food for men and horses was lacking here just as in Ohrid. The crusaders didn't hesitate about harvesting the new ripened wheat. And because the conquering newcomers only spoke Latin, there were frequent misunderstandings, sometimes a total breakdown in communication, especially when it was necessary to speak with the local leaders. Godfrey of Bouillon's army therefore decided to hire a local Bulgarian as interpreter, and he accompanied the crusaders as far as Jerusalem—just the reverse of Ebrard's decision to abandon the Crusade and stay put in Bulgaria. There is no trace of any of this today except in certain chronicles. *C/J* comes across them in the old church at Boyana nestled against the side of Mount Vitocha. He writes carefully in a notebook and will recopy the information into his computer one of these days, yet another brick in the wall, another scholarly presentation to excite his audience at the next Byzantium studies conference at Stony Brook! No one at present has any idea about this place except *C/J,* who is examining every stone with a magnifying glass. Next to a fortified castle that once served as a garrison are the ruins of a minuscule church in the form of a cross lost among giant ferns. It has no relation to the Chrest family, it is simply a sanctuary that commemorates the crucifixion, as was customary between the ninth and eleventh centuries. *C/J* remembered it had been mentioned by the historians in the context of a description of the campaign of Basil II in 1015 and the anti-Byzantine insurrection of Peter Delyan in 1040–1041. What a lot of killing! It seemed likely that the fortress and church had been visited, used, and eventually destroyed by Godfrey of Bouillon. A mute history and legends. You want hard facts? Memory is fueled by the imagination, like jealousy and love—in fact the leading historians today brag about being writers, C/J knows them. What, you don't believe it? Everyone envies Saint-Simon, and who wouldn't prefer to be a grand duke instead of a modest member of the institute! It's the frescoes inside the new church that attract the traveler's attention. The master painter of Boyana (or his school) completed two hundred and forty images, not icons but living faces. Their glances never cease. Today they are still staring out at you from the ancient brick walls that were painted long before the birth of Giotto in 1266.

The sponsor, one Sebastocrator Kaloyan who was nephew to the czar and ruler of the Serdica district around Sofia at the time, can still be seen too. His calm appearance suggests a man of the church more than a political leader. The painter made his face lovingly saffron and sunny against a black background that recalls the profane world outside. The artist also used black for the tunic, beard, and hair of this generous benefactor. His wife Dessislava has a round face with a pointed chin and the same almond-brown eyes that Sebastian associates with Mithra, the mother of Sylvester (herself a distant descendant of the alleged first wife of the crusader), in other words, Sebastian's grandmother. Her kitschy portrait dating from the end of the nineteenth century had always hung in the living room of his Chrest cousins in Plovdiv. No, this oval-faced beauty was certainly not the mythical wife of Ebrard. However, if one overlooked the diadem and the tunic encrusted with precious stones imagined by the painter, the moon-faced Dessislava that Sebastian was looking at was the spitting image of his grandmother. There was the same fine Greek nose, the same round high Slavic cheekbones, and the same thin lips suggested with fine brushstrokes. Notice that the left hand of the sponsor's wife is extended and that an elegantly braided cord of her vermillion robe hangs in the crook of her thumb across the palm. This gesture that tourists hardly notice is something Sebastian has often admired in the gothic art of Western Europe. It reveals the secret Latin influence on the local artist that dates from the Crusades, the Santa Varvara professor is sure of it. During the Crusades, people from far and near spied on, pillaged, and killed one another, yet over time some of them conversed and got acquainted—words were borrowed as well as gestures, colors, and foods (one thinks of Iraqi peasants feeding their pota-

Portrait of Dessislava

toes to hungry GIs). The maturity of the East and the illuminations of the Latins intermingled and sometimes produced a graceful result such as the gothic left hand of Dessislava.

But who today knows anything of Boyana and its artists faithful to the aesthetic canon of Nicaea, the famous Second Council of 787, you remember, that put an end to the iconoclast crisis and authorized the figurative representation of the emperor and his court as well as of Christ and the Virgin? After Constantine V, a true thinker of iconoclasm, and Leo V, the foremost iconoclast emperor, many subtle theologians, such as Nicephorus with his *Antirrhetici*, that Western Latins had no idea of at the time, took up John of Damascus, Theodore of Studium, Gregory of Nazianzen, Anastasios the Persian, and Gregory of Nysse, and they pleaded for a new philosophy of painting, one that Nicaea would officially authorize and that would triumph in 843 thanks to the wisdom of the empress Theodora. Who remembers today that it was in Byzantium at Boyana—especially at Boyana, Sebastian will be sure to emphasize at the next conference in Stony Brook—that the future of painting was decided, a future that would give rise to so many Virgins, crucifixions, annunciations, and pietas throughout Italy and France? But this would be after Boyana, of course, a good while after Boyana!

No one remembered, but so what?

Should one express outrage as do those somber Balkan peoples who are forever neglected by the pretentious Occident? Or should one puff up with the secret pride of being among the innovators who will, one never tires of hoping, eventually be discovered as the unsuspected precursors of genuine values? Passing between these two bitter thoughts, *C/J* calms down as he contemplates *Christ and the Doctors* through the eyes of the medieval painter. With the oval face of an adolescent nobleman, the brown-eyed glance of a young Romeo, and the forehead of a scholar, the young Jesus in no way resembles his model, a real man of his time, according to the realist local historian of art. No, in this adolescent Savior there was both similitude and enigma; he inaugurated a new way of seeing, created a new look. The image that Sebastian saw before him was the incarnation itself because for the people of Boyana to be the image of someone or something meant nothing less than being in a living relationship with that person or thing. He ought to have explained that to this obtuse windbag, but what good would it do? He wouldn't understand a word of course, since after the Turks and then the communists, Byzantium is no longer what it once was, alas!

The image was not sign but sense. Sebastian knew the arguments of the ancients by heart: not *prosti* but *skhésis*. Bizarre how this *skhésis* first designated intimacy for the Byzantine fathers, a tone of affect, and the love and grace of the incarnation. For the profane, the intimacy in question is that of man and woman, what is called sexual commerce, but you understand that in this kind of incarnation, the one Sebastian observes on the walls of Byzantium, the term designates the passion between two men, God the Father and his Son. However, the Byzantine side of all this doesn't end here because the same Father-Son Incarnation that the spectator is asked to contemplate in the Christ image—referred to as its *economy*, the word having, you know, the same root as the word *icon*—the same economy, or if you like the same icon, will be supposed to be active in any profane image no matter what the model. There is a whole history of love between Father and Son no less than between model and image.

The walls of Boyana impressed on Sebastian the economy of a love of another age, another way of seeing. Love of the Beyond in the eyes turned inward of Saint Stephen the Protomartyr. The prescriptive love of a grave destiny in the features and gestures of the archangel Gabriel. The melancholy love of Jesus Christ Evergete. The dramatic love in the face of the Virgin viewing the crucifixion. Or that of a radiant weightlessness in the dormition when she sees herself as a doll-baby in the arms of her son. The infernal love of Christ in hell who does not yet believe in his resurrection, the black features suggesting those of a shipwrecked sailor. And here is another sailor, Saint Nicholas, the patron saint of most churches in the region and the holy guardian of seamen. Are they sailors, the Thracian peasants and Balkan farmers? Certainly not. What then? Are these souvenirs of Homeric heros? Is this nostalgia of Hellenic origins? Or is it a cryptic reminder of a more recent event of that year 1259 when crusaders disembarked at Dyrrachium and elsewhere before swarming onward to their destination in Jerusalem?

The Boyana painter has unveiled for Sebastian one of the first cartoons that ever existed, entitled "The Miracle at Sea." It recounts the exploits of Nicholas during a raging storm. Look closely at this sail and this boat, he ought to say to the local art historian, but he says nothing, the other has already seen them with his detective's eye. It's Venice in the middle of

The Descent of Christ Into Hell

Bulgaria, it's the high sea, the stormy, the desirable, the impossible Europe. Europe doesn't know the passion that is felt for it—then and now she has never even suspected how much. Europe does not imagine how much she is integrated into an imaginary realm criss-crossed by abstruse and gracious paths, paths that have made it fertile without its least knowledge or recognition. Before Byzantium disappears for a time, too refined, too decadent for the barbarian hordes from the South, East, West, and for the Turks, the Latins, and the Santa Varvarois.

Sebastian's Panda continues eastward. With or without crusaders, the essence of Byzantium is hidden within the Church and influenced by the sea. A sea that carries the memory of Ulysses, the one who sought neither glory nor immortality but only to return to his home. In his day what he is blends with his original habitat: palace, island, household, Ithaca, and Penelope and her gynaeceum. You properly *are* if—and only if—you have a home that awaits you at the end of your voyage. But now? Who is he,

The Life of Saint Nicholas: The Miracle at Sea

Sebastian *C/J*, where is he if Santa Varvara is now everywhere—and what if he is a homeless person lost in Time? Ever since Ebrard de Pagan, setting out from Le Puy, crossed Chrest Wood to live provisionally and forever in Philippopolis and established his crypt somewhere in Thrace, and beyond it nothing, Ithaca has very much changed. Penelope no longer exists and insecurity has overtaken all habitats since 9/11 from Paris to Bali.

Those who stay put easily believe that moving around is liberty itself. Sebastian thinks so too, and yet today his voyage is his prison; he is enclosed within it as within an inner sea. The Black Sea is an inner sea, its bitter taste comes from its rocky entrails, heavy with iron and sodium, that make an India ink out of its deep blue waters.

Here in Sozopol the beach covered with minuscule pieces of orangey mother-of-pearl, fine and pliable pieces that have not yet disappeared into the anonymous floury sand, remembers it was once seashell. The ancients celebrated Apollo, the sun healer, and they called the city Apollonia before the first Christians opted for Sozopol, meaning "the saved city." Saved— Apollo, Anaximander, Aristotle? The sand itself holds the memory of its past along with the fishermen who tread over it, still speaking Greek in this country that has been Slavic for more than twelve centuries now. Harmanite Bay is deserted, the German and Swedish vacationers won't invade until July and August, and Santa Varvara will extend out to here as well, as it has everywhere else. Today there is no one. Two laughing gulls wheel between the outcrop of purple rock just off the shore that washes against the bluish peninsula on which the Chez les Peintres restaurant stands chic and empty, the beach strewn with periwinkles into which Sebastian thrusts his tired toes. The traveler doesn't seem to bother them, secluded as he is within his invisible prison, the palace of his memory. Anesthetized outside for the outside. Enveloped in his impression of having always known this spot. Had the patriarch Sylvester visited Harmanite Bay? The haggard scholar relaxes into a transgenerational childhood memory, as the Psychoanalytic Society of Paris would say. Ebrard himself, and grandfather, and father bathed here perhaps—his toes told him so.

C/J had not opened his mouth in two weeks. Suddenly his familiarity with Harmanite Bay made him make a sound, the name of the place: Sozopol. He heard an oddly sad little voice that seemed to hurt him just by crossing his lips. The man shuddered and jumped into the sun-soaked water, which carried him as though he were weightless. He had no consciousness of the movements he was making as his legs and arms alternated between breast stroke and crawl. His body swam on without him, he thought of nothing, certainly not about turning back or swimming to the other side. Where was he going? Only the breast stroke and the crawl knew. Somewhere toward the Caucasus, the petroleum paradise, as it was called? When night fell he was floating on his back. The moon wasn't full, and the north star kept him company as usual. He awoke, shivering and nearly paralyzed, moving with the swell. There was no identifiable shore and waves were beginning to get larger, the black waves of the Black Sea. It was the ideal moment to let himself sink. He felt an urge to vomit, cry, and tap his feet. But the spasm that could have been fatal actually brought back to mind his swimming lessons. The robot was excellent in the pool at summer camp. Technique replaced agony and he began to swim again, fighting furiously. Here it was: the miracle of Saint Nicholas with his Venetian ship as depicted on the walls of Boyana took shape in Sebastian's body in the open sea off the coast of Sozopol.

Along with the cormorants, the dark red sun greeted an exhausted but still living man. He was covered with black iron-laden sand, looking like the Boyana Christ exiting hell, and collapsed on the shore a few kilometers away from the Harmanite beach where his Panda was parked. He slept a full twenty-four hours until the next rising sun, and then stretched his body a good deal before the violet-colored rays began to warm him. Feeling himself again, Sebastian walked back to his Fiat, changed clothes, bought a watermelon, which he devoured with the crude appetite of the homeless person he was, and then set off in the direction of Nessebar.

EBRARD HAD PERHAPS not traveled by water to the Caucasus, but in his day we would not have been able to avoid traveling to Messemvria. Anna must have told him about it. Since the fifth century at least all the great families of Constantinople each built their church on this divinely blessed peninsula, and ever since 863 the well-born never failed to move there once the Byzantine batallions had reconquered the city that had been invaded by Kroum the Bulgarian czar. At the time there was a rush on Messemvria just like the French housing boom of today in Saint Tropez or Ile de Ré. (By the way, if you have a chance, take a look at a current map of Messemvria, known now as Nessebar, a peninsula linked to the mainland by a long promontory, and then look at a map of Ile de Ré since the construction of the Bouygues Bridge and tell me if they don't look the same!) The Greeks mixed with the Bulgarians who were supposed to come back in 917 after the memorable battle of Acheloy, then again in the thirteenth and fourteenth centuries. All that while waiting for the crusaders of Count Amadeus of Savoy to restore the beautiful Messemvria to the Byzantine Empire in 1366. Though perhaps agitated, this history is of the most ordinary kind for Byzantium, which was already a multicultural empire, that is to say, ungovernable—Anna saw it and almost said so herself. As a result of having to finesse multiple invaders and migrant populations, this empire found itself often defeated and forced to give in to nationalist pretentions or turn some against others before eventually collapsing under the brutality of Turkish Islam, its warriors, its rugs, its hammams, and a bloody degeneration that only thrived on yatagan fights and throat cutting.

Sebastian remembered that Sylvester had kept engravings of the oldest church in the area, Saint Sophia, a church built in the fifth and sixth centuries and that was still intact when the patriarch was a boy. How old would those engravings be? Fifty years old? He thought he recognized the ruins not far from a Kodak store with a Coca-Cola and espresso snack bar attached. "No less then two hundred churches or their remains on this little spit of land, you should go some day." That was the only nostalgic remark that Sylvester ever made to his accidental son—in other words Sebastian had not gone as a result of any sustained pressure or propaganda.

The Church of the Virgin of Humility, Eleoussa, from the fifth and sixth centuries, with its domes and vaults of reddish brick contrasting with the grayish white cement walls, enclosed him as one sheltered within a red breast, and he took off his shoes to feel the peony tiles against his arches. Jesus-Pantocrator from the thirteenth and fourteenth centuries with its exuberant chromatic architecture and surviving frescoes was one of the jewels of Nessebar, said the guide (speaking Santa Varvarois of course), and Sebastian was for once in agreement with the local tourist office. From the same period the archangels Michael and Gabriel invited the visitor to duck under the network of arcades beneath its large dome. But it was in Saint Stefan, a church from the tenth and eleventh centuries dedicated to

Holy Mother of God Eleoussa Basilica

the Mother of God whose colorful representations dated from its founding through the sixteenth century, that Sebastian almost felt himself at home.

If he had to choose a home, Sebastian would have laid down his bags and body in Saint Stefan. It was a house that was not all that different from many patrician houses that over the years fishermen had taken over and democratized when it came to the style, abandoning the red brick in favor of fragile walls covered with wood to resist humidity. At the time, as still today, they would suspend strings of sardines from the rafters. They would dry over the summer and be grilled in the winter on a wood fire and eaten with beer or a dry local wine. Brushed by the salt air, they would expand from the heat of the wood embers and release the oily, fishy taste as though freshly caught in summer. Byzantium was definitely a matter of taste, and this was in fact the key to its downfall—Anna knew this all along. Pitted against crusaders, Muslims, Santa Varvarois, and any other kind of warrior, taste is an inexo-

Saint Stefan

rable weakness. Saint Stefan extends the sacred into the profane, unless it's the opposite—the countryside is enfolded within the temple.

Sebastian leaned against a wall bathed in shadows and the perfume of the dry ground, his eyes looking off into the distance, out to the sea filtered through apricot-colored glass, underneath a round sun that amused the laughing gulls poised on sleepy waves.

Tranquil, perfectly Byzantine—Greek even—Sebastian now stopped. Perhaps it was the end of his journey. A possible end in any case. Time regained outside of time.

Enough then for Sebastian. But Ebrard? Ebrard has not yet yielded up all his secrets, and Sebastian does not allow himself to leave things half finished.

Was it necessary to battle the Muslims to the bitter end and completely exhaust their warrior thirst, this male monotheist fanaticism, rather than dream of Anna and progressively pacify oneself on the Thracian plain of Philippopolis, Boyana, and Sozopol? Ebrard had opted for a relative existence, but an existence all the same, renouncing the most radical renunciation of death and refusing war so as to live on, for better or worse, down to Sebastian. The pacific choice of Ebrard was perhaps the first defeat of the West. History only sees in it the defeat of Byzantium, because the West recovered with the Renaissance and the expansion of technology, capital, industry, colonies, and atomic bombs. Again the male monotheist fanaticism, but new and improved, or at least with pretensions of being new and improved, sometimes. All the while, not satisfied with having swallowed Byzantium, Islam continues to advance, and though stopped for a time at Poitiers or Venice, their suicide-killers, their shahids are blowing themselves up today in New York and Jerusalem, in Moscow perhaps, and most certainly in Iraq and Afghanistan. Sure, the humiliated and offended have a right to make themselves heard, and no one, any more than the pill, condoms, or AIDS, can put a stop to the demographic growth of the poor if the faithful believe that God comes from numbers and that One God orders them to procreate and expand their numbers.

Ebrard the pacifist was not a purifier; his renunciation takes on purity within the fraternity of builders who pile up stones, polish, and do the masonry for later or never. Others will say that his renunciation of collective hysteria breaks down into a soft syncretism, into the sweet club of the powerless that exchanges one perversion for another. But perhaps not for just any other. Was this male madness dissimulating a mother madness? Was it the last stage of the journey? Was he wrong? Right? While Byzantium became strung out on intrigues and manipulations with and against its crusader comrades, and the crusaders themselves were targeting it no less than they pursued Jews and Saracens, Ebrard was playing the scholar peasant and planting grains of universal peace. O peace, soft sleep of fathers! However, is Europe not doing the same thing now, proposing its "third way" between Bin Laden and Sharon, Al Qaeda and George W. Bush? Is the European Union a holdover of the Byzantine dream of Alexius I, of the Roman wish of Urban II, of the scepter of the Holy Roman Empire? No, but of Ebrard's dream, yes. Put away your arms and cultivate your garden. That would be too good to be true! Sebastian understands that only Santa Varvara has the means to end war, despite appearances, despite its mafias, sects, drugs, arms trafficking, stock market corruption, and global pollution. Granted, Santa Varvara is in the process of unifying the globe with a banal monoculture, but where are the means to do otherwise? The Ebrard style is far too elitist, too top-down, too European, too Byzantine, in fact, to work.

Must one get used to an omnipresent and omnipotent Santa Varvara?

Sebastian sips his Coke at a table outside the Pizza Hut that stands next to Saint Stefan, confirmation that it wasn't as off the beaten path as one might think. So this woman who was his type, this woman he pursued in this hallucinatory quest as a man without value, without time or roots, with only a painful memory—was it really Anna? Or was it instead Ebrard relayed by Anna? Or was it not Boyana? The churches of Nessebar? Or the pieces of seashell that make up the beach at Sozopol? Time that opens up into space? Sheltered from History such as it is made and recorded today in Santa Varvara. Lifted out of the ordinary passage of time by the extravagance of his solitude as a bastard and murderer, an intellectual crazy about the past and beautiful things that will never belong to this world, it's already been said, but who understood? Sebastian is always in search of nothing in the flesh of the world.

"*Do you speak English?*" A young local woman in a wine-colored mini-dress and high heels extends her cigarette under the nose of the stranger, asking for a light. Antismoking campaigns have not yet made it all the way around the globe.

Her lips are too fat and her sandalwood perfume doesn't really cover up the odor of her armpits. Why not? It's time to face reality. Here as elsewhere prostitutes adore the dollars from Santa Varvara. Sebastian puts his arm around the waist of this heavy beauty, herding her toward the Panda. The animal only obeys the law of his erection. A far cry from sumptuous memory palaces, which now seem to him to have a confused identity. A far cry as well from the sentimental and realistic Fa Chang, have no fear. Sebastian's killer days are over, now that he has met Anna and Ebrard on their own terrain, now that he has found himself in them and pasted the pieces of himself back together in another world. What does it matter; it was not a woman Sebastian was looking for but a world that though *in* this world is yet not *of* this world. Go for the woman who wants the light; it's not important; it's easy. A whiff of sandalwood, swollen mucous membranes, and a discharge that makes him proud of himself. Finally proud and full of initiative.

Silence, My Mother Is Dead &

I am writing to you from Paris, Nor, but I don't know if I'm going to send you this e-mail; it's for myself that I'm trying to conserve the silence, ours and others. So here you are fired up again by the murder of Minaldi, yet one more strike by the serial killer that caused the *Événement de Paris* to send me off to you, to Santa Varvara, or is it someone else? In any case I found you in top form the other Sunday before leaving you: the truly great Commissioner Rilsky! You'll fill me in when I get back. As for me, well, I've not really given up, but it's true that Sebastian's Byzantine dream contaminated me, his wanderings urge me on, and I'm even certain that he's not using his laptop because he's set out not in search of Anna but of Ebrard somewhere in Thrace. I'm pursuing an idea I have that will allow us to scoop him up—you'll see—give me a little more time, perhaps a day or two, no more.

The silence then that we love and in which we love each other. Sure, you're a good talker, a poet even at times, and me, my job is to put anything and everything into words. We really met, once we understood that there was nothing to say. Together we receded from that place where words are too noisy, a place of pathetic aches and obsessive exaltations. This moment of close hugging could have been a colorless resignation, a boredom that annihilates each one in a nameless liar's communion, said a master whom you admire. On the contrary, however, our silence preserves my lucidity and yours, incommensurable and yet not shut off: you're me and I'm you, but we remain quite different inside this reciprocal echo chamber where sentences bump against the wall making clarion sounds, designating thick objects, and remain unable to return to where we are. What name shall we give "it"? It's a challenge to find one, but I'm still trying. *Nothingness* is too melancholic. It well evokes the death of the fusional pretension that lovers are usually seeking and that we are both fleeing, but it has the disadvantage of yawning wide open, defeatist, too Buddhist or too vague. *Ecstasy* is pompous and too weighed down with red marble saints and anorexic ones exalted by painters. *Serenity* is too wise sounding, too philosophical. But *joy* is too childish for big kids like us. *Silence* is a humble term that doesn't rule out language, since it is after all words that it uses to point to the interval that words are unable to grasp. Being sober, it doesn't destroy or get you drunk. It points instead to a respite, a letting go, an abandonment. And yet, how many captures, dominations, and traps are in that modern mantra L-O-V-E! *Silence*, it's an alert word that takes me beyond my borders, my glance, my skin, my sex and my ears and my throat even—always ready to extend the knot of hysteria in secret. And all the while remaining attentive to my body and yours, a word that transports me outside. Silence outside of me, outside of you, an animal crossing, inhuman, astral.

I've known lovers who didn't know how to shut up, who pretended to speak to me about me before carrying on with their exterior monologues about their obsession of the moment, and who ended up evoking the smartalecky mama's boys that they always were, or as you can guess, were never quite able to be. Others shut up in order not to say what they believed was hurtful to me, some perversity or infidelity—it's the same thing—that only degraded them. These cases have nothing in common with our silence, which is not a subtraction but a plenitude without the overflow of illusions. Nor, you are the least pathetic and most inhuman lover I've ever met!

You remind me of my mother, who was stricken by a terrible meningitis that sent her into a coma. I came to Paris to keep her company until the end. The end happened Friday, today is Tuesday, and I've just got back from the cemetery filled with tears and silence. The nighttime face of our sunny silence. My mother was one who inhabited the kind of silence that I've been trying to describe to you. She was the most reserved kind of woman, some would say the least hysterical, and it wasn't because she was depressed. You think that can't exist? But yes, this woman exists, my mother, and don't be shocked if I use the present tense, she's here, between us. Our silence is so transparent that I believe I never felt the need to speak to you about her, or not that much, it's possible. OK, so here I go, yet with a good bit of silence. In mourning, to write what one cannot say is still silence, I know that you understand me.

My maternal grandfather, Ivan, married a beautiful brunette Jewess, Sarah, and they left their native Moscow just before the revolution and went to Geneva, then Paris. If I may indulge in some wild psychoanalysis, I suspect this precommunist cradle with Orthodox cupolas is the only Byzantine magnet that pulls me to follow the footsteps of your Sebastian. Curiously, from the mixture of Slavic blond Ivan and the anthracite Semite Sarah, there came a daughter, Christine, who most resembled those proud Greek figures on urns—red profiles against a black background. Since neither of my grandparents practiced the religion of their ancestors, they turned their daughter over to the unique god of universal Reason. It was a respectable program that had been pursued for a long time in Moscow and Saint Petersburg, ever since Diderot and Catherine the Great, in other words, long before the revolution, though it later did also serve as a counterweight to Bolshevik nihilism—but that's over now, it's finished. In short, the Republic was what mattered, along with Darwin, the only "great man" my mother respected, her "mentor" in the natural sciences, which she taught before giving up to devote all her time to me and my sister and especially to my father, with his overly erratic diplomatic career. You know the tune, however, even though you don't know my mother, misogynist that you are—no need to protest.

Standard oedipal stuff. I've never thought that she truly loved her diplomat husband. But it seems as though she did, since in her will she expressly asked to be incinerated and placed in an urn beside him. You see, the perfect couple! But first there was an Orthodox mass that she asked for in memory of her father, and that I found rather dull; the popes of today don't have their hearts in it, you can see it and hear it, they would do better to convert to Judaism or Catholicism or stop altogether. But no, they spend their time in political disputes and swing their incense holders without conviction—something that is not lost on the faithful who leave all the more disappointed, but they can cry over a lot less in any case. It's a sorry spectacle in many ways, this Orthodox cremation—is it the end of a religion or just the trough before the next wave? It's not my problem. I would have thought the religious service would not have interested my mother either, but it did. She insisted on reminding us that she was the daughter of her father Ivan and on taking her distance from my father's Catholicism: the faithful wife right down to the cremation ashes, OK, I wasn't able to ignore this final message, but she certainly wasn't a submissive wife.

Nor, I'm giving you this last image of my mother; please hold on to it. The Greek beauty of Christine in her coffin. Grave, severe, at peace. None of that mushy, passive Oriental style that she liked to put on to seem like one of those Turkish women that a husband has no reason to fear. A firm, no-frills purity in her cheekbones. Her usual smooth radiant dark skin with no lines. On his deathbed my father was almost smiling. She looked more reserved, not really sad, but with no advance toward anyone or anything outside. The extreme exertion, the surprise at her strange capacity for being alone.

Christine was the most intelligent woman I've ever had the chance to meet. No one ever says that of their mother, but I did in a little speech choked with tears that I muttered before her cremation. And yet the mental acuity of this scientific mind that could have degenerated into pure viciousness softened into a receptive retirement—I might have said generosity, if my mother hadn't detested the strings attached to this word. For example, look how this mother, who didn't hesitate to discuss my professional and intellectual choices with a rough, joking tenderness that always provoked without persuading me, never made the least intrusion into my sentimental life, let alone my sexual life.

She listened to everything that concerned the soul, Slavic or Jewish. She listened to me in that silence that is also ours after making love. A love without grasping. She will have her paradise: a woman who was never a weight to anyone—not even to her daughter, can you imagine? The lightness of Christine. My nights are broken up with nightmares and yet there is also a sensation of peace. Christine: feather, wing, fleeing blackbird who only barely touched us three—my sister, my father, and me. Because really it was we who weighed her down, because we relied on her. But this woman let us believe that she was content to open a path for us, that she didn't suffer or scratch and gave nothing but a caress. "I didn't tie you down, I gave you wings." That was her modest motto, which she'd repeat with a spark of irony in the corner of her eye and her lips, apologizing for having said too much, for having broken the silence. Her complicit silence was only an interval; it left a lot of room to the rest of us; I can hear it still and I am always looking for it. Might this be the ancestral vocation of women, the one that we lost in the celebrated fight for our emancipation that you find (wrongly) so laughable: the duty to be the ground, the sill, the chock, the foil, the launchpad that always gives a child well loved or any beloved creature the chance to take wing? If so, it's a launchpad that risks being scorched by the ascending rocket and thus forgotten. This was a risk that Christine accepted, not with the bitterness of sacrifice but with only a sober, alert silence.

I never heard her speak of herself, let alone command or demand. "How tactless!" she would murmur with nose pinched. In the autumn of her life, my mother didn't set out to find her Russian relatives, Jews and Orthodox, since there weren't all that many left after so many years and so many purges. She looked instead for historical documents about prerevolutionary Moscow: postcards, handbills, chronicles, and various other testimonies. It was the same magnet that pulls me toward orthodoxy, just like Sebastian, as I've already said. The nostalgia of my scientific mother could only come through documents and well-organized files that wouldn't bother anyone. That was her, all right, whether it was researching a neighborhood, a house, or the air that Ivan and Sarah breathed there before moving here.

One day, not paying attention, or perhaps out of one of those secret hatreds that go on between married people, my father threw her treasured documents away. He later claimed to have confused them with piles of junk mail from Picard, Trois Suisses, and other mail-order catalogs. I will not forget the day Christine discovered the disaster. Her dark eyes suddenly went blank. She stood speechless in front of her husband for what seemed like an eternity. Then she locked herself in her room and only came out twenty-four hours later with eyes red from crying. "You know, my daughter, no one in the world has the contempt for foreigners that we have, we the French. A cold contempt, without the least scruple or bad conscience. We're the best at it." Oh, the viciousness of that "we." Promise me not to forget that, OK?

After there was nothing more. Silence.

I had never imagined until that moment that my father might have been xenophobic, anti-Russian, anti-Semitic, or anything like that—he who had devoted his entire life to international relations, who had dragged his little family all over Santa Varvara to serve the Republic, do you understand? Since then, I don't know. There are hatreds, we could call them unconscious, that are better not stirred up. So, anyway, this was the single passionate explosion of my mother, if passion is the word for this folding in on her mute judgment.

Over the fifteen years since I left her house, our courteous, intimate, and relaxed confrontations hardly prepared me at all for the flood of sorrow that has come over me now. I thought I had been vaccinated against mourning after having paid my dues at the time of my father's death. I thought I was armored. You can't imagine, no one can imagine Stephanie Delacour crying like a little girl, poor orphan! Well, she did. I cry in no language, without words, with the memory of her look, her perfume, her solitude, and this silence, her silence, my cradle, my country. I am discovering suddenly the number of things that I will not be able to do now that she's gone. For example, there's no one to send the vacation pictures to that I take with Jerry. They interest no one, these pictures of me and Jerry in the rosebushes of the island, on the beach of Martray or on the dance floor at Pergola. No one but Christine, and she's gone. Maybe you? Lots of other things that I did out of a sense of dignity, and without realizing that it was her sense of dignity that was guiding me, all those less intimate but serious things are becoming distant from me now. At bottom I can tell you that without her I am capable of doing nothing at all.

Don't be afraid, I still have Jerry; I will continue to march on because of him. And I promise you that you will definitely see me again in Santa Varvara. But I won't be the same. I have lost my blackbird, the wing that gave me wings. I am guarding Christine's silence and I'm giving it to you for safekeeping.

Stephanie

P.S.: I hesitate about sending you this e-mail. I wanted to add more, but no, impossible. With mourning comes also a certain laziness.

But here's some new info on Sebastian. You know Jerry, Gloria's son who fills me with tenderness and will always keep me linked to Paris, whether you like it or not. Well, this child that others call handicapped and who blows me away with his computer skills has become a young man to whom I can go with my computer problems, which come up often, as you know. So anyway—get this—Jerry was able to get into the memory of your uncle

Sebastian's laptop! I suggested several possible passwords to him, all derived from dates important to Anna Comnena, of course: her birth in 1083, the meeting with Ebrard Pagan in the spring of 1097, her marriage to Bryennius in the fall of 1097, the beginning of the *Alexiad* in 1138, its completion in 1148. It turns out that the number 1138 was the one; I had guessed it would be: Lake Ohrid, Ebrard Pagan, you know the story . . . But it was Jerry who found out how to break into the network at the University of Santa Varvara, then into the lab's subnetwork, and finally, with the code I gave him, into Sebastian's laptop. I have no idea how he managed to do all that, but anyway, to make a long story short, I can share with you the following:

First: Sebastian is alive and is still writing his story of Anna.

Second: He is traveling in the footsteps of Ebrard Pagan, his ancestor, your ancestor too, if it's true, the impossible sacrificed love of Anna Comnena.

Third: In less than one week he will be at Le Puy-en-Velay. I deduced that from observing his Christian obsessions and how he's made an entirely new world for himself built solely of churches, frescoes, and cathedrals. He is looking for the saint of saints and he is going to arrive smack-dab back at the source of the Crusades, at *Salve Regina*.

Don't ask me to say more, I'll explain everything later. Get going on setting up the necessary secret service agents so you can snatch him up there. Maybe Foulques Weil can help us to coordinate with the French police, even though they seem overwhelmed at the moment with their hysteria over insecurity and violence. So rendezvous at the cathedral in Le Puy. Hurry! See you soon! XO

... to write nothing but what will drive to
despair every one who is "in a hurry."
NIETZSCHE, *Daybreak*

CHAPTER SIX 🙖 What Do They Want? The Macabre
Discovery of a Drowning Victim

It's either one or the other. Either the serial killer named Number Eight is
none other than the Chinese Infinite, like the boss thinks, or someone wanted
to make us think so. But in that case it was someone who knew Number Eight,
that is, the Infinite, very well. It's worth being cautious, in any event. Considering only the first hypothesis, several variations were possible and none of them
could be favored outright by Popov at this stage in the investigation.

The genetic data were troubling, to say the least. The chromosomes of
Fa Chang and those of the Chinese Infinite who deliberately chose to leave
his DNA on his last letter of ideograms showed striking resemblances, the
scientists were in fact meeting to discuss the matter. No one's genetic code
is identical to anyone else's except in the case of cloning, though there was
no reason to rule out contact between the New Pantheon and the Raelians
and the possibility of them cloning someone under the nose of the commissioner. But in the present case the DNA was not exactly identical and,
what's more, the individuals were in their thirties and were therefore made
long before the recent scientific progress in this area. Therefore, such an
extraordinary genetic resemblance would suggest that the drowning victim
and the Infinite were close relatives, perhaps even fraternal twins. And since
Fa Chang had only one known brother—which doesn't mean she didn't
have others, but one always begins with the information one has—the
Infinite might be that brother Xiao Chang, her twin, the math geek, birdwatcher, anti-WTO activist, normal or junkie, but in any case unlocatable
because supposedly on vacation.

Too far-fetched? Let's continue. If so far this hypothesis seemed plausible,
would Xiao Chang have knowingly left traces of saliva, blood, and sweat on
this letter with the intention of being caught? Was it a daring bluff, the last

move of the purifier or the start of a new phase of Vengeance with a capital *V*? Was it the prelude to the Apocalypse for which he would be ready to take responsability? Finally defying the world for all the world to see?

Another mystery: why Minaldi? Professor Chrest-Jones's assistant had contacts with the New Pantheon like everyone else, nothing more. He had been invited to luncheon meetings with the reverends, like most of the intellectuals of this country, where the leading thinkers, preferably occult, are regularly flattered. He had even given a talk on "The Dangers of Globalization for Our Interbred Humanity"—a nonsensical topic, according to the boss, and I guess he knows what he's talking about. Minaldi had gone to brothels controlled by the mafia, i.e., by the New Pantheon. There was nothing exceptional, except perhaps this one detail: the drowning victim Fa Chang was four months pregnant. Was Minaldi the father? His blood type, A, was the same as that of the embryo, though that's not proof, and it's no crime were it true. The boss doesn't seem to want to search further into the DNA of the father of this poor fetus drowned in the womb of the Chinese woman. "We've already bothered the scientists enough with these twins, and I've had all I can take for the moment." Curtain down. Maybe Sue Oliver has another idea?

Popov, who hadn't been sleeping much since the boss got onto this Chinese lead, rubbed his eyes and knocked at the door of his old friend, a well-known prostitute and good friend of the police. "She's the real interior minister," the pundits in Santa Varvara liked to chuckle " . . . and the culture minister as well," added the experts, who knew of the structural connections between sexual liberation and contemporary art.

Sue took her time before opening the door. She was a fright: black bags under sagging brick-colored cheeks, and when she forced her voice to make it audible, which was not always the case, a strong whiff of tobacco and whiskey overpowered her interlocutor.

"I've come too soon, you're not alone?" Popov was distant—still lost among the either-ors that swirled in his head.

"Don't worry about it, back-to-back meetings are my thing, dear. I'm an activist now, you know? Coffee?" Sue offered him her saggy cheek to kiss as she turned to the coffee maker. Someone was pulling up his zipper in the bedroom opposite.

Was it two years ago or more—Popov had lost track of time ever since this serial killer had turned everything upside down in Santa Varvara—that

Sue Oliver had become famous in a tell-all exposé of her sex life to a local journalist? That had been a big event: the in-crowd applauded the New Eve who had finally unmasked the hypocritical and reactionary puritanism of mainstream feminists, feminists who would read her secretly in bed while masturbating. Only a few old-fashioned psychiatrists claimed that Sue was no woman but really thought of herself as a homosexual at the service of every penis in Santa Varvara ready to get it up and on. Who was wrong, who was right? Popov didn't know, and he didn't want to know. The book made him hard, no doubt about it, and no matter what the boss, who found the writing "sober" and the experience "educational," had to say. True, no one expected the boss to react like everyone else, but this time he was going too far. As for the experience, educational was an understatement!

You see, the girl prefers round after round and a kind of stagecraft that is rather unusual in the business, the newcomer is highly appreciated by true connoisseurs. Done up in a medieval harness, with eyes covered, cold and clean, she opens all her holes and counts out loud the cocks that enter her. They file by, as in the army, a Salvation Army of a very special kind. No compunction, no disgust, no pain or ecstasy, of course, just a modern woman content to count. Male organs most of the time, sometimes a few animals, what the heck! The males are machines skillfully managed by women, and, just as mechanically, why not? a woman is a man like another. Sue does not feel her orifices, she merely counts each hard faceless nut, ten hours of communal labor and her vulva is bleeding, sometimes her face and hips, some try to strangle her, they're excited to death, so what, in the end she's had them all, that's what matters. A triumph! Vestal endurance! Intellectual curiosity policed and offered to the great god Phallus! The art of woman in the service of the rights of man! As a revolution it certainly qualified. Humanity finally got out of the twentieth century that had embarrassed itself with fine-tuned psychologizing and other gender studies. The worldwide success fell on Sue and on Santa Varvara, which had created her. (I'm speaking about the success of her book, so cut out your fantasies, I see what you're thinking!) Busloads of men and women, especially women, came from Japan and Latin America to touch Sue's Kenzo suit, everybody's got their shrine and these pilgrims were more drowned in the absolute than the pope prostrate before a relic of the Fatima Virgin. Sue Oliver had become an artist, and a wealthy one, thanks to this publication, and she dressed the part. This was something that even her most envious enemies found normal, even justified, since a sadomasochistic society, they noted, merely gets the star it deserves.

"An explorer, a revelation!" Rilsky didn't stop rejoicing, in his own special way.

Popov, on the other hand, his prick piqued, so to speak, was going to get a taste of the Sue experience live and in person. It was quite a squirt, and more than one, though he was not going to count them, but the inspector was ready to admit it if Sue had recognized it, but no, you must be joking, no face in this huddle, nothing but the holes of the textual artist who takes interest in no one, not even in herself, completely stoned on coke and cocks everywhere, paradise, I'm telling you! The most surprising is that she escaped the irresistible drives of the standard sadist who can only get extremely excited in these kinds of ceremonies—Popov was experienced enough to know that girls like that usually end up cadavers after the paradise of the initiated. But no, in this theater she was the killer, the one who had cut them all, but they loved it and went off mostly satisfied while Sue was left bleeding, perhaps, but smooth and cold and terribly alive, at least on television.

"A militant, you, and of what?" The lieutenant was surprised by the sudden engagement of the one the media had nicknamed "The Goddess of Nothingness."

The door of the room opened and Nicky Smith appeared in his usual suede pants, multicolored check shirt, and high-top boots. To think that this clown was the ringleader of local prostitution, a pillar of Santa Varvara! Ever since Sue's worldwide success, Nicky didn't lose sight of her. "A treasure like Sue is worth protecting." He thought it necessary to explain his new addiction to group sex, Sue style. This was the worst humiliation for a man like Nicky upon entering into Sue's game. Great stuff!

"It's always Mardi Gras at your place, I see. Militant and Carnival at the same time, is that it?" Popov had lifted this snappy repartee from a detective novel along with a chuckle that pretended to be above the rest of humanity, when he was really just jealous.

"You can laugh all you want, but things are serious now. It's between eradication or official brothels; do you think that's any kind of a choice?" Rinsed with coffee, Sue's rough voice became louder and more threatening. But Popov had had enough of "either-or" talk.

"Me, laugh? Me? Did I say something? Listen, baby, calm down. We're friends, you know me, right? Can you tell me what's making you get worked up like that?" Popov trying to play the pal.

Two clans had been fighting it out in the local press, but the police commissioner's right-hand man didn't have time to plow through all those pages, and besides, he had pieced together the main point: the new administration was getting ready to regulate prostitution. Again! Yes, again. Since sex tourism had become one of the major revenue streams of the country, the state didn't look too closely into its share of the megabucks that the local mafia and others were raking in. But there were still some citizens, even here in Santa Varvara, who were appalled by this trafficking in human beings, by the bad example it gave to young people and by the nuisance and noise pollution that it caused in public places, especially in some of the nicer neighborhoods. What was to be done? The abolitionists wanted to eradicate prostitution once and for all. To do so, one had to begin by getting rid of the demand: put the customers in jail and you get rid of the desire and the degrading trade in women will be wiped from the planet . . . or so went the cant.

"Do you know what abolition means, Popov? You don't. Don't play smart with me. In the old days these guys wanted to abolish slavery, nothing more, nothing less; and they did it, in America, for example, are you following me? The Sue that stands before you is therefore a slave in the eyes of today's abolitionists. And what else? I'm not saying that there's not a little exaggeration in this job, as in others; you know well that we're all more or less criminals, I know. But you, have you known sex of the kind they want, "with mutual respect between consenting adults"? Are they crazy? Ever since Toumai sex has come with a big stick. Eros and Thanatos, you know about them? Sex wants to be staged, to be high art, no big emotions, tragedy, comedy, masquerade, a little mothering, lots of low blows, everyone risking something, otherwise what good is it? Even the kiss asses know it. They come for their fill-up at my station!" Sue thought of herself as an anthropologist specializing in the death drive. Ever since her literary success it was said she hung out with intellectuals and participated in seminars, conferences, and high-brow talk shows on television and radio.

Popov was waiting for her to continue; she savored the moment.

"So, me and a few girlfriends, we've formed a delegation. 'Dear Mom and Dad, we declared, we don't need you fussing over us any more;

we're old enough to take care of ourselves. Please let us act and speak for ourselves.' You know how that went over: it didn't. They want to get rid of us and man too."

"You're right, my lovely, and man too. Farewell." Nicky playing the satisfied chief. Some had said that the mafia had orchestrated the idea of the so-called delegation.

"Who is thinking about man today? You, me ... it's a dying species." Popov posing as pessimist.

"Most women won't accept sex without love, said the chief of the feminists. Maybe, but not certain, let's admit it. But what about most men? Do you think men confuse sex and love?" Sue posing as the exceptional female, proud to count on the support of men.

"So, you'll still have brothels, isn't that enough for you?" Popov trying for hygienic objectivity.

"You've got the answer, old boy! Corral us in, cattle on video surveillance 24/7, why not a hospital? But cops in our homes—I'm not talking about you—no thanks!" Sue was getting nauseated.

She was right. Why wasn't anyone talking about the pleasure of men these days? Not gay pleasure, they're doing fine, they're out now, but the other guys. No, no, got to stay mum about that. Popov thought of all those around him who officiated in Sue's tunnels in the Stony Brook forest: truckers, magistrates, building managers, disguised priests, con artists, artist artists, high and middle civil servants, ex- and future ministers, that's happened, every imaginable class, it's below-the-belt democracy, and they're all as happy as kings—sovereigns! Guys! Sue's secrets have spread over the whole planet, but not one newspaper thinks of asking the erection set for their opinion! The top taboo, the supreme shame. It's not the homos in backrooms but the heteros in heat that no one dares talk about!

"I'm going to tell you what shocks me the most." Once started in disgust mode, Sue was hard to stop. "That they want to lay down the law is normal enough; after all, it's their job—all those judges, journalists, union organizers, feminists, and so on. But you know that they're getting off on it, they're bursting inside over it, especially women. You know that women especially are involved in this cause, and they're getting wet between the legs as they contemplate our fate! The abolitionist terrorists, just like the clean moderates in favor of regulated brothels, are getting wet just thinking about you know what without of course saying so! They can barely stand up without exploding, these dames, but I hear them, I know how excited they're getting. You can hear it in their mouths when they speak out to defend us on television; you can read it beneath the lines of all they write in the so-called respectable press and in all that gets served up over and over in articles and petitions between judges, philosophers, and tony women with their hot ideas. And that, I'm telling you, is worse than hypocritical—it's gross, it's garbage." Sue was not really laughing, she seemed genuinely disgusted.

Gross or not, Popov had not come to hear her pontificate about the next delegation of pussy proletariats. Better to change subjects.

"Say, talk about gross, did you hear that the serial killer had struck at the university this time? You know, you and your delegates should go there and do a sit-in or lay-in or something: "Prostitution and the University," some catchy conference like that while you're at it too . . . Someone named Minaldi bit it this time, name mean anything to you?" Popov had needed no help in figuring out that Minaldi used to go to the Artists Club; i.e., the brothel where Sue was boss, with Nicky as supervisor, naturally.

"I don't like television and I don't read. You know me. I write." Sue sounding professional.

"I'm not asking you to read, and it's not a crime to watch television, that's about all you do when you're not doing the other stuff, and I know you, like you said! You didn't kill Minaldi; I know that, so calm down. He was a good customer, that's all." Popov looked her in the eye as he said this.

Sue was no longer sure that her recent literary glory put her beyond the reach of all police investigations, even of the petty parody kind. It's true this Minaldi who was not her type—not at all—used to come for whippings. He'd pose as the head of his lab before going off to his boss's wife; but without his little preliminary workout at the Artists Club the poor guy wasn't up to it, so to speak. What's more, Sue hated, really hated that syrupy psychologizing like the kind you get on American soap operas and talk shows, and this guy would never fail to chew on her ear endlessly over drinks after being whipped into shape. He was a weakling, a puny weakling, that Minaldi. That at least Sue could say to Popov without betraying any secrets, first, because everyone at the Artists Club knew it and because in any case it was written all over this poor Minaldi's face.

"By the way, he didn't tell you he was seeing a little Chinese girl at the university, did he?" Popov with his lubricious leading question.

"You're barking up the wrong tree! The little Chinese girl is a volcano, or was, according to what I've heard from one of my girls, a compatriot, who knew her when she arrived from Hong Kong. That cutey wasn't the type to get bogged down with a Minaldi. On the other hand, your China girl supposedly had a soft spot for his boss in the lab, again according to my own China girl. Top secret! That's why my girl nearly had the whip drop from her hand the other day when the murdered Minaldi came to her under the name of the lab leader. I forgot his name, but I can find it out for you if you don't know it yet . . . Why are you staring? You're not interested in all this? I thought you were, sorry, but what do you want—that's our business: staging the same stuff over and over, you don't think it matters? Of course you do, but it's not your problem, not today, I understand . . . There would be lots to say about your China girl and the lab chief. I could introduce you to her compatriot if you weren't in such a hurry. Interested? No, not Minaldi, certainly not. Wrong tree, I'm telling you. That happens to you, I know . . . see you 'round." Sue was cooperative and a little bothered still; the inspector seemed not to be listening to her, what was up with him anyway?

Popov was in shock; he was no longer listening to the stories and explanations of the new militant leader of sex workers of the world. But he had a scoop that, true or false, was going to blow all the commissioner's hypotheses to pieces. Unless Rilsky himself . . . either . . . or . . . ?

"That's it, my lovely, you're wonderful, you know? She's wonderful, isn't she, Nicky? I'll see you again soon, you two." He had to get out of there, especially with his cellphone, which wouldn't stop ringing. "People are always calling the cops in this damned country. You, the cute couple, you know all about that. I won't keep you any further. Ciao."

It had been raining in Santa Varvara for ten days, a heavy soaking rain that entirely sapped your morale. Sudden but brief interruptions, like the one happening at that moment, allowed the dirty windows of Sue's place as well as the eyes of the men and women of this fucked-up planet to reflect a fleeting hope. But only to enclose them all the more inside a muddy tunnel without exit or even an illusion of exit.

Three Roads to Le Puy-en-Velay: 1 ☙

After Lyon and Saint-Étienne, the national 88 brought him right to Le Puy-en-Velay. Before getting there, Sebastian turned off on to the departmental route 136 near Monteil (just like Adhémar de Monteil). "No, there aren't any bed-and-breakfasts here." The tourist office had found only one at Chaspinhac. The professor was still hoping to put up at Monteil with its greenery, its hills, its valley with steamy mist that sticks to the extinct volcano of Le Puy. One could really breathe here, and this cookstove that smells wonderfully like gratin potatoes, it was a little paradise like no other to be found in the world today, greenhouse effect or no, "No bed and breakfasts in Monteil, my good man," on to Chaspinhac then, a polite nod to the owner, baggage in the little room perfumed with vervain and decorated with locally made lace—"You may notice the touch of fantasy on the backs of the butterflies." Madame Besse takes it on herself to explain the local crafts to this strange visitor who is examining like no other the butterflies in her handmade lace. "I assume you are familiar with the distinctive mark of our Vellave lace." How could that be, Sebastian a lace maker? What next? "Yes, a week, maybe more . . . your place is very charming." He then got back in his car and entered Le Puy from the northwest.

The runaway abandoned his Panda between the Pannesac Tower and the statue of Lafayette and continued on foot via the Avenue de la Cathédrale and the Rue des Tables toward the Notre Dame Cathedral.

"It's strange, one can't say it's exactly beautiful." This from one tourist to another.

"Actually quite ugly, you mean, if compared to those of Paris, Strasbourg, or Chartres," replied the second tourist, possibly the husband, adamantly.

"Can't you see that this cathedral is a drunken ship moored to a volcano in the middle of Auvergne, in other words, in the middle of nowhere? It's the pilgrimage itself that's resulted in this agglomeration of styles, stories, and passageways that have been bobbing up and down from the fifth to the nineteenth century!" The wife speaking a learned, lyrical prose, a leaflet in her hand. "One can see it moving, tilting, and changing with every new glance." She closes her eyes, breathless, dizzy.

"A lava monster that has attracted wanderers from time immemorial. An ideal place for miracles. Or crimes." So says the realist and therefore apocalyptic husband.

Take a look at this canon and his wife; they look like they're battling for a bishop's crook there in that flat wall sculpture. They look like witches come out of volcano flames or from hell." The wife joins her husband. She knows the subject and does not put down her leaflet.

"And those two, man and woman again, looking terrified at the mermaid in the middle, here, here, you see, she separates them, an emblem of lust, that mermaid, you know?"

"This facade is not very Catholic, do you think? Byzantine or Arabic, no?—unless it too came right out of the volcano like the black Virgin."

"Vel- in Velay supposedly has the same root as hell, what did I tell you, we're in hell's cathedral here."

"Do you think it's haunted?" Female visitors are always anxious. Precautionary measures are necessary, a warning to associations and spouses.

"No need to exaggerate, but it's true that this black Virgin looks less like Jesus's mother and more like the black Virgin of the initiated—I told you already that she guides and shelters the profane on the far side of the alchemical vase." The husband spices his words with a little esoteric zest; his wife suspected he was perhaps "one of those"—but what do the initiated do? She does not look his way.

"And what about the animals—foxes, lions, wolves, and bears—that show up amid the leafy sculpture on these walls?"

"You have to imagine that mountains around here were full of such things; men lived with the animals; it was a cruel fraternity." Was the husband alluding again to his experience with esoteric fraternities?

"You, you'll always be obsessed with hunting!" The naive spouse suspects nothing somber. "I think these people were depicting themselves through these animals, like the artists at Lascaux who painted bison and horses on the walls of their cave." She jumped ahead of the interpretations of her husband, one always underestimates the aesthetic side of women, of certain women, at any rate, or so Sebastian had always thought, and here was an example.

"Look, the word *Allah* carved in Arabic into the wall, a nice touch for a bunch of crusaders, don't you think?" The man will dominate the woman with his political mind in the end.

"And these cupolas, this Byzantine facade oxidized by time or who knows what volcanic smoke? This cathedral is rather diabolical, really! A UNESCO landmark, OK, but rather sulfurous, don't you think?" The insistent wife, still anxious.

"You stick to your wispy angelic vision of Christianity when really Christian faith has always been a melting pot—I've told you a thousand times—a permanent alchemy of this and that."

The Cathedral of Notre Dame in Le Puy-en-Velay

"I saw a book in the shop down below. Remind me to go back for it. It was a detective novel: *Murder in the Cathedral* or *The Open Door*, I can't remember which. You interrupted me when I was flipping through the book, you know how you are, now I guess I understand—the title doesn't ring a bell?"

"Everything is written ahead of time, as you know, and what's more, the place seems predestined, I told you so . . . "

C/J, who was listening to them casually, distanced himself and then re-crossed their path, irritated and satisfied not to be entirely alone here at the end of his journey. He had scaled the Corneille rock, volcanic stone with steps of brown and shiny black, pumice stone, olive gray andesite, and jet black quartz. Then he had mounted the one hundred and thirty-eight steps of the large staircase and stood still before the cedar doors of this Roman monument that from the fifth century on had fused the styles of the Orient and the Spanish Moors into a harlequin's coat. The pillars and passageways resulted in four bold bays that used the height well and enlarged the nave that was set on the rock itself—nature and history, lava and faith inseparable, sculpted the countryside of Auvergne that merged with the myths of its men.

Did anyone here still remember Adhémar? Only the cult of the Virgin still breathed in these stones, which had witnessed the first crusaders depart on Assumption day, August 15, 1096. *Dio le volt*: Notre-Dame resounded with the Occitan language then, but since that time the exhortation of the bishop of Le Puy had been engraved in the walls, underneath frescoes, and it filtered now down from the rock and in the Holy Women of the Tomb, it vibrated in the Martyr of Saint Catherine of Alexandria, it rose up to the Archangel Michael on the upper level, it pierced the eardrums of the historian. From the time of the druids this miraculous rock has favored ap-paritions, as everyone knows.

Since one apparition deserves another, *C/J* thought he had the right to one in a place like this, and so why not the son of the Valentinois count who easily carried the knightly armor before being named bishop at this very place? Here he is advancing behind the black Virgin with his coat of arms and a roughly made cross of two pieces of red wool cloth, which the pope had attached to his chest in Clermont. Like *C/J* today, Adhémar cer-tainly liked to lie face down on this Stone of Fevers that had been placed in the church, now framed, a miraculous relic, duly protected. *C/J* kneeled down before it, laid out on the anthracite lava. He felt it warming under his bones, he kissed it as pilgrims waiting for their cure had always done, and still do today—thousands of bodies had lain out on this rough bed, covered it with their feverish imprint.

Ever since the Virgin appeared on Mount Anis, back in Roman times here next to this volcanic dolmen, and the Mother of the Word spoke to the first children of Jesus, the House of Mary slowly but surely replaced the druidic cult and the Catholics took over from the pagans. Is not Le Puy the most ancient Mary sanctuary in ancient Gaul along with Chartres?

The sacristan pretended to blow out the half-burnt candles while looking with the eye of a detective above the half-moon lenses of his glasses. The strange visitor was like a ghost. The temple servant made a sign with his mouth and chin in the direction of Madame Lebon, the leader of the chorus who never failed to make her daily visit to the cathedral before going off to consume her daily bowl of leek soup rigorously prescribed by her nutritionist. A voluminous, imposing figure with a melodious voice advanced toward the ghost.

"Our cathedral is known throughout the world, isn't that right, my dear sir? Classified among the World Heritage sites of France by UNESCO, as you must know." Madame Lebon, though conscious of not being the proper size for a guide, nevertheless hoped to attract the attention of the ghost by the sheer spirituality of her voice. "Rather much better than our lace, which only interests women . . . solitary women, I believe." She let go a contemptuous smile; she is afraid of the ghost and is trying to regain her calm.

ADHÉMAR WORSHIPPED Mary fervently. His *Dio le volt* launched a *Salve Regina* so intense that it tore across the entire planet and the news became known in the farthest islands of Oceania. *C/J* knew all this and everything else reported at the time by Robert the Monk. The chorus resounded in his ears. It was indeed the magic Virgin of Le Puy that protected the massive cavalcade of villains, bourgeois, and knights. It was she who spoke through the mouth of Adhémar: *When the French see that the country is full of noise, that the valleys and plains are full of Turks, do not be surprised if there are sick ones among you. But courage comes to the pious. The Savior, placed on the cross, said that his sons would avenge him with swords of steel. On Mount Tabor, so says the Scripture, four horns will sound on the Day of Judgment. The dead will rise up, and all of humanity will live again. You will find one hundred thousand saints that God has elected. See the Saracens with their cursed brown faces. Hear how they carry on with great noise and cries. May each of you be skillful in striking out and may the riches be taken in the name of the Lord. I take on myself the sins both large and small. In the name of penitence, strike out at the Arabs!* Thus wrote the celebrated chronicler.

A formidable warrior, this Adhémar, a musketeer of Mary and her son long before Richelieu and the cape-and-sword novel of Alexandre Dumas. "All for one and one for all!" is already Adhémar's harangue, which he uses against the hesitant and the cowardly. He sheds a river of tears when fifty of his knights are taken and decapitated by the Saracens, but he also knows how to shut down the tears when his soldiers are taking things too easy and no longer advancing against the enemy. *C/J* agrees with Guibert de Nogent, in the *Gesta Dei per Francos,* who compares Adhémar to Moses; his death, just one year before the conquest of Jerusalem, he compares to that of the Jewish patriarch as well. A Moses of the Puy Virgin: why not? Does the knight Adhémar become a partisan of the peace process? He narrowly escapes the confrontation between crusader princes. He blocks the vengeance of his followers against the heretics. How was this possible? Only Mary could have conferred on him that special aura, *C/J* feels, a moderate authority that will be lacking in all the others. After the disappearance of the bishop in 1098, the princes take things into their own hands, and this would prove fatal. Seeing things from the perspective of today, as *C/J* of course does, Adhémar the Vellave would be a Moses in the spirit of the Oslo summit. (OK, let's not dream, this is only an anachronistic interpretation. Having arrived too soon in a world grown too old, Adhémar was not able to go far, and his companions took care of matters when they declared "the pest" and buried him at the very spot where the prelate and his followers had found the Holy Lance.) True, Adhémar tried to calm things down. Had he sensed the end from the very beginning? Others insisted, however. How many Crusades would there be after the first? Four, five, six, seven, and then what? The rush to the ends of the earth during the Renaissance, then colonial wars, then world wars, and it's not over yet . . . In fact, more than Adhémar it is Ebrard who went most directly to the Mother of the Word in loving Anna and giving his life—a life in death, it is true, but one that lasts and will last right down to *C/J,* among others. A life made of rape, fear, bastardy, solitude, studies, success, treason, nonsense, all that for this, glory and nothingness, war and terror, terrorism, the Shoah, Hiroshima, WTC, kamikazes, crime is a part of it, just look at *C/J*.

"OF COURSE, *Salve Regina*! Adhémar de Monteil and Ebrard Pagan, do those names mean anything to you?" Sebastian sums up all his thinking with these words just for the sake of hearing the voice of this mushy female mass who would have been ridiculous if she weren't so infantile.

"Our Choir is giving a concert at the church next Saturday and of course you will hear the *Salve Regina*. The tickets are only five euros." Madame Lebon begins to talk faster, uncertain if she is addressing a patron of the spiritual arts. "Adhémar de Monteil, who doesn't know him here? Of course only in rather summary fashion, I confess, after all these years how could it be otherwise. And then, you know, the Crusades are not exactly a fashionable topic what with the Americans lately, the fundamentalists, and the rest. They all are much more interested in them than we are. We've gotten over them, you might say. Ever since Vatican II, if I'm not mistaken; but I do often make mistakes in this area. What I mean to say, you understand, is that for us it's ancient history." She was a bit at a loss for words. "We don't do politics here."

Looking still very much the ghost, Sebastian waited for an answer to his precise question. So what about Adhémar de Monteil. Cécilia Lebon became frightened.

"Monteils . . . Monteils. There are some around here, bakers, I think, but to say they'd be descendants, that would be asking a lot. It could be they don't know themselves, so as for me, well, you'll have to excuse me." She was more and more afraid of this deathly stare that wouldn't let her go. "Now Pagan . . . what was the first name again? No, I don't think so. Pagan, Pagan . . . I think I remember a Pagan family in Chamalières. What does he do this Ebrard. . . . how did you say again?"

"That's right, Pagan, Ebrard de Pagan, also called Ebrard de Payns, a nephew of Adhémar and related to Hughes de Payns, the founder of the Order of Templars. A cleric and a crusader as well who settled far away from here, a lover of Anna Comnena . . ."

"Are you certain? A nephew of Adhémar? Say, that goes back a long way, your story. Maybe in Chamalières, but I'm afraid no one could help you here, sir. Your question would require a great deal of scholarly knowledge.

For us simple folks of Le Puy, you understand, well, it's just not our area of expertise, really not at all." This visitor was a lunatic, Cécilia Lebon could tell, having seen many others of the same kind who would eagerly wander up here. At first glance, not dangerous, no, not dangerous at all, but the guide nodded discreetly three times as a sign of agreement intended for the sacristan. "Don't forget our concert Saturday if you're still around then."

Sebastian was no longer looking at her. He was being carried toward the phantom of Ebrard. The soprano voice of Madame Lebon sounded the *Salve Regina*, or so he thought—no, he was certain of it, the woman had receded into her voice. Had she ever existed? The entire cathedral of Le Puy resonated with Adhémar's hymn, and Sebastian joined his murmuring voice in the place of Ebrard's:

> And after this our exile . . .
> O clement, O loving, O sweet Virgin Mary.

The fifteenth of August is already past, and the crowds of pilgrims as well; there are no Japanese tourists even—what day is it?—since when has *C/J* not followed the course of time, the vertical presence of stones, alone in the pinkish air? When they were afraid of the year 1000, the faithful followers of Mary noticed that the day of the annunciation coincided with Good Friday of the year 992, and they came en masse to Le Puy. Now the crowds mass together in Mecca, all of the invisible fervor of Al Qaeda converges at the Black Stone, yet one more, but evidently the right one and the most famous. Anyway, back then the pope had the idea of marking this coincidence with a jubilee celebration, and the first one was held in 1065, Adhémar was not yet bishop then, and the next one (the thirtieth edition) will take place in 2005, according to a placard inside the church, and the following one in 2016, which of these two years are we in today?

SEBASTIAN NO LONGER keeps track of the passage of time. Madame Lebon gives him goose bumps. She's much more ghostlike than the history of the crusaders and Mary's miracles, which have been so irresistible to him for such a long time. But what is a ghost? "A being condemned to impalpability by death, absence, or a change of habits." Who is a ghost? Ebrard who didn't dare make love to Anna or Sebastian who dared strangle Fa? And who condemns him to the realm of the ungraspable? Crime, absence, or modern habits, hypocrite policemen of primary drives, ones, moreover, that don't ask permission to come to the surface or sometimes even to be unleashed?

Who is Ebrard? The ghost of an ideal Sebastian who went back in time and, after having found then left his spiritual father, the papal legate—who can claim more?—comes to take refuge among the volcanoes of Auvergne frozen into a Mary sanctuary. "Hamlet, no, Sebastian, I am your father's ghost!" It is to a son that the ghost speaks, to Sebastian Chrest-Jones himself, persuaded that Ebrard abandoned the Crusades in the name of an interior "Peace of God," and that he halted in Thrace so that the one who will carry his name may live forever. It seems the leader of the Raelians, who claims to be able to clone humans, was born and lived around here, that his very first revelation was produced right here. The volcanoes favor ecstatic experiences and delirium because humans cannot stand the fire of hell unless eternal life is promised in compensation for the lava, to compress it, reassure it, and reignite it permanently—in Auvergne, in America preferably, in Santa Varvara, of course, then everywhere, as is well known.

Do not expect the play to continue now in the shadow of this cathedral. There is no more play. The mass was the last and best version of the filial tragedy, but the mass is over. At most the curate of Le Puy will celebrate it tomorrow in commemoration of the mystery of yore with Madame Lebon in the role of the Queen of the Night and the sacristan in the role of a Papageno tired of all his begettings, which are much less droll than was planned by that optimist Wolfgang. The cathedral in Le Puy is a museum, the tourists celebrate the history of art there, and Sebastian *C/J* himself will soon be classified by UNESCO as a rare specimen, gifted with a pathological memory to be cloned. Everything in the world exists in order to end up in a database. The world is a gigantic hard drive that no one has the time to open. Migrants like Sebastian are the last actants (you notice I say "actants" and not "actors": they don't really play the game, they exhaust themselves in observation, in memorization, in forgetting the games of the past, games invented by those who had a history by believing they were making history).

A line of joyous schoolchildren are crowding under the arches of the sulfurous Notre-Dame du Puy. Unlike the earlier couple, they have nothing to say. They wear their address on their T-shirts: Madison, Wisconsin. Their parents must be Polish, hence their attraction to the black Virgin and all the rest. The type of migrants who notice no ghosts and who spit bits of undigestible popcorn on the stone floor that no one is bothered by. Except perhaps the sacristan, who is tired of his little Papagenos and Papagenas waiting for him back home, and walks with resignation to his broom.

Sebastian is going to descend to the sacristy later. He is going to pause in silence for a long while before the pieta and a head of Christ from the fifteenth century another time. He will not look at the Bible of Theodulf that the bishop of Orléans offered to Mary here in 789. He will maybe come tomorrow, or the day after tomorrow, to see the paintings discovered at the end of the nineteenth century by Prosper Mérimée, a Flemish touch at the heart of the Mary volcano. They represent the grammar and logic with Aristotle, rhetoric with Cicero, and music as well. Madame Lebon insists on it with that celestial voice that has definitely risen beyond her bulimic body.

Today Sebastian will be happy just to take refuge in the music of the Vellave cloister whose construction was observed by Adhémar and Ebrard, in the deep bass notes of its arches that recall the mosque of Cordoba, in the harmony of its red, black, and white, lava and blood keystones. While they were fighting in the area of Ohrid and the Bosporus, here the cultures mixed in quite another fashion, in another peace of God. Sebastian will go as far as Saint-Michel-d'Aiguille, on the neighboring peak that overlooks the chimney of the volcano worn with erosion. They were there, the uncle and the nephew, before departing. They prayed before this Christ reliquary that seems to have come from a Moorish temple rather than from Saint-Jacques-de-Compostelle. There was interbreeding among the crusaders of Le Puy—Sebastian would even say an Arabic presence in the stones. Were Ebrard and Adhémar the only ones to have seen this prefigurement of modern times?

Religions foment war and the historian is ready to admit that they must be abolished. Progressively, slowly. There have been enough gulags! Current events prove it; Sebastian will not go so far as to say they demand it. On condition that the religion of Le Puy is allowed to survive and only disappear at the very last moment of this vast and ambitious cleansing program that would target all superstitions and that it will be necessary to take up one day or other for the salvation of humanity. Has *C/J* completed his voyage? A reverse crusader? A returned crusader. For the moment he remains in Le Puy, next to Mary, next to the black Virgin. He'll do some going back and forth … he'll look … sometimes toward Boyana and Nessebar, certainly, during this time of his that is no longer time. Until the world, and why not Europe first of all, makes itself as Ebrard and even Adhémar wanted, one is permitted to dream, with their military exhortations softened somewhat by the love of Mary.

Mary whose body is incarnated in the volcanic rock or the reverse. The mystery of Christ resides in the alabaster of the black Virgin enthroned at the main altar, a head of little Jesus, black too, sticking out of her pearly robe at an opening at the level of the maternal womb. An all-powerful queen and yet the Daughter of her Son, Mary is a woman who does not frighten Sebastian. Unlike Tracy Jones who allowed herself pleasure with Sylvester without a care for Sebastian. And not to be confused with Fa Chang who took herself for the origin of the world. Mary, herself nothing but love, delivers man from sex, she soothes him. If he had been the victim of some pain, Sebastian would have been able to tell her about it. What pain? Nothing. Everything is limpid here with Mary—no passion: all is enchantment, luxury, calm, and voluptuousness. Mary reassures the warrior, or else she locks his madness inside an impregnable, unsayable, inextinguishable innocence.

Sebastian is sleeping under the arches of the cloister like a baby taking its nap. *Salve Regina.*

2 ☙

The disappearance of Fa, her death, her murder had put Xiao Chang in a state of endless agitation. He had passed into another suprahuman world beyond everything except music, and he rarely left the enclosure of his Walkman, which protected him against society.

"Music is all there is. A language of hatred that leaves the human species on its ass." Madame Lebon did not really grasp this utterance. What exactly did he want, this man who scoffed at her Saturday concert invitation? This time she was really panicked.

The person's Asian face was emaciated. With his scout's backpack, he might have been a pilgrim were it not for the earphones, which he never removed. A strange creature indeed.

"You mean 'a consolation'?" Did she think she'd misunderstood him or did she still hope to convert him?

"Bullshit! Monteverdi makes the dying believe that they're going to traverse death. Yes, the harmony of the spheres takes revenge on your fat humanity, my dear lady! The Mass in B Minor goes straight to your heart like an arrow, you've never felt it? It doesn't surprise me in your case, it reduces your insides to nothing—I won't speak of the outside of which there is precious little remaining. No one left, I'm telling you, after music sails through, nothing but a trembling of ecstasy you say. No, it's only the divine monstrosity taking hold of the world or getting rid of it. Bach is a purifier, therefore he is antisocial." From now on, Xiao was neither Chinese nor Santa Varvarois. Since the death of his twin, he had hitched himself to the universal mathematical absolute without language. A Pythagorian hilarity of human mechanisms!

At Fa's place Xiao had used his own techniques to get the best of the lock that was supposed to protect the apartment. ("The police are clearly not in a hurry. These bastards are not going to get worked up over a little Chinese girl.") Fa didn't see her twin anymore ("You're too complicated for me, Xiao, too Chinese, too naive, too pure. And I have to tell you, you frighten me.") She had not forgotten the torture that her little autocratic brother inflicted on her. OK, Xiao could understand that, even though the war he was waging now had nothing to do with that stupid past, which was frankly over and done with. He was not going to preach to her about the New Pantheon and his campaign against them! When an encounter takes place, there is an understanding that does without explanation and chitchat. But the encounter with his sister never took place for Fa, only for him—if one can call this explosion an encounter. To love one's twin is certainly the most normal thing in the world and the most inadmissible for everyone. Outwardly there's another person—a sister, to be precise—whom one is forbidden to love and who moreover does not love you. Therein is already the making of a tragedy, and in Greece and Santa Varvara it happens; elsewhere it's different, there are individuals much more civilized than that, more free, more like surfers: Egyptians, for example. Here, on the other hand, they say that it is incest: theories and constructions to jabber over and write books about. In reality you love yourself in your female mirror. You love yourself as you were in the immemorial premasculine embryo, when you had only female chromosomes—a din of blood and broken up mass of cells. Those who have gone that far, behind themselves, belong to no one: no sex, no people, no religion, no party, nothing. The ocean of the species, a night of the living. Their biological solitude condemns them to rage, their fated exclusion removes even the shadow of remorse. Pure vengeance and a highway of crime! They are clean, and Xiao knew he was clean.

He searched the apartment. No cop had been snooping around there yet. He only took his sister's computer. Fa dead: it was as unthinkable as was the suppression inside himself of the desire he had for her, ever since the maternal womb, and that he had put down to the point of being sick, a permanent state of near vomiting. She was the Juliet that Romeo carried inside himself. No one had known anything about it. A love to death, the love-hate couple was them, was him. All alone. When the retching made him dizzy and he kicked the calves of Fa and scratched her face, not in fun, as she had first thought, but in earnest, in the middle of a video game, for example, whether he was losing or winning, and Fa stared at him, astonished the first time, then more and more amazed and afterward resigned, she and others understood nothing. Psychotic, hot-tempered, maladapted to his surroundings—such were the judgments made of this precocious adolescent, perhaps brilliant, but alas the product of immigrant parents. The psychologists found nothing better to do than to separate him from his family. A residence, then nothing, neuroleptics. When it was clear as day!

"*It is not solely within our power to love or hate, because our will is governed by fate.* Do you agree, my dear lady?" More and more terrified, Cécilia Lebon was the prisoner of the nervous laugh of the man whose ears were continuously listening for the steps of the sacristan. Where was he, Mother of God?

It was a special ed teacher who had first taught him about Shakespeare and so many other things, nurturing his love for math, for example, situationism, and music. The guy was a pedophile or a homosexual—it was the same. Xiao didn't let himself be taken in, one isn't supergifted for nothing. The fascinated attention that he decided to give to the special ed teacher ended up satisfying the seductive instructor. Xiao left the mentor to his erotic dream, all the while taking advantage of the sentimental protection this unexpected tutor offered him; in the prison of his deep inner ocean the Chinese man clung to his native language—nothing seen, nothing taken. What else was there to do in a prison if not appropriate in his own way Chinese thought, the unfathomable citadel? But this native grotto was situated at such a depth that the subject's brain, which had excelled at mathematics, now brusquely abandoned, began to rot from pain.

From that moment on, Xiao Chang was cut in two.

On one side there was the infinite solitude that most of you take for a desert but, for the literary Chinese person that he longed to become, is only the complement of autonomy. *"An open space but not a desert. To discover that there is no desert is enough for me to triumph over what is oppressing me."* Who said that? Lao-Tze, Zhuangzi, or Colette? We train for paradise by imitating the masters of the past who in their day imitated the habits of animals: *"To jump like sparrows, all the while tapping one's behind."* Funny? Yes, rather. One might say satanic and free. Colleagues seemed to be surprised that the math genius turned away from his calculations in the lab and devoted himself to the odd jobs of his miserable ornithology hobby, which one could hardly call science! Who could have guessed that Xiao Chang was following the lessons of the sages—of Taoist saints, that is; ones who recommended the imitation of birds at the moment they spread their wings to lift off, the dance of the bear who twirls stretching his neck to the sky. *There is little difference between all that lives; so the two-legged saint will communicate with four-legged creatures, birds, insects, genies, and demons of all sorts.* And, like the tigers, he will believe himself among the hilltops of the forest, at the center of a cosmic ring, filled with a spacious fullness. Because there were no bears, genies, or demons in Santa Varvara, Fa's twin made do with birds. There is as much to learn from owls as from tigers, skilled as they are at twisting their necks to look behind; and from monkeys, who know how to suspend themselves with heads down. The first advantage of these games—something that was often written in ancient China and even translated since then into all languages by more or less talented scholars—is that they bestow the lightness needed by one who wants to practice ecstatic levitation. A certain Marcel Granet gives the recipe for this: one who wishes to avoid passions and dizziness must learn to breathe not only through the windpipe but with the whole body from head to toe, he must make himself impenetrable, impermeable, a closed circuit like an embryo preparing to be born. Note the magical grace of the calf that has just left its mother's side. A calf and a chickadee is only an infinite continuity. To blend with the flux of life—*she sheng*: 攝生, "to nourish life," which is not the same thing as to be nourished by a life that would be outside one, no. To nourish life without me or you, without mine or yours, without I or other, nothing but the mutation of living things transforming from one species to another, eating each other, devouring each other, reconstituting, an incommensurable ring. The ancient Chinese called this departure from self "long life," "to die without perishing": a state without time or space in which there is no place for death.

Listening to herons, curlews, great-crested grebes, auks, avocets, little egrets, turnstones, common shelducks, black-bellied plovers, cormorants, black-tailed godwits, black-legged kittiwakes, or their cousins the common black-headed gulls, and following and protecting them, speaking with them and nourishing them, and knowing each of their flights by heart, Xiao arrived at the certainty of having attained this impersonality, the impartiality of which the ancient texts speak: *The life of man between heaven and earth is like a white horse jumping a ditch and suddenly disappearing.* Birth—death? The change is total, instantaneous. But is it all that different from the wholesale changes that occur throughout life at every moment? Immersed in the instant, the mathematical man refused everything that could be divided by calculation or numerically measured. A disciple of Taoism could not limit himself to the mathematics used in a laboratory. Ought he to fly off toward the mathematics of the infinite, an infinite without bound or measure? An imaginary infinite, that which remains to be imagined if the mind were to turn to imagining. From then on all that is not infinite and therefore partial becomes exhausting, deathly, corruptible.

Thus on one side a secret abyss, his joy, his love.

On the other there is this century, this century into which Xiao had the misfortune to be born. It was not the world but the period that deserved to be called barbarous, a malignant tumor. It has been said that man is an idiot, but teachable. From that some have believed in the power of education! Not Xiao. Like others, he believes there is no point in shortening the feet of the crane or lengthening those of the duck. Being violent on the theory of correcting? Nonsense. *Where is the Tao?—There is nothing where it is not! —Show by example, that is better .—It is in this ant! —Can you give another more humble example? —It is in this grass. Smaller still? —It is in this shard. Is that the most humble? —It is in this excrement.* So then, there is neither horror nor crime?

"Yes there is. The time is one of false morals, false laws constructed to exploit small little urges, but those that unleash all the passions that humans possess: the taste for intrigue, the possessive spirit, the rage to dominate, the new world order, the stock market bubble, the destruction of the ozone layer, the neglect of the Kyoto accord, the New Pantheon, the maritime or solar Temple, the labs of Santa Varvara, and plenty of other troubles. It is laws that make criminals, the regulations that provoke anarchy; and if there were no doctors there would be no sick people—Artaud said it before everyone else. And so what?

So the ornithological saintliness of the Taoist of Santa Varvara was unable to simply contemplate how today's chiefs were willing to cage man like a pigeon. With no specific desire, freed from his passion for Fa and the advances of the special ed teacher (or so he thought), Xiao lived out his ecstasy to the fullest in saltwater marshes. But he was not able to forgo all interventions, withdraw to the inner ocean and do nothing by himself. He refused to make do with detesting intellectuals who spoke out against television from television's more fashionable soapboxes, who signed petitions and made speeches in public against society, and most of all against the society of spectacle! It was more advertising for themselves, of course, since it's well known there is no history or event other than advertising, which applauds you when you say "I." Here is the latest Paris fashion (that everyone has forgotten goes back to Montaigne, but oh well): an "I" that has nothing to say except "I'm fucked" or "I'm fucking you/him/her"; the personal pronoun *I* is now a brothel, a market, and "the excited reader flicks off the electricity." Really! In such circumstances, Zhuangzi was brutally clear. Did he not advise stopping up the ears of musicians, gouging out the eyes of painters, breaking the fingers of artisans, and especially tying a cloth across the mouths of all ideologues and enemies?

10–4, Zhuangzi buddy! Xiao Chang himself will shut the traps of the corrupt of Santa Varvara who only reflect the world of desires and isolated individuals of the continuous life, poor potatoes sewn within the sack of their passionate egoisms, oversized egos fixated on their vices! No, Xiao will not purify in the manner of the Confucian sages who called for abstinence, law, morals, and who knows what state discipline: that was the joke that disfigures, that exploits the death in everyone! It has already been stated, in the saint there is no place for death. Xiao will place death outside, he will expel it, he will evacuate it by evacuating the twisted individuals of every species.

"You're cracked, my friend! Not easy to stay in the empty traffic median, even when one is Chinese? Well, perhaps being Chinese here is not the same thing that your ancestors in the Middle Empire knew. Our Santa Varvara is nothing like a silk painting now, is it? Besides, are you Chinese analyzable? That is the question, the real question of this third millennium. But you are cracked, there's no doubt about that, my friend!" Such was the utterly useless diagnosis of his psychiatrist.

Xiao let him rattle on and became a purifier after his own fashion. "Going through with it might allow one to overcome the divide, but it could be dangerous to those in the vicinity," said a therapist who suspected Chang's criminal life. But since Xiao never clearly admitted his acts of purification, and since Doctor Moscovitch had no proof that the serial killer was in fact his own patient, he could not turn him in. All the more since the moral code among psychiatrists is opposed to all denunciation even if certain colleagues in their own practices refused this outmoded moralizing, which was downright inadmissible in the case of homocide or pedophilia, for example. "No scruples are permissible here, proclaimed the citizen-doctors, the public good comes before all else!" In fact, it was an unresolved question within the medical community of Santa Varvara, and as a result the Infinite's psychiatrist took no action. Fa's real disappearance, however, upset the theoretical applecart of Doctor Moscovitch's speculations about practical action serving to mend a serious divide in his patient. This is how, without any scruple, fuss, or delay, but in a manner completely unhinged, that is, 100 percent icily, Xiao Chang got rid of Minaldi and then took off in pursuit of Sebastian until he reached Le Puy-en-Velay.

When I shall die, take him and cut him out in little stars . . . that all the world will be in love with night and pay no worship to the garish sun. The Infinite speaking as Juliet.

The sacristan had finally appeared, to the great relief of Cécilia.

"Should we call the police?"

"Or an ambulance?" wondered Madame Lebon.

So long as Fa was happy to have occasional lovers and found that endlessly satisfying; i.e., ceaselessly and without purpose, with no thought, for example, of establishing a family, her own grotto, her territory, Xiao managed not to become angry. He had bloody gums and hemorrhaging in his stomach and intestines, that's all. But his revenge was following a more vast, noble, and definitive path, it was being written in blood on the very skin of these truants. The New Pantheon was getting carved up like a pumpkin, and it wasn't over yet! There was enough to hate the night itself after having ceased worshipping the garish sun some time ago. You don't see everything covered in gangrene in Santa Varvara like everywhere else: all-powerful networks are tearing each other apart and impose the same horrific conditions that they claim to combat in their rivals as well as among the supposed rebels and opposition, digested and bought off by a power that globalizes all it wants without the least sign of any counterpower? But, of course, you say, and you play at the alternative globalization game, you demonstrate, you write slogans, you make demands, kind and gentle banter, and whatever else. I know, I've been there, illusion and manipulation, little chiefs and insatiable pariahs, masters and slaves. Society secretes its rowdies to let off steam for a weekend, and then everyone is back to their credit cards! A better alternative? Go to court, demand justice? Don't even think of it. All the same, there are no more boundaries, not on the Internet any more than between good and evil. "One must count on one's own power," as president Mao used to say . . . and a few others.

Wuxian, 無限—"No limit": the purification will be without end, fire will burn the territory of the crooks, there is no cave to protect this depraved species of the New Pantheon and their like. Xiao Chang had good reasons to act as he was doing, reasons that were all his own and yet easily borrowed.

The folder "Sent items" inside Fa's laptop was filled almost exclusively with messages to Sebastian Chrest-Jones. There could be no doubt that Fa was hooked on this guy, that is to say, caught hook, line, and sinker. When Stony Brook Lake was dredged and her body was recovered, the papers didn't hesitate to put a racist spin on the story while insisting on their opposition to all racism: "Chinese drowning victim was pregnant." From that point on the story of Fa became utterly clear for her twin. Fa had been wrong not to cut her Romeo into little pieces as Juliet had suggested long ago to old Will: there is no other solution to a love knot; one of the lovebirds has to chop up the other or vice versa. My poor sister got a head start. 無限: *Wuxian*. Infinite, will be, yet again, the *Jinghuazhe* 淨化者, the purifier. The purifier will only join the infinite when he reaches his end. With the killing of Fa, it was done. The ornithologist had reached the end of his war against evil, because Xiao Chang was persuaded that the forces of evil dominated the world and that the source of universal evil came from that which kept him from uniting with his young female. In a word, and to speed things up a bit, it is called *Society*. Whatever it be, with its taboos, conventions, prohibitions, hypocrisies, abuses. And certain of its leading figures in particular, to start with the most corrupt, which is to say the most sociable of all.

"We come here to the principal motor of your psychosis." Doctor Moscovitch had been trying to convince him of this for years. "It is perfectly clear that you cannot stand Law or Society because you cannot stand that a man is not a woman. As a consequence you see injustices everywhere. Which is not exactly false, but rather exaggerated, do you understand?" No, he did not understand, the psychiatrist himself saw that he was confusing concepts, but he was paid to come up with a diagnosis and he stuck by it. "It's simple, you are a Chinese President Schreber," said Moscovitch, sounding optimistic.

"Keep talking! This Schreber, did he really exist? Freud never met him, and in any case there are only anti-Oedipuses; now we're all Schrebers, it's full proof," thought Xiao to himself during all these therapy sessions—who knows if they were useless or if they prevented the worst by at least giving him the feeling of being a modern man. Now Xiao was making no excuses. He knew Moscovitch was not wrong, not totally wrong. It was necessary for Fa to be killed for everything to become clear, and for the Infinite to finish off once and for all with Romeo and Juliet, with the prohibitions of family, and with all of these gangsters that Society allows.

"You are also looking for Adhémar de Monteil, my dear sir?" Ever since yesterday Madame Lebon felt plagued by a welter of terrifying visitors—how in God's name could this possibly end?

"In a way, yes." *Wuxian*: 無限, in other words, Xiao Chang, alias the Infinite, had regained all his lucidity; he had not been so clear-headed since abandoning mathematics in favor of birds.

"Another one of you pilgrims shares your interest, did you know? Lacking any precise address, I made some general suggestions that I thought might be useful—you never know. The gentleman will no doubt come to Saturday's concert." The difference between Xiao, alias the Infinite, in other words, *Wuxian*: 無限, and the historian of the Crusades was that the voice of Madame Lebon did not enchant him in the least. He found it most ridiculous in this deformed, downright ugly mass of flesh. Here was nothing to compare with the grace of Fa—a real minx, the twin, you could see it in her silhouette, her lips, and her black bangs that hung always before her laughing, wet eyes.

"Certainly. Until Saturday then." He was going to make sure that the clown this local chatterbox was speaking of was really Sebastian Chrest-Jones. No joking around this time, the Infinite would not confuse him with Minaldi anymore—or anyone else!

To get to Le Puy-en-Velay, Xiao had traveled more directly than Jerry. The Chinese have an abacus mind that no computerized security filter can combat: everything connects— 感應: *gangying*, "universal resonance." How does one steal the contents of a computer whose information on the hard drive is encrypted with software designed to deny access to that information? Elementary, my dear Professor Chrest-Jones, when one is Xiao Chang and one has no doubt that you are indeed the murderer of his sister, as proven by the e-mails that you've exchanged from work and from home.

Having first identified the Internet sites that his sister's lover liked to go visit (First Crusade, Anna Comnena, Adhémar de Monteil, etc.), Xiao had only to play the hacker; that is, send in a well-built Trojan, a little remote control device that would execute commands from inside the host like a virus. It would copy and divert information to the hacker's memory in a space that he had set up elsewhere. From there Xiao the hacker had only to spy on the host-killer until he connected to the Internet in order to decrypt his information and divert it at will. Once on his hard drive, the Trojan waited for the host to boot up to become active and gain access to files. Thus the mental processes of the historian host become perfectly clear to the Trojan horse; i.e., Xiao, you, or anyone.

Logically, mathematically, the delirium of this memory-obsessed hunter of paternal images named Sebastian Chrest-Jones would lead him from the Crusades, through Thrace, Philippopolis, Byzantium, on a poetic detour through Nessebar and Sozopol, and then finally through an implacable return to the paradise of origins, directly to the point of departure in the Languedoc of his presumed ancestors. Maybe Clermont? Vézelay? Without a doubt, Le Puy.

Nothing was now inaccessible in Santa Varvara, given that Santa Varvara was now global. Xiao Chang, alias *Wuxian*: 無限, in other words, the Infinite, pitched his tent in the valley where the Dolaizon crosses the route of Saint-Jacques-de-Compostelle and adopted the dinosaurlike attitude of a tourist in love with cloisters. He got on the Yamaha 600 Black Frazer 2001 that he had just rented from the local bike shop not far from the station where the Infinite had abandoned forever, and quite willingly, the train that circulated between Saint-Étienne and Le Puy, and rode it back to the center of Le Puy to have a beer at the King's Head, Authentic English Pub.

3 &

The *Salve Regina* that opened the concert threw Sebastian into an unbearable state of anxiety. Among sensitive individuals and some cats music can provoke a neural disorder that even causes epileptic fits. However, such sharp ears are not necessarily those of true music lovers. No code or technical training or disciplined listening can prevent the electrical short-circuit that overwhelms their neural fibers. Among the singularly refined who are affected, one notices a significant number of criminals of all types. Sebastian could no longer stand the obsessive presence of Adhémar de Monteil, especially in the Pergolesi variation that had been pleasingly inspired by the Vellave air. He discreetly left the church where the concert was taking place and was rather glad to see that other listeners were doing the same, though not necessarily for the same reason. Take refuge in the cloister, that was something he could do; and so he happily did take shelter amidst its placid arcades.

The moon was full and the historian leaned his back against a column and contemplated the shiny nocturnal orb. Did he notice that his face was wet with tears? A crying man, carrying along his mortality. He thought he heard footsteps, or perhaps it was a fluttering of wings, swallows returning to their nests under the eaves, bats leaving for the hunt? What did it matter? Here was a man crying, carrying along his mortality.

In via in patria. "Desire the homeland, be conscious of the pilgrimage," He heard himself murmuring. "Join like a foreigner the wisdom that is not foreign . . . since it was far from us, it assumes that which was closest to us." What was that doing here now? Someone was speaking inside Sebastian, perhaps not Adhémar but maybe Augustine. It was impossible to silence him. The historian moved over to the next column with his face still turned toward the moon. *In via in patria.*

Again there was the rubbing of wings or perhaps steps. His eyes were overwhelmed by the moonlight, and he could make out nothing in the darkness of the cloister.

Suddenly there came a shattering noise, a shot rang out, and a bullet grazed the back of his neck. In less than a second there were two or three more gunshots. Sebastian did not have the time, nor perhaps had he the will to react. Blast—the fatal bullet entered his skull through his left ear and lodged itself finally in the old stone of the column that his body now slumped against in a heap.

"We got him, Boss!" said Popov as he turned over the body of the Infinite. "But he had time to put a slug in the skull of the professor."

"You shouldn't have fired, Stephanie. The Colt I loaned you in Santa Varvara was only supposed to be used in cases of self-defense." Rilsky was most concerned by Mademoiselle Delacour, who looked rather pale after taking her shot and was shuffling about unsteadily. "Take my arm and come sit over here, the light is much better."

Put on the alert by Foulques Weil, the local police had been keeping a close watch on the cathedral for several days as well as following all suspicious pilgrims signaled by the sacristan Papageno. Disguised in street clothes among the concertgoers, the special agents had little trouble circling the cloister once Sebastian and the Infinite had stepped inside after leaving the concert at the end of the *Salve Regina*. Now they examined the body of Xiao Chang, alias *Wuxian*: 無很, alias the Infinite Purifier, with all the usual precautions. Stephanie meanwhile continued to stare blankly at the growing puddle of blood that collected underneath the left ear of Sebastian.

"The crime weapon is a CETME automatic pistol, boss. Just as I thought, this guy was in contact with international terrorism." Popov was proud to recognize the weapon at a glance. "No, don't worry. I'm not touching a thing." This he said to the French brigadier general who saw his foreign colleague leaning a little too close to the evidence.

"Yes, like those you find in the Spanish army and elsewhere. Do you remember August 2001 in that village south of San Sebastian? The Basque police arrested eight people suspected of having links to the Basque independence organization ETA, and it so happens they had three CETME automatic pistols in their possession. That was just two days after a toy exploded in San Sebastian—him again—that killed a woman and a sixteen-month-old baby; it was a six-inch toy car filled with explosives and equipped with a timer." Rilsky was intent on distracting the attention of the French police who were at the scene of the shooting so that they would forget about Stephanie. "Herri Batasuna, the ETA's political spokesman, claimed that it was a dirty trick of the Spanish police—why not?—but the Infinite's weapon we've recovered today proves that there was theft going on. Or a hold up ... or a mafia connection between the police and terrorists. It could be ... in any case, it's plausible."

"Excuse me, boss. The ETA has been more into explosives lately—and even toxic gases! Remember the theft in Bayonne of that large stock of capsules of whatever it was called, which, when broken open, would change into a poison gas that could asphyxiate everyone in the Paris subway in less than ten minutes?" Popov was playing Officer Know-it-all and got off track as he tried to hide his excitement.

"That's not what matters here, my friend. Now be logical, will you? Question: Who is using the CETME guns that have come from this theft, holdup, or mafia connection? The Spanish and French underworld, countless independence fighters, and let's not forget the networks of Algerians, Kurds, Africans, Corsicans, Colombians, and followers of Bin Laden, of course, too ... the Infinite is not the solitary figure he would have us believe." There was no way that his deputy was going to upstage the boss with his knowledge of arms and criminal networks. Besides, there was nothing like a convoluted, clunky explanation to calm the nerves.

Ever since the message in Chinese from the Infinite and the recovery of Fa Chang's body from the lake, the police commissioner of Santa Varvara had his idea about the whole thing. First, Sebastian was not Number Eight, now a closed case, the end of a black maelstrom. Xiao Chang decided he had to kill Sebastian once he discovered the historian was his sister's lover, and to do so the purifier was going to do everything in his power to track down this ultimate enemy as a way to conclude his infinite vocation. Second, Sebastian's trail uncovered by Stephanie with the help of Jerry seemed credible and it led to Le Puy. There was no reason for the mathematical ornithologist not to be at least as good a computer hacker as Jerry, so he would be heading toward the same rocky volcanic destination. Rendezvous in Le Puy. Fortunately—point number three—in the wake of their recent security campaign the French police proved more cooperative than ever, and with Foulques Weil's encouragement they were even more on top of things than necessary. With all that in place there was really no reason to fail.

They just had to capture the serial killer while preventing the murder of Sebastian. Easier said than done. Things had happened too fast, not at all the way they'd planned. It was impossible to go back in time before the deaths. The case wasn't a total failure, but as things stood it wasn't exactly a success either. Or perhaps it was a complete success, if one looked beyond the public statements of the commissioner. Of course, the double murder eliminated the chance to put the Infinite on trial and with that the chance for some choice revelations about the New Pantheon. But would a trial in Santa Varvara have been able to make any meaningful revelations about the New Pantheon? "They" would have swept things under the carpet, no doubt. We can say then that it was mission accomplished after all. That's the way things turned out, and Rilsky privately savored his success. First of all, he had finished off the purifier, for now, or until another one took his place. Second, he had put an end to the Byzantine story of Sebastian who had been going too far, who knows where exactly, but too close to Northrop himself—that was certain! And finally, he left the media with their fantastic stories, which did not always prove to be pure pulp fiction. The proof was Stephanie Delacour, who through it all had managed to get over, through, or under the usual wall of journalistic b.s. There was, however, one regret: not being able to save Sebastian.

But was it a true regret? Here was a chance for Rilsky to turn the page on this bothersome uncle who was beginning to dangerously contaminate the nephew with his genealogical quests and other identity crises. It was the obsession of the eighties, all that, and now thankfully over! People would go and search through history, past or present—i.e., in the lives of others—for the stains they were unable to accept in themselves. On the couch, for example. It was easier to cast oneself as the detective, for example, than to undergo analysis.

All said and done, Sebastian didn't get off too badly by dying as he did. Since he had died in his Byzantium, you could say he had reached the end of something—or the beginning. And no one could say whether he had killed Fa Chang and with her his own son in solitary pursuit of his own interior crusade. A criminal as well? It was better that Rilsky be the only one to know for sure and have no proof of it. To review: *Wuxian*, 無限, alias the Infinite, could only have taken revenge on the apostle of migrations whose humanist hypocrisy triggered a powerful feeling of insecurity in the eyes of the purifier, a feeling that structurally justified the mafia of the New Pantheon type that recruited among the ranks of new immigrants, all the while detesting them and so forth. The chain of reasons that can lead to crime is infinite. It was not necessary that this clear accomplice of the foulest individuals, as the purifier considered Professor Chrest-Jones to be, should also be the murderer of his Chinese mistress who happened to be the sister of the Infinite. It sufficed that the brother of the victim be a purifier, a madman of the absolute, a neo-situationist, or something along those lines, for him to send a bullet into his head. A good political argument will win over public opinion, there's no need to go into family histories.

Whether from the right or the left, all purifiers look alike. They think they're above the law. Saints. But let's talk about saints: *socialus est vita sacrorum*, or am I mistaken? The problem is that the Christian-Socialist wisdom no longer works; modern supermen are above all that for fear of seeing themselves too clearly. They protect themselves from their own illnesses by cleaning up society, which, let's admit, often needs cleaning up, and it works; but from there to. . . . Protecting oneself is not purifying oneself—a purist is capable of everything except an honest self-examination. But then there's Sebastian, who succeeded in coming full circle.

Stephanie claims to have seen him crying in the moonlight just before the bullet entered his skull. Very emotional, that Stephanie, especially when she's holding a gun in her hand. But it's not impossible that Sebastian had cried in the end. A nervous type, that Sebastian. On the road, in the homeland. His way of leaving the table and going home, his own brand of elegance, laborious, but . . .

The autopsy of the Infinite would reveal that only an arm was grazed by the shot from Stephanie's Colt. The French were told that it was Rilsky's, that the journalist had no weapon and was only an observer—too close, granted, but the media want to embed themselves everywhere now, you understand. Journalists are getting themselves crushed by tanks for the sake of getting their story "live," there's nothing you can do. Rilsky's nickleplated Remington dealt the fatal blow that struck the serial killer in the temple. In the offical report it would be Popov's. The two shots fired by the French colleagues with their powerful MAB 98B provided by the munitions and explosives unit would alone have finished off this criminal, a dangerous terrorist. With all this crossfire the Infinite had no chance—he was toast. This victory over the mafia and its operations, purifiers included, was thus the success of international cooperation. Rilsky was so pleased with his performance that he took out his mauve silk handkerchief to stifle a mean laugh and malicious half-smile.

As for Le Puy, it began to rain on the town toward midnight on that Saturday after the concert. A soft gray rain that carried on all the next week. Of course the press reported the shooting in the cloister, a banal settling of accounts, it seems, between rival gangs. Even in the wilds of Auvergne, can you believe it! The concertgoers recalled hearing some loud noises, firecrackers or explosions, who could tell; they thought it was a fireworks show, there are so many of them now worked into the historical reconstructions that are staged to amuse crowds of summer vacationers. Journalists call it historical revisionism, you know. The past is reviewed and prettified, why not, if it gives some memories to young people who have not lived enough to have their own? And besides, one has to pass the time, "kill time," as they say, when there's nothing left to do. Others continue to make history in Afghanistan, Iraq, New York, and Jerusalem. Here it's usually calm. Really calm. Cécilia Lebon can tell you that if you come visit the cathedral.

A puffy cloud sailed by between two rain showers in the middle of that sweet night, and the full moon hidden behind it lit up a drunken boat of a scarlet hue. It also looked like smoky blood.

"Ladies and Gentlemen, a terrorist attack has just taken place in the Louvre. The Prefect of the Paris Police asks that you remain calm" ☙

"Hello, my dear! But I thought you were in Santa Varvara, about to arrest the serial killer and put the New Pantheon on trial!" Whenever it suits him, my boss at the *Événement de Paris* can't help directing his sarcasms to the female that I am. I pretend not to understand.

"There isn't going to be any trial, no matter what anyone says." Imperturbable journalist that I am, I bow before objective facts.

"Is it because your purifier, who ended up purified himself, was posing as the prototype of the New Man?" My boss, ever the joker. "You'll at least turn it into a novel for us?"

This guy makes me laugh. It's not that I detest him, I don't respect him enough for that. Lucien Bondy belongs to the class of failed yet unavoidable guppies.

"How's that again?" Audrey always takes up the little nuggets that my boss inspires me to utter.

"Sssht. Let it drop, it's not really any of your business." I am wary of her curiosity. But if I didn't confide a little in Audrey who could I talk to? "So, you still fight for women's liberation, don't you?"

"Used to fight . . . "

" . . . OK, so you've got your cake and your solitude as a nice cherry on top. But really, I'm not getting on your case, I've had my share of crap too. I just want to tell you my discovery—are you ready? Much more than the human female, the male is a mammal that depends on his mother from start to finish. You'll tell me that our ancestor the Lespugue Venus knew that already. Freud pretended to minimize this indelible passion that he was all too aware of—Jocasta and Oedipus, remember them? The good doctor only saw castration fear everywhere, his sole explanation for the forward striving of the stronger sex and his rage to perform. Man is a failed guppy, the Lespugue Venus knew it, perhaps, and our friend Quignard never tires of repeating it, but not today's thinkers. They prefer to kneel down before Papa—who art in heaven. But down here things are different. Are you following me? . . . Unlike the viviparous fish whose eggs develop entirely inside the maternal uterus such that the 'livebearer' exists autonomously from birth, Lucien Bondy is a clingy mammal. What is one to do?" Audrey raises her eyebrows, it's not her problem. Ever since the paparazzi at *Dear Dire* magazine who specialize in scandals, scoops, and other low blows revealed her liaison with her psychic (something she vigorously denied, while the *Événement artistique*, equally indignant, shouted conspiracy), Audrey has been trying to convince me that men don't interest her and that she ignores them. Precisely. It's because she ignores them that she's given herself over to a guru, a being above other beings, a visionary and savant, a healer and thinker, a musician and musicologist, feminine/masculine, a total androgyne, in short, her master whose every word is gospel. Troublesome. I am not going to burst her bubble, her only relation to humanity, or to what resembles the human. I shall continue. "Most women go at it zealously. It's more than a job, it's an enchantment! Some back off frightened. No, I'm not thinking of you! Some persevere in a disappointing cohabitation and finally come to some arrangement. Tenderness and irony, you know the tune, like me with my police commissioner. It's a long march and you got to have emancipated mammals. Bondy's not there yet, as you can guess; he will always be a failed guppy—I'm repeating myself. I love it. Every time he talks to me I'm reminded of one of my old boyfriends, the star talking head on television, yes, the same one you're thinking of—the one I used to admire for his sense of humor, his vast culture, in short, the guy I idealized with that fervor without which lovemaking is only masturbation." I know that my man stories disgust dear Audrey because that's all that interests her—the impossible—so I shall continue. "Until the day I heard Mr. Star-talking-head say on the air that he loved the work of a little sculptress whom I had heard him privately call disgustingly pretentious, *but* whose family connections included ownership of the station that employed my dream man. As my talking head heartthrob continued spouting his admiration and the sculptress continued beaming back her appreciation of his appreciation, my dream man deflated and then disintegrated before my eyes. There was no more man, nothing but a hostage, a victim, a puddle, a white spot, perhaps a baby—and you know I love babies, real ones. You'll say I'm jealous, and I know it's human to defend one's job by whatever means necessary. But the unconscious doesn't reason like you and me. The night after that show I had the most savage dream of my life. My boyfriend was walking toward me, his penis cut off at the root, he was smiling his toothy television smile, I backed up in horror while a voice was trying to tell me that things like that are not definitive, that it grows back like the tail of a lizard—did I perhaps not know this?—there was really nothing to be upset about. I woke up in a sweat—for me it was definitive. I never again wanted to make love with my television star. But we run in the same circles, you know; he's a powerful man and I pretend to respect him. In short, he's another perfect example of the failed guppy. Sad but true. . . . "

"I thought you liked men?" Audrey compassionate. She can't understand me, how could she, my tender little friend who pretends to only love women? Me, I've seen the men's hell, outside over there, as the poets would say. Outside over there, that is to say here and now: that dependence on the mother-mistress, the Dark Lady who rises up in the dreams and erections of supposedly macho seducers, corporate executives, managing editors, and movie stars. Some go homo; the most impulsive or the most phobic, or both, trade in their passion for Mama Superglue in exchange for stronger sports, sadomasochism, life unto death, a regressive loss of self into the immemorial stuff of inorganic matter. But watch out: all of this is presented in the form of chic and shocking little gift packets—subliminal, aesthetic, mystical, academic little packages—all wonderful platters of Platonism! Plato has never stopped producing grandchildren, it's true, every man generates a group of fans that reassures him, raises his spirits and other stuff, whether it's at a restaurant, the stadium, Harry's Bar, wherever . . . Others now pose as worldly fathers of insatiable Lolitas, the ephemeral starlets of *Star Academy* and other reality shows, the cheap drugs of the suburbs. And they amuse themselves in retirement with unbelievable and unbelieving fairies, tactile and coded storms, Coriolanus and Cymbeline for Arabs, Persephone as an anchorwoman in chains. Ah, the hell of men! A long march with no way out through the Abyssinia of maternal power, or how not to escape from the Dark Lady except by getting it up for her and a bit for her cohort of boys and girls, glittery puppets, today's cathode chimeras, easy replicas of the inaccessible, the unavowable, the frightening, the insatiable, the indigestible maternal phallus! I just have to come back to Paris for it to hit me in the face, because Parisians don't bother with political-criminal stories, they pretend to take an interest in money, slush funds, kickbacks and expense accounts, but no, it's not yet Santa Varvara here! We're the regional experts in erotomania, ours is a sort of Byzantium of sex, we're up on things, we know. The male hell, I have to tell you, Audrey dear, is to need and never be able to fuck enough under the magic wand of the Dark Lady, the only imaginary excitement that makes man a Narcissus subject to every recantation, a histrion, a simulacrum. One persecuted and capable of a thousand tricks, a masochist who compensates through sadism, an obsessive stuck on the oral and especially the anal, a paranoid who prefers to remain a nursing newborn, a godfather underneath which hides a sylph. Ah, man, man, man. Popular opinion wants him to be a rock, steel, a pope, a Saddam, a Sharon, a Bush, when he's crumbling into vices, vicissitudes, unmanageable dependencies, and approximate erections, falling with a dried-up soul and frozen heart into a dantesque hell of shivering cold and fear. . . . But how difficult it is to speak of this hell, so bitter and ferocious is the obscure forest in *The Divine Comedy* that revives fear in the mind! It's clear, Paris gets on my nerves, I must look a fright, Audrey is rather kind to put up with my silence.

"Everything will be hell for the rest of us, I see. There will only be a hetero paradise—you know about that now, don't you, lucky lady?" She lights a cigarette, too bad for our failed guppy who's fighting cancer: elementary, my dear Bondy. She finally decides to tease me, but she won't succeed because I'm launched now.

"You know what? A few survivors think they're hetero and look for women so they can masturbate in peace, or so they think, if only they can find some Good Samaritans. And there are plenty. The couple works as the magazines say. Why are there Samaritans? Because the hysteric is depressive, always disappointed by sex and everything else, and looks less for a master to reign over than a tranquil double to give her the illusion she exists, that life is possible and woman too. As for a man who would meet a woman and vice versa, this exploit supposes much more than reciprocal and complementary vices. My goodness, there's a whole alchemy behind it, my dear, and clever indeed would be the man or woman who could recite it for you! No frigidity or impotence: too banal, too simple. But to know how to take care of another to the point of letting a stranger who will always remain foreign reach orgasm and yet not become a victim, and certainly without killing him or her, I mean losing them, like in my dream of the severed penis!" I think I'll stop there.

"Come on Stephanie! Don't worry about it, it's movie sex you're talking about, cocks cut with electric knives and stuff—remember that film, we saw it together? . . . You dreamed of it, that's all!" Audrey thinks she can reassure me, maybe win back for me my TV star, girlfriends often want you to have a famous lover.

I don't listen to her, my awful dream that was not a movie definitively swept away my star, there's nothing to be salvaged there, so now I wage my private battle against Bondy. A stub of penis snipped a few centimeters from his abdomen, no bleeding, white as a scallop: the image invariably comes to mind whenever my boss begins throwing out his wisecracks. I don't want to know what sculptress is holding him hostage, but I know from experience that his aggressive virility is a bandaid over the same sort of profound collapse that I witnessed in my TV star lover.

"You'll at least turn it into a novel for us?" Bondy repeats. He finds me distracted and so insists.

"You . . . at least . . . for us?" What he means is I have too much ambition, that it's not for me, that it's ridiculous, that I would do well to stick to run-over dogs, serial killers, raped women . . . "Stephanie Delacour, our special foreign correspondent in Santa Varvara"—that's fine. A specialist, and even a good specialist, OK. But a writer? Don't make me laugh!

"Maybe, we'll see, a novel. I don't know—maybe some kind of free association." I stay evasive and avoid looking at him for fear he'll see what I think of him.

Ah, novels: he doesn't take them seriously and neither do I! Ever since I returned to Paris it's been impossible to avoid them, we are a literary nation, one thousand two-hundred and thirty-four novels released in September alone, people talk about them on television, at dinner, and even pretend to read them in the subway. Today's fashionable tomes are squeaky clean and trashy, often both at once, rightside up and upside down, hard sex and and ironic sex, and whenever possible clean, trashy, hard sex, and irony packaged as reality literature or "personal histories" as they're called. "What courage! What magnificent prose!" Critics glow, you're pushed to buy some of it, you even read a page or two. That's prose all right. To think the French are getting off on this and are excited to talk about it *urbi et orbi*: literature is the National Front of radical erotism, triumphant or pouting, but always incontinent and chatty. The human chatterbox will always be the emblematic animal of the Republic, prophesied a somber naturalist of the nineteenth century. And so it goes, and more than ever before. "All of society rushes toward the buttocks, the big sinkhole that shakes the world, there's only ass and religion" who hasn't yet understood that? A few rebels hold out, they persevere with their belles lettres, they keep on offering pearls of rhythm and rhyme to the pigs on television, giving poetic faeries, diamonds of love, art, sensitive music, I know one who has even succeeded in turning back evil—did you say evil?—it's been all but laughed away. And really, if you think about it, what better place is there to take refuge than in the beauty of writing that is watched over like a gift-wrapped present in these times when the artistocrats of the high sidewalks, today's "good neighborhoods," are becoming the whores of the Republic or mass-marketed porn authors? So evil, if it's not in the clean-trashy-hard sex-reality literature, only shows the druggy tip of its revolver in police thrillers: a refuge from the apocalypse for the middle classes, the shred of hope for the booksellers in the suburbs. "You can know the source of evil" promises the world of detective fiction. But really salvation is in the style, everything may be pardoned if it's well-written, chant the guardians of the temple of literature; content doesn't matter, the form is all! "Well-written, what does that mean?" reply the avant-garde postmodernists who are still out there, don't forget, turning gutteral Persian into nasal French when they're not busy simply making platitudinous denunciations of their own fathers' pedophiliac actions against their beautiful porcine selves. Ah, the avant-garde!

It's quite a rainbow coalition, the French novel, there's something for every taste—a snake pit too when the television people get involved (and they do, good luck to those who tune in!). I won't. I won't give Lucien Bondy the pleasure, I'll only give a road map, a minor genre, something hybrid, impossible, not even visible, maybe.

"This *Wuxian*, the character in your report, do you think he's part of a new race of men, a nuthead ready to blow up everything like those crazies at the World Trade Center?" Audrey just asked me the same question as poor Bondy, but with an effort at referring to what I wrote. I don't mean that she read it, but she acted as though she had: the sign of a true friend.

"I'm sick of this office. How about we get out of here? What do you say to a drink at the Marly?"

"Or two!"

"You take your car and I'll take mine, I need it later tonight. See you there."

EVERY TIME I come back from Santa Varvara, I like to have a drink on the terrace at the Marly as a way of imagining myself both in the heart of Paris and completely elsewhere, nowhere. Audrey follows me; I think she likes me when she's not resenting my not being like her, a woman who only likes women; but one never knows—according to Kristeva, feminine homosexuality is supposedly endogenous, whatever that means. Audrey hasn't given up hope, she kisses me on the mouth, but then turns to other things.

I have no interest in talking about *Wuxian* 無現, alias the Infinite. How can one talk about a purifier here, before the statue of Louis XIV on horseback? France is out of bounds, we've been spared kamikazes for the moment, though the suburbs are incubating them by the hundreds, they say. Let's not be in a hurry. It's cool to play the wiseman watching from the sidelines. History has given us this respite, so let's try to understand. Where is one when one is understanding? In history? Outside history? In any case, understanding—or what passes for it—is another story. I don't know if I prefer it, but it's all that we have left, here, now, on the terrace of the Marly.

The sunset covers Pei's pyramid in a soft silky topaz while the stones of the Louvre slumber in shadows of indigo. Soon the shadows will efface their stony thickness and the night will reduce the past to a flat drawing or theater decor illuminated for the city's tourists. There aren't many tourists left by the time the museum closes, and they disappear as the moon rises, all but a few dandies who know about dinners at the Marly.

In this sheltered corner, isolated from the major arteries and yet agitated by a cosmopolitan crowd, I rediscover upon each return from Santa Varvara the most inimitable products of French taste. It is not the Revolution with its fraternization and its Terror, nor is it the libertine spirit with its daring and sadism, nor the appetite of Gargantua or the fragrances and palette of the Fragonard family. It is baroque man and his vagabond inconstancy: volatile, mobile, playful. The Versailles court embraced the insolence of Don Juan and the virtuosity of Bernini because it practiced liberty as a comfortable illusion, never as a birthright or absolute claim. Baroque man knew he was an actor without interiority, skillful at changing masks and burning the sets of his spectacles, which were only enchanted islands, dreams or wonderlands never to be confused with reality.

The frivolous ends up deserving its guillotine—that's understood. But what an extravagant superiority over the leaden real and the burden of a fixed transcendence to dare to be inessential! Pei's pyramid is in this sense baroque, it is the empty median of the Taoists translated into French, it has no essence, its inconstant being does nothing but play at reflecting the passage of clouds, the galeries of Le Vau, the colonnades of Claude Perrault, and the spray of water fountains moved with each gust of wind.

"What are you thinking about?" Audrey thinks I'm in Santa Varvara, when really my thoughts are focussed on this very place.

"About *Wuxian,* who had no interiority. The harmony of yin and yang had come unglued in him and became two masks confronting each other as enemy powers, and their unbearable explosion broke him into little pieces. He almost ended up at a psychiatric hospital. Curiously the shrapnel from that explosion was contained by the mechanical envelope he hit upon in his religion of purification. Consumed from within, the "fire of the cave" was transported outside, and I have to say that for me his dirty work as an avenger is not devoid of pleasing aspects. I, Stephanie Delacour, who travel the globe denouncing killers of all kinds find the serial purifier of Santa Varvara fascinating. I admit it, and we know that plenty of people today see in him a hero of the Bin Laden type, someone they'd be happy to name their kids after."

"You're not saying that all terrorists, avengers, kamikazes, and the like have problems with their feminine side and are repressed homosexuals?"

"What do I know? Ask the Institute of Psychoanalysis! *Wuxian* certainly, I've studied his case. What interests me is a little different, you see. Imagine you are torn up inside because you cannot reconcile your yin and yang within yourself—or for some other reason: a humiliation, for example, something sexual, social, or political, and you no longer have any inner stronghold, nothing but a purulent open wound that throws you off, you flee inward and try to save yourself via something outside yourself. How will you proceed? Become an activist? Invent your own religion? Exterminate those of others? Take Prozac, Xolian, Cultopride, Danpharma?"

Audrey loves me all the more when I launch my interrogative mode full of bibbity bobbity boo. But I won't continue chewing on her ear for that. It's just that I don't have a good answer myself.

"Look at this place, yes, here, look around you. *Everything in the world is mutable. You have to love on the fly.* The people who built this place were neither authentic nor immutable. Quite simply they had no interiority, they were nothing but dominoes, wolves, costumes, roles. But they didn't confuse what they were with reality; they knew they were illusions that were to be played and enjoyed, no more. Am I telling you that those who built the Louvre had no religion? And that on the contrary *Wuxian*—Chinese, it's true—patched up his Taoist inauthenticity, itself compounded by a psychic desert proper to him, with an obsessional idea? That the Versailles actors of yesterday have been replaced by today's monomaniacs within a globalized Santa Varvara? That the illusionists have become the doctrinaire? That the wolf costumes of the old masquerade balls have been traded in for the hoods and masks of nationalists and fundamentalists?"

"The monomaniacs, as you say, claim that you, me, and everyone here are just playing: 'idiots who amuse themselves and believe in nothing'; that's what they charge us with . . . "

"You know yourself that they're not always wrong. Remember what you yourself said yesterday about this year's crop of exhibits, videos, and other installations. 'When one reads the *Événement artistique* by our friend Audrey, one wants to call your purifier in help—the new man who will finally save us, right, Stephanie? Don't bother repeating that to her though.' Bondy the Clown is not too far off. But there are different kinds of games. When the actors of the *Île enchantée* burned the set of their show, they meant to say that all was inessential, including their fire, just as the fire in which Don Juan burns is inessential. And that it's up to them, up to all of us, in fact, to renew the show, to reinvent it, nothing more, nothing less. *Wuxian*, on the other hand, when he "sets the house on fire," as the characters that compose his name indicate, sows nothingness, it's the end of the show, and death triumphs in that strange choice."

"You're going to write all that?"

"Are you kidding? I'm going to tell the story as I lived it with no conclusion. Moreover, the "house on fire" who got himself shot in Le Puy is perhaps the real New Man, the migrant nihilist, we'll see. Will he have gotten the better of us, or is it Rilsky who will succeed in setting his paranoid family relations straight? That's the question. Personally, it's Sebastian who, surprisingly, seemed to me most interesting. As you know, that guy was not a part of my newspaper's program. It wasn't on account of him that I was sent to Santa Varvara! As I see it, Sebastian is the Augustinian man, and from what you know of me, my mom and pop, and the rest, you can see I feel closer to him than to the baroque Versailles that I've been trying to sell you . . . I won't talk about that either. Why speak of Augustine in Paris? For whom? For Paul Ricoeur? For Philippe Sollers? People want intrigues, love interests, and the rest . . . What the devil are you trying to get at?"

A waiter proud as a marine grazed us with his tray of full champagne glasses and crystal cups of sorbet; he showed no sign of caring about the historical significance of where he was serving. A swarm of Japanese girls were busy taking pictures of Louis XIV and the Pei pyramid; further off the Carrousel Arch was giving up its pinkish glow in favor of a reddish brown hue as the light dimmed. The mindless pigeons had no idea what place this was that they were stopping in at, no more in fact than the waiter himself. "Hypogeum of thoughts around me, compartmentalized mummies, embalmed in the aromas of words. Thot, god of libraries, a bird-god with lunar crown. And I hear the voice of the great Egyptian priest . . . "

"This conversation is ridiculous, don't you think? It reminds me of the Quaker library episode in *Ulysses*. On top of Mount Knowledge, though less elliptically than in Joyce." Me awake now.

"Listen my smartaleck gal, my adorable ridiculous hairsplitter, you know what saves you? Your little mouth that trembles there in the corner just a bit, your sparkling black eyes. It's true, I recognize your crabby sidewalk of words, the Stephanie Delacour signature, her touch of irony. I may be the only one around to hear it, but here you go . . . " Audrey was happy to let things trail off there.

I liked it too, to see myself as though that were me. How I like to go about incognito. To present something as serious that I don't take seriously. My irony is my haven, just what my boss reproaches me for, and which only means that all of reality has become strange to me, that I am in turn a stranger to reality. As for my police commissioner who bothers you and whom you envy me for—yes, I don't deny it, I know you, Audrey: a deferred irony there too, I assure you he is the only man who has no need for any dramatic leading lady to give him the feeling of being alive. A guppy so unique that if he didn't exist, I would have invented him.

But that's enough for today—basta! That Audrey sure can be sentimental: no idea of going too far! In fact, my irony is precisely the opposite of Audrey's way: the presence of the finite within the infinite sentimental chatter that she so loves. A line in the sand that avoids Audrey's style of tragedy and sets the shiver going again.

"Listen, girl, irony only exists if it's brought up. And you bring it up, so it's yours. The experienced audience knows what's underneath each card, and you well know that the more I succeed in making illusions, the more I enjoy it." Audrey shakes her head from right to left in a furtive sign of disagreement. "I've got to go. Have you seen the time? See you later."

We each returned to our cars, the early darkness of these first days of autumn made the Louvre already look like a cardboard box theater. I had nothing to do, I was certainly not going back to rue d'Assas, I just needed to get away from Audrey. I turned onto the rue de Rivoli and sped toward the Arc de Triomphe and then on to the Défense. It didn't matter where. One is never more alone than when driving without knowing where one is going.

PEOPLE THINK I live in Paris, but it's not true. In Paris there is a whale under every pebble. Time twists under the smallest stone, every individual is a composed past, a novel, you might say, my own Byzantium. The irony of ironies is that Sebastian, dead in his Byzantium in Le Puy-en-Velay, has not left me. Me, Stephanie Delacour of the *Événement de Paris*, to find myself stuck to this guy, to his morbid erotico-Platonic fantasms instead of telling my little life story like everyone else, and everyone knows there would be enough to make the fifty-year-old housewife shed at least one tear if not more! My devotion to Jerry, for example. And that silent passion for the police chief of Santa Varvara, that took some doing!

The son of Gloria, my decapitated friend, who is now my son, my Jerry with his "problems"—people say that to be polite—who suspends the rest of the world, is the only person I shelter from all irony. Now and then, not often, roughly every four or five years, he drops out of life. "He's doing his coma for us," his mother used to say. I could say the same, but I think Jerry is mostly doing his coma for himself. Small things for the rest of us such as an upcoming birthday, the odd voice of the leader of the chorus of which he is a talented member, or, more seriously, any interruption in news from his friend Macha, produce in him a surge of life that approaches seizure. His extreme excitement then tends toward arrest, trauma, the suspension of consciousness, breathing, and heartbeat. It's a demi-death that kills me a little each time too and of which he claims to have no recollection, except for a sacred horror of all talk of hospitals, ambulances, and war. And since it is impossible to avoid these subjects as soon as one turns on the radio or television, Jerry gets up from the dinner table immediately and takes refuge in his computer screen where he can surf at will on the Internet and where he is free to avoid sickness and war if he chooses. He sings in his beautiful tenor voice as though to reassure himself during his imaginary navigations and to let me know that they are indeed imaginary. His kingdom is his own body. Enigmatic Jerry, I wonder at more than I feel frightened by his way of being. A being who is simply there with no intentions or regrets, not for becoming or succeeding, faltering or seducing. A simple present with no *ing* of the present progressive. Nothing but to exist delightfully to the very end, including the very end, with an incommensurable intensity, an excessive delicacy. Living it in all its breadth, without any pretention, music itself in every fiber, in each elementary particle, until the interval in which the unbearable hits him.

"Things didn't go so well when you were in Santa Varvara."

"So well"? Had he just done "his" coma again for "us"? Obviously he won't tell me anything, I'll have to ask old Pauline, but she's out, I'll call her.

Today Jerry devotes all his time to the Internet and his singing. I like to see him absorbed by his passions. They strike me as the luminous resonance of that black suspension where he ejects himself when he leaves us, and himself, when he abandons all effort to be *for*, all effort at be*ing*, when he leads me inside his coma as though it were mine, the death of everything. For now he's content to stay with us, to inhabit his living body and cover me with tenderness, make me endure as well among the living. He will even go and find me new tricks for hacking into the computer of poor Sebastian: "Where are you in your detective work? Do you need my help?" No, thank you, we thought we could save Sebastian from the vengeance of the Infinite-*Wuxian*, 無限. Alas, miracles are not all within my power, you see! It's enough to be able to accompany Jerry in his extraordinary life.

"I have to leave you, I was just passing through, I'm really badly parked . . ."

I leave. One is not as alone as one thinks, in Paris or even in Santa Varvara.

"Stephanie's thriller, it's only an escape," chortles Bondy along with a few others.

Oh, really? Writing it has brought me back to aspects of myself that I don't want to know as mine. A formidable hallucinator of the vast palaces of memory was this professor of Crusades, my familiar, my brother, who inherited the names Sebastian, Chrest, Jones. A man who mocks his knowledge by blowing himself up inside the piece of detective fiction that his life became, or is he mocking detective fiction, all the while using the minor genre as a platform for that memory? A madman, OK; possibly a criminal. Rilsky is persuaded of it, but he will keep his innermost convictions to himself. The investigation is closed. There remains only to write it up.

Where am I? At the wheel of my Rover, alone finally, without the *Événement*, without Bondy, without Audrey, without Nor, of course. Along the Seine, right bank, heading toward Bercy. The clouds look like feathers abandoned by a white swan in the coal-black sky. The bateaux-mouches, those laughable rides for the overgrown children that all tourists of the world are, glide with almost no wake through the muddy brown Seine as though gorged with thick, impure blood. The Grand Library rises up with its four uninhabited rectangular towers that dominate a desert that would discourage everyone including today's Quakers, and I won't be tempted either by the Semiramis shutterbug facade that covers the Institute of the Arabic World or, even less, by the asbestos towers of Jussieu. I double back westward along the Left Bank, toward Orsay; I could easily have a bite to eat at Trocadéro or on the Champs Élysées, at this hour not much would be open anywhere else.

Is not every love story the magic shadow of a searing reality? Anna Comnena and Ebrard in place of Sylvester and Tracy Jones in place of Sebastian Chrest-Jones and Fa Chang? One wonders. Sebastian's story disavowed the Crusades, and the peace of the living survived the programmed reconquest of Jerusalem. Finished, the old eye for an eye; basta, the tooth for a tooth. Chrest the narrator was betting on the countless generations arranged like dominoes from Ebrard to Sebastian. From Le Puy to Philippopolis to Santa Varvara.

Do I mock too easily the tragic destiny of our contemporaries? I know you think that I do, Nor, because you said so—just like Audrey; those who love me tell me that, a compliment, I suppose. In truth, everyone laments the absence of fathers, they don't stand up anymore and do their job, am I right? Thus one gets this deplorable lack of authority, and little by little it goes from school to the police to heads of state . . . enough already! But mothers, when they go AWOL because they're depressed, in love, frigid, overworked, abroad, at home, dead; i.e., because they are simply being who they are and not playing their role, really not at all, well, who cares about that?

Come on, we've not even invented anything to replace the Virgin Mary, unless it's surrogate mothers and pediatric psychiatry, soon we'll have reproductive cloning that will give us photocopy twins without father or mother! Bravo! Techniques, techniques, each one more impressive than the one before. But the soul, the soul? There is no more soul because there is no more mother. And the migrant that flees her or whom we oblige to leave her is not happy, no, he can never be happy. Nor, do you understand? In the large crowd that Sebastian belongs to—I'm not talking about exceptions like you and me—he cannot be happy, do you understand? I'm talking to you! Where are you? In Byzantium, in Santa Varvara? I'm in Paris supposedly. How is it? You want to know? Three quarters of Paris has been invaded by Santa Varvara, the last quarter is slouching as Byzantium did before into an opulent museum culture, a mushy sandcastle civilization, *fluctuat et mergitur.*

Niagara: is it a river or an Egyptian princess? Danton: a teammate of Zidane, Beckham, or Robespierre? Saint Louis: an island, a crusader, or a judge? Television contestants, you all want to be millionaires, but you know nothing about wealth. Santa Varvara condemns you to sacrifice your remaining scraps of memory in the lottery of useless knowledge that could win you that dream vacation for two at some South Seas Island resort. Unlike the television contestant, a biblical contestant such as my first Sebastian in search of his father is a killer killed by the presence of the past.

But the Augustine contestant, my second Sebastian, the traveler with his computer-generated story, reinvents the Crusades and conceives a fabulous pilgrimage. This disoriented migrant, this vagabond who gets caught up in a police thriller and might have ended up in a Santa Varvara jail doing life in prison, maybe even the electric chair, for strangling a pregnant Chinese woman, this head-in-the-clouds professor hits on a reason for being that was his own rebirth. With his imagination he remade the Crusades, and the famous battle to the death to liberate the Holy Sepulchre and the other ancient wars were transmuted into a renewal of the imaginative man himself. Starting with Ebrard and ending up with Sebastian crying in a cloister in Le Puy.

I'm writing the way I drive now, alone at the wheel, watching the landmarks that locate me here and at the same time dispersed completely elsewhere, I'm staying on the road while continuing to dream and speak to my relations in ways that I never do in person, but in a voice that they, Nor or Audrey, may guess to be mine. I don't think it's a novel, no. In France the novel is the rhetorical mode par excellence of perverts, while you each know that I lay claim to only the most exquisite of perversions, that of believing I have none. Americans, Russians, and others fill novels with their psychoses, their melancholy, and the rest gets folded in, lost, and is guessed at. From the beginning and now more than ever, the French have become known for a national specialty: they camp at the intersection of meaning and feeling and pull off feats that tickle the palate, the skin, the penis, the vagina, the ass, whatever you like and whatever they can. Poets, children, adolescents, polymorphic perverts, they get off on novels in the opera of the Flood, the absolute essence of France is a novel! It's undergoing inflation today and rotting into dullness on the screen, in cold households of reconstituted families huddling around Picard frozen dinners and other micowaveable meals. It sometimes happens that the same national marvel plays along and tries to explode the show with its most spectacular excesses—and the most insolent, the most envious, the most monstrous—but that, once brought out on television, are of the most petty, mean, and generic banality, that's all! It's the drug that allows the families to get up, satiated, from their plastic tablecloths and Picard frozen dinners to go to bed certain about having gotten to the heart of the matter.

One has to be downright unconscious to throw a novel into the bookshops of people like that? So for whom does one write? Like everyone else, for one's parents, for or against them. Mine transmitted to me the invitation to hold myself up straight, as if life for them existed solely in this primary sense of holding oneself up straight, that it was possible to polish oneself. Not to become better, nor to rid oneself of the corrupt and the vicious, as that crazy *Wuxian* wanted to believe—one sees where that leads. But to pass on by passing over oneself, by shipping oneself "this side up" for later or never, over paths that lead nowhere. I'm shipping myself on a voyage: I voyage, you voyage, we voyage. It's a voyage that unfolds identities, that goes back in time and doubles back through different spaces, and doesn't necessarily narrate or novelize but remains perhaps more a quest, an enigma.

I don't think I'm going to eat tonight. Having gone around in circles along the banks of the Seine without paying attention, I've ended up near my place after having traveled for hours and hours all over Paris. The Luxembourg Gardens smell a lot like linden even though it's not the season, but that honey scent of linden always surrounds my garden in my sensory memory, in my present impregnated with the past, in my walks with Jerry, doves in the pink walnut trees, bees that confuse their hives with my windows on the rue d'Assas. The fragrance of flowers in bloom, of freshness, of renewal, so light and that yet penetrate glass, iron, stone, my skin, my bones, nourishing me and undoing me.

I park my Rover against the steel door, what time is it? With the time change these first days back in Paris are literally hallucinatory. My own kind of honey.

"ESTELLE PANKOW? But of course I remember you! You're in Paris? Yes, a nice surprise." It couldn't be more surprising. I hardly know her, a rather discreet psychiatrist. What could she want from me? A friend of Hermine's? A messenger from Santa Varvara? "Your international conference on the 'New Maladies of the Soul'? Fascinating! Of course! At my place, of course, it would be a pleasure. No, I've not really got back to work yet . . . still between the two continents . . . not easy as you well know. Yes, rue d'Assas, you don't have the code? Thursday at five, no, I'm not at the newspaper that day, an appointment outside Paris. See you Thursday then!"

I rarely receive guests in my home, I like to keep it my secret garden, but Estelle—where else could I see her? She no doubt has something important to tell me or to get out of me. Tea, Chinese tea naturally, no cake, just the flavor of jasmine and smoked flowers, a Felicity they call it at the House of China near my apartment. I like to go there on my way home, read the paper, have tea, buy some to take home, rub against the polished, coded, meaningless smiles.

"Do I remember Hermine? Can one forget the laugh of a woman so . . . " I hesitate.

"She doesn't laugh anymore. I happen to know she had to be hospitalized for severe depression. After Sebastian's death. The murder . . . But she's better, calmer, now." Estelle Pankow watched each word leave her lips. She would not be indiscreet.

"Is she undergoing psychoanalysis?" I don't know what to say, so I say that.

"Oh, no!" Estelle lets out a hearty laugh and her little forget-me-not eyes sparkle underneath curly hair that hides almost her whole face; she pushes her hair back often with a coquettish gesture. "Not her style. She's gotten involved in the prostitutes' rights movement." I still have no idea why she's come here.

"She's fine then."

"Yes, she wants prostitution to be liberalized. When Sebastian's death was discovered, Hermine got it in her head that he had been the lover of the unlucky lab assistant, you know, the girl Fa Chang who was found drowned. And pregnant." With her two hands, the psychiatrist again pushed her hair back on each side, and her forget-me-not eyes, now suddenly uncovered, stared at me all the more vigorously. "So that a man never again ends up in such a situation, Hermine thinks the only solution is open prostitution. Perhaps you know the work of Sue Oliver?"

So that's it! Was Madame Pankow conducting her own personal investigation to better understand the unconscious and the bodies of our contemporaries? Or was she a spy of the Santa Varvara world syndicate? Did she want to know if I knew if the commissioner knew or why he didn't want to know? And since it was impossible to corner Rilsky—to what end, especially in Santa Varvara where he did what he could against a mafia-riddled regime and an increasingly hardening government?—why not go after Mademoiselle Delacour?

Hermine had insisted that Estelle meet with me in Paris—because she didn't feel up to bothering Northrop, such a close relative, you know, that would have seriously upset her—to find out if I had seen Sebastian in Le

Puy before his death, if I had spoken with him, how he had seemed, that sort of thing.

"I know you won't tell me anything, Stephanie, but I wanted to form my own idea. By myself. And it will make Hermine feel better if I can tell her that I saw you. That's all." Estelle was sweating with curiosity, all the while trying to project an honest calm. I expected nothing more.

Would I tell her nothing? Not really. I'll tell her some things; I won't let her leave without hearing my sincere conviction. A conviction that will only respond very indirectly to Hermine's questions and those of Madame Pankow. But how could one do otherwise? I'm not a cop or a shrink. I see things as I write them, a little bit like Sebastian himself, or almost.

Would Estelle understand if I told her that for me Sebastian was an example of man who had reached his ends, his end—"Western man," Audrey would interject, always militating for who knows what. Estelle scrunches up her forget-me-not eyes. Sure, even a shrink from Santa Varvara can understand this sort of thing. So I tell her my story just as I'm writing it.

On the one hand, Xiao Chang, the Infinite, *Wuxian*: 無限, the man without interiority, the "house on fire" who destroyed everything down to his own soul. On the other, Sebastian, or the house enlarged up to and including the memory of ancestors. Time is not lost with Sebastian, the present has devoured the past that unmakes and remakes it. A pure criminal product of Santa Varvara, this poor *C/J*, a victim of his family epic? Or an antidote to the criminal city, Augustinian man reborn from his memory? The triumph of the infernal unconscious? Or, on the contrary, time replayed against time?

"Listen to this: *'It is therefore incorrect to say there are three times: past, present, and future. It would be more correct to say there are three times: the present of the past, the present of the present, the present of the future. The present of the past is memory; the present of the present is intuition; the present of the future is waiting.'* That sounds familiar to you, doesn't it, Estelle? Sounds like an analytic session, no? That's how it strikes me, but no, they're Sebastian's notes, citations that he collects and recalls within the night of his own time. Our historian made his crusade in the present; there are no more dead leaves or dead letters or embalmed archives. Chrest lived his memory like the very faculty of the present."

"Paranoid hyperamnesia, my scientific colleagues would say."

"In a way. An 'awful mystery,' sighed the author of the *Confessions* way back when. I would see it as the apotheosis of our bulimic present, but one that escapes notice of the rest of us sleepwalkers, hurried consumers of information in bites and clips. Proust lowered into this frightening pit his sounding rope of paper and words, peered at it with his telescope of chagrin. Sebastian, on the other hand, slips entirely into an expanse of time—his 'zone of transit'—that ends up reabsorbing his painful shards. The malaise of a fatherless nomad who is no dupe but who nevertheless drifts, the spasm that strangles all real presence of love, the radical fatal push—I'm speaking about what moves History with a capital H, do you agree?—well, he finally transcended all that in the ocean of his crusader story. He settled his accounts by reinventing Anna Comnena and Ebrard de Pagan, the impossible couple, and yet, reunited—if only under his pen—that is already something, and Chrest didn't ask for more. Do you want to put him on trial for that?"

Estelle Pankow drank her tea.

"Tell Hermine there are no happy foreigners because they're all in mourning for their mothers. I know that's no surprise to you. Newborns know it, and young children too. The old only become old because they forget it. One can remain the ambitious inheritor of one's father from afar, even in exile. In fact, that's what they're for, fathers—to keep you far off, upward and onward. But a mother! She's that feeling presence, that language of taste before the code of ideas, that envelope of aromas—in a word, Love. Reread the Song of Songs! So if you go without the body to body, if this communion of tongues is lost, paradise is lost. Then all that's left is nostalgia. You've noticed, Estelle, how all nomads are melancholic, their songs speak lamentation with every breath . . . "

Estelle smiles—these are words that reassure this specialist of the body. I'm preaching to the converted. She tells me that some of her patients try to reinvent this relationship all the while knowing that it will never be the same. There are mothers—not many, it's true—who may help you in this recommencement exercise. I tell her, "Mine, for example . . . " but Madame Pankow has no reason to believe me, and the smile of her forget-me-not eyes tells me she doesn't. Most mothers, however, trap you; one thinks one will escape, but they keep hold of you, and you butt into the impossible, in other words into the real. Have you noticed that men—there are no women—who feel loved by their mothers are called "heroes"? That's only the beginning of the story. The end is that they kill the maternal model and then kill themselves. Perseus cuts the head of the horrible Medusa, Orestes murders Clytemnestra, Oedipus blinds himself so as not to know that he has slept with his mother. Heroes or criminals? Madame Pankow is getting impatient, she fears that I've forgotten the murdered murderer. But no, I'm getting to that.

"Sebastian was ashamed of his mother. Do you want my opinion? He had a genuine horror of Tracy Jones; she was the cunt who was capable of having a son without asking permission of the father. That's the disgusting wound the historian tried to patch up with cold indifference right up to his death. A scholar? Get real! A phenomenon—a case, if you prefer. His nephew, the police commissioner, was sure of it—it's true, he told me so. You can believe me. He was a matricide, our Sebastian, I can tell you that straight out, and I know I'm not shocking you by saying so. No, not you, a disciple of Melanie Klein! Personally I find our idealist of the Crusades frightening. His passion for Anna Comnena says nothing to me except how guilty he was about having suppressed the mother in him, don't you think?"

Estelle shrugged her shoulders and replied.

"Others would have satisfied their desire for the original breast—I should say their desire to oppose the original breast, as one opposes oneself to a wall by leaning up against it—by inventing the role of a tender mama's boy, the gigolo of wilted matrons, the eternal cherubim of these women. Do you remember Colette? That woman delighted in all who played the role before depicting them as boy toys and suicides. Do you remember her *Fin de Cheri*? Not everyone's denatured who wants to be. Besides, a transgression as natural as incest with mom or her double doesn't shock anyone anymore."

"But that wasn't Sebastian's choice!" Is it so surprising to find in Estelle a sympathetic ear? "It was Anna Comnena that he wanted, the ideal woman made of pure spirit. I wouldn't be surprised if you found clones of Chrest-Jones in a Byzantine monastary prostrate before the Dormition of the Mother of God. And that Orthodoxy wins over Catholics, Jews, maybe even Muslims in the end! The mother finally rebegun! That would take the cake, the end of jihad, the end of history, don't you agree?"

I don't know if Madame Pankow will pass along my message in Santa Varvara, but it's enough for me to convince her that the Augustinian player, my second Sebastian, the traveler with his laptop e-book, reinvented the Crusades and recomposed chimerical loves. Let her leave with that image and let her do with it what she pleases with Hermine, among the gossips in courts and law firms, in relation to the new maladies of the soul, whatever! I've understood his cause. So what if "the fire in the house," in other words *Wuxian*, alias the Infinite, ends up blowing Sebastian's brains out? That's the way it goes. Estelle reads the papers like I do, she watches television: at this stage in the movie it's the purifiers who have the upper hand. As a result, the contest is a long way from being won, but Rilsky is still on duty, and me with him. Sebastian is nevertheless a survivor, although now dead, because this man of memory is the man of the beginning: *"So that there would be a beginning, man was created, before him there was no one."* Again Augustine, but I won't say a word to Audrey, she'll rag on me again for being an Occidentalist, worse, a Christian, me! However, with Sebastian, the Sebastian who remade himself with his story of the Crusades, there are no more repetitive cycles, the "repetitive cycles have exploded," everything recommences when he cries in the cloister.

"You knew that, didn't you? The depressed don't cry unless life recommences: when they are capable of tears they forget to commit suicide, they no longer think of it, they think simply of the difficulty of being. Tears are already life."

"There's just one crack in this sacred edifice Sebastian inhabits and rehabilitates in the irony of his laptop story that tranquilizes his relation to the volcanic madonna: Sebastian does not believe in happiness. This fruit (*frui-fruitio*) that Augustine is tirelessly going on about and his disciple Lacan baptizes with the awkward term *j-ou-i-ssance* is not even sought after by Professor Chrest-Jones. He only seeks the past to remake it, to live it in the present, period. That is his sole enjoyment—nothing beyond that, nothing to come. Nothing! Isn't that outrageous? And what else is there in Paris, in Santa Varvara? Philippopolis? Le Puy?"

It's this faulty and yet enormous plenitude that brought him to tears in Velay, I'm sure of it. Maybe I'm imagining it. Having arrived at his end, his goals, Occidental man—that's right Audrey, I stick by that—or my Sebastian at any rate does not toot his own glorious horn. Perhaps he rediscovers his glory discreetly? By reinventing on his laptop Anna Comnena and Ebrard, by crisscrossing the Balkans from Santa Varvara to the Black Sea to Le Puy-en-Velay?

The messenger from Santa Varvara is still staring at me with her forget-me-not eyes. Like Audrey, like Nor, she thinks that I'm telling her this story of Sebastian and Ebrard and Anna Comnena to test her sense of humor and make her understand that I don't believe a word of it, that I think almost just the opposite, and that I'm interested in entirely different things, perhaps simply in the here and now of my Parisian life.

"So you spin out a detective story and make fun of detective stories at the same time, and you recount the Crusades while discounting the actual crusades led by Santa Varvara itself." Doctor Estelle Pankow is a sympathetic listener, but vigilant.

"A means to do otherwise so as to be free with the other and oneself? No need for Plato, Kierkegaard, or La Fontaine to fall snugly into irony. Gallic peasants are all ironists scattered over various fiefdoms. I'll share a secret with you, my dear Estelle. When he wasn't the ambassador to Santa Varvara, my father used to take us on vacation to the Ile de Ré to introduce me and my sister to salt marshes, rose hips, and the Charentes sense of humor. Do you know the island?"

Go there for the irony, Estelle, my vicious visitor. My superego is the fox of the fable: "Vous êtes le phénix des hôtes de ces bois!"—"You are the best of the beasts of this wood!" What I say is not what I think, my words describe an illusion that is the opposite of my sincere conviction, and I enjoy savoring this discrepancy, which I've made up on my own. An imposter? Not really. Suffice it to say that misunderstanding is rife within contemporary language and within the supposed frank talk that we're told can be understood immediately and would supposedly be the foundation of communities, audiences, and best-sellers. No, I don't think so!

"So irony is your way of opposing yourself to the discord of the world?" Estelle posing as the engaged therapist.

"Since I don't really know where I'm going, I undo the reality of my opposition." I summarize what I suppose a psychoanalytic remark to be, shocking Estelle.

"You're not a believer." Estelle, remaining political.

"If atheism really existed, the ironist would be the radical atheist. Certainly not a purist! Those who deflect words and genres abolish purity itself, no? A prophet? Perhaps. One who doesn't cease pointing at something to come without knowing exactly what, something still missing." I'm playing the philosopher. I pour her some more Felicity.

Dear Estelle Pankow, is she simple enough to confuse my irony with derision? Let's hope not! Derision leaves us with the impression that everything is imposture, as my old TV star lover used to say. I'm not giving him a name, but did he really have one? Only Audrey knows who I'm talking about—no, she's not mistaken—even if there are tons of his kind for whom the world exists only to end up in a joke. "There is nothing sacred for the mind that is essentially corrosive," he used to whisper, even during pillow talk, in case I'd not yet understood, "I'm a born profaner!" At first I found him amusing; in the end he had it all wrong. Not believing him, I ended up not listening to him at all. Nothing to do with irony. It guides you by means of an elevation toward a truth that cannot be stated—"You sang? Well, now dance!"—but percolates through its opposite—"Do what you want, but don't count on any help, least of all from me." The game of life is more complicated and really more mobile and playful—that's what this fox of La Fontaine has to say to all the crows of Santa Varvara. On the other hand, derision is put-down—"I gotcha; you're dead; I'm the worthless master...." In the long run my playful, blasphemous lover profaned himself: a false man who could say everything and its opposite, who ended up saying all was false. His tantrums too—boy, he had some good ones—nocturnal rages and tooth and claw battles with his rivals. Ah, the war of ratings! You can do anything with a false man: laugh, fuck, travel, earn money, sparkle, battle, suffer, have fun, die eventually—why not?—especially die for sure—the images kill me, not you? But not live, no, Estelle, not live! So writing is all that's left . . .

She tired me out, the messenger from Santa Varvara. Truly. But I think there won't be a trial, no, Sebastian has reached his end for good, and Madame Pankow is a witness. We'll see each other again, Estelle, of course; I'm in your country so often, in fact I really never leave Santa Varvara.

COLD SWEATS, FEVER, or a panic attack? I have trouble swallowing, my voice doesn't get out of my throat, and still this whistle in the heart, palpitations, suffocation, my sweaty palms are looking in vain at the bottom of my sack for the telephone that's always going off at the wrong time. I've got it—too late. There's a message. Him again, the failed guppy, my boss. "I'm not stalking you, my dear Stephanie, but I'm expecting an article from you, not a novel. Just the facts, ma'am, got it? Where are we at with the New Pantheon? Basic stuff, OK, and don't tell me I'm harassing you, either sexually or morally, got it? It's just business, and I *am* your boss, he, he!" I'm going to kill him, I'm telling you, one day there'll be murder at the *Événement de Paris*, do you hear me, Audrey?

She's not listening to me. Her face serious, her lips pursed, her squirrel eyes turning left and right, Audrey seems to be listening to strange, barely audible noises and looking down toward the back of the Marly Café. A crowd of bodies presses toward the exit, a shot, two—"Get down!"—people start running, Audrey grabs my arm: "Let's not move. In cases like this, there's nothing to do." Cases like what? People around us are huddled under tables, others are escaping toward the rue de Rivoli.

The proud waiter of a moment ago is now wielding a Heckle PS 9 instead of his tray of peach melbas and champagne glasses. A cop, but of course! He shoves in front of him an ordinary-looking individual with shaved head, jeans, T-shirt, Nikes, walking casually despite the handcuffs and the punch he must have taken given the red drool coming down his chin. "A holdup man!" whispers my neighbor, straightening up from underneath her table. An honor guard of patrons suddenly forms around the holdup man and the waiter-cop; we're delighted to have a good story to tell back home tonight and at the office tomorrow.

Suddenly the handcuffed Nike man halts, falls, and starts having intense convulsions. Epilepsy? "He must have swallowed something, Chief!" cries the young female police officer in uniform, obviously the waiter-cop's associate. Where did she come from? Or had she been sitting here the whole time without anyone noticing, not so strange now with the beefed up police presence these days, and . . . how shall I say? . . . so desirable with all the alerts and insecurity.

"Shit, he's poisoned himself!" The waiter grabs for his phone, he's losing his grip on the situation and needs more information. "You, Jeanne, call an ambulance. His weapon is a CETME from the Vitoria factory, you follow me, ETA commando, or some local branch, who knows, Al Qaeda, Bin Laden—why not, I'm serious, don't laugh, given what's happened lately. Evacuate the Marly, the Pyramid, everything. The whole Louvre, all Paris if you want." He's getting excited, it's his day, why hold back? "Yes, lieutenant." Aside to Jeanne: "I'm talking to the big boss." "Yes, Commissioner!" Now he's yelling into his telephone. "Yes, I can confirm that, the holdup man is neutralized; he's dead as a doornail, in fact. No, I wasn't too rough; I believe he poisoned himself . . . That's what I think too . . . the first domino . . . anything could happen, I agree. When? Right away, tomorrow, here, of course, why not, we're well situated, I think. Anywhere else too, if you want . . . "

A new explosion—under the Pyramid this time—splits my heart. I should have had that MRI done before leaving for Santa Varvara. "You don't take care of yourself, my girl. Who will be thinking of you if you don't, if I don't?" She was right, my mother who is no more, everything passes through the heart, and I knew it too. But when that failed guppy Bondy gets on my case, I can't help it, I run, I forget to take care of myself, and—ta-da—what was bound to happen happens: my heart goes—what a time for this.

The second and third explosions. The Pyramid flies into a million pieces and the glass rains down on the café, Audrey is crying; I am petrified; it's the fault of that damn whistle in my heart; it locks up your vocal chords, you can't open your mouth—not a word, not a sound.

The Marly regulars have disappeared. We're still standing there alone, Audrey and me, two ghosts contemplating the collapse of the World Trade Center and now the cardboard box theater sets of the Louvre biting the dust this evening. Dead or alive? I don't know, we've not yet seen any survivor to confirm one way or another, to dare to think, to know or say anything.

Flames are pouring out the windows of the Oriental Antiquities, Egyptian, Greek, and Roman wings and lapping up the outside walls. Le Vau is going up in smoke and Bernini is turning into a pile of hot coals. "We have to get out of this hell, give me your hand—move, damn it!" Audrey tries to shake and pull me away from there.

A strong odor of gasoline has overtaken the Tuileries; black ash is falling on the pink Carrousel and on the two ghosts that we are, filling our mouths and lungs. I can't breathe; it's the coma. "You've got to try, do you hear me, come on, run!' cries Audrey. "No, not toward the subway—people always get it in the subways—we'll run outside, to the end . . . " What end? I'm a dumb robot and obey Audrey.

"Ladies and gentlemen, please remain calm. A terrorist attack has just occured at the Louvre. We do not yet know the number of victims; there may be many. We fear extensive damage to this centerpiece of our culture, which is engulfed in fire and smoke at this moment. This is the prefect of the Paris police speaking. Please know that we have regained control of the situation. Three terrorists are dead. One of the three, whom we believe to be the head commando, blew himself up in front of the *Victory of Samothrace.* We have taken one of these new crusaders of evil prisoner; the third died of self-poisoning. The Paris fire department is working with other competent agencies to put out the flames. Stay in your homes and remain vigilant. The mayor and myself, as well as the government ministers, are doing everything necessary in the current situation. The president of the Republic, on vacation in Santa Varvara, will address the nation in just a short while. I ask that you remain calm and thank you for carrying out your civic duty. Do not give in to panic!"

Loudspeakers blare this message in the streets of Paris, now emptied of gawkers and rubberneckers. Where have the Parisians gone? Audrey doesn't stop pulling me by the hand. The feet, mechanical, go round. I still can't form a damn word, and my stiff heart, my heart is beating like a wounded bird. Ambulances are racing around in every direction. Paramedics are collecting people here and there, some unconscious, some corpses. A television left on in a deserted café broadcasts a commentary by our ambassador in Santa Varvara; I think I recognize the voice of Foulques Weil, thick smoke blocking his face: "France has not been and is still not a privileged target of global terrorism, ladies and gentlemen. We have done everything in our power to spare our country the vengeance that the forces of evil unleashed on September 11 against the World Trade Center. This incident may have nothing to do with Al Qaeda: an ordinary explosion of a gas pipe, for example. We will know when the investigation is complete, and it is well underway. I give you my solemn word on that. I also wish to assure you that our government and the entire European community—unlike other powers—is doing everything possible to dissuade extremists from attacking our interests." I continue to run like a robot. I can no longer hear the voice of Foulques Weil—I'm pretty sure it was him.

Another explosion. It feels like a bomb. "Do you think it's over?" No response. I've lost Audrey. The flames from the Louvre are spreading over the whole city and advance toward me.

Finally a cry breaks through my lips.

I open my eyes.

It's dark and warm; I'm soaked. Three-thirty at night. My room is a tunnel that leads nowhere. I turn on the radio, listen to the news. Paris is sleeping. As usual, not much is happening here. Only my palpitations tell of the night's events. I get up, open the window; the linden honey smell of the Luxembourg Gardens wakes me up completely.

"Hello, Nor, I'm not bothering you, I hope?"

"Never, you know that. But what time is it? Four o'clock in the morning in Paris—you're not sleeping?"

"No. Yes. Where are you? Are you working?"

"Of course. I'm at the office. I haven't stopped today, and it's far from over. You won't believe me, but HE's started up again!"

"He who, you don't mean . . . ?"

"Yes, the Infinite. Two murders since this morning, still in the cloudy morass of the New Pantheon.

"Good. Sorry, just kidding. But he can't be the same?"

"No, of course not, but it's his clone. He makes a point of saying so in his e-mails to me signed 'The Infinite.'"

"Is he Chinese? Muslim? Santa Varvarois? An antiglobalization militant, a prankster, a postsituationist?"

"I haven't ruled anything out. And you? Tell me about you. What's going on?"

"Nothing. A terrorist attack blew up the Louvre."

"Are you joking?"

"No, not exactly."

"Wait, I can't hear you, can you say that again, please?"

"A terrorist attack. Bombs under the Pyramid at the Louvre, Paris in flames, a nightmare!"

"It's incredible. No. But how. You were thinking you were protected from."

"A nightmare, I'm telling you. I had a nightmare. I'm sorry to get you all worked up. I had to talk to someone about it. How's Minoushah?" Silence.

"You did the right thing. I prefer . . . Wow! . . . The brand of humor of your dreams, you know, is rather frightening."

"I'm not yet able to laugh about it. Weird story, don't you think? I'll tell you the whole thing. I won't be able to stay here. I'm afraid you're going to be thinking again that my place is in Santa Varvara. I'm sure my boss is just waiting till morning to tell me to get on the next plane back to your world."

"That's what I was going to tell you. Infinite or no, I'm waiting for you. There's two of us, counting Shah, who are calling you, can you hear her?"

"I miss her. So the crusade continues?"

"And the investigation is starting up again."

"Can you know where the evil comes from?"

"Detective fiction is an optimistic genre."

"The Louvre will never collapse because we are in Byzantium."

"No one knows what we're talking about."

"They have a hunch, but not about our silence."

"Shhh, don't give it away!"

"OK, so I'm coming. It will be tomorrow for you. Same plane, same time."

"I'll be there."

"Everything's starting over?"

"Another day, another voyage."

"I'm a journeywoman."

"Can't you talk like everyone else? We're under way now—that's already pretty fantastic."

"But for how long?"

"Good question."